Sylvia Day is the *New York Times* bestselling and award-winning author of more than a dozen novels, written across multiple sub-genres, including the international sensation *Bared to You*, the first in the Crossfire trilogy. She has won the RT Reviewers' Choice Award, the National Readers' Choice Award twice, and has been nominated for the RITA twice. A wife and mother of two, she is a former Russian linguist for the U.S. Army Military Intelligence. She lives in San Diego, California. For more information visit **www.sylviaday.com**.

Praise for Sylvia Day:

'*A Touch of Crimson* will rock readers with a stunning new world, a hot-blooded hero, and a strong, kick-ass heroine. This is Sylvia Day at the top of her game!' Larissa Ione, *New York Times* bestselling author

'Angels and demons, vampires and lycans, all set against an inventive, intriguing story world that hooked me from the first page. Balancing action and romance, humor and hot sensuality, Sylvia Day's storytelling dazzles. I can't wait to read more about this league of sexy, dangerous guardian angels and the fascinating world they inhabit. *A Touch of Crimson* is a paranormal romance lover's feast!' Lara Adrian, *New York Times* bestselling author

'*A Touch of Crimson* explodes with passion and heat. A hot, sexy angel to die for and a gutsy heroine make for one exciting read' Cheyenne McCray, *New York Times* bestselling author

'Sylvia Day spins a gorgeous adventure in *A Touch of Crimson* that combines gritty, exciting storytelling with soaring lyricism. Adrian is my favorite kind of hero – an alpha-male angel determined to win the heart of his heroine, Lindsay, while protecting her from his lethal enemy. Lindsay is a gutsy, likable woman with paranormal abilities of her own, as well as a dedication to protecting humanity against a race of demonic monsters. This is definitely a book for your keeper shelf' Angela Knight, *New York Times* bestselling author

'A gripping, touching and scintillating page-turner' *Romantic Times* 4 ½ *Stars*

By Sylvia Day

Renegade Angels
A Touch of Crimson
A Hunger So Wild

A Touch of Crimson

SYLVIA DAY

A RENEGADE ANGELS NOVEL

ETERNAL
ROMANCE

First published in the United States of America in 2011
by Signet Eclipse, an imprint of New American Library,
a division of Penguin Group (USA) Inc.

First published in Great Britain in 2012
by ETERNAL ROMANCE
An imprint of HEADLINE PUBLISHING GROUP

3

Cataloguing in Publication Data is available from the British Library

ISBN 978 1 4722 0074 7

Offset in Times by Avon DataSet Ltd, Bidford-on-Avon, Warwickshire

Printed and bound by CPI Group (UK) Ltd, Croydon, CR0 4YY

Headline's policy is to use papers that are natural, renewable and
recyclable products and made from wood grown in sustainable forests.
The logging and manufacturing processes are expected to conform
to the environmental regulations of the country of origin.

HEADLINE PUBLISHING GROUP
An Hachette UK Company
338 Euston Road
London NW1 3BH

www.eternalromancebooks.co.uk
www.headline.co.uk
www.hachette.co.uk

*This one is for my Marked series readers.
I hope you love it.*

ACKNOWLEDGMENTS

My gratitude to Danielle Perez, Claire Zion, Kara Welsh, Leslie Gelbman, and everyone at NAL for all the enthusiasm shown for my Renegade Angels from auction to publication.

A tip of my hat to Beth Miller for all the little things.

A shout out to Erin Galloway for her input and for just being her.

Thanks to the art department for granting my wish to have Tony Mauro design my cover.

I have mad love for Tony Mauro and his head-turning, kick-ass artwork for Adrian. I'm grateful for the many ways he allowed me to use his art to share Adrian's story.

Thank you to Monique Patterson for feeding my muse.

Huge thanks to Shayla Black and Cynthia D'Alba for reading early drafts of this story and helping me pull it together.

Much love to my friend Lora Leigh, to whom Lindsay/Shadoe pay homage.

Lara Adrian, Larissa Ione, Angela Knight, and Cheyenne McCray are very busy women, yet they generously spent some of their precious time reading Adrian and Lindsay's story. Thank you so much, ladies! I'm grateful.

GLOSSARY

CHANGE—the process a mortal undergoes to become a vampire.

FALLEN—the *Watchers* after the fall from grace. They have been stripped of their wings and their souls, leaving them as immortal blood drinkers who cannot procreate.

LYCANS—a subgroup of the *Fallen* who were spared vampirism by agreeing to serve the *Sentinels*. They were transfused with demon blood, which preserved their souls but made them mortal. They can shape-shift and procreate.

MINION—a mortal who has been *Changed* into a *vampire* by one of the *Fallen*. Most mortals do not adjust well and become rabid. Unlike the *Fallen*, they cannot tolerate sunlight.

NAPHIL—singular of *nephalim*.

NEPHALIM—the children of mortal and *Watcher* parents. Their blood drinking contributed to and inspired the vampiric punishment of the *Fallen*.

("they turned themselves against men, in order to devour them"—Enoch 7:13)

("No food shall they eat; and they shall be thirsty"—Enoch 15:10)

SENTINELS—an elite special ops unit of the *seraphim*, tasked with enforcing the punishment of the *Watchers*.

SERAPH—singular of *seraphim*.

X GLOSSARY

SERAPHIM—the highest rank of angel in the angelic hierarchy.

VAMPIRES—a term that encompasses both the *Fallen* and their *minions*.

WATCHERS—two hundred *seraphim* angels sent to earth at the beginning of time to observe mortals. They violated the laws by taking mortals as mates and were punished with an eternity on earth as *vampires* with no possibility of forgiveness.

Go tell the Watchers of heaven, who have deserted the lofty sky, and their holy everlasting station, who have been polluted with women, and have done as the sons of men do, by taking to themselves wives, and who have been greatly corrupted on the earth; that on the earth they shall never obtain peace and remission of sin. For they shall not rejoice in their offspring; they shall behold the slaughter of their beloved; shall lament for the destruction of their sons; and shall petition for ever; but shall not obtain mercy and peace.

The Book of Enoch 12:5–7

CHAPTER 1

"Phineas is dead."

The pronouncement hit Adrian Mitchell like a physical blow. Gripping the handrail to counterbalance his shaken composure, he rounded a bend in the stairwell and looked at the seraph who ascended abreast of him. With the relaying of the news, Jason Taylor advanced into Phineas's former rank as Adrian's second-in-command. "When? How?"

Jason easily kept up with Adrian's inhuman pace as they approached the roof. "About an hour ago. It was called in as a vamp attack."

"No one noticed a vampire within striking distance? How the fuck is that possible?"

"That was my question. I sent Damien to investigate."

They reached the last landing. The lycan guard in front of them pushed open the heavy metal door, and Adrian slipped sunglasses over his eyes before stepping into the Arizona sunshine. He watched the guard recoil from the ovenlike heat, then heard a complaining growl from the second lycan, who brought up the rear. As base creatures of instinct, they were susceptible to physical stimuli in ways the seraphim and vampires were not. Adrian didn't feel the temperature at all; the loss of Phineas had chilled his blood.

A helicopter waited on the pad in front of them, its whirring blades churning the oppressively dry and gritty air. Its rounded side was emblazoned with both MITCHELL AERONAUTICS and Adrian's winged logo.

"You have doubts." He focused on the details because he couldn't afford to vent his fury now. Inside, he was shattered by grief over the loss of his best friend and trusted lieutenant. But as leader of the Sentinels, he couldn't appear diminished in any way. Phineas's death would send ripples through the ranks of his elite unit of seraphim. The Sentinels would be looking to him for strength and guidance.

"One of his lycans survived the attack." Despite the roar of the aircraft's engine, Jason didn't need to raise his voice to be heard. He also didn't cover his seraph blue eyes, despite the pair of designer shades perched atop his golden head. "I find it a bit . . . *odd* that Phineas was investigating the size of the Navajo Lake pack; then he gets ambushed on the way home and killed. Yet one of his dogs survives to call it in as a vamp assault?"

Adrian had been utilizing the lycans for centuries as both guards for the Sentinels and heeler dogs to herd the vampires into designated areas. But recent signs of restlessness among the lycans signaled a need for him to reevaluate. They'd been created for the express purpose of serving his unit. If necessary, Adrian would remind them of the pact made by their ancestors. They could have all been turned into soulless, bloodsucking vampires as punishment for their crimes, but he'd spared them in return for their indenture. Although some of the lycans believed their debt had been paid by their predecessors, they failed to recognize that this world was made for mortals. They could never live among and alongside humans. Their only place was the one Adrian had made for them.

One of his guards ducked low and pushed through the air turbulence created by the helicopter blades. Reaching the aircraft, the lycan held the door open.

Adrian's power buffered him from the tempest, allowing him to proceed without effort. He looked at Jason. "I'll need to question the lycan who survived the attack."

"I'll tell Damien." The wind whipped through the lieutenant's blond locks and sent his sunglasses flying.

Adrian snatched them out of the air with a lightning-quick grasp. Vaulting into the cabin, he settled into one of the two rear-facing bucket seats.

Jason occupied the other one. "But I have to ask: is a guard dog that can't guard worth anything? Maybe you should put him down to reinforce that by example."

"If he's at fault, he'll pray for death." Adrian tossed the shades at him. "But until I know otherwise, he's a victim and my only witness. I need him if I'm to catch and punish those who did this."

The two lycans dropped onto the opposite row of seats. One was stocky, a bruiser. The other was nearly equal in height to Adrian.

The taller guard secured his seat belt and said, "That 'dog's' mate died trying to protect Phineas. If he could've done something, he would have."

Jason opened his mouth.

Adrian held up a hand to keep him quiet. "You're Elijah."

The lycan nodded. He was dark haired and had the luminous green eyes of a creature tainted with the blood of demons. It was one of the points of contention between Adrian and the lycans that he'd transfused their seraph ancestors with demon blood when they'd agreed to serve the Sentinels. That touch of demon was what made them half man/half beast and it had spared the souls that should have died with the amputation of their wings. It also made them mortal, with finite life spans, and there were many who resented him for that.

"You seem to know more about what happened than Jason does," Adrian noted, studying the lycan. Elijah had been sent to Adrian's pack for observation, because he'd displayed unacceptable Alpha traits. The lycans were trained to look to the Sentinels for leadership. If one of their own ever rose to prominence, it might lead to divided loyalties that could spark thoughts of rebellion. The best way to deal with a problem was to prevent it from occurring in the first place.

Elijah looked out the window, watching the roof recede as the helicopter lifted high into Phoenix's cloudless blue sky. His hands were fisted, betraying his breed's innate fear of flying. "We all know a mated pair can't live without each other. No lycan would ever deliberately watch their mate die. Not for any reason."

Adrian leaned back, attempting to ease the tension created by restraining wings that wanted to spread and stretch in a physical manifestation of his pained rage. What Elijah had said was true, which left him facing the possibility of a vampire offensive. His head fell back against the seat. The need for vengeance burned like acid. The vampires had taken so much from him—the woman he loved, friends, and fellow Sentinels. The loss of Phineas was akin to severing his right arm. He intended to sever far more than that from the one responsible.

Knowing his sunglasses wouldn't hide the flaming irises that betrayed his roiling emotions, he shuttered his gaze ...

... and almost missed the glint of sunlight on silver.

He jerked to the side by instinct, narrowly missing a dagger slash to the neck.

Comprehension flashed. *The pilot.*

Adrian caught the arm reaching around his headrest and snapped the bone. A female scream pierced the cabin. The pilot's broken limb flopped against the leather at an unnatural angle; her blade clattered to the floorboard. Adrian released his harness and spun around, baring his claws. The lycans shot forward, one on either side of him.

Without a guiding hand at the stick, the helicopter pitched and yawed. Frantic beeping sounded from the cockpit.

The pilot ignored her useless arm. Using the other, she thrust a second silver dagger through the gap between the two rear-facing seats.

Bared fangs. Foaming mouth. Bloodshot eyes.

A goddamned diseased vampire. Distracted by Phineas's death, he'd made a fucking major oversight.

The lycans partially shifted, unleashing their beasts in response to the threat. Their roars of aggression reverberated in the confined space. Elijah, hunched by the low roof, pulled back his fist and swung. The impact knocked the pilot into the cyclic stick, shoving it forward. The nose of the helicopter dove, hurtling them toward the ground.

The wailing alarms were deafening.

Adrian lunged, tackling the vampress with a midsection hit and smashing her through the cockpit window. Free-falling, they grappled.

"One taste, Sentinel," she sing-songed through froth, her eyes wild as she struggled to bite him with needle-sharp canines.

He punched into her rib cage, rending flesh and splintering bone. Fisting her pounding heart, he bared his teeth in a smile.

His wings snapped open in a burst of iridescent white tipped in crimson. Like a parachute deploying, the thirty-foot expanse halted his descent with teeth-rattling abruptness, ripping the beating organ free of the writhing vampire. She plummeted to the earth, trailing acrid smoke and ash as she disintegrated. In his hand, the heart still pumped, spurting viscous blood before losing life and bursting into flame. He crushed the fleshy organ into a pulpy mass, then tossed it aside. It fell in burning embers, billowing away in a glittering cloud.

The helicopter whined as it spiraled toward the desert floor.

Tucking his wings in close, Adrian dove toward the aircraft. One lycan peered out the windowless cockpit, his face blanched and eyes glowing green.

Jason shot out of the damaged helicopter like a bullet. He circled back, his dark gray and burgundy wings a racing shadow across the sky. "What are you doing, Captain?"

"Saving the lycans."

"Why?"

The ferocity of Adrian's glare was the only answer he deigned to give. Wisely, Jason banked and came around.

Knowing the beasts would need to be spurred through their innate terror of heights, Adrian compelled the one standing in the cockpit. *"Jump."*

The angelic resonance of his voice rumbled across the desert like thunder, demanding undeniable obedience. Mindlessly, the lycan tumbled into the open sky. Arrowing directly toward him, Jason snatched the guard out of harm's way.

Elijah needed no compulsion. Exhibiting remarkable courage, the guard launched himself from the doomed aircraft in an elegant dive.

Adrian swooped under him, grunting as the muscle-heavy lycan slammed onto his back. They were mere feet away from the ground, close enough that the beating of his massive wings sent sand twisting upward in spiraling gusts.

The helicopter hit the desert floor a heartbeat later, exploding into a roiling tower of flames that could be seen for miles.

CHAPTER 2

There was a walking wet dream in Phoenix's Sky Harbor International Airport.

Lindsay Gibson spotted him at her boarding gate during a cursory surveillance of her immediate perimeter. Arrested by his raw sensuality, she slowed to a halt in the middle of the concourse. A low whistle of appreciation escaped her. Perhaps her luck was finally turning around. She would certainly welcome a silver lining after the day she'd been having so far. Her takeoff from Raleigh had been delayed almost an hour and she'd missed her original connection. From the looks of it, she had barely made her rebooked flight, if the number of passengers standing by the gate was any indication.

Finishing her assessment of the crowd around her, Lindsay returned her attention to the most decadent-looking man she'd ever seen.

He paced sinuously along the edge of the waiting area, his long jeans-clad legs maintaining a precisely controlled stride. His thick black hair was slightly over-long, framing a savagely masculine face. A cream-colored V-neck T-shirt stretched over powerfully ripped shoulders, hinting at a body worthy of completing the package.

Lindsay pushed a lock of rain-damp hair back from her forehead and cataloged every detail. Unadulterated sex appeal—this guy had it. The kind you couldn't fake or buy; the kind that made handsomeness a bonus.

He moved without looking, yet unerringly avoided a man who cut through his path. His attention was occupied by a BlackBerry, his thumb rhythmically stroking over the trackpad in a way that caused places low in Lindsay's belly to clench.

A drop of rainwater slid down her neck. The cool, slow trickle heightened her physical awareness of the guy she was devouring with her gaze. Behind him, the view of the tarmac revealed a gloomy gray late-afternoon sky. Sheets of rain pelted the windows framing the terminal. The inclement weather was unexpected, and not just because there'd been no rain in the forecast. She always anticipated weather conditions with uncanny accuracy, but she hadn't felt this storm coming. It had been sunny when she landed, then began pouring buckets shortly after.

Usually, she loved rain and wouldn't have minded having to step outside to catch the interterminal bus to her connecting flight's gate. Today, however, there was a morose quality to the weather. A weight of melancholy, or mourning. And she was empathetic.

As long as she could remember, the wind had spoken to her. Whether it shouted through a storm or whispered through stillness, it always conveyed its message. Not in words, but in feelings. Her dad called it her sixth sense and he went out of his way to act as if it was a cool quirk to have instead of something freakish.

That inner radar drew her to the luscious man by her gate as much as his looks did. There was a brooding air about him that reminded her of a brewing storm gathering strength. She was strongly attracted to that quality in him . . . and to the lack of a wedding band on his finger.

Pivoting, Lindsay faced him head-on and willed him to look at her.

His head lifted. His gaze met hers.

She was hit with the sensation of being buffeted by the wind, the gusts whipping through her hair. But there was none of the chill. Only heat and seductive humidity. Lindsay held his stare for an endless moment, riveted by the drawing pull of brilliant azure irises, eyes that were as tumultuous and ancient as the fury of the weather outside.

Inhaling sharply, she turned and walked to a nearby gourmet pretzel shop, giving him the opportunity to chase her obvious interest . . . or not. She knew instinctively that he was a man who pursued.

She reached the counter and glanced up at the menu. The smell of warm, yeasty bread and melted butter made her mouth water. The last thing she needed before sitting on her ass for another hour straight was a carbohydrate bomb like a giant pretzel. Then again, maybe the rush of serotonin would soothe nerves jangled by the sensory input from the large number of people around her.

She ordered. "Pretzel sticks, please. With marinara sauce and a diet soda."

The clerk relayed the total. Lindsay dug into her purse for her wallet.

"Allow me."

God . . . that voice. Tantalizingly sonorous. Lindsay knew it was *him*.

He reached around her and she breathed in his exotic scent. Not cologne. Just earthy, virile male. Crisp and pure, like air cleansed by a rainstorm.

He slid a twenty-dollar bill across the counter. She smiled and let him.

It was too bad she was wearing her oldest pair of jeans, a loose T-shirt, and army-issue jungle boots. Great for ease of movement, but she would've preferred to look hot for this guy. He really was way out of her league, from the movie-star good looks to the Vacheron Constantin watch on his wrist.

Turning to face him, she held out her hand. "Thank you, Mr. . . . . ?"

"Adrian Mitchell." He accepted the handshake, with the addition of his thumb stroking across her knuckles.

Lindsay had a visceral response to his touch. Her breath caught and the tempo of her heartbeat accelerated. Up close, he was devastating. Both fiercely masculine and terrifyingly beautiful. Flawless. "Hi, Adrian Mitchell."

He reached down and caught her luggage tag with long, elegant fingers. "Nice to meet you, Lindsay Gibson . . . from Raleigh? Or returning there?"

"I'm heading your direction. We're sharing a plane."

His eyes were the most unusual shade of blue. Like the vivid cerulean at the heart of a flame. Set within olive skin and framed by thick dark lashes, they were mesmerizing.

And they were focused on her as if he couldn't get enough of looking at her.

He raked her from head to toe with a searing glance. She felt bare and flushed, left naked by the undressing he'd done in his mind. Her body responded to the provocation. Her breasts swelled; everything else softened.

A woman would have to soften for him, because there was nothing remotely yielding about his body. From the sculpted definition of his shoulders and biceps to the chiseled features of his face, every angle was sharp and precise.

He reached around her for his change, moving with a lithe and primal grace.

I bet he fucks like an animal.

Heated by the thought, Lindsay caught the extension handle of her suitcase. "So is Orange County home? Or are you traveling for business?"

"I'm going home. To Anaheim. And you?"

She moved to the pickup counter. He followed at a more sedate pace, but there was something inherently determined about the way he came after her. His predacity sent a shiver of expectation through her. Her luck had definitely changed—her final destination was Anaheim, too.

"Orange County is going to be home. I'm relocating for a job." She wasn't going to get as detailed as naming a city. She knew how to protect herself if she had to, but she didn't want to buy any more trouble than she already had.

"That's a big move. One side of the country to the other."

"It was time for a change."

His mouth curved in a half smile. "Have dinner with me."

The velvety resonance to his voice engaged her interest further. He was charismatic and magnetic, two qualities that made short-term relationships memorable.

She accepted the bag and soda the clerk passed to her. "You get right to the point. I like that."

The calling of their flight number drew her attention back to the gate. A short delay was announced, causing the waiting passengers to shift restlessly. Adrian never took his eyes from her.

He gestured to the row of chairs near where he'd been pacing. "We have time to get to know each other."

Lindsay walked with him over to the seating area. She canvassed the vicinity again, taking brief note of the numerous women following Adrian with their gazes. The sense of him being a leashed tempest was no longer so overwhelming, while outside the rain had abated to a heavy drizzle. The correlation was intriguing.

Her ferocious reaction to Adrian Mitchell and his unique ability to set off her inner weather radar cemented her decision to get closer to him. Anomalies in her life always bore greater investigation.

He waited until she was settled into a seat, then asked, "Do you have friends picking you up? Family?"

No one was meeting her. She had a shuttle reserved to take her to the hotel where she'd be staying until she found a suitable apartment. "It's not wise to share that sort of information with a stranger."

"So let me address the risk." He shifted with sleek fluidity, reaching into his back pocket to grab his billfold. Withdrawing a business card, he held it out to her. "Call whoever is expecting you. Tell them who I am and how to reach me."

"You're determined." Also used to giving commands. She didn't mind. She had a strong personality and needed the same in return, or she took the lead. Docile men were fine in certain situations, but not in her personal life.

"I am," he agreed, unabashed.

Lindsay reached for the card. His fingers touched hers and electricity raced up her arm.

His nostrils flared. He caught her hand; his fingertips teased her palm. He could have been stroking between her legs, given how aroused she became from that simple touch. He watched her with an almost tangible sexual heat, dark and intense. As if he knew what her hot buttons were ... or was set on figuring them out.

"I can tell you're going to be trouble," she murmured, tightening her grip to still his questing fingers.

"Dinner. Conversation. I promise to behave."

Holding him captive, she reached for his business card with her other hand. Her blood was thrumming through her veins, roused by the excitement of such an immediate, unruly attraction. "Mitchell Aeronautics," she read. "But you're flying commercial?"

"I had other plans." His tone was wry. "But my pilot dropped out unexpectedly."

His pilot. Her mouth curved. "Don't you hate when that happens?"

"Usually ... Then you came along." He pulled his BlackBerry out of his pocket. "Use my phone so whoever you call will have that number, too."

Lindsay reluctantly released him and accepted the phone, even though she had her own. Setting her soda on the worn carpet, she stood. Adrian rose with her. He was affluent, elegant, mannered, solicitous, and drop-dead gorgeous. Yet as polished as he was, there remained a dangerous edge to him that titillated a woman's basest instincts. Maybe the crowded terminal was provoking her sharp senses. Or maybe they just had a combustible sexual compatibility. Regardless, she wasn't complaining.

Leaving her pretzel bag on the chair, she moved a few feet away and dialed the number to her father's auto shop. While she was occupied, Adrian walked to the gate counter.

"Linds. You're there already?"

She was startled by the abrupt greeting. "How did you know it was me?"

"Caller ID. It shows a 714 area code."

"I'm on my layover in Phoenix, using someone else's cell phone."

"What's the matter with yours? And why are you still in Phoenix?" A single parent for twenty years, Eddie Gibson had always been overprotective, which wasn't surprising considering the horrific manner of Regina Gibson's death.

"My phone's fine and I missed my connection. I've also met someone." Lindsay explained the situation with Adrian and relayed the information from the business card. "I'm not worried. He just seems like the kind of guy who could use a little resistance. I don't think he hears the word 'no' very often."

"Probably not. Mitchell is like Howard Hughes."

Her brows rose. "How so? Money, movies, starlets? All of the above?"

She assessed Adrian from the back, taking advantage of the opportunity to check him out while his attention was diverted. The rear view was as impressive as the front, revealing a powerful back and a luscious ass.

"If you sat still for more than five minutes, you might know this," her father said.

God, she couldn't remember the last time she'd read a magazine, and she had stopped paying for cable television years ago. She rented movies and shows by the season, because even commercials were a luxury she couldn't make room for. "I can barely keep my own life straight, Dad. Where am I supposed to find time to pay attention to someone else's?"

"You're always poking into mine," he teased.

"I know you. I love you. Celebrities? Not so much."

"He's not a celebrity. He actually guards his privacy pretty fiercely. He lives on some kind of compound in Orange County. I saw it on a television special once. It's some sort of architectural wonder. Mitchell is similar to Hughes in that he's a reclusive gazillionaire who likes planes. The media keeps tabs on him because the public has a fascination with aviators. They always have. And he's supposedly attractive, but I can't judge that sort of thing."

And to think she'd picked him out of a crowd. "Thanks for the heads-up. I'll call you when I get settled."

"I know you can take care of yourself, but be careful."

"Always. Don't eat fast food for dinner. Cook something healthy. Better yet, meet a hot chick and have her cook for you."

"Linds . . ." he began in a mock warning tone.

Laughing, she ended the call, then went into the phone's history and deleted the number.

Adrian approached with a ghost of a smile. He moved so fluidly, exuding power and confidence, which she found even more attractive than his looks. "Everything okay?"

"Absolutely."

He held out a boarding pass. Lindsay saw her name and frowned.

"I took the liberty," he explained, "of arranging adjacent seats."

She took the ticket. First class. Seat number two, which was more than twenty rows closer to the front of the plane than she'd had originally. "I can't pay for this."

"I wouldn't expect you to foot the bill for a change you didn't ask for."

"You need photo ID to mess with someone's ticket."

"Yes, but I pulled a few strings." He retrieved the phone she handed to him. "Are you okay with that?"

She nodded, but her inner warning light lit up. With TSA security being what it was, it should've taken an act of God to change her ticket without her permission. Perhaps the gate attendant had simply succumbed to Adrian's allure or maybe he'd seriously greased her palm, but Lindsay never ignored alarm bells. She was going to have to dig deeper where he was concerned, and she would really have to think twice about what she'd hoped would be a short and sweet, hot and raunchy, no strings attached affair.

Frankly, there was no need for a guy like Adrian to go to any trouble to get into her pants. Every woman in the terminal was eyeing him, some with the sort of searching glance that said, *Give me the slightest encouragement and I'm yours.* Shit, even some of the men were looking at him like that. And he handled the prurient interest so deftly that Lindsay knew it was par for the course for him. He kept his gaze moving, never lingering, while wearing an air of indifference that acted like a shield. She'd arrowed right through it with her direct come-and-get-it eye contact, but it truly made no sense that he'd taken her bait. She was rain damp and scruffily dressed. Yes, self-assurance was a lure for powerful men, and she had it, but that didn't explain why she felt as if she was the one who'd been snared.

"Just so we're clear," she began, "I was raised to expect men to open doors, pull out chairs, and pick up the tab. In return, I dress nice and try to be charming. That's as far as it goes. You can't buy sex from me. Work for you?"

His mouth curved in that now familiar almost-smile. "Perfectly. We'll have an hour to talk on the plane. If you aren't completely comfortable with me by the time we land, I'll settle for an exchange of phone numbers. Otherwise, I have a car picking me up and we can leave the airport together."

"Deal."

His gaze held a hint of self-satisfaction. Lindsay kept her similar response in check. Whatever else he may be and whatever his motives were, Adrian Mitchell was a challenge she relished.

CHAPTER 3

I have her. Adrian savored a ferocious surge of triumph. If Lindsay Gibson knew how predatory and rapaciously sexual his sense of conquest was, she might have thought twice about having dinner with him. His first urge upon seeing her had been to press her against the most convenient flat surface and take her swift and hard. To her, they were meeting for the first time. In truth, they were reuniting after two hundred years apart. Two hellish centuries of waiting and craving.

Today, of all days. Life had a way of grabbing him by the balls at the most in-fucking-convenient times. But he couldn't bitch about this—would never bitch about it.

Shadoe, my love.

They had never been apart this length of time before. Their reunions were always random and unpredictable, yet inexorable. Their souls were drawn to each other despite the disparate roads their lives were traveling.

The endless cycle of her deaths and her inability to remember what they meant to each other was his punishment for having broken the law he'd been created to enforce. It was an excruciatingly effective reprisal. He was dying in slow degrees; his soul—the core of his angelic existence—was ravaged by grief, rage, and a thirst for vengeance. Each time he lost Shadoe, and every day he was forced to live without her, further compromised his ability to carry out his mission. Her absence impaired the commitment to duty that was the cornerstone of who he was—a soldier, a leader, and the gaoler of beings as powerful as he was.

Two hundred damned years. She'd been gone long enough to make him dangerous. A seraph whose heart was encased in ice was a hazard to everyone and everything around him. He was a danger to *her*, because his hunger for her was so voracious he questioned his ability to restrain it. When she was gone, the world was dead to him. The silence within was deafening. Then she returned, and the rush of sensation exploded around him—the pounding of his heart, the heat of her touch, the force of his need. *Life.* Which was lost to him when she was.

As they returned to their seats, Lindsay said, "My dad says you're the Howard Hughes of my generation."

Impatience clawed at him. Discussing his necessary but meaningless facade after the events of the day was both perverse and anguishing. He was beyond agitated, his blood flowing thick and hot with fury and driving hunger.

"I'd like to think I'm less eccentric," he replied in a voice that betrayed none of his volatility. Every cell in his body was attuned to Lindsay Gibson—the vessel carrying the soul he loved. The illicit physical needs of his human shell had roused with vicious alacrity, reminding him how long it had been since she'd last been in his arms. He could never forget how good it was between them. A single scorching glance could set off an incendiary hunger that took hours to burn out.

He craved those intimate hours with her. Craved *her*.

While Shadoe's physical form reflected the genetics of Lindsay's family line, he felt and recognized her regardless of the body she was born into. Over the years, her appearance and ethnicity had varied widely, yet his love burned undiminished regardless. His attraction was borne of the connection he felt to her, the sense of finding the other half of himself.

Lindsay shrugged. "I don't mind eccentric. Makes things interesting."

Raindrops glistened in her hair. She was a blonde in this incarnation, with tousled curls that were sexy as hell. The length was short, about four inches all around. His hands clenched against the desire to fist the lush mass, to hold her motionless while his mouth slanted over hers and quenched his desperate thirst for the taste of her.

He was in love with Shadoe's soul, but Lindsay Gibson was inciting a blistering lust. The combined response was devastating, blindsiding him when he was already on edge. His spine shifted with restless awareness, forcing him to restrain wings wanting to flex in sinuous pleasure at the sight and smell of her. Sitting beside her on the plane would be both heaven and hell.

He had the advantage of remembering every one of their past relationships, but Lindsay had only her instincts to go on, and they were clearly sending her signals she wasn't sure how to process. Her nostrils flared gently, her pupils were dilated, and her body language confirmed her reciprocating attraction. She watched him carefully, assessing him. There was no coyness to her. She was bold and self-assured. Definitely comfortable in her own skin. He liked her immensely already, and knew that would be the case regardless of his history with Shadoe.

"Where in Orange County are you heading?" he asked. "And what was the draw worth uprooting for?"

Although Adrian knew her as deeply as any man could know his woman, in most ways he was starting from scratch every time he found her again. Lindsay's likes and dislikes, her personality and temperament, her *memories* were unique to her. Every reunion was a rediscovery.

She peeled back the flimsy plastic top to her soda cup and took a sip. "Anaheim. I work in hospitality, so Southern California tourism is right up my alley."

He gave the appearance of reaching into his back pocket. With his hand behind him, he summoned a straw and then presented it to her. "Restaurants or hotels?"

How did she take her coffee? Did she even enjoy coffee? Did she sleep on her back or her stomach? Where did she like to be touched? Was she a night owl or an early riser?

Lindsay stared at the straw, then arched a brow at him. She accepted it and tore into the protective paper, but was clearly wondering when he'd picked it up. "Thank you."

"You're welcome."

There was so much to assimilate and an unknown amount of time in which to work. Once, she'd come back to him for twenty minutes; another time, twenty years. Her father always found her. The leader of the vampires was as drawn to her as Adrian was, and Syre was determined to finish what he'd started. He wanted to make his daughter immortal through vampirism, which would kill the soul connecting her to Adrian.

That would never fucking happen as long as Adrian was breathing.

"Hotels," she answered, returning to his question. "I love the energy. They never sleep, never close. The endless flow of travelers ensures there's always another challenge to tackle."

"Which property?"

"The Belladonna. It's a new resort near Disneyland."

"Owned by Gadara Enterprises." It wasn't a question. Raguel Gadara was a real estate mogul rivaling Steve Wynn and Donald Trump. All of his new developments were heavily advertised, but even without the publicity, Adrian knew Raguel well. Not just through their secular lives, but also through their celestial ones. Raguel was one of the seven earthbound archangels, falling several rungs below Adrian's rank of seraph in the angelic hierarchy.

Lindsay's dark eyes brightened. "You've heard of it."

"Raguel is an old acquaintance." He began planning the steps required to research her history from birth until this moment. There were no coincidences in his world. He found Shadoe in every reincarnation not due to chance, but because they were destined to cross paths. But to move so near to his headquarters and end up in an angel's employ ... ? Raguel owned properties all over the world, including resorts closer to her home on the East Coast. It could not be accidental that circumstances contrived to bring her to Orange County.

Adrian needed to know the opportunities and decisions that led her so directly into his life. The discovery process was one he undertook whenever she returned. He looked for routines or patterns applicable to her former lives. He gained knowledge used to build her trust and affection. And he searched for any sign that they were being manipulated, because the time was fast approaching when he would have to pay for his hubris. He had committed the transgression he'd censured others for: he had fallen in love with Shadoe—a naphil, the child of a mortal woman and the angel her father had once been—and he'd succumbed, countless times, to the decadent sins of her flesh.

He had personally punished her father for the same offense. He'd severed the wings from the fallen angel, an act that took Syre's soul and made him the first of the vampires.

The consequences of Adrian's hypocrisy would eventually catch up with him; it was an inevitability he'd accepted long ago. If Raguel was the means the Creator intended to use to rebuke him, Adrian needed to know and be prepared. He had to ensure that Shadoe would be taken care of when his time came.

His gaze met those of his lycan guards, who were sitting a few rows away on either side. They were observant, curious. They couldn't help but see that he was reacting differently to Lindsay than he did to other women. The last time Shadoe's soul had been with him, neither of the two lycans had been born yet, but they knew his personal life. They knew how little attention he paid to the opposite sex.

He would need more than two guards now that he could resume his hunt for Syre, and Lindsay would need her own dedicated protection. Adrian knew he'd have to manipulate that carefully. She was young—twenty-five at most—and starting out on her own in a new place. Now was the time for her to broaden her horizons, not find out that her new lover was micromanaging her life.

Lindsay rolled her straw between her fingers, her soft pink lips hovering momentarily before parting for a sip.

A wash of heat swept over him. Even the knowledge that he would lose her again, that he was forsaking his duty once again, couldn't dampen the rush of desire quickening his blood. He wanted those lips on his skin, needed to feel them sliding across his flesh, whispering both raw and tender words as they teased him mercilessly. Although the Sentinels had been forbidden to love and mate with mortals, nothing could convince Adrian that Shadoe hadn't been born to belong to him.

She talked to her dad on the phone . . .

He grew very still.

Adrian kept his face impassive, but he was intensely alert. Shadoe's various incarnations had always been raised by a single-parent mother, never by a father. It was as if Syre had marked her soul when he'd begun the Change that would have transformed her into a vampire, ensuring that no other man would ever take his paternal role in her life. "Are your parents in Raleigh?"

A shadow passed over her features. "My dad is. My mother died when I was five."

His fingers flexed restlessly. The order of her parents' deaths had never been mutable.

His long-stable world had canted that morning, and Lindsay Gibson continued to challenge his balance, causing the objects around him to begin a slow slide away from their predetermined place. The lycans had been growing more agitated by the day, the vampires had crossed a precipitous line with the death of Phineas and the attack in the helicopter, and now Shadoe had returned after an interminable absence with the most basic pattern of her reincarnations altered.

"I'm sorry for your loss," he murmured, adopting the customary remark offered to grieving mortals who so often viewed death as a sorrowful ending.

"Thank you. How about your family? Big or small?"

"Big. Lots of siblings."

"I envy you. I don't have any brothers or sisters. My dad didn't remarry. He never got over my mom."

Adrian had become adept at winning over her mothers. Men, however, tended to give him a wide berth regardless of any efforts he made to put them at ease. They instinctively sensed the power in him; there could be only one Alpha in a designated space, and he was it. Gaining acceptance from her father might take some work, but it would be worth the time and investment. Familial support was just one of the many avenues he utilized to gain her complete and total surrender, which was the only way he could bear to have her. No holds barred.

He touched the back of her hand where it rested lightly on the armrest, relishing the charge he got from the simple contact. He heard the elevated beat of her heart as if his ear were pressed to her chest. Over the paging of flight information, boarding calls, and gate changes, the strong and steady rhythm of her heartbeat was crystal clear and deeply beloved. "Some women are unforgettable."

"You sound like a romantic."

"Does that surprise you?"

Her lips curved gently. "Nothing surprises me."

His heart ached at that smile. He'd gone too long without her, and his wait was hardly over. While she couldn't fail to feel the pull between them, she didn't love him. He'd have only her body for a time, which would soothe the sharpest edge of his need but still leave him wanting.

His attention diverted to Elijah, who'd pushed to his feet and moved off the carpeted waiting area to the main concourse. The lycans were uncomfortable in enclosed, crowded spaces. Adrian could have chartered a flight or waited for one of his own planes—either action would have spared his guards their discomfort—but he'd needed to send a message to any vampire stupid enough to think he might have been weakened by the aerial ambush or the loss of his second: *Come and try me again.*

"You love surprises," she guessed.

Adrian looked at her. "Hate them. Except when they're you."

Lindsay laughed softly. A forgotten warmth stirred in his chest.

A young woman pushing a stroller and carrying a fussy infant headed toward the gate counter via the carpeted pathway directly in front of them. As she argued with a toddler dragging a small carry-on, Adrian's phone rang. He excused himself from Lindsay and stepped a short distance away.

The caller ID on his phone showed a number, but no name. "Mitchell," he answered.

"Adrian." The icy voice was instantly recognizable.

Primal aggression spurred Adrian's pulse. Lightning split the sky in tandem, followed by the roar of thunder. "Syre."

"You have something that belongs to me."

CHAPTER 4

Turning his head with feigned nonchalance, Adrian searched for surveillance. Was it possible Syre had found his daughter first and was tracking her? "What might that be?"

"Don't be coy, Adrian. It doesn't suit you. Lovely brunette. Female. Petite. You will give her back—unharmed."

Adrian relaxed. "If you're referring to the rabid, foaming-at-the-mouth bitch who attacked me today, I broke her heart. Crushed it in my fist, to be precise."

There was a long, terrible stretch of silence. Then, "Nikki was the kindest woman I've ever met."

"If that's your definition of 'kind,' I've been too lenient. Try a stunt like that again," he warned smoothly, "and I'll put you all down."

"You haven't the authority or the right. Watch that God complex of yours, Adrian, or you'll end up like me."

Turning away from Lindsay's vigilant gaze, Adrian breathed carefully through his seething wrath. He was a seraph, a Sentinel. He was expected to stand above the vagaries of human emotions. Betraying otherwise—through his tone of voice or actions—exposed an unconscionable vulnerability. What was done could not be undone; his mortal love tethered him to the earth, holding him away from the serenity of the heavens.

"You have no idea what I'm authorized to do," he said evenly. "She attacked in broad daylight, proving that one of your Fallen ranks—maybe *you*—fed her in the last forty-eight hours. That opens the door for me to defend myself and my Sentinels in whatever manner I see fit. Think harder before sending another suicidal minion my way. I'm not Phineas; you and I have already established that a fight with me is one you can't win."

It was the truth . . . albeit oversimplified. Syre lacked the formal combat training that honed the Sentinels, but he'd had centuries to perfect guerrilla tactics. He was also older and wiser for his mistakes, and growing as restless as the lycans. His vampires would follow him into Hell if he asked them to. All of which made him exceedingly dangerous. While Adrian knew he could best Syre again, it would not be as easily accomplished the next time.

And Lindsay Gibson would be caught in the middle.

"Maybe winning isn't the goal," Syre taunted.

Casting a possessive glance at Lindsay, Adrian was acutely aware of the misery he was destined to bring into her life. But he couldn't walk away. Between himself and Syre, he was the lesser of two evils.

"If you've got a death wish," Adrian said, as thunder rumbled across the sky, "pay me a visit. I'm happy to assist."

Lindsay frowned at something, and he followed her

gaze. The woman with the antsy kids was still fighting with the elder. The boy's voice rose to a volume that drew attention from everyone in the immediate area.

The vampire leader laughed. "Not until I'm certain my daughter is free of you."

"Your death will take care of that."

Adrian would forever curse the weakness that had driven him to Syre when Shadoe was fatally wounded. He'd mistakenly believed the Fallen leader's love for his child would ensure he would act in her best interests, but Syre's thirst for vengeance was as all-consuming as his thirst for blood. He would do anything to prevent his daughter from bringing happiness to the Sentinel who'd punished him. He'd attempted to turn her into a vampire like himself—a soulless, bloodsucking creature who would have to live in darkness for eternity—rather than allow her to love Adrian with her mortal soul.

Once Adrian had realized Syre's intent, he'd stopped the Change, with unforeseen consequences—her body had died, but her naphil soul had been immortalized. The partial Change had caused Shadoe to return again and again in an endless cycle of reincarnation, because, unlike a mortal, her soul was half angelic but independent of wings. Mortal souls died with the Change and angel souls died with the loss of their wings, but the nephalim had neither vulnerability. When Shadoe's body had been prevented from completing the transformation, her naphil soul survived to remain tied to the individual who'd sired her into vampirism. Killing her father should free her by severing Syre's hold on her soul; only the vampire who initiated a Change could complete it.

But time was Adrian's enemy. He had only Lindsay's

uncertain life span in which to work. It was a terribly small window for an immortal.

"Selfish bastard," the vampire hissed. "You would rather Shadoe die than live forever."

"And you would rather she suffer your punishment, even though she doesn't deserve it. You broke the law, not her."

"Didn't she, though, Adrian? She lured you to fall as well."

"The decision was mine. Therefore the fault is mine."

"Yet you don't suffer as we do."

"I don't?" Adrian challenged softly. "How would you know what I suffer, Syre?"

He looked at Lindsay again. She watched him from her seat with those dark eyes that seemed to catch everything. They were far too worldly for a person of her age.

Her brows arched in silent inquiry.

He affected a reassuring smile. She was as attuned to him as he was to her, but she couldn't recall the history between them that had created the affinity. He would have to take care not to cause her concern or distress. His mercurial emotions were a sign of how far he'd fallen. They were a testament to how human his love for her had made him. The heavens lamented his mortal weakness through the weather—raining when he mourned, thundering when he raged, the temperature fluctuating with the heat or chill of his moods.

"You covet her soul," Syre purred, "because it's the one thing that binds her to you."

"And to you."

"Yet you won't let me bring her into full awareness. Why is that, Adrian? What are you afraid of? That she'll weaken you all over again?"

Nearby, the defiant young boy kicked his mother in the shin. She cried out. The startled baby in her arms flailed backward. Off balance and clearly beyond frustrated, the frazzled young woman lost her grip on the child.

Adrian rushed forward, forcing himself to move at a natural human pace—

—but Lindsay caught the infant first. Too swiftly. So damn swiftly it seemed as if the baby had never been in danger of hitting the floor at all. The mother blinked, her open mouth betraying her confusion at finding Lindsay directly in front of her instead of seated a few feet away.

"Don't forget," Syre continued, "that soul you prize is clawing to the surface with every incarnation whether I help it along or not. Can you get to me before my daughter regains sentience? What will Shadoe think of you when it all comes back to her and she remembers the pain of the many lives you've cost her? Will she still love you then?"

"I don't forget anything. I certainly won't forget what you owe me for the losses I've been dealt today." Adrian killed the call, his focus narrowing on the woman who'd just revealed a colossal complication with her preternatural speed. Shadoe's naphil gifts were strong in Lindsay, suggesting a deeper entwining of the two women than had been manifested in previous incarnations.

He was running out of time. Souls grew in power with age and experience. It was an inescapable fact that Shadoe would one day have the strength to overpower the soul of the vessel she occupied.

None of them was prepared for that.

Shoving the phone in his pocket, Adrian closed the distance between them.

*   *   *

Adrian Mitchell had immaculate feet.

From her ridiculously comfortable seat in first class, Lindsay stared at the end of Adrian's long, stretched out legs and realized she'd never paid much attention to a man's feet before. Usually, she thought they were ugly: callused skin, crooked toes, absently trimmed and yellowed nails. Not Adrian's. His feet were flawless in every way. In fact, everything about him was precisely symmetrical and expertly crafted. It was arresting how *perfect* he was.

Looking up, she met his gaze and smiled. She didn't explain her preoccupation with his sandaled feet. It didn't seem necessary, considering the way he was looking at her. The sexual attraction was a given. It was hot and edgy and made her body go a little haywire, but there was something softer in his regard, too. Something tender, almost intimate. She responded to it with fierce propriety. A primitive part of her was growling, *He's mine.*

"You're not eating your pretzel," he noted, with that low sonorous articulation that made her want to settle in and stay a while.

He was so stringently contained, rigidly controlled. Even when she sensed turmoil in him, he gave no outward indication of it. His voice was always smooth and even, his posture relaxed and confident. Even when he'd been pacing, he had done so leisurely. The combination of that tight leash and his unrestrained sexuality was a potent turn-on.

It was her nature to make waves and stir things up, and she was going to do that with him. She was going to dig beneath that calm surface, because she was pretty damn certain still waters ran deep in him.

"Do you want it?" she offered. "I don't want to ruin my appetite."

His eyes sparkled with amusement and she realized he had yet to smile fully. Her life was dark enough as it was; she usually went for guys who were lighthearted and fun-loving. It was a testament to his appeal that his subdued intensity didn't dampen her interest.

"What would you like for dinner?" he asked.

"Anything. I'm easy." The moment the words left her mouth, she regretted them. "That came out wrong."

"Don't ever worry about what you say around me, as long as you're honest."

"Honesty is my policy, which gets me in trouble a lot."

"Some trouble is worth getting into."

She twisted within her slackened seat belt, canting her torso toward him. "What kind of trouble do you get into?"

"The epic kind," he said wryly.

The faint touch of humor hit all her hot buttons. "I'm intrigued. Tell me more."

"That's third-date material. You'll have to stick around."

What would it be like to keep a man like Adrian? *Just for a little while* . . . "That's extortion."

He looked completely unrepentant. "I'm ruthless about getting what I want, which leads me back to the topic of what to cook for dinner. What's your guilty pleasure?"

"You're cooking?"

"Unless you object."

Her mouth curved. Adrian was clearly used to getting his way with no questions asked. "I should probably deny you at some point, just to keep you in your place."

His gaze smoldered. "And where would that be? The place where you'd like to put me."

"The place where I set the pace."

"I like it already."

"Good." Lindsay gave an approving nod. He was becoming more approachable by the minute. More real. "As for dinner at your place, I'm okay with that. But I want you to decide what's on the menu. Impress me."

"No allergies? Nothing off-limits?"

"I'm not a fan of liver, bugs, or meat that's still bleeding." Her nose wrinkled. "Aside from that, you've got carte blanche."

Her stipulations elicited his first real smile. "I'm not a fan of blood either."

The sensual curving of his lips caused heat to spread outward from her tummy, pushing languidness through her limbs even as it gave her a potent headrush. She felt flushed and totally smitten.

It figured that the one guy to set her off like a rocket was also one who obviously had a lot more to him than met the eye.

As if what met the eye wasn't enough . . .

"Why do you need bodyguards?"

Adrian lifted his shoulder in an offhand shrug, his gaze trained on Lindsay as it had been since they'd entered his local organic grocery. She was long and lean, athletic. Her body was a credit to the Creator, and she kept it in prime shape. The way she carried her weight on her feet was notable for its predaceous grace. While her outward appearance was relaxed, he sensed the edge to her. His mood was affecting her strongly, yet she rolled with it, maintaining an admirable level of control.

She was in a lot better state than he was.

Shadoe's return was shredding his equanimity. Shopping for dinner ingredients seemed absurd, considering the violent need tensing every muscle in his body. Here, finally, was the one woman who made him hunger and crave and *feel* as no other could. The one woman capable of making him acutely aware of every second of his two hundred years of celibacy . . . and he couldn't have her. Not yet.

"Notoriety leads to unwanted attention," he explained with studious evenness.

Which was why he avoided going out in public when Shadoe wasn't with him. He did so now because it served a variety of purposes—it continued his campaign to appear unfazed by the morning's attack, it established normalcy and intimacy with Lindsay, and it gave her the opportunity to select the ingredients she preferred.

She glanced at the lycans who stood on either end of the produce section. "Dangerous attention? Your bullet catchers are pretty big guys."

"Sometimes. Nothing for you to worry about. I'll keep you safe."

"If I scared easily"—Lindsay picked up a sweet potato and dropped it into a plastic produce bag—"I wouldn't have left the airport in a strange city with a guy I don't know."

She knew him, even if she didn't realize why or how. It was obvious she relied on her gut instincts more than black-and-white reasoning, and that intuition was filling in the blanks on his behalf. She'd taken one look at him and set her sights. No hesitation. Just a straight-up, in-your-face *I want you* look that had volleyed the ball into his court with a rapid-fire salvo.

Lindsay gestured at the nearly overflowing handbasket he was carrying. "I'm looking forward to watching you cook all this and seeing if I can pick up a few tips on how to prepare tempura, which is one of my favorite dishes."

"Do you cook?"

That made her laugh. "Stovetop stuff. Nothing complicated. With a single-parent dad and a crazy college schedule, I've eaten out more than I've eaten in."

"We'll change that." He reached for a Mayan sweet onion, then deliberately allowed it to tumble from his grasp.

She snatched it out of the air with nearly the same speed he'd used to catch Jason's flying sunglasses earlier.

"Here you go." Lindsay tossed the vegetable to him, then turned away as if nothing extraordinary had happened.

His hand fisted and the onion burst within his palm like a raw eggshell. As the fragrant juice flowed over his fingers, he cursed and willed the mess into a waste bin across the room with a terse thought.

Lindsay pivoted at the sound, turning so fluidly that her canvas messenger bag didn't sway from her side. She'd withdrawn the large carryall from her checked luggage the moment she tugged it off the baggage carousel. Her haste had roused his curiosity. Why not carry it on the plane if the need for it was that immediate?

Adrian studied her. Her economy of movement was impressive. And worrisome. "You have great reflexes."

Her gaze shifted downward. "Thank you."

"You could have played professional sports."

"I thought about it." Grabbing a bag of carrots, she placed it in his basket. "But I lack stamina."

He knew why. Lindsay's mortal body wasn't built to sustain Shadoe's naphil gifts. What he didn't know was if she had just the speed or if there were other talents.

A sense of urgency swept over him. He had to take out Syre as soon as possible.

Even knowing how drastically, perhaps catastrophically, the world would change when he killed the leader of the vampires, Adrian wasn't deterred. Shadoe took precedence over everything. He'd made the mistake of putting himself first the night he attempted to circumvent her death; he would not be so selfish a second time.

But the cost would be high.

His mission was to contain and control the Fallen, not execute them. When he ended Syre's life, he would be pulled from the earth for disobeying his orders, leaving the Sentinels without the captain they'd served under from their inception. The two factions—vampires and angels—would both be leaderless for a time, throwing the world into temporary chaos. But Shadoe's soul would be freed of its enchainment to her father, and Adrian's hypocrisy would be at an end. The mistake he'd made so long ago would finally be rectified.

In many ways, his actions would rebalance the scales. He and Syre had both proven unworthy of their leadership. Both the Fallen and the Sentinels deserved captains above reproach, individuals who could lead by example.

His cell phone rang. Pulling it out of his pocket,

Adrian saw it was Jason. He apologized for the need to take the call, but Lindsay just shooed him off and continued on without him.

"Mitchell," he answered.

"Damien's flight is about to take off. He'll be home in a couple hours."

Adrian knew everyone was moving as swiftly as possible, but that did little to temper his impatience. Phineas's death demanded swift retaliation, but he needed detailed information to begin his hunt. Damien had been the first Sentinel on the scene and he would have the surviving lycan in tow. They would be his starting point. "I have Shadoe."

A pause. Then a whistle. "The timing is perfect. Gives us some leverage if Syre's finally decided to go rogue."

"Yes." Adrian's spine rippled with tension. As distasteful as it was to use Lindsay as a lure to gain access to Syre, there was no denying that she was the best means of manipulating her vampire father into a vulnerable position. "We're in public now."

"Should I tell Damien to report to your office in the morning?"

"I want to see him the minute he comes in. This is our primary focus until we find the one responsible."

"Gotcha."

"And the pilot? Do we know what happened there?"

"He was thrown off the roof just before we cleared the stairs. It's all over the local news in Phoenix now."

Shit. Adrian rolled his shoulders back. "Have HR send me his file; I want his family well taken care of. And get PR on damage control. His loved ones don't need to be hounded by the media now."

"I'm on it, Captain. Catch you in a bit."

Goaded to get Lindsay back to Angels' Point as soon as possible, he returned his attention to her and found her gone from the produce section. He approached the second lycan. "Why is she out of your sight?"

"Elijah's with her."

"Get the car and wait out front."

The lycan nodded and left. Adrian walked the length of the front of the store, looking down each aisle for short golden curls and a svelte figure. He spotted Elijah standing at the back wall, a formidable sight with his wide stance and crossed arms. Lindsay wasn't with him.

Closing the distance between them in less time than it took to blink, Adrian asked, "Where is she?"

"Bathroom. Where's Trent?"

Adrian was struck again by the confidence and command with which the lycan carried himself, an innate self-assurance that had enabled Elijah to swan dive out of a plummeting helicopter despite his terror of heights. It was also responsible for drawing attention to him as a possible Alpha in the lycan ranks.

Deliberately testing him, Adrian replied with provocative disregard and vagueness. "Obeying orders."

Elijah nodded curtly, hiding any adverse reaction he might have had to the nonanswer. "There's a demon in the store. One of the night clerks."

"Not our problem." North America was Raguel Gadara's territory. It was the seven archangels' responsibility to police demons. Adrian had been created solely to hunt renegade angels. Aside from Sammael—or Satan, as he'd become known to mortals—most demons were unworthy prey for a Sentinel.

"I think this one might be a concern. He was trailing the woman around the store."

"Keep an eye on him. And escort Lindsay to me the moment she comes out."

"You want me to watch her? What about you?"

Stopping when they were shoulder to shoulder, Adrian turned his head and met the lycan's gaze. He knew Elijah wasn't concerned about his well-being so much as curious about Lindsay's importance. "I can manage on my own for a few minutes."

He continued on, stopping in the Asian food section before rounding the endcap. He was halfway through the baking supplies aisle when Lindsay appeared at the end. Elijah was directly behind her.

"We have everything we need," Adrian told her, "unless you have some requests."

She paused midstep. Although her pose appeared casual and relaxed on the surface, he felt the razor-sharp tension in her. An inexplicable breeze ruffled the thickest blond curl draping over her brow.

He sensed the demon behind him before Lindsay spoke.

Her brown eyes turned as dark and hard as black onyx. "Back away from him, asshole."

Power rippled down Adrian's spine and spread outward, disabling the security cameras in the store with an electrical surge. Elijah bared his canines in a savage snarl.

"Call off your dog and bitch, seraph," the demon hissed behind him. "I don't want any trouble."

"Bullshit," Lindsay snapped. "I can *feel* the evil in you."

Adrian made a quarter turn, affording him a simultaneous view of both Lindsay and the creature she was bristling at—a dragon whose hands flexed beside his thighs, preparing to expel the not inconsiderable firepower Adrian sensed in him. As far as demons went, he was merely a nuisance to a being of Adrian's age and power, but the rapaciousness with which he regarded Lindsay and the disrespect he showed her was intolerable.

"If you apologize to the lady for your rudeness," Adrian said softly, "I might refrain from eviscerating you."

"Fuck." The dragon held up both hands, his eyes darting. "I'm sorry, lady. Just tell her to stand down, seraph, and I'll walk out of here."

The demon's mortal guise was that of a sandy-haired, ponytailed teenager with baggy clothing and a name badge that read SAM, but there was a reptilian coldness to his gaze that betrayed a far darker interior. Dragons were a nasty class of demon, prone to terrorizing mortals for sport before making a snack of them. But this guy was Raguel's problem; Adrian had bigger game to hunt.

Adrian flicked his wrist dismissively, already bored with the delay. "Go."

"I think not," Lindsay growled.

A streak of silver raced past Adrian's eyes. His gaze followed with equal speed.

For an instant, the dragon swayed with a throwing dagger protruding from his forehead and his mouth agape in a frozen look of disbelief. Then his body disintegrated into embers, falling into a pile of ash half the height of the man. The suddenly anchorless blade cut through the debris and clattered to the floor amid a stunned silence.

Adrian crouched and picked up the small knife, which shouldn't have been able to wipe out a dragon; the breed had an impenetrable hide. If "Sam" had suspected for even an instant that he was under attack, he would have shifted to protect himself. But Lindsay had blindsided him as well as Adrian.

A hot surge of desire rocked Adrian back on his heels, followed swiftly by the fury of a man who'd just watched his reason for breathing put herself in incalculable danger. He stood and looked at her.

She returned his gaze with a tight smile. "Looks like we both have some explaining to do."

CHAPTER 5

"**A**re you planning on using that?"

Lindsay fingered one of the throwing knives she carried in her messenger bag and made no apologies. When they'd deplaned at John Wayne Airport, she'd met Adrian's guards and had realized they weren't human. They also weren't *in*human or evil, because she would have felt it if they were—just as the clerk at the grocery store had caught her eye like a neon sign. To be safe, she'd grabbed her arsenal sack the moment her suitcase appeared on the luggage carousel.

She shrugged, deliberately affecting a nonchalance that mirrored his. "It calms me to have it in hand."

She'd been slaying malevolent nonhuman . . . *beings* since she was sixteen and had long since stopped losing sleep over it. What was eating at her now was Adrian. That heinous thing in the grocery store had known him—had *deferred* to him—had shown *fear* when Adrian threatened him. While she, batshit crazy as she was, found herself feeling safer around Adrian than she had at any time since she was five years old.

God . . . She knew how to look away, how to wait for prime opportunities. She knew where Sam worked; she could have gone back at a better time and taken him down in privacy. Instead, she had exposed herself as completely as if she'd ripped off her clothes.

She had done it because she couldn't *not* do it. She'd been too young to save her mother, but in the years since, she had sworn she would never stand by and watch another innocent die. The look in Sam's eyes as he backed up was one she knew: he was spoiling for trouble. No way in hell could she let him leave in that frame of mind. She'd never stop wondering who ended up bearing the brunt of his humiliation and frustration, and whether she could have prevented the consequences.

"It calms you to carry a weapon," Adrian repeated, studying her from his seat beside her. His sleek black Maybach purred up the side of a hill, following a winding road that left the city behind.

"What are you?" Her heart was beating too fast, forcing her to acknowledge how wound up she was. With rigid focus, she made her brain stop spinning around what she didn't understand.

She couldn't slide back toward that dark precipice in her mind, that place where insanity whispered along her subconscious like a lover. Her childhood therapist considered her one of his greatest successes. He thought she was remarkably well adjusted for a woman who'd witnessed the brutal murder of her mother at the tender age of five. He didn't know that when the foundation of her reality had been torn from her, she'd forged a new one. An existence where creatures with inexplicable powers worked in grocery stores and ripped open the throats of parents in front of their children. She'd become a warrior in that world of black and white, that world of humans and vicious inhumans.

Yet Adrian and his bullet catchers made a lie of what she'd come to accept as the truth. What was he? What was *she*? Where did she fit in a construct where beings who weren't inhuman also weren't evil?

Lindsay swallowed past the lump of uncertainty and confusion clogging her throat.

Adrian's lips pursed so slightly the action was almost imperceptible. The hot, pulsing energy charging the air around him was totally at odds with his insolently apathetic demeanor. He sprawled elegantly in the bucket seat, sleekly graceful and inherently lethal. When Adrian had issued that softly voiced threat to Sam, she hadn't blamed the whatever-the-fuck-he-was for looking like he was going to piss himself. While there hadn't been even the tiniest fissure in Adrian's composure, he had felt like a tornado to her, a violent and sweeping unstoppable force of destruction.

If death had a face, it was Adrian's when he was pissed: a terror made more horrifying by its impossible beauty.

"You don't know what I am," he said, the unique resonance of his voice even more pronounced, "but you knew what the store clerk was?"

"The only time I like showing my hand first is when there's a knife flying out of it."

He moved so swiftly. One instant, he was arm's distance away; the next, he'd immobilized her. Her hand holding the knife was pinned at the wrist to the leather seat, while the other was locked to the seatback in an iron grip. His blue eyes were aflame, literally glowing in the darkness.

Her heart raced in awe and mad fear. She had no idea what he was, but she knew he could break her far too easily. Power radiated from him like a heat wave, flushing her skin and stinging her eyes. "Let me go."

Adrian's gaze was hot with rage and sex. "You'll find me to be amazingly lenient with you, Lindsay. I'll concede and bend for you in ways I won't for anyone else. But when it comes to your safety, there can be no games or evasion. You just took out a dragon who didn't attack you first. Why?"

"A dragon?" Shock stuttered her breathing. "Are you kidding?"

"You didn't even know what he was before you killed him?"

Realizing he was serious, Lindsay deflated into the seatback, all fight and resistance leaving her in a rush. "I knew he was evil. And not human."

Just as she knew Adrian wasn't, either. Not human but not vile. Capable of being terrifying, yet he didn't incite the chilling and paralyzing fear that had afflicted her when her mother was killed. Lindsay searched for it, waited for it to rise and choke her with sick dread. But the anxiety never came. The tempest she sensed in him lacked violence, but even that—his effect on her inner radar—was unique. She read him as she would the weather, as if he was one with the wind that had spoken to her for as long as she could remember. There was a familiarity about him that she couldn't explain or deny. And though he subdued her, he did so with an unbreakable but gentle grip, the look on his face filled with longing and torment . . . Everything about the way he dealt with her humanized him.

Whatever he was, she saw him as a man. Not a monster.

Adrian stared at her, his jaw taut. Above them, the panoramic glass roof afforded a backdrop of black sky and stars. The moment lengthened into two, then three, with neither of them capable of looking away. Finally, he whispered in a language she didn't recognize, his voice throbbing with an emotion that elicited a quiver of warm surprise. His head bowed. His temple touched hers, nuzzling. His lips brushed against her ear, his hair drifting like thick silk against her brow. His scent—the earthy, wild fragrance of the air after a storm—enveloped her. Her lips parted on gasping breaths and she sought his mouth blindly, overcome by an inexplicable hunger for the taste of him.

He shoved back, reclaiming his seat. His head was turned away from her as he asked in too calm a tone, "How did you know?"

Lindsay sat unmoving, devastated by that moment of tenderness and yearning so fleeting she wondered if she'd imagined it. She struggled to pull herself together, swallowing hard to find her voice. "I can feel it. I know you're not human, either."

"Do you intend to kill me, too?"

His menacing purr set her teeth on edge. She straightened. "If I have to."

"What are you waiting for?"

"More info." She deliberately flipped her small blade up and down through her fingers, trying to regain her center of balance by engaging in a familiar activity. She wasn't going to tell him about the wind and the way it spoke to her. For all she knew, it could be a major weakness he'd know how to exploit. "You're . . . different. Not like the others."

"What, exactly, constitutes an 'other'?"

"Vampires."

"Vampires," he repeated.

"Yes. Sharp teeth, claws, bloodsuckers. Evil."

"How long have you been killing vampires?"

"Ten years."

A long stretch of silence. "Why?"

"Enough questions," she shot back. "What are you?"

"I can hear your heart racing," he taunted softly. "You're smart to be wary. You don't know what I am or what I can do. And you've lost the element of surprise. Now I know what you're capable of."

Lindsay smiled without humor, rising to the challenge. He was in a volatile mood, and it whipped against her senses like the lash of tropical rain. "You have *no idea* what I'm capable of. You haven't seen anything yet." Leaning toward him, she repeated, "What. Are. You?"

He turned his attention ahead. "When we get to the house, I'll show you."

Lindsay stared at him and played loosely with her knife. He'd gotten the drop on her moments earlier, taking her completely unawares, and even that wasn't enough to put her on full alert. He disarmed her in every way, despite knowing how dangerous he was.

Whatever else she discovered about Adrian Mitchell, it was irrefutable that he beguiled. And that was more hazardous to her than any claws, fangs, or scales he might reveal. A damned sight scarier, too.

She focused on his magnificent profile. Even after receiving the entirety of his attention for the last few hours, she was still arrested by the strength of his jawline and the aristocratic line of his nose. And she loved the shape of his lips, which were so beautifully etched they were a work of art in their own right ...

Mental images of that seductive mouth brushing across her skin, whispering heated, erotic words and curving in full smiles seized her heart in a fist. In her mind's eye there was an entire repertoire of intimate, shadowy images that were so moving they were almost like memories. Arousal swept over her skin, tightening her nipples and spurring a slow, hot trickle between her legs.

Tearing her gaze away, she looked out the window and fought to regulate her erratic breathing. *Fuck.* What was *wrong* with her? She was a mess. A quivering, pissed off, turned on, jittery mess.

The distance between the sprawling hillside properties was widening the higher they climbed. Soon the infrequent streetlights disappeared, the evening sky swallowing them whole except for the narrow swathe of the headlights. She reminded herself that Adrian was a known personage and her father knew where she was, but those safeguards didn't calm the part of her mind screaming, *He's not human.*

The car slowed when they reached a wrought-iron gate bisecting the road, cutting off further public access. She surveyed their immediate surroundings, her gaze pausing on a rough-edged granite slab on the shoulder that was sandblasted with the words ANGELS' POINT. A frisson of unease slid down Lindsay's spine.

A burly guard stepped out of a gatehouse. He looked at Adrian's driver—Elijah—and nodded, then retreated back inside to open the gate. The Maybach drove another half mile or so before the house came into view. As dark as the night was this high above the light pollution of the city, Lindsay had no trouble seeing the home. It was drenched in floodlights to the extent that the evening was lit like daylight. It would be impossible for anyone to approach the house from any side or from above without being seen.

The residence scaled the side of the cliff in three tiers, each with its own wide wraparound deck. Distressed wood siding, rock terraces, and exposed wooden beams made the house seem almost as if it was part of the hillside. She knew nothing about architecture, but Angels' Point screamed affluence—as everything about Adrian did.

The car rolled to a stop, and her door was opened by yet another guard. Lindsay was about to step out when Adrian appeared before her with his hand extended. She couldn't help but notice his speed, which he apparently felt he no longer needed to hide, but she made no comment. She appreciated him dropping the pretense of being human, but she wasn't going to praise him for it.

Her feet crunched atop the gravel driveway. She was attempting to absorb the grandeur of the house when movement in the periphery of her vision turned her head. A huge wolf prowled by.

Gasping in surprise and instinctive trepidation, Lindsay flattened herself against the side of the car. Adrian caught her by the elbows, the shield of his body filling her with indefinable comfort and relief. The beast sniffed a tire, then lifted its majestic head and studied her with undeniable intelligence. Her startled senses kicked into overdrive, prepping her body for defending herself.

"You won't need that," Adrian murmured, making her realize the readiness with which she held her knife.

Elijah rounded the hood of the car. A low growl rumbled from his chest as he stared at the wolf. The beast stepped back, lowering its gaze.

More wolves appeared. An entire pack, or perhaps two. Lindsay didn't know how many wolves made up a pack, but there were at least a dozen of the multicolored beasts padding around the driveway. Their size was imposing. Each one looked as if it ate an entire cow every day.

Lightning streaked across the sky, perfectly mimicking the electrical charge around Adrian.

Jesus. She exhaled in a rush.

The otherworldliness of both the place and the man beside her made her shiver. The wind caressed her, ruffling her hair but carrying neither a warning nor reassurance. She was on her own and feeling like she'd fallen down the rabbit hole—confused, fascinated, stoned.

Adrian gestured toward the house. "Come inside."

She followed his lead. They entered through a double-door entrance, crossing over a slate foyer to reach a massive sunken living room. An enormous fireplace dominated one wall; Lindsay was fairly certain her Prius would easily fit inside it.

"Do you like it?" he asked, releasing her and watching her carefully, as if her opinion mattered.

The interior of Adrian's home was a thoroughly masculine space, decorated in shades of brown and taupe, with splashes of a burnt red that reminded her of rust.

Renewable green materials had been liberally used—carved woods, thick cotton linens, dried grasses. Directly opposite the front door was a wall of windows overlooking the smaller hills and valleys below. In the distance, city lights twinkled with multihued fire, but the metropolis seemed worlds away from this transcendent place. To call the residence amazing would be an understatement. It suited Adrian so well. For all his urbanity, she sensed an earthy connection to nature in him.

She kept her bag close to her side and faced him. "What's not to like?"

"Good." He gave a regal nod. "You'll be staying here indefinitely."

His imperiousness was stunning. "Excuse me?"

"I need to keep you where I know you'll be safe."

I need to keep you ... As if he had the right. "Maybe I don't want to be kept."

"You should have considered that before you killed a dragon in a public place."

"You're the one who gave me away. Or your bodyguards did. If I hadn't been with you, he never would have paid any attention to me. So if I'm a target, it's your fault."

"Regardless of who's to blame," he said calmly, "Elijah noticed you were being followed. There was a brief span of time while you were in the restroom when Sam's whereabouts are unaccounted for. It's possible he notified someone that he saw you with us. If he did, his disappearance will raise suspicions and we'll be the first place to start looking for him."

She frowned. "Why would a chick hanging out with you interest him or anyone else? You're rich and hot as hell. I'm sure you're seen with women all the time. Are you talking about him calling the paparazzi? Or more dragon dudes?"

Adrian gestured down the hallway with a graceful extension of his arm. "Let me show you to your room. You can freshen up; then we'll talk."

"*You'll* talk," Lindsay corrected. "I'll listen."

His hand came to rest at the small of her back and she felt the power thrumming through him—tremendous energy restrained by a cyclonic force of will that awed her.

He was something different in this place. The power she'd felt in him from the beginning was sharper, more refined. Or perhaps it was just more apparent. Perhaps he made it so deliberately. Either way, the agitation he'd exuded in the Maybach was tightly leashed now. Why would he betray that disquiet to her, a stranger, but restrain it in his own home, where he should feel the most comfortable?

She looked around and realized they weren't alone. There were others with them: more muscular guys as well as some who were elegantly built like Adrian. A few women, too—all were stunning enough to rouse feelings of jealousy and possessiveness. All together, there were a dozen spectators hanging around the fringes of the room, sizing her up with examining and somewhat hostile glances.

She pushed her hand into her messenger bag and wrapped her fist around the hilt of a second blade. She was outnumbered by a huge margin and, as a human, definitely underpowered. Her pulse raced with foreboding.

"Lindsay—" Adrian's hand encircled her other wrist and instantly her heartbeat slowed, calm radiating outward from the place where he touched her. "You don't need those. This is the safest place on earth for you. No one will harm you here."

"I would make it as difficult as possible," she promised, speaking to the room at large. A possibly empty threat, considering she had no idea what the hell she was dealing with.

"Be careful. You're mortal. Fragile."

She shot him an arch glance. She could hold her own against any other "mortals," even men triple her size. For Adrian to call her "fragile" reaffirmed her belief that, whatever he was, he was powerful in a way she hadn't known existed. "We still haven't established what *you* are."

He exhaled, relenting. "You spoke of vampires. What other creatures do you know of?"

"Dragons. Thanks to you."

He released her and stepped back. "If there were angels, would they be the good guys or the bad?"

Lindsay's mind spun. Angels had a biblical connotation, and she'd turned her back on religion long ago. She'd had to. She got too pissed off thinking about anyone having the ability to prevent her mother's death, yet doing nothing.

She forced her tense shoulders to relax. "Depends on whether or not they were actively killing the vampires and dragons."

Sleek tendrils of smoke drifted up from behind him. The mist spread outward, taking on the shape and substance of wings—pure, pristinely white wings touched with crimson tips, as if he'd trailed the edges through freshly spilled blood.

Lindsay stumbled backward, barely catching herself with a hand against the wall. The purity of his true form threatened to blind her. Power emanated from him with a warm radiance that was tangible; she felt as if she was basking in the noonday sun.

Tears stung her eyes and her knees weakened. The hallway spun with a terrible sense of déjà vu, millisecond flashes of Adrian with wings. Different clothes ... altered hair length ... various backdrops ...

For a moment, she feared she would pass out. And then it all coalesced into one thought: *an angel.*

Shit. She was so far removed from piety, the concept existed in a totally different universe. Even now—presented with his wings and glorious golden glow—what she felt was less about reverence and more about primitive, sinful lust. If anything, she'd grown more enamored with Adrian as his wings unfurled, because seeing him without his facade exposed him as openly as she'd exposed herself in the store.

She'd been peculiar all her life. Faster, stronger, capable of sensing minute changes in the wind that told her when something *wrong* was nearby. As a child, she'd often felt like a mutant, always having to be conscious of how quickly she moved. The last decade had been spent trying to be "normal" while hunting dangerous things to kill. She'd given up hope of having a serious romantic relationship. The need to hide an integral part of herself had left her utterly alone in the most fundamental of ways.

Now she faced someone who knew she was different. Someone who just might accept her being that way because he was different, too. She'd been unable to confide in anyone about the underworld she knew existed. But Adrian knew ...

"You were going to let that dragon walk away!" she

accused, shielding her sudden vulnerability behind anger. Just by knowing that she hunted, Adrian *knew* her—in a deeply intimate way that no one else did. He was suddenly precious to her for that reason, this ethereal being of impossible beauty.

"Your safety was my primary concern."

"I can take care of myself. You should have taken care of him."

"I only hunt vampires," he said smoothly. "And as I said, he was a dragon."

The front door opened and her gaze flew to it. Elijah walked in, carrying the groceries. He paused on the threshold, his handsome face impassive as he took in the tense scene before him. A lock of his thick brown hair slashed across his brow, framing eyes like emeralds. Although she hadn't seen him smile even once, she didn't get an unfriendly vibe from him. He just seemed watchful and sharply curious. Definitely smart. He was canny, she bet, and hard to catch unawares.

She felt Adrian come up beside her. The scent of his skin teased her with her next inhalation. *He's an* angel. *And he hunts vampires . . .*

"I know you're hungry," he murmured. "Let's get you settled, so you can come talk to me while I make dinner."

The thought of a celestial winged being slaving over a hot stove for her was bizarre, yet there was an eerie sense of rightness in being with Adrian this way, as if the intimacy of him preparing a meal for her was recognizable.

God, she had to get a grip. She had to figure out the new rules and how to either deal with them or circumvent them. She couldn't afford to be ignorant, and she certainly wouldn't have anyone dictating where she would stay and when she could go. Somewhere out there, the vampires who'd killed her mother were certainly terrorizing someone else. They'd taken such pleasure from the pain and fear they had wrought; she couldn't see them quitting until someone put them down. She wanted to be the one to do it, and she wasn't going to stop hunting until she knew for sure they would never destroy another child's innocence the way they had hers.

"Okay," she agreed. "But, like I said, you're the one doing the talking."

"Who is she?"

"I don't know." Elijah leaned his forearm against a top bunk in the lycan barracks and looked at the men and women gathered around him. "I don't see how Adrian knows. She just showed up in the airport and he's been all over her ever since. I've never seen him glance twice at a woman, but he can't take his eyes off her."

"Maybe she's just his type," Jonas said, showing the limits of his sixteen years with his naïveté.

"Seraphim don't have a type. They don't have emotions like we do. They don't lust or hunger or crave." At least that's what Elijah had been taught as a pup, and what he'd observed with his own eyes. But tonight, during the ride home from the grocery store, he'd felt a raw energy radiating from Adrian that betrayed an emotional response to the threat Lindsay Gibson had faced in the dragon. And there was a sharp, intensely possessive edge to the way Adrian managed her. He acted as if she meant something to him, while she clearly had never met him before in her life.

"Still, she's hot." Jonas shrugged. "I'd do her."

"Don't even joke about that," Elijah snapped. "He'd shred you. He was ready to take down a demon, in public, just for looking at her wrong."

"Which would've ticked off Raguel," Micah pointed out, rubbing his hand over his jaw thoughtfully. "You know how pissy the archangels get over their territory, especially with the seraphim. Not to mention the possibility of irritating the demon's liege. Adrian would have stirred up a lot of trouble for a woman he supposedly just met."

"Why her? She's human." Esther's tone was scathing, inciting the other females to nod.

"She slew a dragon like she was swatting a fly." Elijah met the multitude of verdant gazes aimed at him. "She moved faster than I've ever seen a mortal move, but you're right, Esther. She's human. I can't smell anything else in her."

"But there has to be," Micah guessed, catching on to what was left unsaid.

"Yes," Elijah agreed. "I overheard her tell Adrian she can sense demons and vampires, and she's been hunting them for ten years."

A rumble of disbelief moved through the pack.

His mouth curved wryly. "Adrian was showing her his wings when I walked into the house. There's a story there. It would be good to know what it is."

"What should we do?" Jonas asked, looking to Elijah for the answer, as all the lycans in the room did.

The others turned to him too often. It was a burden Elijah didn't want, one he couldn't afford to bear. Everyone seemed to forget that he'd been transferred to Adrian's pack for observation. He told himself they were simply used to him being bullheaded. He just needed to break them of the habit of letting him do things his way all the time. But even that implied a power he shouldn't be capable of wielding.

"Keep your heads down," he answered finally. "Keep your noses clean. Jason made the suggestion that Phineas's death might have been lycan related. We don't want to give them any excuse to keep thinking that way."

Esther snorted. "Jason's never trusted us"

"And he's second-in-command now," Elijah reminded. "His opinion matters."

He looked down the length of the long, narrow room. It was a utilitarian space, filled with rows of olive green metal bunk beds and matching footlockers. Of all the packs, Adrian's was the least comfortable. Most of the others were in the remote areas where the Sentinels kept the vampires contained, locations where a lycan could run and hunt and pretend to be free. But Adrian's pack was considered the most prestigious. The Sentinel captain paid and fed his lycans well, but, more important, he hunted only the most egregious offenders, the most vicious, cunning, and dangerous vampires. And any lycan worth a shit hungered for worthy, challenging prey.

Elijah rolled his shoulders back. "My advice: listen carefully to everything said around you. Nothing is too unimportant to take note of. And, please, think twice before you do anything that attracts attention to you."

Growling their assent, the group dispersed before they were discovered. Collusion and mutiny were serious charges none of them wanted to face.

Micah stayed behind, running a hand through the striking red hair that carried over to his wolf pelt. Before speaking, he glanced over each of his powerful shoulders to search for eavesdroppers. Then, he leaned in and whispered, "She could be our ticket to freedom."

Elijah stiffened. "Don't say another word."

"Someone has to say it! We shouldn't have to live like this—fighting against our very natures and repressing our instincts. I saw you carrying Adrian's fucking *groceries*. You're better than that. Better than him!"

"Stop." Elijah turned away. There was nothing he could do. An uprising would lead only to the deaths of everyone he cared about. "He saved my life today."

"He'd take it just as easily."

"I know. But right now I'm indebted to him."

"I can't *not* try, and we can't succeed without you. I know you see what an opportunity this woman is. If Adrian is attached to her, who knows what he might give up to see her returned to him safely."

"He wouldn't give up his control over lycans!" Elijah sank heavily onto a bottom bunk. "If you think our protection has made the Sentinels weak, you're delusional. They're seraphim trained to overpower other seraphim, the most powerful celestial beings aside from the Creator. Adrian lives and breathes his mission. The Sentinels train every day as if Armageddon is tomorrow. They would slaughter us all."

"Better to die as lycans than to cower as dogs."

Elijah knew Micah wasn't the only lycan feeling reckless. Many believed the power struggle between the angels and vampires was no longer a lycan problem, and that a revolution was in order to secure the freedom they felt was their due. Elijah didn't disagree, but he also didn't have a mate or pups to fight for. He had only himself, and hunting vampires was what he lived for. Working for Adrian gave him the intel and resources to do what he did best.

"We're not cowering," he said quietly. "We're responsible for containing former seraphim. That's huge."

"It's servitude."

"What would we do with ourselves if we didn't have that? Where would we go? You gonna take a desk job? Have a commute? Have human toddlers over to your house for playdates with your pups?"

"Maybe. I'd be free. I could do anything I wanted."

"We'd be hunted. Every day we'd be looking over our shoulders, waiting for Adrian to walk in the door and put us down. Running isn't freedom."

The redhead sat on the bed opposite him. "You've thought about this—a lot, it sounds like. Unfortunately, I have to pack—I'm heading back to Louisiana on a hunt—but we'll talk more when I'm home again."

"There's nothing to talk about. Escape would be futile. Stop pushing."

"I'm your Beta, El." Micah grinned. "It's my job."

"I don't need a Beta. I don't have a pack."

"Keep telling yourself that. Still won't make it true. You control your beast, and somehow, that makes it strong enough to dominate the rest of us. I know you feel it, too, the way every lycan instinctively looks to you. We can't help it. That makes you boss whether you like it or not. We can stir shit up on our own, but when it comes down to it, we need a leader, and you're the only one who exerts the force necessary to become one."

Elijah stood. His uniqueness might be their one saving grace. If they couldn't band together cohesively without him, that might just save their lives. He knew what was said about him: his ability to rein his beast in at all times was an anomaly among lycans. Fear, anger, pain—they could all trigger an unwanted shift, but he never altered unless he chose to. As far as he was concerned, that might make him a mutant, but it didn't make him an Alpha. It sure as hell didn't make it acceptable to lead his kind to slaughter.

"You're asking me to lead a charge into a bloodbath," he said, "knowing it's pointless. Not gonna happen. Ever."

"It's too late to avoid, El. Centuries too late."

CHAPTER 6

As Lindsay licked a crumb from her lower lip, the thoughts sweeping through Adrian's mind were unrepentantly sexual. She was a beautiful woman—a tigress with her golden hair and dark, watchful eyes— but what roused him at that moment was the gusto with which she ate. She alternated between using chopsticks with skill and eating with her fingers, her enjoyment evident in her soft hums of appreciation and hearty appetite.

"This is *really* good," she praised.

Her fervency made him smile inwardly.

Sentinels were created to be too neutral to relish anything with such passion. The highs and lows of human emotion weren't meant for them. They were the weights that balanced the scales, the sword that leveled the field.

She held a shrimp up by the tail. "My dad took my grandma out to a teppanyaki restaurant for dinner once. She totally dug the flames and flying spatulas until the chef did this fancy maneuver that ended with a shrimp flicked onto her plate. I thought it was *awesome*. The guy had mad skills But my granny just stared at the shrimp for a long minute—the stare of death, I'm telling you—then she *tossed it back*. She was so insulted. To her mind, the chef should have learned some manners before working in a nice establishment."

Adrian's brows rose.

Lindsay rocked back on the bar stool, laughing. "You should have seen the guy's face. My dad bought him a couple shots of sake just to soothe his pride."

Her laughter was infectious. The sound was so open and free he couldn't fight a smile any longer. His mouth curved for the first time in centuries. He liked her. He wanted to get to know her better.

But he had to maintain the appearance of a calm, unaffected host. Both for her sake and for the benefit of his Sentinels. He could feel their wariness and distrust. Although they would never voice the accusation, they knew Shadoe weakened him. Their concern for his well-being could foster a dangerous resentment if he wasn't cautious. His unit was comprised of seraphim who were better than him, angels who didn't suffer the same emotional frailties he did. They didn't fully understand what a vulnerability Shadoe was to him, because they couldn't grasp the mortal love he felt. If a Sentinel came to believe their mission had been overly compromised by Lindsay, they'd kill her and be justified in doing so.

Focusing on deep-frying the vegetable tempura, Adrian resisted glancing at Lindsay too often. She sat on a stool on the opposite side of his granite-topped kitchen island, nursing her third glass of water. He found himself aroused by the way she swallowed. Two hundred years of celibacy had taken their toll. During Shadoe's dormancy, he craved no woman's touch. But when her soul returned, his repressed need and hunger surged to the fore, all the more voracious for having been contained for so long. He was aching to taste her, push inside her, make her writhe beneath relentless thrusts of his cock.

But that would have to wait. Lindsay needed to trust him first, then want him as much as he wanted her. When he finally had her, there would be no restraint. And he didn't expect she would allow him any. Not as fierce as she was. When she gave herself, it would be with abandon, he suspected. This woman with the heart of a warrior and a soul radiating such pain.

He would simply have to be patient through the necessary prerequisite steps: keep her safe, make her strong, win her trust.

"You're not eating," she noted.

"I am, actually. Just not in the same manner as you do."

"Oh?" Her tone was deceptively neutral. "What's your way?"

Her grip on her lacquered chopsticks changed, became lethal. He could snap her spine with the slightest touch, yet her sense of right and wrong coupled with her need to protect others goaded her to prepare for an offensive move in a no-win scenario. He admired that fighting spirit and strength of conviction.

Adrian considered his answer carefully. It would do him no favors to have her see him as a parasite like the vampires. "I absorb energy."

"From what? How?"

"There's energy all around us—in the air, the water, the earth. The same energy harnessed by wind turbines and hydroelectric plants like the Hoover Dam."

"Bet that comes in handy."

"It's convenient," he agreed, returning his attention to cooking the last of the batter-coated shrimp and vegetables.

His energy levels were thrumming now, as they always did when Shadoe was near. Her proximity—the unique force of two souls in one vessel—allowed him to achieve the greatest levels of power of which he was capable. Life-force energy from souls was the primary source of seraphim sustenance and the reason why the Fallen had turned to blood drinking—they still needed life-force energy to survive, but the stripping away of their souls forced them to obtain that energy through direct means.

"So," Lindsay began, "you hunt vampires."

"I do."

"But the guy in the grocery store, he was a dragon."

"He was."

She took a deep breath. "Are there also demons? I mean, angels and demons always seem to go hand in hand."

He pulled the last of the tempura out of the oil with a strainer, then turned the burner off. "The dragon was a demon. There are other classifications of beings that fall under that designation."

"Vampires?"

"There are some creatures who have fangs and drink blood that are demons. But they're not my problem. My responsibility is other angels—fallen angels. The vampires I hunt were once like me."

"Like you. Angels. Really." Her lips thinned. "But aren't demons everyone's concern? They're the bad guys, right?"

"My mission is sharply defined."

"Your mission?"

"I'm a soldier, Lindsay. I have duties and orders, and I follow them. I expect those whose job it is to hunt demons feel the same way about their responsibilities. It's not my place to intercede and I wouldn't regardless. Frankly, I have enough on my plate."

"But someone is taking care of them?"

"Yes."

She stared at him a moment, then nodded slowly. "I didn't know. If someone's vibe is off, I've taken them out."

Adrian's grip on the counter tightened. It was a miracle she was alive today. "How do you sense this vibe? How does it feel?"

"Like I'm walking through a Halloween fun house and I know something is about to jump out at me. My stomach quivers and the hairs on the back of my neck stand up. But it's really intense. There's no mistaking it for anything else."

"Sounds scary. Yet you hunt the things that scare you. Why?"

Lindsay set her chin atop steepled fingers. "I don't have aspirations of saving the world, if that's what you're asking. I hate killing. But I can feel the evil in these things for a reason. I can't turn my back on that. I wouldn't be able to sleep at night."

"You feel you have a calling."

She took a slow, deep inhalation. The silence stretched out. "Something like that."

"Who knows that you hunt?"

"You and your guards, and whoever you tell."

"All right. This is a no-brainer, but I have to say it anyway: you're going to have to trust me," he said softly. "I have no chance of helping you otherwise."

"That's what you intend to do? Help me?" Her shoulders went back. "Did you know about me when you saw me in the airport?"

"Did I know you could sense demons and vamps, and were actively hunting them?" he clarified, deliberately narrowing the scope of her query so he could answer honestly. "No. I saw you, I wanted you, and you made it clear there was a possibility I could have you. I acted on that."

Lines bracketed her mouth and eyes. A muscle in her jaw twitched with tension. "And that sort of coincidence just rolls right off your back?"

"I happened to be in the same place you were at the right time. After that, we met because you sensed I was 'different,' right?"

"Actually, I thought you were the hottest man I'd ever seen. The vibe came later. As for right place/right time, I should have been on an earlier flight. I missed my connection."

"And I was attacked by a vampire this morning, which resulted in the crash of my helicopter and a need to travel commercial. See?" He shrugged. "Random chaos."

"You're an angel. Aren't you supposed to preach about a divine plan or something?"

"Freedom of choice, Lindsay. We all have it. Today you and I were affected by the ramifications of other people's choices." He held her gaze. "But you don't really want to get into a theological discussion with me. You want to avoid talking about the events that led you to hunt. I'm not going to push you—yet—but we're at an impasse until I know what's going on with you."

She stared back. "You're so sure I have a story to tell."

"I saw you in action. It takes years of practice to learn how to wield a blade like that. Who taught you?"

"I taught myself."

Fierce admiration heated his blood. "What materials are you using to forge your blades? You must use at least trace amounts of silver."

"Yes. I figured out most . . . *things* have a negative reaction to it."

"Dragons don't. In fact, aside from two points of weakness, they have an impenetrable hide. Your blade would've bounced right off of him if he'd shifted."

Lindsay held up her left hand and showed the pad of her thumb. A straight crimson line betrayed a recent injury. "Some creatures have a negative reaction to my blood, too. I always smear a little on my blades before I toss them, just in case. The blood by itself won't kill, but it gives my weapons a chance to get the job done. Found that out the hard way."

Adrian's mind spun with the implications. She was mortal, but even if she'd been a naphil like Shadoe, her blood shouldn't have any effect on others.

She continued to eat, blissfully unaware of his confusion.

Reining in his thoughts, he said, "So you dedicated what had to be a substantial portion of your free time to learning how to kill things that frighten you. You have a strong sense of right and wrong, Lindsay, but no one who's sane begins killing things without provocation. No matter how evil you sense someone may be, you had to have witnessed that evil firsthand to resort to lethal force. Something tipped you off, and something else keeps you motivated. Vengeance, perhaps?"

"And you want to help me get it?" Her expression was wary and assessing. "How would you do that, exactly? *Why* would you?"

"Why not? Our goals are the same. You've been lucky so far, but that won't last. One day soon you're going to take down a demon or vamp who has friends who'll hunt you, or you'll miss your target. Either way, your days are numbered."

"Can you teach me the difference between vampires and demons?"

"So you have a preference." He crossed his arms. "I can point you in the right direction and give you backup. I can train you how to hunt more effectively and show you how to kill without relying on surprise. Right now you're floating aimlessly, waiting for random encounters. I can give you focus and specific targets."

Lindsay leaned back in her chair. "You don't even know me."

Her proclivities, while deeply troubling, provided him with an ideal excuse to keep her close. "I'm holding the front line in a battle in which I'm outnumbered. I can use every soldier."

"But this isn't all I do. I have a regular life and a job."

"So do I. We can work out the logistics together."

She caught her lower lip between her teeth. After an interminable moment, she nodded. "Okay."

Perfect. He enjoyed a moment of sharp satisfaction. Then he heard the front door opening. A moment later, Damien stepped into view.

Adrian's focus shifted to the expected report on Phineas's death. "Join us."

The Sentinel entered the kitchen. He glanced briefly at Lindsay, then turned his attention to Adrian. "Captain."

Introducing them, Adrian made a point of identifying Lindsay as a recruit.

Damien's seraph blue eyes returned to her. "Ms. Gibson."

"Call me Lindsay, please."

"Speak freely," Adrian prompted Damien, giving the Sentinel a look that told him to hold his questions about Lindsay's incarnation of Shadoe until later.

There was a moment of hesitation; then Damien began relaying the details. "I didn't get a lot of usable information out of Phineas's surviving lycan. The beast was incoherent with grief. He did say that the vampire who attacked them was sick. I'm not sure if he meant physically ill or mentally twisted. The attack was especially brutal, so it could very well be the latter. Phineas's neck was gnawed down to his spinal cord."

Lindsay cleared her throat. "Lycans? As in werewolves?"

Adrian glanced at her. "Werewolves are demons. Lycans share a bloodline with them, which allows them to shape-shift in a similar manner. But unlike weres, they were once angels."

"And as a heads-up," Damien added grimly, "they get very offended if anyone calls them werewolves."

"Angels." Lindsay's eyes were wide and dark, the irises a mere sliver of brown around dilated pupils. "Why didn't they become vampires?"

"Because I needed reinforcement," Adrian said. "We came to an agreement—I would petition the Creator to spare them from vampirism if they agreed to help me keep the vampires in line."

"Were they part of the same group of angels, the vampires and the lycans?"

"Yes."

Her only sign of disquiet was the way she twisted her

glass of water back and forth on the countertop. "I'm sorry about your ... Phineas."

"My second-in-command. My friend—no, more than a friend. He was like a brother to me." Adrian had retracted his wings during dinner, but they unfurled again, flexing with his inner agitation and thirst for battle.

Her gaze followed the upper curve of one wing, softening. He felt that tender look as if she'd touched him directly.

She slid off the stool and stood. "Do we know enough to hunt the bastard who killed him?"

Her use of "we" didn't escape him. "We will."

Damien shot her another look, this one less antagonistic than the previous. "From what I could gather, Phineas was ambushed. He stopped only to feed the lycans."

"Where is the surviving guard?"

"I put him down."

"I didn't authorize that."

"It was him or me, Captain." Damien straightened his shoulders. "He charged me. I was forced to defend myself."

"He assaulted you?"

"He tried. In my opinion, it was a deliberate suicide."

Elijah had been correct in saying that no lycan would be able to watch their mate die on purpose—they couldn't live without each other. But if the surviving lycan planned on dying shortly after ...? "Phineas's wound—you said his throat had been gnawed on. Is it possible the bite wasn't inflicted by a vampire?"

Damien's head tilted to one side. "Are you asking if it could've been a lycan mauling? Yes, it's possible, although I would wonder about the lack of blood at the scene. There was some initial arterial spray, but otherwise, he was drained."

It was concerning that Phineas had walked into a snare. Sentinels weren't susceptible to hunger, so it was the lycans' prompting that led him to pull over where danger awaited him. If Jason's speculation about a lycan uprising had merit, Adrian was facing a battle certain to spill over into mortal lives. He couldn't afford to rule anything out. "Report to Jason now, then see me in the morning. I want to go over this again after you two put your heads together. That will be all for tonight."

The Sentinel bowed slightly and left the kitchen.

Lindsay stifled a yawn behind her hand, reminding Adrian that she was mortal and her body was still running on eastern time.

"Let me escort you to your room," he said.

Nodding, she rounded the island, her movements fluid and graceful, despite her exhaustion. "You and I need to talk tomorrow, too."

"Yes."

She came to a halt in front of him and crossed her arms. "You said you wanted me."

"I do." The urge to pull her close, to take her lush mouth and discover the taste of her was riding him hard. A purely human reaction he couldn't control. They'd never worked together before, in any of Shadoe's previous incarnations. Shadoe herself had remained neutral, preferring not to choose between her father and Adrian. This would be the first time they'd work in alignment, pursuing similar goals. The thought of sharing his true purpose with Lindsay, of being known in all ways for whom and what he was, affected him in ways he couldn't have foreseen. "Want" seemed too tame a word for the power of his attraction to Lindsay Gibson.

Her lashes lowered, veiling her eyes. "How bad a sin is it to lust after an angel?"

"The sin is mine, for lusting after you."

Her throat worked on a swallow. "And if it goes beyond just lusting? Am I going to get struck by lightning? Or worse?"

"Would that deter you?"

"I'd hoped I'd earned some brownie points by ridding the world of things like the dragon."

"I'll help you earn more." He couldn't wait to get started. Already, she'd proven herself to be remarkably resilient and adaptable. In a matter of hours, she had learned that the vampires and humans she'd thought she knew were only a small piece of a much larger underworld. And she had taken it all in stride, because she was a survivor, a fighter, a woman he anticipated having by his side in the days ahead.

"Will I need them?" Lindsay fell into step beside him. "You didn't answer my question, so I'm thinking I will."

"The sin is mine," he repeated, leading her down the hallway to the room set aside especially for her. He always made room for her in his homes, as a reminder to himself of both his fallibility and his capacity for humanity. For him, the two were joined. He couldn't have one without the other, and he had neither without Shadoe.

They reached Lindsay's bedroom door. He opened it for her but didn't move inside. As unavoidable as his transgression was, it was resistible—for now. It wouldn't be for long. Not after going without her for as long as he had. And Shadoe's innately assertive sexuality only upped the stakes. Whether she reincarnated during bawdy, adventuresome epochs or in eras of inhibition and repression, she was always quick to seduce him. And he was always quick to fall.

Lindsay stepped into her room, but hesitated just beyond the threshold. She spoke over her shoulder. "It probably wouldn't."

Adrian arched a brow in silent query.

"Deter me," she clarified.

He was smiling when she closed the door.

CHAPTER 7

"You're going to teach her how to hunt her own family? Her friends?" Jason asked, following Adrian into his office.

"She's already doing that." Adrian rounded the desk. "And she'd continue with or without us. This way, I'm giving her a chance to survive."

Jason whistled. "After all these years, you're still an angel."

"Did you doubt it?"

"No. But there are some who wonder if Syre's daughter makes you ... human."

Not Shadoe herself, but his love for her. Mortal love was not for angels, whose objectivity must be absolute. "Those who have doubts should take them to the Creator. I need the trust of everyone in this unit. If I've lost it, I've lost my usefulness."

"You're well loved, Captain. I can't think of one Sentinel who wouldn't consider it an honor to die for you."

Adrian settled into his chair. "As I consider it an

honor to lead you all. It's a responsibility I don't take lightly."

"It's just hard not to feel restless." Jason scrubbed a careless hand through his blond hair. "Our job is to baby-sit the Fallen forever. 'They shall never obtain peace and remission of sin. They shall petition forever, but shall not obtain mercy.' Sometimes the punishment seems as much ours as theirs."

"So be it. We have our orders."

"And that's everything to you."

"As it should be for you. What are we, if not Senti-nels?"

Jason hesitated a moment, then smiled sheepishly.

"Right." Adrian returned the conversation to his immediate concern. "I want Lindsay put into the training rotation as soon as possible."

"How? She's as fragile as an eggshell. She may hold her own with other mortals—maybe even a vampire or lycan with the element of surprise—but hand-to-hand with a Sentinel? Very few beings can survive that."

"We all know our own strength. It'll be good for us to pay more attention to how we use it."

"At what cost?"

"She'll be an asset." Adrian swiveled his chair around, absently noting the lightening of the sky that signaled the coming dawn. "No one sees her coming. That stealth can be useful to us in a variety of ways."

"Use her as bait?"

"As a distraction."

"She'll definitely be that."

Adrian addressed the slightly mocking note he heard in his lieutenant's tone. "Do you have a problem with your orders?"

The smile left Jason's face. "No, Captain."

"In the last forty-eight hours, the two highest-ranking Sentinels were attacked. You saw the minion on the helicopter—she was diseased—and Damien mentioned possible illness in his report on Phineas's attack. I've ordered updates from all the Sentinels in the field. I want you to sift through them as they come in and see if there are similar mentions there."

"What are you thinking?"

"One or more of the Fallen is giving their blood to enable these minions to come after us in daylight. Syre called me about the pilot, so he was aware of her location, but he sounded genuinely surprised by my assertion that I was attacked unprovoked. He suggested that it wasn't in her nature to make such a move."

"You know you can't trust him. He jacked her up with some kind of drug, then called to see how you fared in your run-in with her. How else would he know she was with you?"

"Right. That was my thought from the beginning— that he was playing innocent to dodge the blame. We both know he wouldn't call me about just any vamp, so his interest alone speaks to his guilt. But when I mentioned the attack on Phineas, he didn't say a word. I didn't expect him to take responsibility for it, but the lack of any acknowledgment whatsoever . . . ? No denial, no questions to fake ignorance, nothing? I find that really fucking strange. He can't trust me any more than I can trust him, so he'd never admit that his control over the Fallen is slipping. Maybe he's feigning cluelessness about the attacks, but if he's not and he really has no idea what's going on, there could be a cabal or even a coven of vampires out there who are setting us up to war with one another. They can't take Syre down, but they know I can and that I will if he's gone rogue, which would leave the field wide-open for a coup."

Jason's brows rose. "Hoping you'll do the heavy lifting? Fuckin' A. It would be poetic justice if we completed our mission because of a vampire revolt."

Adrian had ceased to think in terms of justice and injustice long ago. "I need to know if Syre is behind these attacks or not. Regardless of his culpability or innocence, we can use the information to weaken his hold on the Fallen. Either he's deliberately jeopardizing their dreams of redemption or he's jeopardizing them through neglect. Neither is helping their cause."

"Their *hopeless* cause. You want to turn the Fallen against Syre?"

"Why not? As you said, a revolt would benefit us. Especially if he's making it easy to incite one."

"I'm on it." Jason left.

Adrian decided a workout was what he needed to shed his lingering restlessness. Lindsay would wake soon. He needed to have a clear mind to solidify his plans for her before then.

Lindsay stirred from her dreams before she was ready. Part of her mind still clung to sleep, longing for another touch of wickedly knowledgeable hands, another whisper of firm lips across her throat, another brush of silky white and crimson wings ...

Her eyes opened on a soundless gasp, her heart racing and her skin hot. She was painfully aroused, her thoughts filled with flame blue eyes and raw, sexual words spoken in a purring voice of sin.

Scrubbing a hand over her face, she kicked the covers

off and stared at the exposed wood beams above her head. Her future had taken a monumental detour when she'd caught Adrian Mitchell's eye. Her life had been so black and white before—get up, go to work, come home, and in between kill anything that set off alarm bells. Now everything was so complicated.

Lindsay rolled out of bed and crossed the massive bedroom to a private bath that was the size of her old apartment back home. There was a fireplace by the bathtub and a stunning mosaic in a shower that had six showerheads. She'd never even stayed in a hotel as luxurious, yet she felt comfortable and at ease. Despite the opulence, the overall effect was soothing. The soft yellow and blue palette kept the space light and airy, a look she gravitated to because her life could be so dark.

After washing her face and brushing her teeth, she returned to the bedroom and found her gaze drawn to the unadorned wall of windows facing the west. The view was of rocky hills covered in dry native brush. The vista inspired feelings of remoteness and isolation, but she knew the city wasn't far away.

She dressed, pulling on a pair of yoga pants and a ribbed tank top.

"Don't get used to this," she warned herself, even as she walked toward the windows. As she neared, the huge center pane slid leisurely to one side, opening the way for her to step out onto the wide deck. The morning air was cool and crisp, luring her outside. Clutching the wood railing in a white-knuckled grip, she took a deep breath and absorbed the enormity of her change in circumstance. The sun rose at her back and a soft breeze buffeted her from the front. Below, two more tiers of the house jutted over a steep craggy drop, but she couldn't look for more than a moment, her fear of heights kicking in with a vengeance.

The rush of anxiety startled her. Not because she was feeling it, but because she realized she *hadn't* been feeling it until now. All her life, she'd felt rushed and agitated. The sensation was magnified by proximity to nasty creatures, but it was always thrumming inside her regardless. The expectation that she was waiting for *something* to happen, waiting for the other shoe to drop, had been a part of her existence forever. And now it was gone, leaving behind an unfamiliar but welcome calm. Whatever might happen next, right now—at this moment—she felt grounded and peaceful. To make it even better, she was actually enjoying the serenity.

As she backtracked away from the edge, a large shadow swept across her back and raced along the railing. She glanced up. Sucking in a sharp breath, Lindsay turned completely around.

The sky was filled with angels.

Against the pale pink and gray morning, they dipped and spun in unique, mesmerizing dances. At least a dozen, maybe more, gliding around each other with such grace and skill. Their wingspans were enormous, their bodies so sleek and poised. They were too powerful and athletic . . . too *lethal* to inspire piousness, but they stirred reverence nevertheless.

She moved around the corner of the house, discovering that the deck widened extensively at the rear, forming a landing area of sorts. Awestruck and faintly afraid, she remembered to breathe only when her lungs burned. She'd thought she was in over her head with Adrian when he was just a man. Now—

He stood out even among angels. His pearlescent

wings glimmered in the rising sun, the crimson tips streaking across the horizon as he picked up speed. He shot upward like a bullet, then plummeted straight down, spinning in a blur of blood red and alabaster.

"I think he's trying to impress you."

Lindsay dragged her gaze away. She found Damien standing beside her, his hands on his hips and his attention on the aerial acrobatics taking place above them. He was gorgeous: long and sculpted, with his dark brown hair cut short, and sleek, framing eyes nearly as blue as Adrian's. But unlike Adrian, there was a stillness about him—like an ocean becalmed. His wings were on display, which she suspected was an intimidation tactic. They were gray with white tips, reminding her of a stormy sky. Framing his smooth ivory skin, they created the effect of a classical marble statue brought to life.

"It's working," she confessed. "I *am* impressed. But don't tell him I said that."

A surge of air and the flap of great wings preceded Adrian's landing in front of her. His feet hit the deck almost silently, something she barely registered because he was bare chested and barefoot.

Holy shit.

Wearing only loose black pants and those glorious wings, his luscious body was on full display. Rich olive skin stretched taut over hard, lean muscle. Her hands ached to stroke his beautifully defined biceps and pectorals; her mouth watered with the desire to lick the fine line of hair bisecting his ridged abdomen. As real as her dream had felt, the reality of him was far more devastating. He'd been crafted by a master hand and honed by battle, and she couldn't stop her mind from translating all that raw masculinity into hot sexual fantasy. The sheer force of his sex appeal was enough to rock her back on her heels and shorten her breath.

"Good morning," he greeted her, with that low resonance in his voice that damn near curled her toes. "Did you sleep well?"

She dismissed the déjà vu she was feeling as a lack of coffee combined with the remnants of her very erotic dreams. "I was very comfortable. Thank you."

"I thought you might sleep for another few hours yet."

"It's nine o'clock back home. For me, that *is* sleeping in."

"Are you hungry?"

Knowing he didn't eat food himself made his thoughtfulness even more meaningful. "I'd like some coffee, if you have it. And a few moments of your time."

"Of course." He shot a speaking glance at a man standing guard, one of the brawny ones. The guy gave a curt nod before entering the house. "Would you like to go inside?" Adrian asked.

"And miss the air show? No way."

That earned her a slight smile. She was determined to coax a different sort of smile from him—an intimate one like he'd given her in her dream.

As he gestured toward a teakwood table set nearby, his wings dissipated like mist. "Damien."

The other angel followed, his wings vanishing just as Adrian's had. Adrian pulled a chair out for her, then rounded the table and sat next to Damien.

Lindsay was situated so that she faced the east, which set the two impossibly gorgeous angels against the backdrop of sunrise. She took a deep breath, knowing she was at a crossroads. "I've taken a serious and sudden detour here. I relocated to California for a job. I had plans, including a hotel reservation last night that I didn't cancel and will have to pay for. I—"

"I'll take care of that."

"I don't want you to take care of it. Just listen." Her fingertips drummed on the armrests of her chair. "I appreciate the offer you've made to train me, and I want to take you up on it. I'd be stupid not to, since I'm self-taught and apparently blind. I can feel what's not human, but I can't narrow that down to what I should—and want—to be hunting. That said, I need to be self-sufficient. I need to have my own place, pay my own way, and come and go as I please."

"I can't allow you to put yourself in danger."

"Can't *allow*?" Lindsay would've laughed, but this was a deadly serious turning point in their association. She was well aware that he was a being not of this world, a man of immense wealth in his mortal guise and even greater power as an angel. But she would not be subservient to anyone. Especially him. If she didn't set the ground rules now, it would be too late.

The guard returned with a tray bearing a carafe, one mug, cream, and sugar. He set them down in front of Lindsay, then resumed his position nearby. Lindsay wondered why angels would need protection, especially protection provided by individuals who radiated less power. From what she'd gathered from the conversation over dinner, lycans were guarding the angels. There was apparently some kind of organizational structure to this supernatural underground she'd been brutally introduced to as a child. She realized she knew little about the things she'd been hunting, which had made the killing so much easier. She was going to have to put them into context now, possibly humanizing them in the process, while still slaying them.

Not for the first time, Lindsay wished she could go back in time. If she hadn't begged her mother to take her on that damn picnic, Regina Gibson might still be alive now.

"I'm sitting down with you," she went on, "in an attempt to discuss this situation reasonably so we can brainstorm ideas to meet the challenges while still giving me some independence. But if you're going to take a my-way-or-the-highway stance, I've got nothing more to say to you aside from good-bye. I don't want to be a sitting duck out there, but, frankly, I'd rather take my chances under my own free will than to lose my autonomy."

Damien shot a sidelong glance at Adrian, but Adrian never took his eyes off her. There was a faint lifting to one side of his mouth, as if he was tempted to smile. "Point taken."

"All right then. Any suggestions?"

He leaned back in his chair, sliding his long legs forward to assume a graceful sprawl. Her attraction to him presented yet another hurdle. She'd been looking forward to exploring their chemistry before she knew what he was. Now . . . ? Well, it was going to be very complicated. She didn't have long-term relationships—she barely had time for herself—and she'd never had a fling with a man she worked with, to avoid the postbreakup awkwardness. She knew if she was still living with Adrian after their affair was over, she would have to watch him date other women. She'd never lived with a lover before, let alone with a former lover who had a new girlfriend. Just thinking about Adrian looking at another woman the way he looked at her incited a possessiveness that startled her with its intensity, especially considering how short a time she'd known him.

She poured herself a cup of coffee and sweetened it, needing her brain cells to hurry up and start firing.

"You do realize," Adrian began, "that you can't continue to straddle your two lives? If you want normalcy, I can see that you have it. Raguel Gadara takes the safety of his employees very seriously. I can arrange for you to move into one of his residential properties. Between work and home and the cessation of your killing, you should be fine."

"I can't quit. Not until I find who I'm looking for. Maybe not even then. I can't imagine going through life knowing those things are out there terrorizing others, and me not doing something about it."

Something flashed in his eyes. Triumph, maybe. "The alternative is for you to stay here, train hard, and focus on hunting."

"Isn't there some sort of compromise? Can't I live off-site, train on the weekends, and call you for backup when something sets off my freak-o-meter?"

"Even if I could afford to reserve one of my men for the purpose of identifying classification for you, we don't hunt indiscriminately. We police the vampires, but we can't exterminate them."

Lindsay's blood went cold. "Why not?"

"Their punishment is to live with what they are."

"And we humans are ... what? Collateral damage? We have to live—and die—with what they are, too."

The airborne angels began to land. She watched them with both wonder and fury. These beautiful creatures seemed so magical and powerful, yet they were allowing the parasitic vampires to live.

"We hunt every day," he said. "We kill every day. Is it such a bad thing that we focus on the ones causing the most damage?"

She looked at him over the rim of her mug. "Fair enough. Maybe I can join you on my days off."

"Raguel hired you for a reason. What position did he hire you for?"

"Assistant general manager."

"A big job at a big new property. I'm certain you're extremely qualified, but I imagine it's quite a step up for someone your age."

Lindsay licked coffee from the corner of her mouth. "And he's paying me too well."

"Because he expects you to be ambitious, hungry, and willing to put in some long hours."

She nodded, resigned. The new job alone would take up all her time. That was one of the things that had made the position so appealing—she might actually get to have a regular life, using her livelihood as an excuse for why she wasn't hunting as much. A cop-out, yes, but she'd convinced herself that she was taking the best option open to her.

As angels alighted all around him, Adrian remained the calm center of activity. But he wasn't the eye of the storm. He *was* the storm. He was the dark clouds on the horizon, beautiful from a distance yet capable of great violence.

Lindsay realized she was sitting in the midst of angels, drinking coffee and talking about her new job. Normal, she was not.

"Okay." She took a fortifying sip. "Wow . . . All those hours of studying. For what?"

"I can't believe you would give up your dream so easily," Damien said, examining her. "Mortals wither without dreams."

"Hospitality wasn't her dream," Adrian explained, sounding so sure. "An ordinary life was, or at the very least, a semblance of one."

"Is that so wrong?" she asked. She wanted a steady man in her life, the chance to fall in love, hang out with friends, and clock in at a job where she didn't get coated with ashes. But she also felt guilty for wanting ignorance. What kind of person would rather not know about other people's suffering just so they could be happy themselves?

"It's not wrong. Far from it. You've never felt comfortable in the mortal world, have you? You're too beautiful and confident to be a loner, but you never really felt like you fit in." He looked at her with those knowing eyes, seeing right through her. "There's no shame in wanting to feel acknowledged for who you are and at ease in your surroundings."

"I certainly don't fit in *here*." But she couldn't deny that, deep down, she felt as if she did. And that Adrian was a large part of the reason why. He knew what she did and he accepted her without hesitation. That gave her a sense of fulfillment she'd never had before.

"Don't you?"

"Not yet." But she thought she might.

God . . . What would it be like to work alongside others who fought the same fight she did, to not feel so utterly alone in this vicious, lethal world she'd been initiated into with her mother's death?

Reaching up, Lindsay rubbed the back of her neck. "This decision should really be much harder to make—

for both of us. I'm going to slow you down and be a liability."

"Agreed," Damien said.

Adrian lifted one shoulder in an artlessly elegant shrug. "There's a use for every talent."

"I need income," she pointed out. "Regardless of choosing one life over the other, I won't accept a free ride."

"Mortals," Damien drawled, "are so obsessed with material wealth."

Adrian's mouth curved in a ghost of a smile. "Every day, I'm sending teams all over the world. The duty of making those flight and hotel reservations falls to whoever is unfortunate enough to be near me in the morning; I can't assign it to my office staff at Mitchell Aeronautics without rousing suspicions. Today, that individual will be you. Barring complete ineptitude or profound dislike, we'll keep you busy with that task indefinitely. We can negotiate your salary and rent. I provide cell phones, expense accounts, and transportation to all of the Sentinels. You can choose to maintain your own cellular service, but you'll be carrying two phones."

"Sentinels?"

"All the angels you see around us."

Lindsay's gaze swept over the wide deck. "How many of you are there?"

"One hundred and sixty-two, as of yesterday."

"Total?"

He nodded.

A short laugh escaped her. "No wonder you're willing to put up with me. You need all the help you can get."

"We have the lycans," Damien rumbled.

She looked at the guards dotting the perimeter of the

deck. The disparity in their physical build compared to the angels helped to distinguish them. The angels were lithe and lean, which probably helped them aerodynamically, while the lycans were thicker and more muscular.

Adrian glanced at Damien. "I want to search the area around where Phineas was attacked, and I think it's time for me to visit the Navajo Lake pack again."

Damien nodded and stood. "I'll send a reconnaissance team ahead to secure the base."

"No. That would allude to fear and distrust, which isn't a message I want to send."

"Send a different message then," Lindsay suggested. "A real one, letting them know you're coming."

Both angels looked at her.

She waved one hand in a careless gesture. "I don't know what's going on, so maybe I'm off base, but it sounds like you're going someplace that poses a risk and you don't want the people you're visiting to know you consider it risky. So . . . let 'em see you coming. Announce it. That shows fearlessness—you're handing them the opportunity to do whatever it is you're worried about. But first, run with Damien's reconnaissance idea, but on the down low. Canvass the area without them knowing. Put some people around to scope the place out before you send the message that you're coming. Then watch what they do when they get it."

Damien's gaze narrowed. "Lycans have a strong sense of smell. They would know they were being watched."

"So send some lycans you trust to do the job." When she was met with heavy silence, her brows rose. "You don't have any lycans you trust? Then why are they your bodyguards? Keeping your enemies close?"

Adrian gestured for Damien to leave with a jerk of his chin.

Lindsay watched the angel depart. "Alrighty then. Teaches me to speak out of turn."

Unfolding from his chair, Adrian stood. "It's a sound, intelligent plan. I look forward to utilizing your input today and in the future."

"Flatterer." She wondered where he was going and what she was expected to do in his absence. She needed to call her father, then take some time to figure out what she was going to do about her job.

He came around the table. "Would you come with me for a few moments?"

"Yes."

He pulled the chair out for her, then set his hand at her lower back. The heat of his palm soaked through her thin tank top, perversely sending goose bumps spreading across her skin. He led her to the railing, away from the others. She was highly aware of his shoulder pressing against the back of hers, and of his scent, which was absolutely delicious. If she could, she'd press her nose into the crook of his neck and inhale deep into her lungs. The fragrance of his skin was addictive, intoxicating . . . Familiar.

"Do you trust me?" he asked softly, his breath gusting softly over the shell of her ear.

"I don't know you," she whispered back, racked by a shiver of delight.

They stopped at the end of the deck.

"Okay then." There was amusement in his low tone. "Will you give me the benefit of the doubt?"

Lindsay faced him. He stepped closer, into her personal space. Close enough that only an inch separated them, and she had to tilt her head back to look into his face. His wings materialized, shielding them from prying eyes. Her gaze slid over him, drinking in the leanly muscled expanse of his torso. The tight lacing of his abs stirred a deep, raw hunger to see them tighten in pleasure as he thrust into her. Sexual awareness sizzled across her skin, tightening her body. She licked dry lips and his eyes followed the movement. She nodded.

"Good." He caught her close, one arm banding around her shoulder blades, the other hitching beneath the curve of her ass.

Every hard inch of him was pressed up tight against her. She felt his cock stir against her lower belly, inciting an answering ache between her thighs.

Her arms went around his neck. *"Adrian—"*

"Hold that thought," he murmured. "And hold on to me."

He leaped over the railing.

CHAPTER 8

Lindsay screamed as they plummeted. She scrambled to wrap herself around Adrian's lean frame, her legs flailing. His lips pressed to her temple and she fell silent, the terror draining out of her, rushing from her body at the point where he kissed her. His wings spread and they caught air, soaring.

"Aerodynamically," he said calmly, "I need you not to wiggle."

Ticked off that he'd given her no warning, she nipped at his neck with her teeth. "You scared the shit out of me!"

"Why?"

"I'm afraid of heights!" Her legs pretzeled around his.

"You're afraid of falling," he corrected, nuzzling his lips against her cheek. "I would never let you fall."

Bullshit. She was falling for him already. Lindsay wondered if he had any idea how annihilating his occasional displays of tenderness were. They knocked her on her ass every time. She might have some defense against the searing intimacy if she thought it was a seduction tactic, but his behavior seemed devoid of ulterior motive. His actions seemed innate ... or irresistible. The thought that he couldn't help but be tender with her scared her more than flying without a plane. Fear and arousal created a potent mixture.

Burying her face deeper into his neck, she clung to his powerful body, feeling every contraction of muscle as he climbed over a rocky hillside. He held her securely, so tightly no air passed between them, with a surety and confidence that soothed her anxiety. Flushed by surging adrenaline, she grew hotter by the moment despite the chill of the morning and her bare arms. Her breasts grew heavy and her nipples puckered into tight, hard tips.

As they banked to the right, her shirt rode up. Her breath caught at the feel of his bare flesh touching hers. His skin was hot, the hard muscles beneath it flexing as he beat his massive wings. Her hair whipped the sides of her face and her eyes closed. The wind sang with something akin to joy.

The rippling of his washboard abs against her flat stomach was undeniably sensual, the rhythmic clenching perfectly mimicking how he'd feel while fucking her. The hard length of his erection was a demanding pressure, making it impossible to ignore her own growing arousal.

She writhed, rubbing against the thick rigidness of his cock.

They dropped several feet. She screeched. He muttered something foreign with the vehemence of an expletive.

"Behave," he admonished, tightening his hold to the point of immobilizing her.

"You're the one with the hard-on."

He tugged her chest even closer, crushing her breasts against him. "Your nipples prove I'm not the only one."

They crested another hill, then swooped downward, landing neatly in a small clearing on the far side. Lindsay didn't let go right away. Instead, she did what she'd wanted to do earlier: she pressed her nose against his skin and inhaled. His fingers shoved into her hair, his palm cupping her scalp and holding her near.

He breathed roughly. "How you tempt me, *tzel*."

"Should I be insulted or turned on when you call me things I don't understand?" Her tongue fluttered over his throbbing pulse; then she scraped her teeth gently across it.

Adrian groaned. "Do that again and I won't be responsible for the gravel you may later find embedded in your back."

"Ouch." She stepped back. Glancing around, she realized he hadn't brought her here for an isolated tryst. The dry brush and rocky ground wasn't at all conducive to taking their clothes off.

"Sentinels and lycans have very keen hearing," he explained, restoring his immaculate appearance with a single swipe of his hand through his hair. "If I want to speak to you privately, I need to do so away from the house."

"What do you have to say that you don't want them to hear?"

His wings dissipated. "It isn't what I have to say, but the manner in which I say it. And how I look at you when I say it."

Her brows rose questioningly.

His brilliant blue gaze swept over her, lingering on

the hardened points of her nipples. She pulled her shoulders back and let him look.

Adrian's expression softened. "I don't bring women to the house. The lycans don't know what to make of your presence and they're paying close attention to me, looking for cues."

Lindsay tamped down the warmth wanting to spread through her. After a lifetime of feeling out of sync with the world, she was now somewhere she felt comfortable, a place she alone fit into. Was it possible her square peg had finally found a square hole? "Of course you don't bring women here. How could you explain a legion living under your roof and a pack of wolves prowling the perimeter? Unless there are others out there like me . . . ?"

"No," he said softly. "I can safely say that you are unique in the entire world."

"But you'd invited me over for dinner before I killed the dragon."

His arms crossed, which tightened his biceps and made her hot for him all over again. "Some things you just know. I knew when I saw you that bringing you into my life was inevitable."

"Even as a human with nothing special about her."

"There was always something special about you, even then."

She turned her back to him. Her affection for him was building irrationally fast and she couldn't seem to stop it. "I can't see how I'll be more than a pain in the ass for you."

"As you said, they don't see you coming. You can be a lure for vampires, and I can use you to my advantage. Is that answer acceptable?"

Lindsay looked over her shoulder at him. Mercenary and ruthless: she didn't begrudge him that. She understood the need to be that way. If using her to draw in vampires was the way she could be helpful, she'd go along with it. Innocent people were dying. Victims with families, including little children like she'd once been. She wished someone had been mercenary and ruthless in saving her mother. "An artery to use for bait? Yes, that would be acceptable to me. But I want to know more about the whole angel-turned-vampire thing. And the angel-turned-lycan thing. Knowledge is power and all that."

"Agreed." He waited until she faced him. "Shortly after Man was created, two hundred seraphim were sent to earth to observe and report on their progress. These angels were known as the Watchers. They were a scholarly caste and they were given strict orders not to interfere with the natural progression of Man's evolution."

"They were only supposed to 'watch.' I get it."

"They didn't obey."

She smiled wryly. "I figured."

"The Watchers began to fraternize with mortals, teaching them things they shouldn't know."

"Such as . . . ?"

"The creation of weapons, warfare, science . . ." He waved one hand in a markedly casual gesture. "Among many other skills."

"I'm following."

"A warrior caste known as the Sentinels was created to enforce the laws the Watchers were breaking."

"And you lead these Sentinels?"

"Yes."

"So you're the one responsible for turning the fallen

angels into vampires," she accused, her heartbeat quickening with anger and horror.

"*They* are responsible for what they are. *They* made the choices that led to their fall." He studied her with those fathomless eyes. "Yes, I administered the punishment. I stripped the Watchers of their wings. Wings and souls are connected, and the loss of their souls led to their blood drinking. But I'm not accountable for their mistakes, any more than a police officer is responsible for the crimes committed by offenders."

"A better analogy would be a penal system that releases criminals who are more dangerous after incarceration than they were before it." Lindsay ruffled her curls in frustration. "Why do they have to drink blood? You don't, and they were once angels like you."

"They're still physiologically seraphim. Severing their wings didn't make them mortal. They can't ingest the food you eat. We look similar to mortals on the outside, but we are not the same. We aren't built the same. Your bodies create energy through physical chemical processes; we aren't designed that way."

She nodded slowly. The wings—and the way they appeared and disappeared—were more than enough proof of how different they were. "And what do the lycans do? How do you use them?"

"They scent vampires in hiding, raid nests, and herd vamps into sparsely populated areas where they'll cause the least amount of damage to mortals."

"You said there are a hundred sixty-two Sentinels now. The rest . . . died?"

His chest lifted and fell with a deep breath. "They were casualties, yes."

"How many lycans are there?"

"Several thousand from an original twenty-five, because they can breed."

"And how many vampire casualties have there been?"

"Hundreds of thousands. But they're still ahead, because they can spread vampirism to mortals much faster than the lycans can reproduce."

"While you've been stuck with a static number, minus the ones you lose along the way?" Lindsay exhaled in a rush, overwhelmed by the enormity of the task Adrian faced. "Why can the fallen angel-vampires spread their sickness? I don't understand why that's okay."

"I don't have an answer for that. If I was to hazard a guess, I would say it has something to do with freedom of choice. The choice of the Fallen to refrain from sharing their punishment, just as they should have refrained from sharing their knowledge. And the choice of the mortals who are Changed into vampires."

"You're assuming the mortals have a choice."

"There are those who seek the Change. Most especially ones who are ill or crippled in some way. Ones who want to live, no matter the cost."

She shuddered. "Who wants to live like that? I'd rather be dead."

Adrian took a step closer. Then another. "The better question is, who wants to die like that? Most mortals don't survive the Change. Of those who do, many become feral and have to be put down. The Fallen don't have souls. When they spread their affliction to mortals, who do have souls, the Change causes irreversible damage. Some minions can survive without a soul, but most lose their empathy and then their minds."

"You call them minions?" Her nose wrinkled. "Even the term is disgusting."

A breeze ruffled his hair, luring a thick black lock to hang over his brow. The slight blurring of his sharp perfection made him look younger than the early-thirties range she'd originally pegged him for.

Lindsay now knew what an illusion that was. His eyes, so brilliantly hued, were ancient. The length of time he was discussing so casually was unfathomable to her. Ages. Eons. Trying to imagine the history he'd seen was almost frightening.

"You're here," she said carefully, hooking her thumbs in the waistband of her pants, "to punish angels who taught mortals things they shouldn't know yet . . . but you're going to teach me things I wouldn't know otherwise. Do the rules that applied to the Watchers not apply to you?"

"I'm going to teach you how to better defend yourself, but within the limitations of your mortal body. Basically, nothing you couldn't learn elsewhere from mortal masters of self-defense."

"Good." She released the breath she hadn't known she was holding. "Now that I know the basics, I want to go with you when you leave."

He shook his head. "I don't know what I'm dealing with. Until I do, it's too hazardous."

"There's someplace safer than by your side?" she challenged.

"By my side is the most dangerous place for you to be."

The temptation he presented proved that, but . . . "I'll take my chances. Besides, I'm already packed."

When his face took on an arrogant look of command, Lindsay held up a hand. "Think carefully," she warned, "before you answer."

Adrian paused. The stillness that settled over him was absolute.

She'd known within moments of meeting him that he was used to giving orders and having them obeyed without question. He was going to have to get over that with her.

"Your way or the highway?" he asked with dangerous softness.

Lindsay lowered her hand. "I do what I do—I kill heinous things—to avenge *someone*. I do it for the victims, because they couldn't do it for themselves. If I can help someone who has a name and a face, friends, a life I've seen . . . Do you understand? You said you would give me a focus, and that's the kind of focus I want. I want to help you find whoever killed your friend."

"I'm not hunting today."

"Bullshit. You're going after information. You want to see if you can pick up anything around the scene where your friend was killed. And if you find something, you're not just going to call it a day and come home. I don't need to be trained to be helpful. I'm lethal already."

"With the element of surprise," he qualified. "In hand-to-hand combat you'd be dead before you could blink. And when word gets out about you, you'll be hunted. You're not ready for that yet."

"No one can be totally ready for that. And when my time comes, it comes. Everything happens for a reason."

"Now *I'm* calling bullshit."

"You have to take me with you," she said in a voice that brooked no argument. Then she gave him "the look," the one she'd given him in the airport to snare his interest. She wasn't above using her feminine wiles to get her way.

He smiled. A *full*, seductive smile that rocked her back on her heels. "You can't manage me, Lindsay. I'm more than happy to be the recipient of your persuasive skills, but not if you'll be pissed off when it doesn't get you what you want."

That smile was kicking her ass. Crackling electricity raced across her skin, making the hair on her nape stand on end. "Adrian—"

"No." The curve of his mouth straightened abruptly. "I won't make a tactical error because of my craving for you. My mission—and, most of all, *you*—are too important to risk."

The tightness that constricted her chest was fueled by respect. She had a sudden crazed desire to crawl all over him naked. "I have responsibilities, too, Adrian. I know those things are out there. I wish I didn't. I wish I couldn't feel them coming. But I can, and there's an accountability that comes with that curse. But that's all about what's in it for me. For you, I can be useful and I can watch your back."

"I'm a Sentinel. I can take care of myself." As firm as his voice was, it was softened by the warmth in his extraordinary eyes.

"I won't stay here if you won't let me come. Childish, I know, but it's all I've got as leverage."

"You're blackmailing an angel."

She shrugged. "So sue me."

His wings materialized, flexing along with his jaw. "I can detain you."

"And then my father will create a big stink about me falling off the face of the earth and you'll have even more trouble on your hands. Hey—don't get your wings in a twist. It was partly your idea to keep him in the loop. Besides, I know you want to catch the ones responsible, and every day that passes, the trail grows colder. I don't know if you have the same sixth sense I've got or not, but if not, we both know I can find them real quick. And they won't see me coming. I'm just an average, everyday artery to them."

"Blackmail works both ways, Lindsay. I want something in return."

"Oh?" She was instantly on alert. The glimmer in his eyes was too ... triumphant, almost as if she'd played right into his hands.

"Your reason for hunting—the *someone* you're avenging—I want to know who it is."

"I was talking about a generalized 'someone,'" she prevaricated.

Adrian studied her for a long moment, then said, "Very well. I'll take something else, then."

"What?"

"This—"

He was kissing her before she could blink, having moved so fast it felt like she'd missed entire frames in a film reel.

She was shocked into stillness. He sealed his mouth over hers, his firm, sensual lips pressing softly. The gentleness was unexpected, considering the tightness with which he cupped her face in his hands. His tongue slid along her bottom lip, then slipped inside. The silken caress in her mouth made her shiver, then moan. Adrian kissed with the leisure of a man who took his time making love, which was a luxury she'd never had time for. Sex was for scratching an itch and for feeling human for a few stolen moments. It had never been this slow, deep melding. And this was only a kiss. What the hell would he be like in bed?

Her toes curled. Her hands caught his waistband, hanging on for the ride. Behind her closed eyelids she absorbed the taste and scent of him, the feel of him so close. She felt as if he'd found a way inside her. She was aware of nothing else. Just the feeling of him sifting through her like curling smoke . . .

Lindsay wrenched away with a curse. "Were you just *inside my head*?"

"I needed to know if your past was a liability." Adrian licked his lips as if savoring the flavor of her.

The primitive gesture did crazy things to her insides, but she was too furious to be swayed by it. "So you violated my privacy by digging in my brain to find the personal things I didn't want to talk about?"

"Yes."

"Fuck you." Lindsay would've loved to walk away in a huff, but she was stuck by their location. She wondered if he'd planned that all along.

"I know who you want," he said, "and I assure you, you're going to need my help to snare her. You're definitely going to need my help getting her to identify her accomplices."

She stared at him, wondering how it was possible to feel violated and hopeful at the same time. He'd seen the attack in her mind, seen that Amazon-sized bitch with the flame red hair and skintight black leather outfit. "You didn't recognize the two guys with her?"

"There are thousands of vamp males with spiky, crayon-hued hair like that. Even body size and ethnic features aren't much help when the memory is as fractured by terror and grief as yours is." His wings flapped restlessly, as if her remembered pain affected him. "At some point during the attack, you stopped seeing and started focusing on feeling. That's what resonates most in you—how it felt to watch your mother bled dry, how it felt waiting for your turn."

Which never came. There hadn't been a scratch on her when she broke away screaming for help. The damage they'd inflicted had been entirely mental and emotional. Watching her mother being drained of life. Hearing the lurid taunts. Feeling the pressure of claws against her flesh as she was being held down . . .

"But you know the woman?" she pressed, needing a clue. Anything at all that could help her find the vampires responsible for the event that had forever changed her life.

"Oh yes. Vashti is unmistakable. She's second-in-command of the vampires."

"Second-in-command . . . Vampires like that are running the show? And that's not enough to wipe them all out?"

"It's enough to wipe *her* out, and her accomplices." Adrian's mouth thinned into a grim line. "You and your mother were ambushed in broad daylight. The Fallen are the only vampires who aren't photosensitive. They can bestow temporary immunity to minions by sharing their blood, but either way, one—or more—of the Fallen is ultimately responsible for the attack. Considering that, it's a wonder you survived. They should have killed you, too, to protect their identity."

"I wasn't enough of a threat, I guess. Stupid move on their part." She blew out her breath in a rush. As pissed off as she was at Adrian for picking her brain without her permission, she also wanted to kiss him senseless. He was now the key to unlocking the mystery of that day. She now had the "who"; she just needed the "why."

Then she could kill the fuckers and close that chapter of her life. "So, now that we've gotten the extortion portion of this discussion out of the way, I'll be going with you."

"You will follow orders implicitly."

"Yes. I promise." Lindsay made a gesture of an X over her chest. "Cross my heart."

Adrian beckoned her with a crook of his finger. "We need to head back."

Her body hummed with excitement and growing exhilaration. She suspected that if he ever flew with her over longer distances, she just might orgasm midflight. Like a biker bunny who got off on the vibrations of a Harley-Davidson. Adrenaline had always made her hot. Adrenaline combined with Adrian was an inferno. Her gaze took him in, sliding over him from the top of his dark head down to his bare feet ... which weren't quite touching the coarse ground.

She was so screwed.

CHAPTER 9

Syre swiveled his desk chair around and faced the carefully crafted Main Street scene outside his office window. Reminiscent of a Norman Rockwell painting, the small town of Raceport, Virginia, was modernized by the dozens of Harley-Davidson motorcycles lined in neat rows along the curbs.

"Adrian admitted he killed her? He just came right out with it?"

His lieutenant's normally melodic voice throbbed with anger and sorrow. Vashti paced like a caged animal, her stiletto-heeled boots clicking rhythmically across the hardwood floor.

"Yes," he answered quietly.

"How are we going to retaliate? What are we going to—?"

"Don't do anything, Father."

The eerie calm in his son's voice broke Syre's heart more than fury would have. Pushing to his feet, he faced his only living child. Torque lingered in the shadows by the threshold, avoiding the advancing rays of the sun that slanted over Syre's desk and cut the room in half.

"Nikki wants—*wanted*—peace between us and the Sentinels." Torque's handsome features were ravaged by grief, his sloe eyes red rimmed and his mouth bracketed with deep-set lines. "She would never wish to be the cause of a war."

"Your wife didn't cause this," Vash snapped. "Adrian's brought war on himself."

Syre clasped his hands at the small of his back. "He claims she attacked him."

"Fuckin' ridiculous."

"I would agree, but he said she was foaming at the mouth. Rabid. And he didn't recognize her—he has no idea he killed my daughter-in-law. How is that possible, unless her appearance was drastically altered? Nikki's been missing for two days. Who knows what was done to her during that time? She could've been poisoned with drugs." He looked at his son, who'd often witnessed just how horribly a minion's unique body chemistry could react to certain human drugs.

"Maybe it's not Nikki, then," Vash said quickly. "Maybe it was someone else."

"It was her," Torque confirmed hoarsely. "I felt the moment her life slipped away."

Syre nodded, knowing that the usual bond between vampire and minion was doubly strong when love was involved. He himself felt Shadoe's deaths keenly, no matter the distance between them. "What do we know about the abduction?"

Torque scrubbed a hand over his face. "She was dropped off at the airport around ten o'clock. I called the coven at midnight, because she was late picking me up in Shreveport. Viktor was sent to look for her. Nikki was gone and there was a trace scent of lycan dogs around the helicopter."

Looking at Vash, Syre commanded, "Track the lycans. Bring them to me."

"I thought you'd never ask." Her amber eyes were cold and hard as stone. A half century past, a pack of lycans had ambushed and killed her mate. She now harbored hatred so poisonous it was killing her in slow degrees. "I can get them to tell us what Adrian's orders were."

"*If* Adrian had something to do with it."

Torque frowned. "Who else would be responsible?"

"That's the bigger question."

Vash cursed under her breath. With her waist-length red hair and black leather bodysuit, she embodied popular-fiction descriptions of vampiric beauty. She never hid her fangs, arguing that some mortals paid for vampire teeth veneers. "Adrian told you he killed Nikki. What more do you need?"

"Motive." Syre arched his neck to relieve the building strain there. His fangs descended with the stretch, just as his former wings used to express his mood. "At his deepest core, Adrian is a Sentinel. That sounds simplistic, but it's really not. He's like a machine—he has his orders and he doesn't deviate from them. That adherence to accountability is his greatest strength—and his most predictable weakness. He wouldn't suddenly go rogue; it's not in his nature. To strike this way—this would be a countermove, not a first assault."

"Maybe his orders have changed," Torque suggested wearily.

Vash snorted. "Maybe he's lying. He might've made

up the self-defense story to cover his ass, with the ultimate goal being to piss us off and make us retaliate, so he has an excuse to come after us. Maybe he's sending a message."

"You forget, he still answers to the Creator," Syre said wryly. "And if he wanted to make a statement, he would have pinned a note to Nikki's broken body and left her on my porch. He wouldn't leave any room for speculation. My guess? Someone wants us to blame him. More disturbing, he thinks I sent Nikki to him in some compromised state of mind, so the reverse is true: we're being blamed for Nikki's actions. Who has the most to gain from a war between vampires and angels?"

"The lycans." Vash exhaled harshly and began to pace again. Her long-legged stride ate up the twenty-foot distance between walls, back and forth, at a speed that would give most mortals a headache to watch. "Underhanded and clumsy suits the dogs, I suppose. But I didn't think they had the balls—or the brains—to wriggle out of the Sentinels' collar."

Syre smiled grimly. It was a testament to Adrian's leadership that he'd kept the lycans in his service for so long. Somehow he managed to keep each successive generation indentured by the bargain he'd made with their ancestors.

To this day, Syre admired the Sentinel leader for his foresight. The lycans' finite life spans enabled them to breed. Unlike the vampires, who were sterile. Or the Sentinels, who were forbidden to procreate. Adrian needed those lycan pups to supplement his Sentinel ranks, which had never been reinforced.

"Remember," Syre said grimly, "the lycans are descended from our fellow Watchers. They're distantly related to you and me, so certainly some of our rebellious temperament exists in them. And while they were little more than beasts when they were first infected with demon blood, their mortality has given them an advantage—we remain the same while they've evolved."

"So a renegade lycan or few sets us up to war with the Sentinels. Why? Mass suicide? Their sole purpose for drawing breath is to serve the Sentinels. They're stuck right in the middle."

"Maybe they no longer want to be. Find the ones responsible for Nikki's abduction and we'll ask them, but hold off on taking down any Sentinels for the time being."

"We're justified," Vash argued.

"Do as I say, Vashti."

"As you wish, Syre." Pivoting, she went to the door. She moved like the huntress she was, with precision and deliberation. Syre trusted her with his life, just as he'd trusted her with Shadoe's in her original incarnation. Vash had trained his willful daughter, instilling some much-needed discipline in her, and together the two women had been responsible for the eradication of thousands of demons.

Vash hugged Torque before passing him, murmuring a promise to hunt down the bastards who'd killed his wife. Then she left, taking her agitated energy with her. In the sudden stillness that descended in her wake, Torque's shoulders drooped as if the weight of the world was upon them. He'd Changed Nikki because he had fallen in love with her, bestowing immortality so that she'd always be with him. Forever. Unfortunately, immortality was no safeguard against a Sentinel.

Torque crossed his arms and glared, his eyes glowing

a molten amber. "Avenging Nikki is my right, not yours or Vash's."

"Absolutely. But I need something looked into, and it's too delicate an assignment to trust to anyone else."

Stepping deeper into the room, Torque halted when the tips of his steel-toe boots touched the line between sunlight and shadow. His brutally short hair stuck straight up in opposing directions, the thick Asian locks bleached nearly white at the tips. It was a style that suited both the exotic features he'd inherited from his mother and his sharp-edged lifestyle. While Syre nurtured small towns that attracted motorcycle enthusiasts, ensuring a steady flow of fresh blood to local cabals and covens, Torque managed an expanding chain of nightclubs that offered haven to fledgling minions.

Approaching his son, Syre clasped him by the shoulders. There was so much of Shadoe in Torque's features, all the haunting similarities of twins. Now his daughter was stripped of her genes along with her memories. Once the spitting image of her mother, her incarnations bore the trademarks of someone else's lineage. Although he loved Shadoe regardless of her exterior, there was a part of him that felt as if he was losing her mother anew every time their daughter was reborn with another woman's face.

"I know this is a terrible time," he said softly, "but I have to ask you to drop off the map. In addition to Adrian's comments about Nikki attacking him, he made a reference to Phineas that concerns me. I need you to find out what's happened in the last forty-eight hours."

"I'll see to it." Torque set his hands over Syre's. "I need something to focus on now, or I might do something we'll all regret."

Syre pressed his lips to his son's forehead. He understood all too well. He'd barely survived the loss of his wife and Shadoe. If not for Torque, their deaths would have killed him long ago. "When we spread the word that you've gone under in mourning, no one will question your absence."

It was heartless to use his son's grief to further his agenda, but he didn't have the luxury of passing up perfect opportunities.

God, he felt old and callous. So old that he didn't recognize the youthful face staring back at him from the mirror on the wall by the door. He looked to be only ten years older than Torque, who most people would guess was in his mid- to late-twenties.

Torque spoke gruffly. "How does Adrian maintain control when he's losing the love of his life every few hundred years? Can you be sure he's got it together? Shadoe's been gone a long time, Dad. It has to be fucking with his head."

"That might be true if he gave a shit. Letting her die again and again . . . never having any memory of her family and the people who love her? That's cruelty, not love."

"I don't know." Torque's eyes reflected his inner torment. "I think I'd do anything to get Nikki back, whatever the cost."

"He's not like us. If you'd heard him on the phone . . . so calm and unaffected. He's a seraph in every sense of the word. The soul is everything to him. He can see no purpose in existing without one. You say you'd do anything, but if you were faced with the choice, I know you'd make the right one."

"You can't know that. *I* can't know that. I feel like ripping apart every Sentinel and lycan who crosses my path."

"That's precisely what Nikki's death was designed to do—make us wild with rage. We have to be smarter than that. If we gather intel first, we can move with precision instead of shooting in the dark. Think of how it would benefit us to cause a rift between the Sentinels and the lycans. All we need is proof that the dogs are conspiring against their masters. We turn that over to Adrian and he'll do the dirty work for us."

"What am I looking for?"

"You'll know it when you see it. If something's off, you'll catch it."

"Suggestions for where to begin?"

Syre held his wrist before his son's mouth, offering the potency of his Fallen blood to assist him on his way. Although Torque's naphil state gave him an advantage over minions, he was still disadvantaged when compared to the Fallen. Drinking a pint or two of pure Fallen blood would negate that deficiency for a few days.

Hissing as Torque's fangs sank into his artery, Syre closed his eyes. "Phineas will be near Adrian. Go to Anaheim. Start there."

"Don't like flying?" Lindsay queried, eyeing the white-knuckled force with which Elijah clutched the armrests of his seat.

He looked at her with those beautiful emerald eyes. "Not especially."

"You have to admit, taking a private jet is way better than flying commercial."

"No." He paled as the plane banked slightly. "I don't."

Her mouth quirked. She looked around the luxurious cabin, her palms rubbing over the tan leather of the bucket seat she lounged in. Adrian sat a few feet away, deep in conversation with Damien and a blond guy—Jason—who was smokin' hot, as all the angels appeared to be.

She returned her attention to Elijah, who sat across from her on the other side of a table. A table. On a plane. The aircraft was about as cozy as an RV. "You got stuck with babysitting duty, didn't you?"

He just looked at her.

"I'm sorry about that," she said, feeling bad for him. "I won't give you any trouble."

"You say that, but I can tell Adrian isn't happy about bringing you."

Lindsay finished his thought. "And you think that means he's acting under duress, which makes me troublesome?"

Again, he just looked at her with those keen eyes. A hunter's eyes, watchful and assessing.

Knowing she had to mitigate any speculation that she was a weakness, she said, "Come on. You know him better than that. He's not the type of guy who does anything he doesn't want to do."

Elijah lifted a thickly muscled shoulder in reply.

She set her elbow on the table and her chin in her hand. "You don't talk much, do you? I think I'm going to like you, if only because Adrian trusts you to watch his back, but I think for more than that. Hopefully, you'll grow to like me, too."

"I prefer to face danger only on the hunt."

Lindsay had to absorb that a moment before she understood. "You think you'll get in trouble for being friendly with me? If Adrian intended to be territorial, he wouldn't have assigned you to babysitting duty."

Elijah's face gained more color as his attention

shifted from his fear to their conversation. "There's a big difference between ordering me to take a hit for you and allowing us to be . . . friends."

Looking over her shoulder again, she found Adrian watching her. He was dressed in tailored khakis and a black dress shirt that she knew must be worth a month's pay for her, at least. The sleeves were rolled up and the collar undone, exposing just enough of his olive skin to captivate her. So far she'd seen him casually dressed in the airport, half naked just that morning, and now urbanely elegant. Of course, he was stunning in all ways. She was so infatuated with him that she had difficulty looking away. It was Adrian who broke the contact first, smoothly returning his attention to his men.

Lindsay looked back at Elijah. "See? Not territorial at all."

"We have the same bloodline," he whispered. "Not all of the beast in us comes from demons."

Momentarily taken aback by the notion, she eventually nodded her comprehension. Adrian definitely had some wildness in him; she felt it thrumming just beneath the surface.

"You're not surprised." His verdant gaze narrowed. "He told you what we are."

His tone was pitched so low she had to lip-read as well as listen. She was amazed he was able to speak that quietly with a voice as deep as his.

"I got the Cliffs Notes version," she replied, lacking the practice to speak as softly as he did, but trying her damnedest. "I'm still not sure I understand the whole hierarchy thing, though. I mean, clearly the Sentinels are bad-ass, or else they wouldn't have been able to subdue the Watchers to begin with. Unless the Watchers didn't put up a fight . . . ?"

"I don't know. Perhaps not as much as they would have, had they known what they would become."

"What do you mean you don't know? You can't remember?"

His lips pursed. "I wasn't there. Lycans aren't immortal. I'm only seventy years old."

Her mouth fell open. Her idea of a seventy-year-old man *so* did not fit with the serious hunk of beefcake sitting across from her. His thick sable hair hadn't even one strand of gray in it and his strong, handsome features were unmarred by lines. "Wow," she said.

Silence descended. Surprisingly, it was Elijah who finally broke it. "Why do you hunt?"

Lindsay thought about her answer for a moment. It was a topic she never discussed, because talking about her mother's death meant reliving the memories of it. But Adrian knew now, and in this new world she was living in, her past was relevant to understanding her. That was something she didn't take lightly. She had never been fully understood before and hadn't realized how much she craved acceptance until she'd found it in Adrian. Taking a deep breath, she answered, "I was a victim of a vampire attack."

"Not you directly, or you'd be dead."

"A family member."

Elijah nodded. "Me, too."

"Is that why you're fighting the good fight?"

His dark brow arched. "As if I had a choice. But yes, that motivates me."

"Yeah." Lindsay sighed. "I don't have a choice, either. I thought I did, but I was deluding myself."

"What are you?"

"Huh?"

"How did you know that was a demon last night?"

"Oh." She winced. "I'm a human—*mortal*—with bad luck, I guess you could say." She used to wonder what it would be like to be blissfully ignorant like other mortals were, but it'd been a long time since she had entertained such thoughts. It was pointless, like wondering what her life would be like if she were a cat.

"What is it you see?"

"I don't *see* anything. I feel things. Like a ghost walking over my grave, if you're familiar with that saying."

"You went straight to Adrian the moment you saw him. Is that why?"

"No. I picked him up because he's hot." She embellished the half-truth with a smile, keeping her sense of the weather and its connection to Adrian close to the chest. "I'm a woman, too, you know. Heterosexual. Good-looking guys attract my attention."

"You don't find it coincidental that you happened to pick out the one angel in the terminal?"

"Absolutely. I said the same thing to Adrian last night, but he had some six-degrees-of-separation explanation."

"Hmm . . ."

"Pretty much my reaction, too, but what do I know? I'm not religious."

"So says the woman who now lives with angels."

"No shit." Lindsay grinned. "Did you see Adrian's face when the dragon went down?"

Elijah's eyes lit with amusement. "Yeah."

The plane began to descend. She rubbed her hands together. "I hope we find whoever it is we're looking for."

"We will." His face hardened, taking on the fierce cast of a predator.

"You like hunting, don't you?"

"Yes. This time especially." His irises took on a preternatural glow. "In addition to Adrian's lieutenant, this vamp is responsible for the death of two lycans."

"Friends?"

"Something like that."

Lindsay wondered how many people Elijah called friends and suspected it was a small, elite group. She rolled her shoulders back and exhaled audibly.

"You all right?" he asked, blanching as the plane dropped swiftly.

"I will be."

For the first time, she was actually looking forward to killing something. And she didn't feel nearly as bad about that as she thought she should.

CHAPTER 10

Lindsay stepped out of the plane, slipped on her sunglasses, and looked around. "Holy shit."

A warm hand settled in the small of her back, followed by Adrian's murmur. "What?"

She turned all the way around, slowly, until she faced him directly. "Where is the *ground*?"

The runway ended . . . in midair.

"We're on a mesa."

"No way."

"Yes way."

"Who's crazy enough to build a landing strip on a mesa? If the pilot overshoots, you're toast."

His mouth twitched, making her long to see him smile again. "Come on."

He led her to the airport's small parking lot, where two sleek dark town cars awaited them. Jason and Damien climbed into the back of the first vehicle, while Elijah slid into the front passenger seat of the second one.

"Saint George, *huh*?" she said as Adrian opened the door for her. "I've never been to Utah before."

"It's a beautiful state." He took the seat beside her and shut the door. The cars rolled into motion. "The southern half has some gorgeous red rock formations."

"Where are we headed?"

"Not far. A little town called Her-ah-kun."

Lindsay frowned. "Her-ah-kun? Weird name."

Again, he almost smiled. "It's spelled like 'hurricane.'"

A storm. Oh man . . .

Resolve strengthened her. The city's moniker couldn't be a coincidence, not on top of everything else that had happened to her since she'd left Raleigh.

As they descended into the city, Adrian grew still and silent, but she felt his volatility gathering force with every mile that passed. His best friend was dead. As stoic as Adrian appeared, it was clearly a loss he felt deeply. His pain humanized him, made him more man than angel. It also made her wonder where he sought comfort when he needed it, or if he internalized everything. Surrounded by angels who would die for him, he still seemed so alone.

She set a hand on the seat between them and surreptitiously linked her pinky finger with his. Although he gave no outward sign of it, Lindsay felt the surprise that jolted him. He caught her hand in a fierce grip, his gaze trained out his window. She draped the top of her canvas messenger bag over their joined hands, shielding the contact from the rearview mirror's reflection. He gave a quick squeeze of gratitude.

Oddly moved by being a source of comfort to him,

Lindsay contemplated the closeness that had developed between them already. They were opening up to each other in ways they didn't with others they'd known longer. Why? Why had Adrian planned on taking her to his home last night? A restaurant would have been the wisest choice to prevent her from discovering his secrets. And why was he so *intimate* with her? So tender . . .

Why did she let him? Why wasn't she more guarded with him, as she was with everyone else whose path she crossed?

She stared sightlessly at the passing vista, wondering why she seemed to attract the strange and weird. Why did she move so fast when she was only human? Her dad had taken her to the doctor for every runny nose and minor rash. She'd had her share of dental and bone X-rays, routine blood work, and even a CAT scan when she'd gotten a concussion from falling off a friend's backyard playground. There was no medical explanation for her abilities. But she was undeniably different, and her anomalies were fostering an affinity between her and Adrian. She couldn't decide if that was a blessing or not.

They pulled off the road and into the parking lot of a small country hardware store. As the car slid smoothly into a marked space next to the vehicle carrying Jason and Damien, Lindsay looked around to gain her bearings.

"We're here," Adrian said, before exiting the vehicle.

Her door opened, and Elijah stood there, tall and impressively intimidating. Although he was a muscular man with broad shoulders, he wasn't oversized, yet his presence made him seem so. Like Adrian, he clearly was someone you wouldn't want to piss off.

Stepping out, Lindsay took a deep breath and scanned her surroundings. Hurricane seemed to be a small, one-main-street sort of town. In addition to the hardware store, there were a couple fast-food establishments, one chain grocery store, and a couple mom-and-pop shops.

The wind whipped through her hair, screaming. She gasped and took a step back from its vehemence. Elijah caught her arm to steady her.

Adrian was beside her before she could catch her breath. "What do you feel?"

She shivered. "This place crawls."

"A nest, perhaps?" Damien said, joining them.

"I don't know what that is."

"A group of rogue vamps," Adrian explained.

Great. Just what she'd always wanted. "There are definitely more than a few."

Damien looked at Adrian. "You weren't kidding. She's hypersensitive."

Adrian gave a curt nod.

She pulled herself together. "Do we want to dig around now? Or wait for reinforcements?"

Jason gave her a thorough once-over. "Can you pinpoint their location?"

She nodded, knowing the wind would steer her in the right direction if she gave it a chance. "The closer I get to them, the more I'll feel it. I just need to wander around a bit."

"No." Adrian turned away as if that was all there was to say on the matter. "Now we know Phineas wasn't followed; he walked into a nest. We can take it from here and track without risking her."

Lindsay debated her next move. Challenging him in front of his men wasn't an option for her, but she also wasn't going to be denied the chance to help "for her own good."

When no better idea presented itself, she went with the only solution that came to mind—she walked away.

She headed toward the main street, figuring the road most traveled was the best place to start; plus she was hoping the highly visible location would prevent Adrian from restraining her—she wouldn't put it past him. She didn't doubt that he was capable of tossing her over his shoulder and putting her where he felt was safest. As it was, she felt his gaze on her. For better or worse, her senses were as focused on him as they were on finding their prey.

Elijah fell into step beside her. His eyes were shielded behind shades, but she knew he was surveying the area with a predator's meticulousness. "FYI: there are usually consequences for defiance."

"I figured. I'm a big girl; I can handle it. Are *you* going to be okay?"

"I'm not supposed to let you out of my sight."

"So you're damned if you come with me and damned if you don't." Her lips pursed. "What do you think he'll do?"

He shrugged. "Not sure. Insubordination is usually fatal, but I suspect he'll go easier on you."

Apprehension rippled through her, intensifying the disquiet caused by the frantic wind. She was certain Adrian was capable of things she couldn't even imagine; he wouldn't have been placed in charge of the Sentinels otherwise. Still, she didn't fear him—after all, it was her safety he was concerned with in the first place. Worrying about the consequences wasn't going to get her anywhere. The only thing she could do was what she'd always done: put one foot in front of the other and keep moving forward.

Fortunately, that reasoning seemed to be doing her good now. With every step she took, Lindsay grew more comfortable. However Adrian felt about her mutiny, he was giving her the lead. She appreciated that. It gave her credit for having a brain and some experience. Considering the cavernous gap between her abilities and his, his show of trust meant a lot to her.

As she and Elijah walked past a Dairy Queen, she glanced through the windows. There were families and teenagers inside, laughing and eating and living so happily unaware. Lucky bastards.

"Do you have a girlfriend?" she asked. "Or a wife? Kids?"

"I'm not mated."

She resisted the urge to see how closely Adrian was following. It would actually be better if she were alone; a group of intimidating hot guys in a town of this size was a dead giveaway that something unusual was going on. "Is that who you lost? Your mate? Sorry—I shouldn't pry."

Elijah looked at her. "If I'd lost my mate, I wouldn't be alive now. Lycans languish when their mates die. Death follows swiftly."

"Oh. Like wolves? The real ones. I read that they mate for life."

He turned his attention forward again. "Yes."

"That happens to humans, too, you know. With couples who've been married a long time. The surviving partner usually doesn't last long after their spouse passes away. Does the same thing apply to vampires? And Sentinels?"

"Vampires pair up, but not for life. Sentinels don't date."

"Ah, well . . . They've got a lot to hide and it's not like they can commingle among themselves—there aren't enough of them. I can see why one-night stands would be the best route under those circumstances."

"To my knowledge, they don't even have sex. Period. They don't seem to have a craving for it as far as I can tell. I've always gotten the impression the urge was beneath them."

Lindsay grinned, knowing damn well Adrian craved sex. The man practically dripped it from his pores. "You're just not their type, I guess."

"Sentinels are never without lycans nearby," he insisted quietly. "I would have heard something from someone."

It was the unwavering conviction in Elijah's tone that caught her, followed by recollections of how collected the Sentinels were. She had yet to see one laugh or really smile. They didn't even raise their voices, whether with excitement or anger. Not that she'd been around them long enough to make a comprehensive study of it . . .

"You've got to be kidding," she said.

"Why would I?"

She was surprised to realize she believed him. He was one of those guys who just didn't bullshit. Which left her confused. She knew masculine interest when she saw it—not to mention Adrian had come right out and said what his intentions were. What else could he want from her, if it wasn't to explore the attraction between them?

They reached the end of the main drag, where the road veered to the left, turning into a more residential area. Signs said the turnoff for Zion National Park was close.

"So are you looking for your soul mate?" she asked. "Does it work like that? Only one person in the world for you sort of thing?"

"No. No. And no."

"I hear ya. This is the wrong kind of life to want any sort of long-term relationship. I threw out that possibility a long time ago." The wind whipped through her hair. "We're close."

He looked at her. "Care to explain the crazy gusts of wind that follow you?"

"We're in a place called Hurricane. What do you expect?" She jerked her chin at a rocky hill across the street; then she darted across the road at full speed.

Elijah stayed directly on her heels. "Lycans sense danger in the air before we catch scent of it," he pressed.

She still considered her weather radar too personal and too revealing to share. She wasn't sure *what* exactly it revealed, but it said something about her she'd rather keep to herself—for now.

Her hand slid under the flap of her messenger bag and gripped the hilt of a throwing knife. They passed some sort of monument, a stone pillar with a brass plaque. There were small homes fanning out in a horseshoe behind it. Old homes from the fifties or earlier.

"Do you scent equally well in both forms?" she asked, raking the area with an examining gaze.

The next minute she was bumped in the thigh, drawing her attention to a massive chocolate-colored wolf beside her. She supposed that answered her question.

"Wow." She was seriously impressed. "How did you do that so fast? And where are your clothes?"

He gave her a look that she pegged as exasperated.

"Fine," she conceded, reaching out to touch his fur to see if it was soft or coarse. It turned out to be somewhere between the two. The lustrous cocoa pelt was relieved by patches of white on his chest and paws, making the overall package both beautiful and regal. "You're a really good-looking wolf, you know."

Elijah snorted.

Lindsay moved forward, noting how still the air had suddenly become. Almost stagnant. Protecting her by not blowing the scent of lycan and angel around. Somehow, she knew the angels had taken the high ground. She didn't look up, but she suspected they were on the hilltop above her.

"I'm thinking basement," she said, to which Elijah chuffed in agreement.

They moved forward, circling around the horseshoe. An elderly lady sat in a swinging bench on a covered porch. She smiled and waved as they passed, apparently not the least bit concerned by the humongous canine beside Lindsay. Considering the thickness of the woman's glasses, Lindsay assumed she couldn't see all that well. It was the only explanation—aside from senility—for dismissing a pony-sized wolf prowling around.

A gravel path marked by two squat brick lampposts appeared before them in the space between two homes. They followed it around the hill. At the end was a surprise—a home marked by antebellum-style architecture and a dilapidated bed-and-breakfast sign.

An icy breeze caressed the back of her neck.

"You've got to be kidding," she groused aloud.

While it was obvious the building was no longer in use as lodging, it retained a dignity and style that belied its use as a vampire "nest." A gardener and a fresh coat of paint was all that was needed to revive the exterior.

As they neared the small opening in the brick fence surrounding the property, a massive shadow and the flap of wings announced Adrian's graceful landing in front of her. "That's far enough, Lindsay."

Her brows rose. "Think nothing of it. Glad I could help."

His features softened. "Thank you."

Jason and Damien landed on the other side of the fence in the front yard. To the right was the hill. Behind them, about a half mile away, were the road and the horseshoe-shaped street of vintage homes. To the left were acres and acres of undeveloped land. The nest was hiding in plain sight. Not that Lindsay was overly surprised. The things she killed were usually normal-looking on the exterior. Freakishly so.

She hung back, staying a good twenty feet away from the fence. Elijah sank onto his haunches beside her. The angels moved forward—Adrian in the middle, Jason to the left, and Damien to the right. Two more wolves appeared, startling her. She wondered where they'd come from, then remembered the two drivers, one for each town car. Or a lycan for every angel. One was a mixture of charcoal gray and white, and the other was a rusty brown and taupe. Both panted softly, as if they were barely containing their eagerness.

Yet the three beasts surrounded *her*. Leaving the angels to fend for themselves.

She reached down and stroked Elijah's huge head in silent gratitude. The other two took up positions behind him, giving him the lead. Only his ears and eyes moved. Although his stance appeared casual, she knew he could explode into powerful movement in the blink of an eye. All the hunter traits she'd observed in him as a human were multiplied in his lupine form.

Her attention moved to the angels, who approached the house with their wings flexing at their backs. That surprised her. Why expose such a vulnerability when they weren't flying? Jason and Damien might be able to retreat by air if they were capable of taking off vertically, but Adrian was on the porch, caged in by two-story-high columns and an overhanging roof.

Adrian entered the house through the front door, while the other two found alternate ways in that Lindsay couldn't see from her vantage. Quiet blanketed the area. She shifted from one foot to the other, twirling a throwing blade in one hand and playing absently with Elijah's ear. "I have a really bad feeling about this."

The wind screeched across the vacant plain, making the fine hairs on her arms stand up. Then all hell broke loose.

Glass shattered as angels exploded out of draped windows in unison, followed by a veritable horde of vampires.

"Holy fucking shit!"

The flood of vamps poured toward her, surging over the short wall. Lindsay tossed the blade in her hand, nailing a foaming-mouthed vampire right between the eyes. She kept on throwing, one right after the other, retreating as the lycans lunged forward, forming a barrier to protect her.

She looked for Adrian over the writhing mass of limbs. *Oh man . . .*

He was cutting a swath through the throng . . . literally. Had she thought his wings were vulnerable? They were *deadly*. He wielded them like blades, slicing through limbs and torsos, spinning with lethal precision. The sight of him and the other two angels was riveting. Their wings flared like capes, snapping wide, then curving fluidly around their bodies. The burning embers of vanquished vamps spiraled around them in glittering clouds. She couldn't take her eyes off their eerily graceful, macabre dances.

A high-pitched yelp yanked her attention back to the lycans, and the suicidal vampress who'd latched on to the back of Elijah's neck. Resisting his violent efforts to shake her off, the wild-eyed bitch held on even as Elijah threw himself to his back and writhed, grinding her into the ground beneath him.

Lindsay looked frantically for the other two lycans and found them with their jaws full. Steeling her courage, she leaped into the fray. A male vampire darted toward her head-on, playing chicken. Knowing that changing course would only weaken her footing, she charged ahead with a dagger in hand. She staked him in the heart, then used the protruding hilt for leverage to flip over his shoulder and land on the other side.

She continued without breaking her stride, diving forward as Elijah straightened. Her fist collided with the vampress's jaw and it gave way with a sickening crack. Dislodged from her hold, the vampress hit the dirt on her back. Elijah rounded on her with a roar, grabbing her by the throat and ripping the flesh to the spine. Lindsay finished her off with a throwing knife to the forehead.

A gunshot echoed off the hillside, followed by the unmistakable whine of a ricochet.

She pivoted. A woman stood on the steps of the

house with a shotgun, pumping another round into the chamber. She took aim at Adrian and pulled the trigger. As the report reverberated through her, Lindsay's lungs seized, preventing her from screaming the warning that howled inside her horrified mind.

Adrian whipped one wing around, deflecting the bullet with the harsh *ping* of metal on metal.

The gun disappeared from the vampress's hands and appeared at Lindsay's feet.

It took a half minute for Lindsay's brain to lurch into full understanding. Then she caught up the weapon and pumped the fore-end, firing at a vampire charging one of the wolves. She got off six more shots, providing cover for the lycans. When the last chamber was spent, she wielded the shotgun like a club, whacking a vamp attempting to get up from where he'd been sprawled on the ground.

Risking a glance at the house, she searched for Adrian.

He was surrounded on all sides and kicking some serious ass. But the chick on the porch had retrieved another shotgun—a sawed-off one this time—and was lifting it to aim . . .

Lindsay darted through the opening in the fence, dodging flying bodies and barreling through ash piles. A vamp flew at her from the right and she ducked beneath his sailing body, startling herself with her own agility. She grabbed the last throwing knife from her bag and prepared to hurl it.

The barrel of the gun swung toward her.

Lindsay caught the nearest vampire and hauled him in front of her. The shotgun discharged with a deafening *boom*.

The vamp jerked against her. Agonizing pain radiated through the forearm she had wrapped around his waist. She dropped to her knees in an exploding cloud of ash, the vampire disintegrating from the fatal shot.

The three lycans tore up the stairs and attacked the shooter.

Lindsay gulped in air but couldn't breathe past the pain. She kept her gaze averted, afraid to look at her arm.

A vamp galloped on all fours out of the black pit of the front door and leaped toward Adrian. She took him out with the final blade still clutched in her uninjured hand. His ashes billowed over the yellowed, weed-infested lawn just as Adrian slammed his fist into the frothing maw of a snarling vamp.

The vampire hit the ground, unconscious. A second later, Lindsay joined him.

CHAPTER 11

Lindsay woke in a shadowed room. She blinked the sleep out of her eyes, her head turning to figure out where she was.

Her cheek touched the cool cotton of the pillowcase and she saw Adrian. He sat to the left of her in a round low-backed chair covered in silver damask. He was bare except for a pair of loose-fitting white pajama bottoms and whatever he might be wearing underneath them. He watched her with a searing intensity, his mouth straightened into a dangerous line. Although he didn't move a muscle aside from blinking, she felt a tornado churning inside him.

"Hi," she croaked past a dry throat. She must have pushed her body too far; she always felt like hammered shit when she exerted herself beyond her limits.

He reached for the clear glass pitcher of water on the bedside table and poured a large ration into a waiting tumbler. Then he stood and helped her sit up, propping her back with some pillows before handing her the drink.

She accepted with a grateful smile. There was a thick cushion of white gauze bandages on her left forearm. Beneath them, pain throbbed dully. She downed the entire contents of her glass and passed it back.

He picked up the phone beside her and punched a button, ordering room service. They were in a hotel, she realized. The windows to the right of the bed were at least two stories tall and had Tiffany Blue drapes drawn across them. There was a large sitting area beside her and a massive entertainment center at the foot of the bed. Considering the size and opulence of the room and the grand piano she saw through the open living room doorway, they were in . . .

"Las Vegas?" she queried.

Setting the phone down, he nodded. He poured her a refill and returned the tumbler to her.

She blew out her breath. "How long have I been out?"

"We were in Hurricane the day before yesterday."

Yikes. "Is everyone okay?"

His gaze bored into her. "You were the only one seriously hurt."

"That's good."

"The hell it is," he growled, his voice rumbling through the room like thunder, rattling every loose object. "I told you to stay put."

Here we go. "That was my plan, too. Until the vampire on the porch aimed a shotgun at you. Then I couldn't stand still."

"Why the fuck not?"

God, he was sexy when riled. She'd never seen him show anything besides total self-possession, but he was visibly seething now. "Because you needed someone at your back. Everyone else had their hands full. I couldn't take the risk that you'd be spread too thin and leave an opening."

"I could survive it."

"You don't know that! You told me yourself that you've had casualties. You're not indestructible. I wasn't going to stand around and watch you die."

If there was any mercy in the world, she'd never have to watch another person she cared about die.

"So you decided to make me watch *you* die?" *Again* . . .

The unspoken word slid insidiously and inexplicably through Lindsay's mind. She winced and pressed her palm against a suddenly throbbing temple. Adrian took the glass from her other hand—the hand that should have been too weak to hold it—and bent to press his lips to her forehead. The pain left her like a receding tide.

"If only you could bottle that talent," she murmured.

Remembering the ninja/*Matrix* vault she'd done over the vampire, she freaked herself out with her own coolness. How the hell had she known how to do *that*?

"You're going to drive me insane." Although his voice was once again smooth as silk, the turbulence inside him hadn't abated. He straightened.

"Can you open the curtains?"

Adrian hit a button on the nightstand and the drapes parted, revealing an overcast sky and drizzle. In Las Vegas. Not that it never rained in the desert city, but at this time of year . . . ?

She looked at him, knowing his mood was once again affecting the weather, which affected her in turn. "You were really worried."

His hands went to his lean hips, exposing the entirety of his perfect torso and delicious biceps. His wings materialized, extending with a sinuous grace. He was so damn beautiful. So fierce and proud. He was like catnip to her. She wanted to roll around with him in a blissful stupor, breathing in that scent of his that drove her wild.

"When you fell to the ground—" He exhaled harshly, his lashes lowering to hide the sudden flaring of his brilliant eyes. His arms crossed his chest and his feathers ruffled, giving so much away with his restless movements. "Yes, I was worried."

"You shouldn't care so much. You don't know me."

"Speak for yourself. You risked your life for me."

He was right. A hard-driving fear of losing him had spurred her into charging a vampire holding a shotgun. It had been a suicide run for anyone, especially for a weak human. But he was . . . Well, he was invaluable to her.

In such a short time, he'd given her a sense of belonging. He knew the worst and best of what she was, and passed no judgment. As much as her father loved her, Eddie Gibson didn't know the truth of what she'd seen the day her mother died or how she hunted because of it.

Lindsay tossed the covers back and swung her legs off the side of the bed. Her *bare* legs. She froze, realizing she was wearing only a ribbed tank top and boy-shorts underwear. Although she was decently covered, she was suddenly conscious of her need to shower, brush her teeth, and shave her legs. "I have to freshen—"

The clicking of the door latch told her Adrian had already left the room.

Vash raced through the forest, darting through dappled sunlight and around bald cypress. Ahead of her, she could hear the harsh and heavy breathing of the lycans she pursued. Flanking her, three of her Fallen captains gave chase with the same penetrating focus she did. The underbrush rustled beneath their feet as they traversed miles in minutes, the fire of vengeance scorching their veins.

I need only one . . .

One of them would tell her what she needed to know about Nikki's death.

She heard one stumble, then fall. The lycan's roar of frustration brought a smile to her lips. Reaching over her shoulder, she gripped the hilt of her katana and slid it free of the scabbard slung across her back. The whisper of the blade against the sheath was thunderous to her ears, as she knew it would be for the lycan. The sudden kick of his heartbeat made her fangs extend in anticipation.

Leaping over a fallen pine tree, she closed the distance between them—close enough to smell the fear underlying the lycan's natural scent. It was her favorite fragrance, sweeter even than the smell of their blood.

The charge from the left caught her completely unawares.

Vash was tackled into the trunk of a nearby tree, her blade flying from her hand to spin madly through the debris of vegetation littering the forest floor. The massive old-growth pine shuddered in protest, leaves falling around her like rain.

Dazed by the ambush, it took her a moment to register the threat. The red wolf was lunging toward her again before she even had a chance to summon her blade.

She could only tense for the blow and pray it didn't kill her.

Then she'd be able to kick his ass.

*   *   *

Adrian stood at the window overlooking the Las Vegas Strip and struggled with the roiling emotions he shouldn't be feeling. When the door opened behind him, he turned, expecting Lindsay. Instead he found Raguel Gadara entering the penthouse suite as if he owned the place—which he did. The world-famous Mondego Hotel and Resort was the archangel's property. Regardless, Raguel ranked far below Adrian's station in the angelic hierarchy. He should show more respect.

"Raguel."

"Adrian. I expect you are comfortable."

"You would know if I wasn't."

The archangel hesitated a moment, then dipped his head with the expected deference. His smile was dazzlingly white within the framework of skin as smooth and rich as the finest milk chocolate. There was a smattering of tight gray curls at Raguel's temples, but that telltale sign of aging was an affectation to disguise his immortality. Unlike Adrian, the archangel embraced the media attention that came his way.

Raguel withdrew a cigar from his pocket and offered it to Adrian.

"No."

The archangel's grin widened. He was dressed in a loose guayabera and linen pants, but the man-of-leisure appearance was as much of a guise as his gray hair. Like the other six archangels, Raguel was intensely and ruthlessly ambitious. "That minion you brought along with you . . . He is sick."

Foaming mouth. Reddened eyes. Nearly mindless. The infected were like zombies. The nest had been partially filled with them—the diseased living alongside the healthy. Adrian had interrogated the vampress with the shotgun, questioning her about who was responsible for the attack on Phineas the day before. How many of the Fallen were feeding them? Only a few of the members of the nest had been photosensitive. The rest of the group—a rough guesstimate of nearly one hundred minions—had been able to charge into the light of day.

The woman had laughed for long minutes, gasping for breath. Then, with her amber eyes bright with malice, she'd hissed, "How does it feel to be hunted, Sentinel? You'd better get used to it."

In the end, she'd revealed nothing at all. He'd severed her head with frustration eating at him and fear for Lindsay still riding him hard. The sight of her crumpling to the ground had broken something inside him. He remembered nothing of what he'd done between her collapse and the moment he determined she would live. If Lindsay Gibson died before Syre, the cycle of Shadoe's reincarnation would continue—another round of waiting for her return and the numbness that accompanied it. But more than that, watching Lindsay fall had elicited a different kind of horror. He'd just discovered her, just begun getting to know her, just started envisioning a few years of hunting with her at his side. Faced with losing the myriad possibilities that lay between them, he'd found a unique hell.

Fear. That's what he'd felt. He hadn't recognized it at first because he'd never experienced it before. He knew it now because he had lived through it via Lindsay's memories; he'd felt the raw terror that had frozen her from the inside out. What she recalled of her mother's murder was a nightmare capable of warping the minds of adults, let alone that of a child of five—a blood-splattered picnic, a mother's pleas for mercy for her daughter, a sunny summer afternoon shattered by a child's screams. The images of crimson dripping from blades of grass and the remembered feel of claws almost breaking fragile skin were so vivid in her mind they'd imprinted themselves in his.

It was nothing short of miraculous that Lindsay Gibson had matured into the woman she was—strong and sane, determined and compassionate. It was one of the many great ironies in his life that the woman who was his downfall was also responsible for restoring a little of his tarnished faith. She proved that redemption was always possible, no matter how dire the circumstances or how insurmountable the odds.

And so with his heart racing with fear, he'd joined her in the backseat of the town car and gingerly lifted her unconscious body into his lap. Her decimated arm had lain across her chest, the bone exposed and tendons flayed. The flesh sizzled as the blood he'd squeezed out of a slice in his palm worked its miracle, mending the rent tissues and rebuilding what had been blown away by the shotgun blast. Had she been hit directly, he wouldn't have been able to save her arm. He couldn't give her back a lost limb; he could only heal what was still alive.

She'd risked her mortal life for his.

"He's not the first diseased minion I've seen lately," Adrian said, forcing his focus back to Raguel. "I need to figure out what's wrong with him and how widespread the illness is."

"Perhaps the vampires' time has finally come. Jehovah does love his plagues."

"I considered that and I can't rule it out, but I think it

more likely that they're trying to combat their photo-sensitivity with a new drug that has horrendous side effects. There were too many minions in that nest capable of tolerating sunlight." Another alternative was that Syre had sent large quantities of Fallen blood to Hurricane. Considering how close the nest was to the Navajo Lake pack, it was a very real possibility. But that wasn't a speculation he would share with Raguel at this time, if ever.

"Would you like me to have his blood tested?" The glimmer of avarice in the archangel's dark eyes belied the altruistic nature of his offer.

"Yes." Adrian intended to have a full blood workup done at home, but he still had to make the trip up to Navajo Lake. Meanwhile, he needed answers and he needed them now. Although it had been proven to be a vampire attack that killed Phineas, it was still necessary to finish the lycan population reduction the lieutenant had started.

"I will see to it. If I can be of further assistance, just let me know."

Adrian arched a brow. "You're being helpful."

"It pays to be useful." Raguel smiled enigmatically.

"I'll keep that in mind. If there's nothing else . . . ?"

With a slight mocking bow, the archangel left without getting what he'd really come for.

Adrian stared at the door after it closed, knowing Raguel had visited for one reason and one reason only: to see Lindsay. To see Adrian with Lindsay. To see how vulnerable she made him. The conversation itself could have been managed over the phone.

It wasn't just the vampires who would smell blood and circle like vultures.

*   *   *

Fresh from the shower, Lindsay stood in front of the brightly lit vanity mirror and examined her left forearm. Twisting it to and fro, she noted the baby pink hue of the hairless flesh. Although it looked tender, the muscles and tendons beneath had been strong enough to wash her hair with. Her fingers and hand flexed smoothly and with only slightly compromised strength.

Her arm was *regenerating*. A fucking miracle.

She exited the bathroom wrapped in a towel . . . and found a lover's gift waiting on the bed—champagne-colored silk pajama pants and tank top with a luxurious full-length robe in the same hue. The matching lace thong sealed the deal.

She stared down at the ensemble for a long moment, then removed her towel and dressed. She couldn't fight the flare of desire the feel of the silk evoked, but it was tempered by everything she knew *and* everything she didn't know. Adrian was intricately complicated, and she had more than enough complications in her life.

Belting the robe, she moved to the door and stepped out into the living room. Its massive size froze her in mid-step. Aside from the grand piano, there was also a full-sized kitchen, dining room, and billiards table. Through a glass partition, she spotted an indoor swimming pool.

"Food's here," Adrian said, drawing her gaze to where he sat on the couch. His bright white pants were a sharp contrast to the blue of the upholstery. The way his legs were propped on the mahogany and glass coffee table, crossed at the ankles and barefoot, was gracefully erotic. He stood when she entered, his gaze sliding over her in a heated caress.

He was so human-looking . . . if not for his impossible beauty and sensual elegance.

Lindsay went to the dining table and lifted the domed lids from the plates one by one. Pancakes, eggs, bacon and sausage and ham, hash browns, orange juice and coffee. A feast for two, but he wouldn't be eating. She, however, would eat every bite. She always ate for an army after one of her power binges.

"You look beautiful," he murmured as he resumed his seat and retrieved the iPad lying on the cushion beside him.

She sat and picked up her fork. "Thank you. So do you."

His dark head tilted in acknowledgment.

"Why are we here?" she asked while slathering butter in between each layer of pancake.

"We're regrouping."

"You mean to say I'm holding you back."

He looked down at whatever was on the screen. "No."

"I'm grateful for whatever you did to my arm."

"You're welcome. But if you ever put yourself in danger for me again, I'll make you sorry you did."

She shot him a glare he didn't see, while secretly wondering if she was crazy. No sane modern woman would listen to that chauvinistic bullshit and hear a sensual threat in it. But she did, and some primitive recessive gene made her body tingle in response. "Don't threaten me."

"It's not a threat. I won't lose you. I've lost too much already."

Wincing, she remembered he'd just lost a friend who had been like a brother to him. Her affront drained away. Struggling to find something to say to fill the sudden void, she floundered and managed a lame "Thank you for the clothes." After a mental smack upside the head, she added, "They're lovely."

"I'm glad you like them," he said, too neutrally. His control appeared absolute, but the softly howling wind outside and the steady rain told her otherwise.

Lindsay couldn't bear his turmoil. She was as scrambled as he was—*vulnerable*—but she couldn't hide it the way he did. And she couldn't let him hide it, either. He knew her secrets, and she needed to maintain that openness now that they'd achieved it. "Although they're clearly not suitable for wearing in public. Are you leaving me behind?"

Without looking up, he replied, "We'll be heading out tomorrow. Together. Until then, you need to eat and rest."

"They're not really suitable for resting, either." She poured syrup over her pancakes and began to eat.

He lifted his head to study her. "Aren't they comfortable?"

She swallowed her food. "Sure."

Adrian's brows rose in silent inquiry.

"They're also very sensual." She stabbed her fork into a sausage link. "Designed to be sexy for the wearer and for the beholder. But I heard angels might not be wired the same way—sexually—as we mortals are, so maybe you weren't thinking along those lines when you bought them."

Very calmly, he turned off his iPad and set it on the seat beside him. "You've been talking to Elijah. I would prefer it if you would pose your questions to me."

"Well, see, that's the problem. I don't know what to ask." She bit the end off the link with more gusto than necessary.

"Perhaps because there's nothing to question."

"I doubt that," she said, chewing. "Are you leading

me on? Maybe you picked me up because you needed a female companion for media purposes or a date for an upcoming event. Then I surprised you with the dragon and you're not sure what to do with me now."

He set his elbow on the couch arm and settled in, displaying his body to even better advantage. He might be an angel, but he knew his assets and her weakness for them, and he wasn't above exploiting both. "Oh, I know what to do with you."

"But you didn't do it the other night. And apparently you haven't been doing it for a long time—if you've ever done it." *Oh god.* She was getting turned on by the idea of him being a virgin. The thought of training a man like Adrian—the things she could teach him . . .

"So," he murmured, "the fact that I'm not promiscuous disturbs you?"

"Ha!" Lindsay wagged her knife at him. "There's a big difference between discerning and celibate."

"Maybe the celibacy exists because of the discernment."

"Is that your answer?"

He examined the fingernails of his right hand. "I didn't know there was a question on the table."

"Okay, here's one. Are angels forbidden to have sex?"

"No."

Her gaze narrowed. "Any truth to the rumor that lust is beneath you?"

"What do you think?"

"I think *I* want to be beneath you. And I thought we were headed there—eventually—but I'm sensing there's a whole lot going on I don't know about."

His tongue slid along his bottom lip, making her as damp as if he'd licked her with it. "Let's head there now."

Lindsay wiped her mouth with the napkin in her lap, then pushed back from the table. She moved toward him with a deliberately slow and sultry stride. Her hands went to the belt of her robe, her fingers sliding through the silken knot and loosening it. Reaching the coffee table, she allowed the robe to slide to the floor. She smiled when Adrian's breath hitched. He straightened, planting his feet wide on the floor and revealing the thick length of his aroused cock. The act of the tease was enticing on its own, but his physical response took her quickening hunger to another level.

She was yanking an edgy tiger by the tail, and from the sharp, rapacious hunger in his gaze, Adrian was getting ready to pounce. And bite.

Leaning over him, Lindsay balanced herself with one hand on the back of the couch and allowed her camisole top to gape open. When his gaze slid to the view, she used his distraction as an opportunity to snatch his iPad.

Straightening, she returned to the table. She resumed eating while using the browser to Google some choice keyword phrases. Like "angel sex" and "sentinel angels" and, finally, "watcher angels vampires." She was briefly distracted by an article speculating that male Watcher angels had been capable of endless erections, but the deeper import of what she discovered was what, exactly, the Watcher angels had done to get damned with vampirism—they'd lusted after and fucked mortals.

While she read, Adrian sat on the couch, still and silent. She didn't look his way, but she sensed the coiled expectancy in him and heard it in the rumble of thunder outside. Inside the air-conditioned suite, it felt like the hour before a heat wave broke with a summer storm— unbearably hot and humid, crackling with bated energy.

All the turbulence inside him was primed to explode. She knew he needed the release, just as she instinctively knew she could take him to that point of exposure. But at what cost?

She forked the remnants of her hash browns into her mouth, then sat back, chewing thoughtfully. Their gazes met and held.

"As I suspected, I didn't ask the right question," she said, after finishing off the orange juice. Now fed, her body was recharging so swiftly she felt light-headed. "Are *you* forbidden to have sex? Is that the sin you were talking about the other night? Not the lust itself, but the culmination of it?"

Adrian set his elbows on his knees and steepled his fingers together. "I don't suppose my telling you to leave the consequences to me will satisfy you?"

What would satisfy her was *him*, hot and hard and deep inside her. But there were consequences, and then there were *consequences*. "Could you lose your wings and soul and become a vampire?"

"I could lose my mind wanting you."

"You can't be serious." He was killing her.

"I can't?" He set his chin atop his fingers.

"No. You can't. And I'd be an idiot to think I'd get away scot-free. My life doesn't work that way. I pay for everything. In fact, I might have been paying for this"— she gestured between them with an impatient flick of her wrist—"my whole life. I mean, who has the shit happen to them that's happened to me? When I was born, maybe someone said, 'Yep, that's the one who's going to fuck with Adrian's perfection.'"

He straightened abruptly, his gaze haunted. "Lindsay—"

"You're the most powerful warrior in the highest rank of angels. I've seen how the others look at you. They trust you. Admire you. To have the power you do, and to look like you do ... someone up there loves you madly. I'm not going to be the one who screws you up." Pushing back from the table, she stood, feeling agitated enough to run five miles just to burn energy.

Adrian stood, too. "The decision belongs to both of us. There's something between us. Something precious and powerful. I want it. I want you."

His wings materialized, fanning wide. The pearlescent expanse shimmered so beautifully it made her eyes sting. She hadn't cried since her mother died, but Adrian had brought her close to tears more than once since she'd met him. The way he made her feel important and valuable, the ease with which he accepted her just the way she was ... For his tenderness alone, she couldn't allow him to take the fall for her. He made her feel human; he made her *feel*—period. She was so vibrantly alive when she was with him, as if she'd been half asleep her whole life and was finally stirring. But the humanity he'd returned to her was forbidden to him and she couldn't afford to forget that. *He* couldn't afford for her to forget.

"I like sex as much as the next gal," she said, beginning to pace. Adrian was a seraph, just like the Watchers. Same class of angels, same offense—same punishment? She had no reason to believe Adrian wouldn't suffer the same fate, and he apparently wasn't going to give her one. "It can be a lot of fun and a great stress reliever. In a twisted way, I'm flattered to get you so hot and bothered. But it's not worth sucking blood over. It's not worth losing those gorgeous wings. Trust me—the buildup is the best part. You're not missing anything."

He moved, traversing the space between them in the blink of an eye and blocking the path of her pacing, forcing her to confront him directly. She stumbled to a halt just before she ran into him. Thunder boomed directly overhead, rattling the silverware on the table.

His arms crossed his powerful chest; his irises glowed with pure blue flames. He bared his teeth in a predatory smile. "Prove it."

CHAPTER 12

Lindsay shook her head emphatically. "No."

Adrian caught her by the shoulders when she made a move to step back. The moment he touched her, he was reminded of the fragility of her mortal body.

And she'd risked her life for his.

He wanted her so much he ached with it. His own vulnerability where she was concerned both enraged and humbled him.

"Don't look at me like that," she muttered.

"I need you, *tzel*," he said softly.

"No, what you need is for me to be the one strong enough to say no and try to talk some sense into you." Her gaze lifted beyond his shoulder. Pulling free of his grip, she circled him. "I should have realized before . . . You're having a rough time right now. You've been through a lot in a short amount of time and you're not thinking clearly. You're being reckless. Shit, you took on a nest with suicidal odds."

She was exquisite. Her hair was still damp, giving the

thick curls the hue of pure honey. When she'd come for his iPad, he'd been riveted by her predatory stride—the sensual sway of her hips, the soft rustling of silk as she drew closer. A golden lioness on the hunt. More than a match for him. More than willing to take him on . . . until she discovered the risks he faced.

Lindsay Gibson was holding back for his benefit, because she was worried about him.

Anticipation tightened his spine, the weighted expectation for a touch he wasn't sure was coming but hungered for anyway. When her fingers brushed tentatively over feathers on his right upper wing, his eyes closed as the barely-there caress moved through him.

"These are beautiful," she whispered in a voice filled with awe. "Oh! I thought they were one pair. But there's . . . *three*? Oh my god. You have *six* wings."

He could only nod, his throat too tight to speak.

Her touch grew bolder. She stroked along the upper curve and the wing stretched slightly in bliss. She gasped and stumbled back. "I'm sorry."

"Don't stop."

There was a pause. "They're sensitive? But you deflected *bullets* with them!"

"Nothing manmade can wound a seraph's wings."

She stepped forward again, splaying her fingers and running them lightly over his feathers. "Watching you in action was amazing."

He knew from the low pitch of her voice that the memory was an arousing one, a lingering effect, perhaps, from her time as Shadoe. Or maybe that's just who *she* was. Lindsay was a warrior in her own right.

Eager to soak up the heat of her focused attention

and admiration, he unfurled his wings slowly, a silent encouragement for her to continue touching him.

"Every angel I've seen has had a unique set of wings," she murmured, torturing him with her gentle petting. "Jason's are dark. Damien's are gray. There are some similarities among the others, but no one has wings like yours. The touch of red at the tips . . . Gorgeous. Does it signify anything? Or are wing patterns randomly individual, like fingerprints?"

"The stain appeared when I severed the wings from Syre. I was the first to spill the blood of an angel."

"The first ever?"

"Yes."

Lindsay touched the nape of his neck, then slid her fingertips between his wings down the length of his spine. His back arched with a serrated groan, his body trembling.

"Is this—?" She cleared her throat. "Is this erotic to you?"

Reaching behind him, Adrian caught her right hand. He pulled it beneath his wings and around to his front. She was forced to step closer, her breath near enough to sink through the down to his skin beneath. He wrapped her fingers around the rigid length of his cock.

She made a soft sound, one he recognized as a cry of vulnerability. Ruthless, he pressed his advantage, stripping the pants from his body with a terse thought and pressing her palm against his bare flesh.

There was a moment of breathless stillness. He waited for her to jerk away or take over.

Her voice, when it came, was quiet. "You did that with the shotgun, too, didn't you? You took it from the vampire and sent it to me. You did it with the straw in the airport. You can move things, just by wanting to."

"Yes."

Her hand closed around him.

His arms fell to his sides, his fists clenching. The clean scent of her body and the rich undertone of her arousal permeated his senses. Lindsay was intoxicating—certain to be addicting.

"You're burning hot," she whispered.

"You make me that way." His blood had gone cold the moment he'd learned of Phineas's death. It had turned to ice when Lindsay had collapsed to the ground with blood splattered all over her. It wasn't until now, under the heat of her touch, that he finally felt . . . *human* again.

She fisted him at the root, then stroked to tip. "And big. God, you're so thick and long. I want this. I want *you*. So badly. From the moment I first saw you."

"Take me." His voice was a rasp.

"I can't."

His jaw clenched. She had every right to be afraid. She was smart to be. It was only going to get more difficult from here.

Lindsay pumped him again, harder. Then again.

"Yes," he growled, thrusting into her hand. "Jack me off. Make me come."

"Jesus . . ." She released him.

Adrian shook with his hunger. He *needed* her touch. Two hundred years without it had left him dead in all the most fundamental ways. Now every sense and nerve ending was alive again, and desperate for her.

She came into view, rounding his right wings.

He stood there, exposed in every way.

Her gaze locked with his. "Tell me the truth, angel. Is this just you and me? Or is this you, me, and a motive I haven't figured out yet?"

"Just you and me." His chest tightened with the half-truth. In reality, everything stood between them. His mission, her father, the rules that would deny him the solace of Lindsay's body . . .

Tell me the truth, angel.

He choked on the truth. It wrapped around his throat and squeezed so tightly he could barely breathe, let alone give her the disclosure she deserved. *I'm going to pit you against your own people. I'm going to train you how to kill your father. I'm going to send your soul from this earth once and for all. My love will destroy you, and me, and everything we care about. I can't stop it.*

She slid her recovering left arm around his waist, tucked beneath his wings. Her right hand reached for him again. His breath hissed out between his teeth.

She stroked him firmly. His wings trembled as lust surged through him. The next pump of her fist was so perfect it was painful.

"Faster." He gasped, pulling her closer with an arm around her shoulder.

Lindsay widened her stance, stabilizing herself with her arm at his waist. She faced him directly, standing perpendicular to his body. He was seared by her proximity. The side of his torso was tucked between her breasts, while her thighs were planted on either side of his. Anchored, she used the leverage she'd gained to fist his aching cock with greater power and speed.

Adrian's head fell back in supplication. His wings lifted and curved around them, sheltering their precious intimacy.

All the while her hand moved on him, her grip strong and the tempo steady. His chest lifted and fell with rapid, heaving breaths. Her breath, too, came quick and hot, gusting over his chest. Her nipples were hard and tight against him, her hips moving in quick, needy little circles. He pressed his lips to her forehead, his eyes stinging.

"You get thicker before you come," she breathed. "And harder."

Her hand flew as she worked him, pumping him, her speed preternaturally quick—and just what he needed. Two centuries of pent-up desire demanded release *now*. Then he could seduce her properly. He would lure her into his bed, where he could wrap himself around her and pretend that nothing and no one existed but the two of them. No consequences, no deception, no inevitable and eternal parting.

"Yes," he panted against her perspiration-damp forehead. "I'm almost there . . ."

Need coiled around his spine and pooled like molten iron at the base of his cock.

Ever his temptation, she coaxed him with a voice made husky by her own desire. "Show me. Come for me, Adrian. Come hard."

"Keep touching me . . . don't stop."

"I won't. I can't. Let me see you—"

His entire body jerked with the first wrenching spurt. *"Lindsay."*

She made a soft sound of hunger as he shuddered through the explosive climax, her arm tireless as she brought him off with the dedication of a woman who wanted nothing more than to pleasure him.

I love you. The words clawed their way up from the depths of his soul, threatening to escape.

Unable to stem the rush of feeling, Adrian smothered the truth with the softness of her mouth.

Lindsay's knees buckled the instant Adrian's mouth sealed over hers.

He turned in her embrace, cupping her face with gentle hands. As ferociously lustful as he'd been while desperate for orgasm, he was devastating with his tenderness now. His lips were light against hers, his tongue a velvet lash. She caught his wrists, so lost to the scent and taste of him that she didn't realize they were moving until her back came up against a wall.

"Thank you," he whispered, before licking into her mouth.

A low whimper escaped her. He moved his head slowly, from side to side, sliding his parted lips back and forth across hers. His fingers pushed into her hair and kneaded her scalp. Heated delight coursed through her, permeating her overeager body and soothing her frantic desire. Growing languid under the surprisingly delicate onslaught of his mouth, she reached for his lean hips, pulling him closer.

"Stay out of my head," she warned.

"It's not your head I want to get into right now."

The feel of his cock against her belly, still hard as steel, made her breath catch. Adrian breathed into her mouth, filling her lungs with air from his own. The intimacy was more potent than his fingers sliding down and across her shoulders, pushing aside the thin straps of her camisole. Her back arched, offering her breasts.

In her mind, she knew it was wrong to be this way with Adrian. She knew she had to stop, that she had to make him stop. Her hands fell away, her palms pressing flat against the wall. But the feel of his touch on her bare skin, his fingertips following the line of her waistband before slipping beneath her top, was sublime ... so perfect ...

She gasped out a laugh, her stomach concaving to flee his questing fingers.

His beautiful lips curved against her mouth. "You're ticklish."

Adrian's delight was palpable, reverberating through her and shaking her resolve. He gripped her waist and tugged her into an exuberant embrace.

Oh god ... she couldn't take him like this. Sensual. Playful. His brilliant eyes no longer stormy but lit with joy—because of her. It was a level of intimacy she didn't know, had never experienced in her previous brief sexual encounters. She hadn't known what she was missing ...

"Adrian."

"Hmm ... ?" He kissed her temple, then moved lower, to her ear. "Where else are you ticklish, Linds?"

"We—" The flick of his tongue along the shell of her ear made her shiver. Her hands fisted. "W-we shouldn't be doing this."

"You don't have to do anything," he purred, cupping her swollen, tender breasts.

A low moan escaped her. She turned her face toward the wall of windows beside them. The sun was shining brightly, sparkling through the rain droplets clinging to the glass—a reflection of his mood and how she'd lightened it.

He caught her nipples between thumb and forefinger, tugging lightly. "Such tiny, delicate nipples for such lush breasts. I'm going to tongue them until you come."

Her hips thrust forward without her volition, her sex clenching in greedy demand. "For a virgin"—she gasped—"you're damn good at seduction."

Adrian paused, his cerulean eyes glittering with amusement. "You think I'm virginal?"

"Are you saying you've done this before?" Jealousy ate at her, cooling her blood. "I thought you'd grow fangs if you got some."

His mouth curved in a purely male smile. "There's only you, *neshama*. You alone bring out this side of me."

She had no idea what he'd just called her, but it struck a deep chord with her, and the way his voice sounded when he said it gave her butterflies. "Adrian . . . Shit. I'm going to burn in hell for this."

"For leaning against a wall?" He licked erotically into her ear. "No, you won't."

"I'm trying to do the right thing," she protested, even as she couldn't seem to find the will to push him away. Not when one of his wickedly talented hands was sliding into her pants while the other was pushing up her camisole and baring her chest.

"This was inevitable. *We* are inevitable." His gaze lifted to look into her dazed eyes. "You know it."

"Why aren't you afraid?"

"I'm more afraid of not having you than of paying for the privilege." He cupped her possessively through the lace of her thong.

Her head fell back, all resistance leaving her as his finger teased along the sensitive crease of her thigh where skin met the edge of lace. There was a vibrating anxiety inside her, a piercing hunger and longing that scared her more than the ramifications of what they were doing. The steamy sensuality that clung to him enveloped her, stoking her desire until she couldn't think for wanting him. She wanted his touch so badly—*craved* it.

Adrian supported her spine in the cradle of one large hand and arched her toward him. She held her breath, waiting. He blew a cool stream of air over her puckered nipple, and the light constriction of her thong disappeared along with the garment itself. His hot, wet tongue stroked across her at the same moment his fingertips parted her and stroked across her clitoris. She shuddered violently and cried out, so damn turned on she thought she might combust. She was feverish, damp with sweat and the slickness of her arousal.

He gave a rumbling sound of approval. "Soft and wet. And waxed. Nothing to get in the way while I eat you for hours."

Not wax. Laser. But why argue? He liked it. And she liked that he liked it. She also liked the feel of his feather-light touch circling the trembling entrance to her body, and his tongue fluttering over her hardened nipple. She liked the way his wings curved nearly to the wall, forming a shield of white that made her feel safe and protected. Cherished.

Reaching up, Lindsay ran her hands through the thick strands of his black hair. She lifted one leg and slung it around his hip, opening herself further. "Touch me," she gasped, writhing as his cheeks hollowed with a quick tug on her breast.

"I am." His breath gusted warmly over the cooling wetness left from his mouth.

She growled.

Two long, elegant fingers pushed inside her. "Is this what you want?"

Pulling herself up with a grip at his nape, she took his mouth, ravishing it; then she nipped along his jaw down to his throat. Her lips parted over his throbbing pulse, her tongue stroking over it, plumping the thick vein. Then she raked her teeth across it.

He groaned, catching her with an arm around her back. "You're so fucking hot. You're driving me insane."

Her hips pumped and circled, riding his fingers. She tossed his words back at him. "Get me off. Make me come."

Adrian's mouth slanted across hers. His thumb pressed against her throbbing clitoris, massaging it with every plunge of his fingers. She sobbed her pleasure into his mouth, her short nails digging into the rock-hard muscles of his shoulders. He caught her tongue and sucked on it, making her sex clench hard on his working hand.

The silky soft stroke of his chest hair across her aching nipples was killing her, finishing the job begun by his tenderness. Everything about the way he touched her was reverent. Worshipful. Even in the midst of the rawest sexual encounter she'd ever had, she felt like it was all about her. About being with her in every intimate way possible.

The orgasm hit her like lightning. She quaked in his arms, climaxing violently, the delicate tissues of her sex rippling along wickedly knowledgeable fingers that curved and rubbed in a way that kept her coming.

Lindsay could only hold on to him, tears squeezing past tightly closed eyelids. Her panting breaths exchanged with his. All the while he kissed her as if he'd die if he didn't.

She'd barely stopped shaking when his fingers left her and she was lifted against him—naked, her clothes gone the way of his ... wherever that was. Entwined, they spun in a controlled rush; then the cool surface of the dining table was beneath her buttocks and she was reaching back, propping her torso up with her arms canted behind her. Adrian pushed her knee aside with one hand and took his cock in hand with the other. The broad crown was tucked against her.

His eyes, shimmering with raging blue flames, stared into hers. "I've been starving for you, *neshama sheli*."

She'd barely sucked in the shaky breath required to ask him what he said when he began the hot, hard slide into her, pushing her to lie back, blanketing her with the scorching heat of his body. Writhing to accommodate him, she gripped his hips, trying to slow the relentless stretching impalement.

"Jesus—" She gasped, her back arching. "Why the hell are you built like a porn star if you're not allowed to have sex!"

His laugh swept over her, leaving goose bumps in its wake. It was such a rich, deep sound—infinitely beautiful and soul stirring. Her heart swelled as if she lived and breathed to hear that sound from him.

He sank to the root, touching the end of her. His wings extended and flexed luxuriously, reminding her of the sensual stretching of a well-fed feline. Their eyes met and held; so did their breaths. He cupped her face in that breathless moment, staring at her in a way that melted her.

"*Ani ohev otach*, Lindsay," he whispered, before taking her mouth and filling her burning lungs with his exhalation. He rotated his hips, sinking a fraction deeper. She swore she felt every inch—every ridged vein and every beat of his pounding heart.

She held his nape with one hand, licking across his

lips, shaken by the absolute surety that she was right where she'd always longed to be and hadn't known it. "Adrian, I—"

The sound of resonating chimes froze her. And him.

They clung to each other, breathing hard, his penis a thick, throbbing presence inside her. The full import of what she was doing and who she was doing it with hit her like a deluge of ice water.

The sound came again, followed by a brusque knocking. A damn doorbell.

She gasped a sound of relief, then whimpered as Adrian began to withdraw. His gaze never left her as he pulled out with aching slowness and a tightly clenched jaw. The moment he fell heavily from her body, she scrambled from the table and ran to her bedroom.

He redressed her in her pajamas before she slammed the door shut, but nothing so simple as clothes could make her feel less raw and exposed.

CHAPTER 13

Adrian pushed shaking hands through his hair to straighten it before looking into the oval foyer mirror. Although the sleeveless Asian-style tunic he'd summoned fell to his midthigh and hid his erection, his flushed face and bright eyes, along with lips swollen by Lindsay's fervency, betrayed his mortal weakness.

He stared at his reflection, regulating his breathing and willing his countenance into the tight, austere lines he was expected to present. He tucked his wings away, knowing they'd betray his roiling emotions as surely as his gaze did.

The bell rang a third time, followed by another round of knocking. He yanked on the levered handle of one of the double doors, then walked away as the door began its automated glide back into a locked position. As he crossed the room, he mentally crushed some of the most fragrant flowers in the massive floral arrangements scattered about the vast suite. The cloying scents couldn't hide the lush smell of sex from the powerful nostrils of an angel, but at least he could show respect by making the effort.

"Captain," Jason greeted him in a slow, knowing drawl.

"You have news for me?" He went into the kitchen and washed his hands, rinsing away the now beloved smell of Lindsay's desire. His blood still raged from the remembered feel of her body's tight hot clasp. That bright moment of connection would have shattered him if she hadn't made him laugh, which he hadn't done in so long he couldn't recall the last time. He'd forgotten how potent their affinity was. He couldn't remember it ever scorching him so completely. He felt as if he'd been run through a forge, heated until he was molten, then refashioned into something new and untarnished.

"Where's Shadoe?"

He turned around, feeling an odd agitation at the use of a name he couldn't yet explain to Lindsay, and found Elijah with Jason. The truth of what he'd been doing before their intrusion wouldn't escape the notice of a lycan's more primal instincts. Lindsay's scent was all over him, and from the flaring of Elijah's nostrils, the lycan recognized that.

"*Lindsay,*" Adrian emphasized, "is still recuperating."

Jason studied him openly. "But she's been up. She . . . ate."

"Like a lumberjack."

"How's her arm?" Elijah asked, his face studiously impassive.

"Healing nicely."

"Good." The lycan gave a brisk nod of satisfaction.

Adrian crossed his arms, appraising Elijah. There was no longer any doubt the lycan was an Alpha, not after watching him with the other lycans when they cleaned out the Hurricane nest. Also no doubt he was dangerous—his inherent dominance and ability to draw other lycans into following his lead could only result in trouble. For now, however, he was committed to Lindsay. She'd saved his hide—more than once, he said. He would repay that debt by protecting her with his life and, right now, that was just the level of loyalty Adrian needed to keep her safe.

"I just wanted to check with you," Jason began, moving to the dining table, "about our plans to head back up to Utah tomorrow. Is that timeline still doable?"

"I said it was." Adrian's voice was low and smooth, but he had to make a concerted effort not to clench his fists as Jason paused before the very spot where he'd been buried inside Lindsay just moments earlier. "Six o'clock sharp I want to be on the road."

"Okay." Jason set his hand on the table and looked at him. "Helena's in Vegas. She wants to see you."

"I'll meet with her as soon as I change. Elijah, stay with Lindsay."

Adrian headed toward his bedroom on the opposite side of the living area from Lindsay's. He closed the door and sat on the edge of the bed, exhaling harshly before picking up the phone and hitting the button that connected him to her room.

It took her a long time to answer. "Hello?"

"Linds . . . Are you okay?"

She sighed. "No. I'm pretty far from okay."

His eyes closed. Her embarrassment and confusion were tangible. "I have to go out. Elijah will stay with you. When I get back, you and I will talk."

"All right."

"If you need or want anything while I'm gone, charge it to the room."

"Oh god." She groaned. "Please don't buy me off."

"Wouldn't think of it. You're priceless."

There was another long pause. When her voice came again, it was laced with steel. "You're right, Adrian. You can't afford me. The price is too high. I won't let you pay it."

He looked at the closed door and cursed under his breath. She needed his attention and reassurance after what they'd just shared, but with the others here he could do nothing to soothe her. There were things he couldn't yet say, but could show her, if only they had privacy. "We'll talk when I get back," he said again.

"Be careful."

"Stay out of trouble." Adrian returned the receiver to the cradle and pushed to his feet. The sooner he took care of business, the sooner he could return to Lindsay.

Lindsay took a second shower. When she came out of the bathroom, there was another outfit laid out on the bed. This one was on a hanger and covered by a boutique's protective bag. She revealed the garment inside, finding the outrageously priced tags still attached. It was a beautiful ensemble, with chocolate-hued palazzo pants paired with a multihued turquoise and gold shell. Expensive and elegant, so suited to Adrian's taste. A makeup case sat beside it, filled with brand-new MAC makeup. And lying innocuously on the bed beneath it all was a money envelope branded with the hotel's logo, filled with a two-inch-thick stack of crisp hundred-dollar bills.

She ran her hands down her face with a groan. She was in so far over her head she was drowning. Adrian was too much for her. She couldn't handle it. Couldn't handle *him*. The looks he gave her, the way he spoke to her and touched her ... whatever the hell they were doing wasn't a fling for him. And no matter what she said, no matter how hard she tried, he was determined to have her at any cost.

She dressed and made herself presentable, then settled into the seat Adrian had occupied earlier and called her dad.

"Eddie Gibson, Gibson Automotive," he answered.

"Hey, Dad." She heard the whirring of air tools in the background, and her throat tightened with homesickness. Her father didn't know about the darker aspects of her life, but he knew she was unusual and he loved her unconditionally anyway. "It's me. Sorry I didn't call sooner."

"Hey, baby. Are you feeling better?" His beloved voice was gruff with concern.

Frowning, she asked, "Better? Yes, I feel good. Great, actually."

"I'm glad to hear it." A relieved sigh crossed the line between them. "I was worried when I couldn't get ahold of you. Every time I tried your cell, it went straight to voice mail."

"Yeah. I haven't charged it since I got here. It might've died."

"Tell Adrian I appreciate him calling and letting me know you're all right. If he hadn't done that, I'd probably have called the national guard to hunt you down."

"Adrian called you?" A tingle moved through her. With everything else he had on his plate, he'd taken a parent's concern into consideration and went out of his way to alleviate it. His thoughtfulness touched her deeply.

"Yesterday. Told me you were knocked out by a stomach bug. You should take it easy for the next couple of days and drink lots of liquids. And you might consider investing some time in Adrian Mitchell. He sounded like he really cares about you. Could be something there."

If only. She'd finally met a man she didn't have to lie to or hide from, and she couldn't have him. "Are you taking care of yourself?"

"Knowing you'll nag me if I don't, yes. Went over to Sam's last night and played poker, too."

"Good." She'd been pushing him to get out more. A poker night with the guys was a good first step.

"Where are you? The caller ID says Mondego Resort."

"It's a Gadara property," she explained, having noted the Gadara Enterprises logo on the bedside phone as she dialed.

"So you're already back in the saddle then. You need to take care of yourself. You've always pushed yourself too hard."

"Look who's talking," she shot back. "I'll make you a deal: every time you take a day off, I'll match it with one of my own."

He laughed, and she absorbed the sound with delight. "All right. Deal."

"I love you. I'll call again in a couple days, but if you need anything or just want to chat, I'll make sure my phone is charged."

"Will do. Love you."

Returning the receiver to the cradle, Lindsay stood and moved to leave the bedroom, grabbing her messenger bag on the way out. The living area had been devoid of masculine voices for a while now, but she still took a deep breath of courage before opening the door. Hearing her father's voice had helped her get her focus back, but the feelings of vulnerability and exposure remained. Adrian got to her. As much as she wished it otherwise, she had so few defenses against him.

Lindsay found Elijah waiting by the couch, standing with his arms crossed. He was a big, formidable presence. His olive green T-shirt and loose-fitting jeans did little to hide the power of his body. There was such a sense of solidness and steadfastness to him; he was the kind of guy you could trust with your life. He reminded her of Adrian in that respect. Adrian, too, was august and stalwart in an extraordinary way. The feeling he gave of anchoring her was the most difficult aspect of him to resist. She desired him, she liked him, she trusted him. And when she was with him, she felt peaceful, which was a state of being the vampires had stolen from her that long-ago nightmarish day.

Adrian had given her equanimity back to her. But to return the favor, she had to let him go. As much as he gave to her, she could take everything away from him in a single selfish moment.

"Hi, El." She smiled at the handsome lycan. "How are you?"

"Alive." Elijah's deep voice rumbled across the room. "In large part, because of you."

"Whatever. You were kicking ass. I just tried to be more than a helpless human."

"Helpless." He snorted. "No, you're not helpless. You're fucking crazy."

Lindsay nodded grimly. "For the most part."

His brilliant emerald eyes swept over her in a clinically examining glance. "How are you feeling? Is the arm hurting you at all?"

She approached him with her hand extended. The pinkness of the flesh was fading and a light dusting of peach fuzz had sprung up since she'd taken her first shower earlier.

Elijah looked at her arm and whistled. "I thought for sure you'd lose it."

"It was bad, *huh*?"

He shot her a wry glance. "Yeah. It was nearly blown off by a shotgun."

Lindsay remembered the searing agony and hugged her arm, massaging the phantom pain. "How did he do it?"

"Wish I knew."

Since he seemed so fascinated by it, she offered, "You can touch it."

"No way."

One brow rose. "I don't bite."

"I'm not pissing Adrian off. Curiosity killed the wolf, too."

"Seriously. You're totally overestimating any possessive tendencies on his part. Besides, how would he know?"

"He'd smell me on you."

The other brow rose to match the first.

"Seriously," he parroted drily. "Hate to embarrass you, but I smell him all over you."

Her stomach knotted. "Did you also smell me on him?"

"Yep."

"Shit." She shook out her hair with agitated hands. "If I wanted to pack up and run, would I have to ditch you? Or would you let me go peaceably?"

"Try to ditch me." He growled softly. "See how far you get."

"Do you have orders to detain me?"

"No. But I won't let you out of my sight."

Because she trusted him, she let him see her turmoil. "I'm playing with fire and I'm going to get burned. I could live with that, but Adrian—he doesn't need this kind of heat. He's still recovering from Phineas's death."

"He's a big boy. He can take care of himself." Elijah's features softened. "Worry about taking care of you."

Her gaze moved to the table. She remembered vividly what it felt like to have Adrian inside her. The edge to his voice had been as intimate as the physical act, and the foreign words he spoke resonated inside her, striking her in a way that was distantly familiar. She didn't know their meaning, but she knew they were words spoken from one lover to another. They were as potent as tangible caresses, drifting softly over her skin like a warm breeze. If she was the only one to face consequences, she would take him. Keep him. Make him hers. But it wasn't that way. He would suffer . . .

She exhaled in a rush. "My self-preservation warning light appears to be on the fritz."

"So I noticed the other day."

"Are you hungry?"

"I could eat."

"Let's go pig out, then ride a roller coaster until we vomit." An adrenaline high or two was the only thing that might save her from bolting. She was strung too tight. If she didn't loosen up, she was going to snap.

Elijah sighed. "You saved my ass for this?"

"It's either that or run away. Your choice."

"Fine." He swept his arm toward the double-door entrance to the suite. "But I'll warn you now—you really don't want to puke on me."

She started walking, eager to escape the place that had too many dangerous memories. "Why not?"

"I'll puke back," he said, pulling the door open. "I guarantee I eat more than you."

"Eww." Lindsay was about to step out to the hallway when a dapper African American man filled the threshold.

She stumbled to a halt, arrested by his megawatt smile. He was instantly recognizable. He was also her boss. "Hello, Mr. Gadara."

"Good afternoon, Ms. Gibson. You are just the person I wanted to see."

Adrian entered the Hard Rock Café and asked for Helena Bardon. The hostess offered him a bright smile and tried to engage him with small talk, but he offered only monosyllabic answers, his thoughts firmly on Lindsay. The pretty brunette continued to flirt with him as she led him to Helena's booth, but her warmth quickly faded when she spotted the blonde sliding from the bench seat to greet him. He knew what the hostess saw—a stunning, statuesque, radiantly beautiful woman with waist-length blond hair and seraph blue eyes.

"Adrian." Helena pulled him into a warm embrace. "When I heard about Phineas, I was so worried about you."

"I'm managing."

Her delicate nostrils flared as she studied him. "Your Shadoe has returned to console you."

He gestured for her to sit.

"You know I don't judge you," she said softly, returning to her seat.

"I know." After all this time, Helena remained pure of heart and soul. Her piety was so unassailable; she seemed untouched by the world they lived in. He envied her that serenity.

"Does she truly bring you solace?"

"Solace and torment, pleasure and pain. All of it in the extreme. It is sublime and it is hell, and I need it to exist. I need her." There were few Sentinels he could speak so freely to. Helena's unwavering faith gave her an impartiality few could lay claim to.

A waiter intruded and they ordered. They would push the food around for appearance's sake, then box it up for their lycans. When they were alone again, Helena leaned back in her seat and suddenly looked very weary.

"How can I help you?" he asked. He didn't show how her unrest affected him, but it did. Deeply. She'd always been one of the immutable things in his existence. But then, so had Phineas.

"By commiserating." Her delicate hand rested on the table. "Have I told you that one of my lycans, Mark, claims to be in love with me?"

Adrian stilled. "No."

"Yes. Well, that's what he believes."

Recovering, he said, "I'm not overly surprised by the possibility. You're a beautiful woman with a gentle soul."

"You know where the praise for such things should be directed, but thank you." Her fingertips drummed lightly into the tabletop, a revealing action she seemed to be unaware of. "I made every attempt to be respectful of his feelings, however inconvenient they are. He's done his job very well because of them. Mark has risked himself in ways and situations no other lycan would have."

"Has he become a problem for you?"

"No." She sighed. "*I* have."

Reaching out, he caught her hand, stilling its fidgeting. "I'm listening."

"I knew he had . . . needs. I understand the lycan breed. It's just . . . I refused to see how he handled those needs and he made every attempt to hide his activities." Her fingers tightened on his. "But the other day, when I heard about Phineas, I called Mark in after I'd already given him the afternoon off. When he returned, I smelled—I smelled a woman on him."

"Helena." His chest tightened with sympathy.

"I was furious, Adrian. As I have never been before. I raged at him. Said cruel and deliberately hurtful things. Accused him of being weak and flawed. And more . . . so much more. I couldn't stop. Ugliness poured from me and I couldn't stop it. I made him hate himself. He was already suffering guilt and shame on his own, and I added the burden of my pain to his."

"You were jealous." And now she knew what few Sentinels did—that they were as possessive as the lycans and vampires could be. The trait, it seemed, was inherent in the seraphim and was passed on to the Fallen. "It could've been worse. It would have been, had you been sleeping with him."

"And that's the dilemma I come to you with." Her chin lifted. "You, of anyone, know how I feel. All this time, I believed the urges of the flesh were beyond us. That lust was one battle we didn't have to fight."

"We're meant to be tested—you know that."

"Yes, but as I attempted to explain the situation to Mark, to apologize for the hurt I'd caused him and to prepare him for a transfer away from me, he caught something I had missed. We are forbidden to mate with mortals, Adrian. Lycans, vampires—even demons—are not mortals."

He released her hand and sat back, removing himself from the role of friend and returning to that of her commanding officer. "You're hoping for a loophole."

"Don't judge me!" she snapped, too upset to maintain courtesy. "How can you even presume to, after coming here with the scent of a mortal woman all over you?"

"What did you expect me to say? Ask yourself— honestly—did you come to me for commiseration? Because you know you have it. My heart breaks for you. But if you came for absolution, I can't give it to you."

"Why not?"

"If I gave you license to make the mistakes I've made I'd be no better than Syre. I won't lead you to damnation, Helena. It's my responsibility to do everything in my power to prevent your fall."

"Do as you say," she said bitterly. "Not as you do."

Her fulminating glare cut into him. In just a few short moments, he'd become her enemy. As deeply as her anger hurt him, he could do nothing differently. "The answer to your question doesn't lie with me. You know that."

Helena's lush lower lip trembled. "I ask, and hear nothing."

"The conclusion I drew from that," he said gently, "was that the silence was answer enough."

She sucked in a deep, shaky breath. "I thought you would help me."

"I'll try. But not in the way you want."

A tear formed, then fell down her flawless cheek. Her pain radiated from her and echoed through him. She slid out of the booth. "I need a moment to collect myself."

He nodded and watched her weave her way through the dining room and turn down the hall to the restrooms. He pulled his cell phone out and dialed.

"Jason," he said when the lieutenant answered. "Find Helena's personal guards and recall them immediately."

"I'll see to it personally. What's going on?"

"We'll discuss it later. If you haven't recovered both guards within a half hour from now, I need to know."

"Gotcha."

The food arrived and Adrian sent it back to be boxed. It took the waiter several minutes to see to it, and Helena failed to return during that time. But Adrian had known the chances of her doing so had been fifty-fifty at best. He understood what she was going through and he knew what he would do if there had been anyone capable of stepping between him and Lindsay—he'd grab her and run, buying what precious little time he could before they were caught.

He tossed cash on the table to settle the bill. He collected the bagged food containers with one hand while rubbing at the constriction of his throat with the other. He'd given Helena an hour's head start. It was a pitiful concession, but the only one he could make before the hunt for her and her rogue lycan would begin.

Adrian hoped she'd had the foresight to have Mark

waiting nearby. The alternative—that she might have thought, for even a moment, that he would condone her decision—was too painful to contemplate.

If he'd fallen that far in the eyes of his Sentinels, the trials they would face in the days ahead would be insurmountable.

CHAPTER 14

Vash wiped the blood from her mouth with the back of her hand and bared her fangs at the lycan she'd pinned to a pine tree with a silver-coated blade. Forced into his human form by the silver's poisoning of his blood he slumped naked with his head hanging, breathing shallowly.

"You know whose blood this is," she said again, nursing her own myriad collection of deep bites and gouges. She waved the rag with the telltale bloodstain on it under his nose. "Which one of your packmates took the pilot from the airport in Shreveport?"

"Fuck. You. Bitch," he gasped, gripping the hilt of the sword but too weak to pull it free of the wood behind him.

"We'll be at this all day."

He looked up at her from beneath a hank of red hair that was lighter than hers by a few shades. "I'll be dead in an hour. And you'll have nothing."

"You really don't want to keel over before you tell me what I want to know."

"Barking up the wrong tree." He managed a croaked laugh at his lame pun.

"You're a real comedian." She gripped his chin and forced his head up. "I see recognition in your eyes. If you'd just spill the name, your pain would be over."

He flipped her the bird. "See this, too?"

Vash stared at the lycan with a clenched jaw, wondering if he could possibly be responsible for the death of her mate. It was a question that haunted her with every lycan she met. She had to believe the responsible party was still alive and out there somewhere, waiting for her to exact retribution for the atrocities committed against her beloved Charron. "How many vampires have you killed, dog?"

"N-not enough."

"He's young," Salem said beside her, momentarily distracting her with his latest blinding hair color of primary blue. It was fortunate for him that he possessed classical bone structure; there was a regal quality to his handsome face that transcended whatever crayon hue adorned his head. He was also a badass motherfucker. If he hadn't been, the bull's-eye on his noggin would have seen him killed long ago.

She examined the lycan's face. Beneath the agony and exhaustion that marred it, she could see youth. Perhaps he was too young. "How old are you?"

"Suck my dick."

Bending forward, she aligned their gazes. "I'm teetering on the brink of releasing you, stupid. Don't fuck it up."

The redhead glared. "Fifty."

Not him. He would have been a five-year-old pup at the time of Char's death. She yanked her blade out of the tree and watched the lycan crumple to the forest floor. "Go to the asshole who kidnapped my friend. Tell him Vash is coming for him. Tell him he can meet me like a man, or he can cower like a dog and find himself with my blade in his back."

The lycan's skin began to ripple with the shadow of fur, a last-ditch attempt to save himself by shifting into his lupine form. In the process, his altering flesh would knit back together faster than it would without a shift.

"You're letting him go?" Raze asked, his massive biceps bulging as he cleaned the lycan blood from his blade.

"If he makes it out of the woods alive, he deserves to die another day."

She turned away and began tracking the path the two lycans had taken as they fled from her. The two Fallen captains fell into line behind her.

A mile away, Raze caught her arm and looked down at her through his sunglasses. Vash was a tall woman, but the captain towered above her. "Syre wanted us to bring the lycans back to Raceport."

"That one isn't going to crack, not even for Syre. If we want him to be useful, we need to give him his freedom."

"The chances of him making it back to civilization are practically nonexistent," Salem pointed out drily.

Her returning smile was grim. "He's motivated. He was willing to die to protect whoever it is we're after. He's going to want to get back and give a heads-up that we're coming, and when he does, he'll lead us right to the one we want. If necessary, we'll help him along and make sure he survives long enough to give us a trail."

They located the remnants of the lycan's clothing two miles farther. In his pants pocket, they found his wallet. Pulling out his Mitchell Aeronautics identification card, Vash smiled and waved it. "I thought so. His home address is Angels' Point. I *knew* Adrian was involved. Now maybe we'll be able to prove it."

"Mr. Mitchell."

Adrian paused as he moved past the Mondego's registration desk. "Yes?"

The front desk clerk reached for the phone. "Mr. Gadara would like to see you when you have a moment."

He gave a curt nod and continued toward the elevators. His cell phone beeped with a text message just before the doors opened. He pulled it out of his pocket as he stepped inside the waiting car.

The principal's on the move, via Gadara. Heading to airport to intercept, but may have to follow to CA. Will report ASAP.

Because he was partially distracted by planning the logistics of the hunt for Helena and her lycan, it took Adrian a split second to register who'd texted—Elijah— and who the principal was—Lindsay. "Shit."

He thrust his hand out just before the doors slid closed, then exited the car in a rush. "I'll see him now," he said to the front desk clerk, who directed him to another elevator, which required a key code from the occupant or the front desk to activate it.

The elevator had only two stops—Raguel's office and the roof. The doors slid open directly into a massive reception area that kept visitors at bay until Raguel was ready to receive them. Adrian set the bag of food on the receptionist's desk, then walked right through to Raguel's office.

"Adrian." Raguel rose gracefully to his feet from behind his desk and waved off his secretary with an insolent flick of his wrist. Behind him, a wall of windows offered a panoramic view of the city, creating an impressive backdrop for the overly ambitious archangel. "I am afraid the test results have yet to come back."

"You're fucking with the wrong seraph."

"Ah, I see." Raguel's smile was knowing. "You are here about Ms. Gibson. I had assumed your thoughts were focused on more pressing matters."

"Right now my thoughts are focused on making your life hell. You don't want me to do that. Where is she?"

"There is no emotion at all in your voice, yet your words are so fierce. Which is it, Adrian? Does Ms. Gibson's departure truly upset you, or have you simply failed to acquire suitable social skills?"

"You can't bait me, Raguel. Where is she?"

The archangel sank back into his seat with an elegant economy of movement. "She took my helicopter to the airport, where I believe she intends to catch a flight to California. She was most eager to begin her work as the Belladonna's assistant general manager."

"Your interference in my matters is exceptionally foolhardy. I thought you were smarter than that."

"I had no right to detain her. Once she stated her desire to leave, I had no choice but to allow her to go. What would you have had me do? Restrain her?"

Adrian's back rippled with his aggravation. "You didn't have to assist her."

"She works for me. How could I not help her when she asked?"

"Did she ask? Or did you offer?"

"What does it matter? She accepted eagerly." Raguel's smile was filled with calculation.

Pulling out his phone, Adrian sent a quick text to Elijah. *Find the principal. Protect her until further notice.*

"I am more than happy to lend you my helicopter as well," Raguel offered.

"Perhaps. If something pressing comes up." He was almost decided that he shouldn't go after Lindsay even when it became possible for him to do so. She would be safer if he stayed away. He no longer needed her to lure Syre—the vampire leader was giving him all the excuse necessary without her help.

And maybe letting Shadoe go was the lesson he'd never learned. Maybe she'd been his test at selflessness and he'd failed to pass it over and over again. Maybe freeing both Shadoe's soul *and* the vessel carrying it was the true sacrifice he was expected to make. There was no reason Lindsay Gibson couldn't live a life separate from him. He'd given her the choice between relative normalcy—a secular job and the cessation of her hunting—or training with him. If she'd chosen the former, there was no good reason for him not to let her go. He knew where she was; he could keep Syre away from her until the time came when he could end this.

That time was coming soon. Very soon.

In the interim, he had Helena to contend with. Finding her wasn't something he would delegate to anyone else. He respected his Sentinels too much to not see to them personally. And when he did find her and separate her from her lycan, it would be best if he could look her in the eye and tell her that he'd made the same sacrifice to his happiness that he was demanding she make to hers.

"You surprise me," Raguel murmured. "You have risked so much for something you relinquish so easily."

"You don't know me, Raguel." He pivoted to leave the room. "But I know you. Your ambition will be your downfall. Especially if you make an enemy of me."

"I believe you will find," the archangel called after him, "that I am a friend worth having in your corner."

"Unlike you, I don't have a corner." Adrian stepped into the elevator and faced Raguel, baring his teeth in a feral smile. The archangel's territory extended only across North America; Adrian had no such limits.

The elevator doors closed, shutting out the look of sharp consideration on Raguel's face.

Shadoe had never run from Adrian before. From the first time she'd seduced him past all restraint, rules, and better sense, she had been ferociously determined to keep him enthralled. It had taken her a long time to break him down initially, a relentless and passionate assault on his senses that led to him falling on her in a mindless rut, driven past all reason. Since then, her incarnations had been consummate seducers and she'd relished his every surrender.

Until now.

Now he was alone, stripped of the people he'd relied on for support. First Phineas. Then Simone. Lindsay's departure was equally hard to take. He'd found comfort in her presence and he missed her already. But Adrian refused to allow his losses to impact his ability to carry out his mission.

He did concede, however, that they were likely the first of many signs that his retribution was nigh.

*   *   *

Lindsay was still kicking herself when her plane landed at John Wayne Airport. It wasn't like her to run. She was a doer. A woman who faced things head-on. She didn't like leaving things to chance or not knowing the score.

Yet the minute an escape route had been opened to her, she'd bolted. Not because she was frightened. No—that was a lie. Everything about Adrian Mitchell scared the shit out of her. The way he affected her was damn scary. She was so used to making do by herself, keeping to herself, and he got under her skin so deeply, she was already beginning to forget what it felt like without him there. She couldn't forget, however, what it felt like to be herself. The experience had been freeing, and now she was returning to the cage of the "real" world.

The sense of loss was almost like grief.

But she would learn to deal with it. Having Adrian's soul on the line was powerful motivation. He was too valuable to waste on her.

The wind, that fickle bitch, taunted her with soft whispers. *Adrian . . . Go back to Adrian . . .*

"Fuck you." She exited the terminal with no more than the designer clothes on her back, her cell phone and emergency charger she'd bought at McCarran Airport, and a ridiculous amount of cash in her messenger bag. She intended to pay back every penny she spent, but she hadn't had the luxury of leaving the money behind. Not while Adrian had her suitcase at his house. Which made it inevitable that she'd see him again. At the very least she had to retrieve her luggage. She could ask him to send someone down the hill with it and spare them both the awkwardness, but she wouldn't. They had unfinished business, and he deserved the courtesy of hashing it out in person.

She headed to the nearest taxi stand. For a single surreal day, Adrian's life had felt like it could be her life. But that was a ridiculous fantasy. His existence was filled with private jets, presidential suites, Maybachs, a home that was showcased on television, dragons, demons, vampires that foamed at the mouth, skies filled with angels, guys that turned into wolves, and regenerating limbs. Meanwhile, she was a mentally scarred, slightly crazy, middle-class mortal with a death wish. Nary the twain shall meet.

Downtime to get her head on straight and catch her bearings—that's what she needed. Then she could plan her next steps. Steps that would lead her away from Adrian. The temptation he presented was too great. She couldn't trust herself around him.

Sliding into the backseat of a cab, Lindsay directed the driver to take her to the Belladonna hotel. Mr. Gadara had offered her one of the finished suites until he could make arrangements for her to move into one of his residential properties. She'd been surprised by how sweet he was. For such a powerful and well-known public figure, he seemed remarkably down-to-earth and approachable.

She pointedly ignored the fact that whatever sort of being was driving the cab was sending out the kind of malevolent, inhuman vibes that would formerly have put him on her hit list.

"It's your lucky day," she murmured, meeting the curious glance the driver shot her through the rearview mirror.

Lindsay pulled her phone out of her pocket and

turned it back on. She wasn't surprised when it chirped a multitude of voice mail and text message alerts. Steeling herself against a suddenly knotted gut, she read the text messages first.

No trouble til I get there, pls (this is Elijah BTW)

"Aw, fuck," she muttered, feeling like an asshole for leaving him holding the bag. If he got in trouble because of her ... Well, he just better not or she'd be pissed at Adrian for not being fair.

Then Adrian. *Call me.*

She dialed his number.

"Lindsay." His voice, modulated and smooth, made her grip tighten on her phone. "Are you in Anaheim?"

"Not yet. I just landed."

"You shouldn't have left," he said with the arrogance she was beginning to adore. "That said, it's best that you did. Something's come up. It'll be a day or two before I can get to you. Elijah will join you until then. Don't ditch him again."

Even across the cellular waves and despite his steady tone, which gave nothing away, she knew he was troubled. She could feel it. "What's going on? Are you okay?"

"I'm ..." His voice trailed off. "No. I'm not okay."

Her spine straightened. "What's wrong?"

"I'm not in a place where it would be safe to discuss it." He exhaled audibly. "I wish I could speak freely. There are things I want to get off my chest that only you would understand."

"Adrian." She leaned forward, prepared to tell the driver to turn around. "I'll come back if you need me."

"Always," he said, so simply, as if it wasn't deeply profound that a being of his power was reliant on her for anything. "But not now. You'll be safest at Angels' Point."

"Actually . . ." Lindsay found herself hesitating to put the necessary distance between them. It didn't seem like the time—not while he needed her. But she couldn't lie to him or hold off the inevitable, either. Whatever it was they had between them, it was based on baring sides of themselves they exposed to no one else. "I'm on my way to the Belladonna. I'm going to stay there until I can find a place of my own. You said I'd be safe with Gadara."

There was a short pause. "Keep Elijah with you at all times. Stay in the hotel as much as possible and *don't hunt.*"

"I won't. I know we need to discuss the logistics first." She'd need his help to take down the vamps who had killed her mother. As reckless as she could be at times, she didn't have a death wish, and she didn't want to inadvertently endanger Adrian by crossing a line or breaking a rule she wasn't aware of.

"When you left Vegas, were you leaving me as well?"

Her stomach tightened. "I felt like I had to. I . . . want you. If it was just sexually, I'd be okay. But the more I'm with you, the more I like you. I'm not as good at fighting those kinds of feelings. I can't say no to you, and we both need me to."

The silence stretched out this time. Long enough that Lindsay feared she'd lost him. "Adrian?"

"I'm here. You just . . . surprised me. Your decision to leave in order to protect me is unexpected."

"I'm not worth falling over," she muttered. "I promise you that."

"I disagree." Although his tone didn't alter, she sensed a change in him. "I like you, too, Lindsay. You fascinate me. For someone of my years, that's a rare gift. I intended to let you go, if you agreed to stop hunting. But I've changed my mind. We'll pick this up when I get back and reach a compromise."

Lindsay's brow arched. Adrian compromising on anything wasn't something she pictured easily. He always seemed to end up getting what he wanted. He was a favored son, this warrior angel with his bloodstained wings. And he captivated her completely.

"I have to thank you," she said, "for calling my dad. He would've worried himself sick."

"It was my pleasure."

"It means a lot to me that you thought of it."

"I can't help but think of you," he said in a low, intimate tone. "I haven't been able to stop since we met."

God . . . she felt the same way. They were in such deep shit with each other. "Whatever you have to do, please be careful."

"Don't worry, *neshama*. Nothing can stop me from finishing what we started today."

"Are you ever going to tell me what you're calling me?"

"Ask me again," he purred, "the next time I'm inside you."

Shivering against a sudden flare of sexual heat, Lindsay said a hasty good-bye and ended the call.

She knew she'd done the right thing by leaving, but that didn't stop her from regretting it. Especially now that she knew he needed her with him to listen and offer support.

Damn it . . . she had to get a grip and think, but her lungs were constricted by a ferocious pressure to return to him. Although her mind knew the most reasonable and selfless course was to stay away, there was a driving need inside her demanding she go back and take him. Claim him. Make him irrevocably hers. The rapacious urge was so intense, it frightened her.

She'd never had trouble holding to her decisions, but with Adrian it felt like she was battling with herself ... with a high risk of losing. He was a glorious being, proud and dangerously beautiful. His sole purpose was hunting the very creatures she hated and wished dead. If she destroyed him, if she derailed the work he did—which was so important to her—she'd destroy herself. But knowing the consequences didn't seem to quiet the furiously whispering devil on her shoulder.

Holding to her chosen course of action by more willpower than she should have needed, she sent Elijah a text message: *c u @ the Belladonna*.

She was glad he was going to be with her. He was a straight shooter. He'd help her keep her head out of the clouds, where angels flew and mortals had no business treading.

"This is for the best," she told herself, earning another wary glance from the driver.

The verbal reinforcement didn't help as much as she wished it would.

"Whatever the most disastrous thing you can imagine is, the reality is worse." Torque shoved a pillow behind his back and leaned into the headboard attached to the wall. He was careful to keep his leg away from the slender shaft of sunlight sneaking through a tiny parting in the blackout curtains of his motel room. "Word on the street says Phineas is dead—from an unprovoked vamp attack."

There was a long pause, filled only by his father's deep and steady breathing. "Dead? Are you certain?"

"As certain as I can be without hearing it from Adrian himself. He's been out of town since I arrived. My guess is that he's hunting down those responsible."

"Without a doubt."

Torque allocated unlimited resources to the cabal he'd managed to infiltrate into the area, which gave him—and his father—access to fairly accurate reports of Adrian's and the other Sentinels' activities. Of course, Adrian kept a high profile on purpose, and Torque had long suspected that the cabal members had gone unmolested only because the Sentinel leader willingly looked the other way. *You can see me coming and I'll still get the jump on you* seemed to be his message.

"I was hoping to meet with him," Torque said, toying with a throwing star, "to let him know we had nothing to do with this."

"*No.* He might see you as a fair trade for Phineas—someone he loved and relied upon for someone equally valuable to me."

"A small sacrifice to keep a war from erupting."

"That isn't your decision to make."

"Isn't it?" Torque threw the hira-shuriken at the wall, absently noting the star's position in relation to the wallpaper pattern. His father was too protective, to the point that Vash served as his second-in-command to keep Torque out of the direct line of fire. While Torque understood the motives—and the paranoia that fueled them—it didn't make the bitter pill any easier to swallow. He wanted to serve the vampire community to the fullest extent he could. There wasn't anything he wouldn't do or sacrifice to see them thrive and flourish.

"I've already lost one child. I won't lose both of you." Torque could imagine his father's head leaning heavily into the headrest of his office chair. "Come home, son. We have the information we need. Now we need to figure out what to do with it."

"We should send Vash on cleanup duty. If we police ourselves first, maybe that will reinforce our innocence."

"Yes, you're right. You can take over the hunt for Nikki's abductors."

"I'd like nothing more, but there's something else." Torque threw another star, embedding it in the wall directly beside the first. "Adrian's been spotted with a woman recently."

Again, a lengthy stretch of silence. "You think it's Shadoe?"

"I haven't known him to show interest in any other women. Have you?"

"Phineas is gone. Adrian will be deeply aggrieved, maybe enough to break a cardinal rule. We need to be certain of the woman's identity before we take her."

Torque's hand relaxed. "I'll keep digging until I know for sure."

"If it's your sister, we need to bring her home."

"Of course. I'll keep you posted." Pulling the phone away from his ear, Torque turned it off and tossed it on the bed beside him. The hunt for intel distracted him from the grief he couldn't bear to deal with now. When he'd Changed Nikki, he had done so because he wanted her immortally by his side. Nikki's life was a sacrifice he hadn't expected he would have to make. Living without her was killing him. He now understood the venom that coursed through Vash's veins over the loss of her mate. His agony fueled him, keeping his focus sharp and his need for retribution simmering in his blood.

A couple more hours until dusk, and then he could

hit the streets again. And god help any Sentinel unfortunate enough to cross his path.

Adrian had just reached Mesquite when his phone rang. "Mitchell," he answered.

"Do you have an idea of how long the vampire was infected before you captured him?"

The somberness of Raguel's voice snared Adrian's complete attention. "No. Why?"

"The vamp is dead, and the blood sample degraded during testing. It was, I am told, as if his blood turned into a 'motor oil–type sludge' in an instant."

"I'm very sorry to hear that." *Furious* was more apt, but he made certain that wasn't evident in his tone.

"Whatever you are dealing with," the archangel went on, "is apparently lethal and perhaps fast-acting, depending on when the subject was infected."

"Thank you. Your help is appreciated."

Ending the call, Adrian looked at Jason and Damien. They were waiting nearby, looking bleak and disheartened beneath a flashing neon keno sign. Adrian wished he could have spared them this hunt for one of their own, but he couldn't risk losing Helena or her lycan if they decided to split up. Already Helena's second guard was traveling separately from the couple, stopping less frequently and swiftly pulling ahead.

"We need to capture more minions," he told them. "Infected and not."

Jason's golden good looks were made stark by concern. "What's going on?"

"Perhaps the end of the vampires is finally nigh." Adrian returned his cell phone to his pocket. *Jehovah does love his plagues,* Raguel had said. Perhaps the arch-angel had been onto something.

"What a blessing that would be," Damien said grimly, following Adrian around the corner of the casino parking lot in preparation for takeoff.

Adrian didn't voice the rest of his thoughts.

Or we are about to be tested in ways that may yet see the end of us all.

CHAPTER 15

Lindsay fingered the keypad on her cell phone and debated the wisdom of calling Adrian. She'd been strong the first few days and refrained from contacting him, but the night before had been hard. She had roused from sleep at three in the morning, her thoughts filled with memories from a dream so vivid she still recalled it eight hours later.

She'd been standing with Adrian in a lush valley. A massive river had flowed beside them, providing the water necessary to support the miles of grasses spreading outward from its banks. The sun was bright and fierce, the air humid and almost too hot. Adrian wore only coarse linen pants and leather sandals, his hair long enough to hang to the tops of his broad, powerful shoulders. His head was tilted back, his eyes closed, his sensual mouth thinned with frustration or displeasure. There was a blade in his hand—a thick, sturdy weapon that reminded her of a medieval sword or glaive, like King Arthur's Excalibur. He spun it deftly, absently, his skill apparent in his easy familiarity with its weight and length. He was both regal and fierce. Heartrendingly beautiful.

As the wind slid lovingly through his hair, he looked at her with such torment. She felt pierced by his gaze, as if he'd stabbed her with the weapon he wielded with such obvious agitation.

Ani ohev otach, tzel, he'd said to her dream self. *I love you, shadow. But I cannot have you. You know this. Why do you tempt me? Why do you flaunt what I crave, yet am forbidden to possess?*

Her sorrow over his pain had constricted her lungs and created an ache so overwhelming it roused her from a dead sleep. She'd bolted awake to find tears wetting her face and pillow, and the remnants of sympathy and grief twisting in her stomach. He'd been talking to her, as if she was the source of his agony, yet she couldn't imagine doing anything to elicit that devastated look on his face. She would die before she ever wounded him so deeply.

Spending the rest of the night alone in her suite at the Belladonna had felt nearly as desolate as when she'd talked to Adrian on the phone four days earlier. The urge to call him again was becoming too forceful to resist. She was worried about him and missed him more than she should.

She sucked in a sharp breath, fighting through a rush of greedy desire and feelings of possession she had no right to. She'd lived her entire life struggling to find a place for herself on the outside looking in at the "normal" people, but it had taken only a couple days to get irrevocably used to fitting in somewhere. Forging it alone after that acclimation was damn hard; wondering if Adrian might be feeling equally adrift was even harder.

Lindsay hit the DIAL button on her phone and lifted it to her ear.

He picked up almost instantly. "Lindsay—is everything all right?"

The knot in her stomach loosened at the sound of his warm, confident voice. "I called to ask you the same question."

"Ask me . . . ?" His voice faded. "I—"

"Adrian? Are you okay?"

"I'm sorry. I'm still getting used to being asked that question. It's been a rough couple of days, but it'll soon be over."

Her heart faltered a beat. He was so collected and smooth, so pulled together and in command of himself and others; she could see how easy it would be to assume he was always all right. Whom did he lean on when his burdens wearied him? With Phineas gone, did he have anyone?

He'd given her an outlet for her private self. If she could return the favor, if he trusted her enough to do so, she'd consider it an honor. "You don't sound happy about that."

"Someone I care about is hurting, and I will have to inflict more pain on her before all is said and done."

Jealousy dug its claws into her, a response so alien and unwelcome it unsettled her deeply. "I'm sorry. I wish there was something I could do."

"Just hearing your voice and knowing that you're thinking of me is enough."

Lindsay felt a fierce rush of pride that she might continue to be a source of comfort for him, despite everything that stood between them. "I dreamt about you last night."

"Did you?" His voice took on a seductive smoothness. "Will you tell me about it?"

"You asked me to leave you alone. To stop tempting you." Sighing heavily, she slumped over the table. "And some horrible part of me didn't care that I was hurting you by making you want me. I was almost giddy over your anguish. It made me feel powerful to have such a hold on you. I wanted you—whatever the cost."

He exhaled slowly. "The dream disturbed you."

"Damn straight it did! I hate that I would think that way for even a moment. I *don't* feel that way. I won't."

"Lindsay." He paused. "I know you don't. It was just a dream."

"Which means that somewhere in my subconscious that thought exists." She shoved a hand through her curls. "I don't want to be that person, Adrian. I don't want to hurt you, but look at me. I can't even go a few days without calling you, even though I know we need to keep a professional distance between us."

"You are not that person." The gruff note of vehemence in his tone took her aback. "Just as I'm not the Adrian you dreamt of. If anything, the roles in your dream were reversed. You're asking me to let you walk away, and I won't. I know you want me, and I'll exploit your desire to the fullest—I want you that badly. With every day that passes, with every conversation we have, I want you more. It burns in me, Lindsay. I ache for you."

"Adrian—" Her eyes closed on a sigh. "I'm so sorry we met."

"No, you're not. You're only sorry that there are risks involved."

"I should run while I can." She'd moved so far away from her dad for the same reason, because she knew it was too dangerous for him to be around her. She would never forgive herself if something happened to him because of her hunting, just as she'd never forgive herself if Adrian paid a price for being with her.

"I'd find you," he said darkly. "Wherever you'd go, however you'd hide . . . I would find you."

A knock came to the adjoining door, yanking her rudely back into the here and now. "I should let you go."

"I'll see you soon, *neshama*. Stay out of trouble until then."

"No worries there. You're all the trouble I can handle right now."

She hung up, then called out, "Come in, El."

Elijah entered. His hair was still damp from a shower and slicked back from his forehead. He was dressed in his usual loose jeans and T-shirt, and his gaze raked the room as it always did whenever he entered one. The man was a warrior through and through.

"Are you hungry?" she asked, even though she knew the answer already. The guy ate like a . . . wolf.

"Starved."

"Can we please not have room service again? I need to get out of this hotel. It can't be *that* dangerous to hit up the Denny's around the corner, can it?"

"*Hmm . . .*" He glanced out the window at the cloudless, sunny day. "All right. Bring your bag of tricks."

Lindsay stood. "I know it sucks for you to be stuck with me, but I'm glad you're here."

She adored Elijah, despite the fact that he was a constant reminder of Adrian and the life she could have shared with the angel, if only they were friends and not crazy with desire for so much more. After losing her mother, she couldn't bear to lose anyone else she loved, and with her hunting, her life was too dangerous to pledge to someone else. It wouldn't be fair to anyone. But Adrian was special. He shared the life she did, and she resented that she couldn't even *try* to have a relationship with him. After all the times she'd wished for someone who could know and understand why she hunted, she'd finally found him—only to discover they could never be together. Even the wind seemed to mourn that injustice, howling softly every time she stepped outside.

"This is a good place for me to be," Elijah said, rolling his shoulders back as if the muscles were too tight.

"You're bored out of your mind."

"Yeah, but I need to keep a low profile now."

She winced. "Because of me? Because I took off?"

"No." He exhaled audibly. "I used to be a member of the Navajo Lake pack. Then I was sent to Adrian for observation. Right now, the less I'm observed, the more likely it'll be that they forget I was any trouble at all."

"I didn't peg you for the troublemaker type." He was too stoic, too honorable. He took his commitments seriously, as evidenced by the fact that he'd jumped on a plane to come after her in spite of being terrified of flying.

"I don't think I am."

"*Hmm* . . . Let's head someplace to eat, and you can tell me about it."

"I'm up for the food, not for the talking."

She shot him a wry look. "After nearly a week in my company, you still haven't figured me out yet?"

Elijah gave a long suffering sigh and gestured toward the door. "It was worth a shot."

*   *   *

Lindsay managed to let Elijah mow his way through two full stacks of pancakes and six over-easy eggs, before she pressed him for more information. "So why do people think you're a troublemaker?"

He dropped a pat of butter onto his hash browns. "I said I was being observed, not that I'm a troublemaker."

"Okay then." She pushed aside the remnants of her breakfast. "What are you being observed for?"

He shoveled a massive forkful of potatoes into his mouth. After he chewed and swallowed, he said, "There are some who think I show Alpha traits."

"Alpha. Like top dog? King of the hill? Master of all he surveys?" She nodded. "Totally."

He paused with another heaping forkful suspended halfway between his plate and his lips. "You're not helping."

"What?" She leaned back into the booth. "What's wrong with that? Better than being a Beta male for sure. I mean, they have their uses and all. But really, women are looking for sexy, hunky Alpha males. We like that take-charge, take-no-shit, bad-boy vibe. It really does a number on us, which I'm sure you've noticed in the course of your seventy-some-odd years of living."

Elijah exhaled in a way that conveyed endless patience. "Women aside," he said drily, "it's not good to show Alpha traits when you're a lycan."

"Why not?"

He stared at her for a long moment, as if debating what to say or whether he should say it at all. "The Sentinels are supposed to be the only Alphas. The lycans are supposed to look to them for guidance, not to each other."

The gravity in his voice sobered her. Lindsay waited until their waitress had topped off her coffee and moved on to another table, then asked, "What happens if it's decided that you're an Alpha lycan?"

"I'll be separated from the others and ... I don't know. Alphas don't come around very often, so I don't know what happens to them. I've heard rumors that they're kept together and used for non–field assignments, like interrogations, but frankly I don't see how that would work. You can't put a bunch of Alphas together and expect them to play nice. But maybe that's the point—make us kill each other, so the Sentinels don't get their hands dirty."

"I can't believe Adrian would condone that."

"After working with him, I'm not sure he's fully aware of how the lycan system is run." He grabbed the top half of an English muffin and eyed the amount of butter already on it. "He's out there in the trenches, more so than any other Sentinel I've seen. He's always on a hunt. He hadn't been home in almost two weeks when you saw us in Phoenix. We'd taken out a rogue minion just a few hours before we ran across you."

"He's been away from home for days now."

Elijah opened two jelly packets and scraped the contents onto his muffin. "Yeah. Hunting is what he lives for. It's his way."

She blew out her breath. It was her way, too. The only way she knew. "Okay, you'll think this is crazy, but ... what about going into business with me? Bounty hunting maybe? Private investigations? You'd still be hunting. Plus, I've got a score to settle that I could really use your help with. We both know I need someone to be the level-headed voice of reason."

He paused in the act of chewing, staring at her, then washed down his food with half a glass of orange juice. "You think I can just quit?"

"Hey, I'd have to quit my job, too."

"The only way out of working for the Sentinels is death."

Lindsay's pulse stuttered. "What are you saying? You're prisoners? Slaves?"

He resumed eating. After he swallowed, he said, "I think I'm gonna bring another lycan on board."

"Okay, ignore the big question. I'll worm it out of you eventually. As for another lycan, do whatever you think is best. I trust you. I don't suppose it's a woman . . . ? I'd feel a lot better about you having to babysit me if you had some fun doing it."

His green eyes sparkled with laughter.

Realizing how that sounded, she groaned. "That came out wrong."

"No, it's not a woman. Just someone who could use a little time away, too."

"Is he an Alpha?"

Elijah shook his head. "He's not. Thank god."

More than anything he'd said, it was the relief in his voice that gave Lindsay chills.

Adrian exited Yellowstone into Gardiner, Montana, just after dusk. He'd located Helena and Mark early in the morning, then held Damien and Jason back until nightfall, giving the two lovers one last day together.

It was a concession the Sentinels obeyed without question but couldn't understand. Love in the mortal sense was unknown to them. They didn't grasp the desperate desire, the aching longing, or the purity of joy a mortal felt in finding the other half of his or her soul.

Adrian knew those extremes far too well, but this time with Lindsay was novel in many ways. He couldn't stop thinking about her, couldn't stop comparing her incarnation to the ones that had come before. He was used to starting from scratch, but there were always certain constants he'd come to expect. Lindsay deviated from the pattern to such a degree that he could find few markers with which to map their interactions. It was all new and uncharted. And he was captivated by the mercurial emotions she roused in him.

"What are you going to do, Captain?" Damien asked as they entered the small town on foot.

"Arrangements have been made for the lycan to join the Hokkaidō pack."

"I still think you should put him down," Jason said. "If ever there was a time to make an example out of a lycan, this is it. When this gets out—"

Adrian cut him off with a look. "It's not going to get out."

He'd tracked Helena's other lycan guard first, catching up to her halfway to Cedar City en route to the Navajo Lake pack. Her destination showed the strength of her self-preservation instincts. Given the opportunity to flee while the Sentinels were distracted by Helena's desertion, she chose to head to the nearest pack instead. Without hesitation, she had agreed to never speak of Mark and Helena again for the rest of her life. For her loyalty and common sense, Adrian had offered her reassignment to his pack, a promotion she'd readily accepted. He had learned long ago that positive reinforcement was a far better motivator than fear and intimidation.

"Once Mark is in Japan and Helena is Anaheim," he continued quietly, "we're all going to forget the last four days. None of us wants to deal with what will happen otherwise."

A Sentinel and lycan affair. The two running away together. The consequences of that choice. All of it would be a ticking time bomb, giving ammunition to the malcontents. With the recent spate of vampire attacks and the infection he'd witnessed in Arizona and Utah, he couldn't risk unrest among the Sentinel ranks now. The balance he'd preserved for so long was crumbling around him. If he lost control of the Sentinels, nothing would save the world from the chaos that would ensue.

Because of the pressing need for secrecy, he'd conducted the entire hunt thus far without any technological help, unable to risk leaving a trail by using Mitchell Aeronautics resources. Being able to track Helena's rental car via GPS would have shortened the hunt, but he hadn't been in a hurry. Affording her a few days of whatever happiness she could find while on the run was such a small concession, and it was the only one he could make. The longer she was AWOL, the more volatile the situation became.

"You and Helena can't be the only ones to form attachments," Jason said.

"No." Everything seemed to be coming to a head at once. Or maybe it felt that way because he was still reeling from Lindsay's decision to leave him. She was being selfless for him. He had to try to be the same for her, which might mean letting her go.

"You can't be surprised," Jason went on. "We've been on this mission forever."

"I'm only surprised it took this long." Adrian looked

at Damien, who lifted both shoulders in an offhand shrug that neither confirmed nor denied whether his opinion aligned. "But what are the alternatives? Dereliction of duty? The forfeiture of our wings? Preying on the mortals we were created to protect? Who the fuck wants to live that life?"

Damien exhaled harshly. "You'd have to ask the Fallen about that."

They walked through Gardiner, then beyond to the rental cabins where Helena was holed up. Adrian had shadowed her and her lycan by air during the night, following them along the winding back roads and small towns they'd traveled through until they'd stopped near dawn.

Reaching into his pocket, he wrapped his hand around his cell phone. He wished he could talk with Lindsay now. Her mortal heart might not understand why he would part two lovers, but that heart would know it killed him to do so. She wouldn't see his sympathy and compassion as weaknesses. Even if she argued against the actions he was forced to take, it would soothe him just to hear her voice and unvarnished reasoning, strengthening him for the pain he was about to inflict on a friend he loved.

When his phone vibrated with an incoming call, his grip tightened on it in surprise. He slowed his stride, wondering if Lindsay had actually felt compelled to call him by the force of his desire for her to do so.

The caller ID told him it was the Point. He answered.

"We might have a problem," Oliver said without preamble.

Adrian stopped. Oliver never labeled anything a problem unless it was very much a problem. "What is it?"

"I just talked to Aaron. He went to Louisiana on the hunt for a rogue we've been tracking. They were ambushed by Vash and two of her captains. Aaron was wounded enough to put him out of commission for a while. He has no idea what happened to his lycans while he was regenerating. He's been searching for them for three days."

Looking at Jason and Damien, who could easily hear what was being discussed, Adrian saw the despair he felt reflected on their faces. Too much. Too fast. Like dominoes, everything was toppling in rapid, unstoppable succession.

"You sent a team to retrieve him?" Adrian asked.

"Yes. But after Phineas and the attack on you, I thought you should know it was the lycans Vash was after."

"Is it possible they're the ones responsible for Charron's death?"

"I thought of that. Too young, the both of them."

"Keep me posted." Ending the call, Adrian started forward again, spurred by the driving need to get back home, where he could regroup and take the offensive. He could only hope that compiling all the information he'd obtained over the last week would lead to an understanding of what the fuck was going on and why everything had gone to shit in a matter of days. "Let's get this done," he said to Jason and Damien.

As they neared the cabin, he freed his wings. The metallic odor that teased his nostrils was instantly recognizable. No light shined from the unit, intensifying Adrian's foreboding. He raced the final distance to the door, disengaging the lock with a thought before he reached for the knob. The stench of congealing blood hit him with enough force to rock him backward a step. He willed the lights on, even though he didn't require illumination to see.

With a curse, he averted his gaze from the carnage that was more horrifying under the harsh glare of flickering fluorescent lighting.

Jason stepped into the cabin and froze. "Fuck me," he gasped, before pivoting and stumbling out the door.

Damien entered next. His sharp inhale betrayed his shock and dismay, but he remained at Adrian's side, his gaze darting around the room as he took in the entirety of the grisly tableau before them.

Knowing he needed to provide strength to the two Sentinels, Adrian scrubbed both hands over his face and rolled his shoulders back. He turned his head forward again, breathing through his mouth. The sight of a wing lying on the floor blurred, then cleared as tears coursed down his face. The other wings were scattered about the room as if they'd been tossed away like so much trash. One hung off the end of the bed, the soft pink and gray feathers now stained with blood. They'd been clawed from Helena's back, leaving two rows of three stumps protruding from her graceful spine.

The fallen Sentinel lay prone on the bed, her sightless eyes trained at the door, her golden hair plastered to her cheeks and back with dried sweat and blood. Her lycan lay sprawled on the floor at the foot of the bed. Two unsealed punctures in his neck explained the sickeningly white pallor of his skin. Adrian doubted there was a drop of blood left in Mark's body.

"This is hell," he said gruffly, shaken to his soul by the waste—the *wrongness*—of it all.

Damien looked at him. "Why didn't it work?"

"Why would it have? She wasn't punished. Her wings were taken by her lycan lover, not a Sentinel. He was bitten by a—" Adrian walked over to Helena's body and peeled back her upper lip. He stared for a long moment. "Her canines aren't elongated."

"Maybe they retracted when she didn't fall completely."

Adrian's gaze lifted skyward, corrosive grief burning through his veins. His fingers sifted through the once glorious strands of Helena's hair. She'd been more than a friend. She had been proof that failure was not inevitable, that it was possible, if they were strong enough, to serve their mission without forfeiting their faith in the process. Now that hope was lost, withering in an agonizing death along with a seraph whose heart had been so pure that only love could destroy it.

For the first time, he thought perhaps the Sentinels hadn't been tested so much as served as test subjects to answer the question: Was the Watchers' fall unavoidable?

"You're right, Captain," Jason said, remaining on the porch. "This can never get out."

Damien ran a shaking hand through his dark hair. "We need to clean this place."

His hands fisting at his sides, Adrian continued to survey the damage. More than two lives had been lost here. A seraph had willingly mutilated herself in an attempt to fall. Then she'd tried to turn her lycan. If they'd succeeded, they would both be vampires now—a new class of vampire. And they would have opened the door to others to try the same. The mere knowledge of what they'd done held immeasurable power.

"Something went wrong here," Adrian thought aloud.

"Maybe ingesting lycan blood affected her fall. Maybe he could have Changed if she'd fed him her blood sooner. Maybe there was no way for them to succeed. We can't know unless it's tried again. Perhaps again and again. Whatever possibilities this desperate act might inspire in others must die here, with them."

Although he spoke as if it could be contained, Adrian knew the idea would merely lie dormant for a time, waiting for another fertile mind to conceive of it.

He knew, because the idea had once been his, long ago.

And not so long ago.

CHAPTER 16

"She's here in Anaheim." Torque shielded his eyes against the headlights of a car pulling into the parking spot in front of his ground-floor motel room. "But Adrian's been gone almost a month, barring a one-night visit over a week ago when he was seen out with her."

"It can't be Shadoe then," Syre said with a sigh of regret.

"I can't say that for certain. She has a lycan guard. If she leaves the hotel for any reason—which is rare—he's with her. It's possible that Adrian just doesn't want to put her at risk while he's hunting."

"Leaving her with one guard? Away from the Point?"

"She's working for Raguel and living on his property. She doesn't need a lot of protection when she's under the wing of an archangel."

Syre exhaled harshly.

Torque frowned at the sound, hearing a wealth of disquiet and frustration in it. Not what he would have expected from his father while discussing Shadoe's possible reincarnation. "What's wrong? What aren't you telling me?"

"You remember what Adrian said about Nikki? About her appearance and behavior?"

"Like I'd forget fucking lies like that."

"Torque . . ." Another weighted pause. "I've received two reports of similar sightings. These came from within our own ranks."

"Sightings of what?"

"Disease. Infection. You haven't heard anything?"

"No. But the cabal here is successful because of its discretion. They keep to themselves and stay focused on watching Angels' Point." Torque's spymaster cabals, known as the kage, were comprised of his most trusted minions, those who took orders without question and deeply respected that he was the son of Syre. "What kind of infection are we talking about?"

"Unreasoned aggression, mindless thirst. Adrian's description of foaming at the mouth and bloodshot eyes has been corroborated."

Torque sank onto the edge of the bed, his heartbeat quickening. "Nikki was only gone two days . . ."

His father's worn, comfortable desk chair creaked over the cell phone receiver. "If it's not possible for you to definitively establish the woman's identity by the end of the week, I want you to come home. Depending on how widespread this sickness is, we could be looking at an imminent war with the Sentinels. We need to be prepared."

A young family of tourists walked by Torque's window, laughing and chattering with little regard for the lateness of the hour. He turned his head away from the simple happiness he would never know and looked at the clock on the nightstand. "I think it's even more important that I find out who this woman is. Think about it, Dad. What if Adrian's behind everything that's happening? What if he's deliberately staging these attacks to give him the excuse to come after you? It would make sense if the blonde is Shadoe."

"A blonde?"

The pain in his father's voice iced Torque's blood. If the woman was his sister, they were as far from looking like twins as could be. "Yeah. And I'm dying my hair now to get the blond out. How ironic is that? I've got a job interview with her tomorrow and we'll see what happens. That's why I asked you to overnight the Fallen blood to me. I have to head out in daylight."

"Did it arrive?"

"Yes. I've got it."

"Vashti should be there shortly, if you need more. I'll be waiting to hear reports from both of you."

Torque was tired of waiting. "I'll be in touch as soon as I can. In the meantime, think about the possibility of Adrian orchestrating these attacks and the illness."

"He wouldn't go to the extent of killing Phineas. They were as close as brothers."

"Anyone will sacrifice a lot, Dad, if they're desperate enough. It can't be a coincidence that Vash is tracking Nikki's abductor right back to the Point. While you're investigating the reports of sick minions, see if you don't also hear reports of vamp abductions." Torque scrubbed a hand over his face, feeling weary and irritated by the chemical stench of hair dye. "I think what you're hearing are carefully planted rumors, but if there's any truth to them and Adrian is involved, he has to be abducting vamps to infect. And if so, someone out there is missing those who've been abducted. Like I'm missing Nikki."

Missing her so badly it was eating him alive. Inside, it felt like he was screaming at the world through sound-proof glass.

"I'll look into it, son. As always, I'm grateful for your counsel."

"Yeah, well, I wish we had better things to talk about."

Lindsay glanced at the clock. She had fifteen minutes until her next interview. Although she knew she shouldn't, she wanted to call Adrian. The phone call she'd just ended—the one to the bladesmith who fashioned her custom throwing knives—made her want to hear Adrian's voice. She spent a moment spinning her phone around and around on her desk; then it rang. When she saw Adrian's name on the caller ID, she snatched it lightning quick.

"Hey," she answered, too fast. "I must have thought you up."

"Lindsay." He exhaled harshly. "I needed to hear your voice."

Her smile faded instantly. "What's wrong?"

"Everything. I . . . I lost a Sentinel last night."

"Adrian." She sagged back into her desk chair, knowing how seriously he took his commitment to his mission and his Sentinels. "I'm so sorry. Do you want to talk about it?"

"She did it to herself. I put her in a position where she felt like taking a fatal risk was her only option to being happy, and she paid with her life."

"She had a choice," Lindsay argued. "It's not your **fault she picked the option she did.**"

He breathed softly into the phone. "Do you believe in leading by example?"

"Yes."

"Then I have some culpability. And truthfully, I envy her strength of will. I've faced the choice she did. I didn't—I *don't*—have the courage to do what she did."

The steadiness of his voice was more alarming than if he'd been noticeably upset. "She's dead. That's not courage; that's nuts. You need to come home. You've been away too long, and you're tired. You need a break."

"I need you."

Her free hand curled around the arm of her chair. She couldn't help wanting to be the friend he needed. Just as she couldn't stop wanting to talk to him about her new job, her weapons, her day—anything and everything. Because he *got* her. And she was pretty sure he felt that way about her in return. "You know where I am."

He said good-bye and she hung up, her heart heavy with worry.

The dreams she had about him each night kept her connected to him. She felt almost as if she was seeing him every day, as if they hadn't been apart since she'd left Vegas.

The night before she'd dreamt of them making love in a horse-drawn carriage. They'd been in costume. Something historical, like she'd seen in movie adaptations of Jane Austen stories. She'd climbed onto his lap, pulling up yards of skirts and underskirts while he unbuttoned a pair of breeches. As she'd enveloped his rigid length within her, he cupped her face in his hands and kissed her, disheveling her upswept hairdo and freeing strands of long dark hair. Gripping her hips, he'd thrust upward with barely restrained ferocity, driving her toward orgasm with single-minded determination. His eyes had glowed with that preternatural blue flame as he grated, *"Ani ohev otach, tzel."*

I love you, shadow.

Lindsay was frightened by her understanding of a language she shouldn't know. She was confused by both the vast differences in each dream—exotic locations and an endless spectrum of clothing from all time periods—and the repetitious similarities. Adrian was always with her. He was always in love with her, and she was always insatiable. Their time together was always marred by a pervasive sense of desperation and her greedy determination to conquer him no matter the cost. She was always a woman who loved Adrian with a dangerous disregard for the consequences, yet she was never the same woman. Her appearance, her culture, her language and background—it was all mutable.

Lindsay straightened, taking a deep breath to clear her mind. She was growing more scattered as the days passed. More restless and unable to concentrate. She needed to resume hunting. Until she made peace with her past, there would be no peace for her in the present.

The phone on her desk beeped a notice that her next interviewee had arrived. A moment later, a handsome young Asian man appeared on the other side of her clear glass office door.

She gestured him in with a smile.

He entered with a quick and confident stride. "Good morning."

"Hi." Lindsay stood, shooting a quick glance at his application to read his name. *Kent Magnus.* She liked the sound of it. As they shook hands, she felt herself responding to him immediately and surprisingly—he wasn't human, but he wasn't making her hair stand on end either. He was dressed in a loose pair of khaki Dickies pants and a short-sleeved black dress shirt. His smile was wide and charming, and when they shook hands, his grip was dry and strong.

Good or bad, she couldn't tell, because she was hit with the overpowering feeling that she'd met and talked to Kent before. "Have a seat, Mr. Magus. Please."

He waited for her to sit before he did. "The Belladonna is impressive."

"Isn't it?" A fact that made Lindsay's discontent only more annoying. Her job was a fabulous, once-in-a-lifetime opportunity, and she wasn't appreciating it the way she should be. "You're applying for the night auditor position."

"Yes, that's right."

"I have to say, you're overqualified."

"I'm hoping the position has room for advancement . . . ?"

Lindsay gripped her armrests. The especially strong sense of déjà vu his presence evoked made the room tilt. The previous address he'd listed on his application was Virginia, a state she'd driven through many times. It was possible she'd crossed paths with him at a gas station or diner at some point. She blinked through the black spots dancing before her eyes, then made a concerted effort to get her brain firing on all cylinders.

Kent wore his hair cut short. Like hers, it was the same length all around. He also had a great build, with broad shoulders and thick biceps, but he wasn't as big as a lycan. She made a mental note to have Elijah classify him for her.

"There's definitely room for advancement," she assured him. "I noticed you're new to the area. I confess I'm worried about whether you'll decide to stay or not. The West Coast is very different from the East Coast."

"Have you traveled to the East Coast often?"

"I just moved from North Carolina." Unable to shake off her wooziness, she stood. "Would you care for some water?"

He stood when she did, displaying the etiquette she expected in men but had found sadly lacking in most of the applicants she'd seen over the last two days. "No, thank you. So you and I were practically neighbors."

Pulling a bottle of water out of the minifridge in the bookcase behind her desk, Lindsay was relieved to feel less disoriented after standing. She took a long drink and noted his wedding band. An inhuman who was married. That threw her for a loop. "The hours are from eleven p.m. until seven a.m., and the days are Tuesday through Saturday. Will that be a problem?"

"Not at all. I'm a night owl."

"Your wife, too?" She didn't mean to pry, but she also didn't want to train a night auditor only to lose him a short time later.

All charm and humor left his face. His beautiful amber eyes revealed a deep sadness. "My wife recently passed away."

His application said he was twenty-six. Far too young to have suffered such a loss. Then again, maybe he was thousands of years old like Adrian. Or even several decades like Elijah. "I'm very sorry."

He gave a short nod. "I want a fresh start, in a new place, with a new job that keeps me busy at night. If you hire me, I promise you won't be sorry."

Lindsay sucked in a deep breath, feeling sympathy for Kent Magus, regardless of whatever kind of being he was. She knew how hard the nights were when dealing with the loss of a loved one. It was easy to stay busy during the day, but nighttime was when one closed ranks with family and settled into private routines—dinner, favorite television shows, before-bed rituals. His confidence and quiet dignity were two traits she very much admired, and his earnestness suggested that he gave a hundred percent to everything he set his mind to. She also acknowledged the possibility that she liked him *because* he was something "other" yet had loved and lost and grieved, just like she did. Just like Adrian did. Her angel had shown her that not every preternatural creature was bad.

"How soon can you start?" she asked.

Kent's smile returned. "Whenever you say. I'm ready when you are, Ms. Gibson."

"Call me Lindsay."

The minute Lindsay spotted Elijah waiting for her in the Belladonna's expansive lobby, she knew something was wrong. It was visible in the set of his shoulders and the grim line of his mouth. And he was pacing—prowling, actually, like an agitated panther. Scratch that—like a wolf.

Her heart sank into her stomach. "What's the matter? Is it Adrian?"

He shook his head, his hands going to his hips. A low growl rumbled up from his chest. "Remember that friend I told you about? The one I wanted to have reassigned to partner with me?"

"Yes."

"He went on a hunt in Louisiana right before we left for Utah. I just found out he was missing until this afternoon."

"Is he okay?" Lindsay crossed her arms tightly, knowing Adrian was taking hits left and right, and suffering for them.

"He's half dead, I'm told. And he's asking for me." His verdant gaze was sharp as he looked at her. "I need you to stay put. Don't leave the hotel until I get back or someone else comes to watch you."

"I want to go with you, El. I don't want you going alone, and I know you don't want to leave me here. If you do, you'll be worried about me and your friend at the same time."

"I didn't want to ask you," he said gruffly. "Micah's at Angels' Point."

Her breathing quickened as she remembered the morning Adrian had taken her flying over the hills around his home. Her body responded to the memories as if she was experiencing them all over again. The wind had been happy that day, whistling with a joy she so rarely felt in it. Or maybe the joy had been hers.

Abruptly, the fragrance of the massive floral arrangements decorating the lobby became cloying. The soaring ceiling seemed to close in on her. Everything about the hotel felt entrapping. She didn't fit in here. As much as she was trying and giving it her best shot, she was still—and would always be—a misfit in the "normal" world.

"It's okay," she assured him, as much for herself as for him. "If you need another reason to take me, I'll remind you that I need to get my suitcase anyway. It's a good time for me to get that done."

Elijah nodded. "Do you want to change or need to grab anything?"

"Yes to both."

Fifteen minutes later, they were climbing into her powder blue Prius hybrid, which had been delivered by the car transport service just the day before. Elijah sucked up all the space in the vehicle, even with the passenger seat shoved back as far as it could go. She felt bad about cramping him, but she liked her car. She'd told Adrian she had no aspirations of saving the world, but she did try to not pollute it or drain its natural resources.

They hit the road. Elijah was a great side-seat driver, telling her where to turn in time for her to maneuver across lanes.

"You're twitchy," he noted when she rubbed her damp palm against her jeans—again.

"I'm worried about all the bad stuff that's been happening since I met you and Adrian. It's a lot more than usual, isn't it?"

"We're always busy, but it's definitely getting more intense."

"God." She exhaled in a rush. "I'm sick over Adrian. He's lost too many of his friends lately and he's not getting a chance to grieve properly with everything falling apart at once."

"Mortals don't mate so quickly."

She shot him an arch glance. "Not sure where that came from, but I have to disagree. Haven't you ever heard of a one-night stand? Some mortals mate within minutes of meeting each other."

"Not mate as in fuck," he corrected drily. "Mate as in take a bullet."

"I'd take a bullet for you. And while you're very hot, I don't want to mate with you."

"You're nuts, you know that?"

She shrugged. "And you're my friend. So what does that make you?"

He stared at her profile for a long time, then finally turned his head to look out the passenger window.

As they climbed the hill toward Angels' Point, Lindsay's cell phone rang. She pulled it out of the cup holder where she'd dropped it and answered, fumbling to hit the SPEAKER button. "Dad. How the heck are ya?"

"Missing you. How are you?"

"I'm hanging in there. Hiring staff for the grand opening and trying to stay out of trouble."

"How's Adrian?"

Recalling the weariness she'd heard in Adrian's voice, she sighed and said, "He's having a rough time."

"But you're still sticking with him. That's hopeful. It must be serious between you two."

Glancing at Elijah, Lindsay spoke the truth because she knew both men had her best interests at heart. "Actually, I kinda put on the brakes."

"Why?" Unlike Adrian, Eddie Gibson revealed every emotion in his voice. The undertone of disappointment was unmistakable.

"We're ... incompatible."

"Did he say that?" Now he sounded pissed.

"No," she said hastily. "He wants to go for it. I just see the trouble ahead, and it's best to cool things off now, before we're invested."

"You're already invested, baby," he argued. "Or you wouldn't be worried about trouble ahead."

Her lips pursed. *"Hmm ..."*

"You've been keeping guys at arm's length your whole life. I was happy about that when you were younger, and later on I figured if your dates were worth anything, it wouldn't be so easy to cut them off. But shutting Adrian out isn't easy, is it?"

"Dad, can you please not psychoanalyze me? Or at least save it until you've tried dating again."

"That's why I called. I'm taking someone out to dinner tonight."

Lindsay's hands tightened on the steering wheel. For a moment, she couldn't decide what she was feeling. It wasn't all good. She was surprised and scared, dismayed and hurt, happy and excited.

"Lindsay?"

"Yeah, Dad." Her voice was too husky. She cleared her throat. "Who's the lucky lady?"

"A new customer who came in today. She asked me out after I changed her oil."

"I like her already. She's obviously smart and has great taste in men."

He laughed. "Are you sure you're okay with this?"

"Totally," she fibbed. "I'd be mad if you didn't go. You better have a good time, too. And wear the shirt and slacks I got you for your birthday."

"Okay, okay. Got it: Go. Have fun. And don't dress like a bum. But you have to do something for me, too— give Adrian a shot. A real one."

She groaned. "You don't understand."

"Listen," her dad said in his no-nonsense voice. "Adrian Mitchell is a big boy. He can take care of himself. If he doesn't see a problem, don't make one. You deserve to be happy, Linds, and no relationship is risk-free. I'm dipping my toes in the dating waters again. But you—you've never jumped in at all. I think it's time you took the plunge."

"I love you, Daddy, but the metaphors are killing me."

"Ha! I love you, too, baby. Be good."

"I'll want a rundown tomorrow," she warned.

"As if I kiss and tell. Talk to you later."

Hitting the END button, she looked at Elijah, who met her gaze. Her dad was finally putting himself out there. She thought she'd be happy about that. She was—mostly. But there was a part of her—an admittedly childish part of her—that felt as if her dad was leaving her mom behind. Which was something Lindsay still couldn't do.

"You're close to your sire," Elijah noted.

"We're all the other one has, if that makes sense."

Nodding, he said, "Explains why Adrian has lycans guarding him."

Her foot lifted from the gas pedal. "*What? Why?*"

"Adrian assigned lycans to watch your father. I didn't know why. Now I do. He's doing it for you, because your sire is important to you."

"When did he set that up?"

"In Vegas."

Lindsay pushed harder on the gas, thinking it would be better not to be behind the wheel at the moment. "Why would my dad need guards?"

"Anyone important to Adrian is at risk of being used against him."

Getting to her dad would get to her, which would get to Adrian. "If something ever happened—"

"Don't worry." Elijah offered a reassuring smile. "Adrian asked me to pick the team, and I suggested the best of the pack. They'll keep him safe."

She might have kissed him, if she hadn't been driving. "Thank you."

"You're welcome. You should thank Adrian, too."

"Yes," she said softly, her heart softening further. Adrian's fall wasn't the immediate concern; it was her own fall that was imminent. "I should. I will. Shit, everything's a mess."

"Yep."

Which reminded her why they were driving to the Point to begin with. "Do you know what happened to your friend? Why he was missing?"

"He was ambushed and left for dead. It took him a couple days to make it to the highway, where he was found."

"Jesus," she breathed. "Was it vamps?"

Elijah gave a curt nod and gestured for her to turn left up ahead.

"Fuckers. I want to kill them all." Even as Lindsay said the words, the depth of hatred in them surprised her. Her life had changed so much in the last couple of weeks. Vampires were now hurting her friends, and they were responsible for making it impossible for her to have Adrian. She couldn't think of one good reason for them to exist. They were like fleas or mosquitoes— disgusting, worthless, bloodsucking parasites that were better off extinct.

She pulled up to the wrought-iron gate and gatehouse that protected the Point. The guard took one look at Elijah and let them in. It was midafternoon. The sun was still high in the sky, affording her the opportunity to check out all she'd missed the first time she'd driven through the elegant gate. The wolves stayed on the other side of a rise in the road, keeping themselves hidden from public view. When she crested the top, she saw them dotting the native landscape. So many of them. So majestic and imminently dangerous.

Pulling around the circular driveway, she parked. She tried to expel some of her tension with a swift, audible exhalation.

Elijah was out of the car in a controlled yet powerful rush of movement, opening her door before she had released her seatbelt. He waited until she climbed out, then pointed to a large hangarlike building set atop a hill about a half mile away. "I'll be there. You can come up when you're done grabbing your things, or wait for me here. If I'll be more than an hour, I'll send word."

Lindsay caught his arm before he turned away.

He stared down at her hand, which she pulled back quickly. "Sorry. I didn't mean to put my scent on you. I just— I'm sorry about your friend, Elijah."

His gaze lifted to hers and his features softened. "I know you are. Thank you."

"If you need anything, I'm here for you." She offered a commiserating smile, then headed toward the double-door entrance. She'd just lifted her hand to knock when the door opened.

"Ms. Gibson."

A tall, sinewy redhead filled the doorway. His hair was long, hanging past his shoulders, but there was nothing effeminate about him. He brought to mind a Viking warrior of old, grim faced and resolute.

Lindsay hesitated. "Hi. I just need to grab my stuff; then I'll get out of your way."

He stared at her for a moment, assessing her in a way that suggested he found her lacking. Then he gestured her in.

She knew he was an angel. All the Sentinels had the same flame blue eyes, although only Adrian's ever gave off heat. The Sentinels were works of art, really. It was rather intimidating being surrounded by dozens of perfect, gorgeous beings.

Since the redhead declined to say anything further, Lindsay headed straight for the bedroom she'd used when she'd spent the night. Everything looked the way she had left it—the bed was made and her toiletries were neatly arranged on the bathroom counter. When she'd last walked out of the room, almost two weeks earlier, she had expected to be back that night. The loss of what she might have had if she could've joined Adrian's world tightened her throat and made it hard to swallow.

In hindsight, the plans she'd made to live in this sumptuous space, with its balcony that led to a deck where she could watch angels take flight with the sunrise, and its owner, who was the most magnificent creature on earth, seemed preposterous. But she had held the dream for a moment, and she missed it terribly.

Lindsay looked at the bed as she moved past it, remembering how she'd fantasized about seducing Adrian there. Her imagination in that regard had been especially vivid, yet nowhere near as raw and searing as the real deal had turned out to be.

"I've got to get out of here," she muttered, fighting the fierce desire to stay—forever. Fighting the aching longing to embrace the angel, his life, and the possible friends—like Elijah—who would understand what drove her.

Packing in record time, Lindsay grabbed the handle of her suitcase and wheeled it out of the house. She had to pass a large number of Sentinels who'd crawled out of the woodwork to get a look at her. She now understood why they eyed her the way they did. She was the interloping human who was fucking with their leader's head. Despite their palpable animosity, she paused on the threshold of the open front door and faced them.

"I'm rooting for you guys," she said. She wanted to ask them to take care of Adrian for her, but she didn't have the right to do so. He belonged to them, not her.

The front door shut behind her with a soft click of finality. She didn't cry; she refused. She would *not* feel sorry for herself for doing the right thing for Adrian. For the world, actually, which was dependent on him but didn't know it.

Popping open her trunk, she collapsed the telescoping handle of her suitcase and lifted the carry-on from the ground. The wind kicked up, swirling in a funnel that encompassed only her. She was held motionless in the churning embrace.

Stay, stay, stay, it crooned.

"I've caused enough trouble," she shot back.

Don't go, Lindsay. Lindsay . . . Lindsay . . . The wind ceased abruptly, leaving a vacuum in which her name cracked like a whip.

"Lindsay."

Her head turned. Adrian stood beside the open rear door of the Maybach, which sat idling at the start of the circular part of the driveway. The wind was all over him like a lover, riffling through his dark hair, which had grown at least a half inch since she'd last seen him. He looked rakish and beautiful in a black long-sleeved henley and dark blue tailored slacks. His face was serenely composed and his posture relaxed, but she sensed the raging turmoil in him. His gaze dropped to the suitcase in her hands and an icy surge of desolation washed over her, making her shiver. She'd never felt such hopeless despair, such heartrending guilt and pain. His and hers.

Tears stung her eyes. She could scarcely catch her breath.

God. Of all the things she had to give up, why did it have to be him? She'd give up food. Chocolate. Water. Air. If it meant she could have him without restriction for any amount of time.

He shattered his stillness by lunging toward her and breaking into a dead run.

The carry-on fell from her slackened grip and hit the gravel drive. *"Adrian."*

She'd barely taken a few steps when he snatched her up, tackling the breath from her lungs.

His wings burst free in an eruption of crimson-stained alabaster, and they surged into the air.

CHAPTER 17

Elijah entered the lycan barracks and was met with chilling silence weighted by the expectation of imminent death. The rows of neatly made bunk beds stretched on endlessly, the far side of the room extending away from him even as he traversed its length.

He followed the sound of a beeping heart monitor, but he knew where he was going without that guide. Micah had one of the private rooms at the end, those that were set aside for the mated pairs. The door was open and a handful of lycans, including Esther and Jonas, formed a gauntlet to the threshold.

They watched him with haunted and beseeching eyes. He looked away from their crushing expectations, hating their belief that he was some kind of messiah. Just because he held absolute control over his beast didn't mean he exerted a similar level of control over other lycans' fates and circumstances, but that's what so many hoped for and believed.

Entering the room, he found Micah in bed, stuck with

multiple intravenous lines and tended to by Rachel. She stood when Elijah approached and met him partway, looking as pale and thin as her mate.

Swallowing past the tightness in his throat, Elijah asked, "How is he?"

She ran a shaking hand through her dark hair and jerked her chin in a silent gesture for him to step outside. Back in the barracks' great room, she said, "He's dying, El. It's a miracle he's even alive now."

He scrubbed at his eyes with his fists, trying to rub out the sting of grief.

"He's been waiting for you," she went on. "Honestly, I think that's all he's been waiting for."

Elijah looked at her helplessly.

She swiped tears from her cheeks. "He really loves you."

Pushing past her in a desperate rush, he reentered the room and took the seat she'd vacated. He scooched it closer to the bed, then reached out and gripped his friend's cold hand.

Micah's eyes slitted open. Turning his head, he met Elijah's gaze. "Hey," he whispered. "You made it."

"That's my line."

A slow smile briefly transformed the lycan's features, but was quickly gone. "Had to tell you . . . Vash—"

"Vash did this to you?"

"She's looking . . . for you."

"Me? Why?"

"A vamp in Shreveport . . . missing. Your blood was there."

"I've never been to Shreveport."

A violent shiver racked Micah's emaciated frame. "Yeah, well . . . your blood was."

"Stop talking. Get some rest. We'll catch up later."

Micah's once clear green eyes were cloudy with pain and weariness. "No time. I'm going, Alpha. This is it."

"No."

"Watch your back. Blood . . . It's yours."

Elijah looked at Rachel hovering in the doorway. She nodded grimly. *His blood.* At an abduction scene in a town he'd never visited.

A high-pitched wheeze from the bed drew his attention back to Micah.

"I'll be all right," Elijah said gruffly. "Don't worry about me. Worry about getting better."

Micah's hand tightened on Elijah's with surprising force, his claws extending enough to break the skin of his own palm and Elijah's. Blood, hot and slippery, pooled between their joined grips. "Listen. You're the one. Hear me? It's you. Get Rachel out . . . Get them all out."

Elijah jerked backward. "Don't put that on me, Micah."

"She trusts you—" The redhead erupted into violent, hacking coughing that left flecks of blood on both his lips and the pristine whiteness of his sheets.

"Rachel will be fine. I promise you that."

"Not Rach—" He gasped. "Adrian's woman . . . trusts you. You can abduct her . . . Leverage."

Elijah pulled free of Micah's grip, furious and sick that his best friend would dump this shit on him now. On his fucking deathbed. "Don't do this," he hissed. "Don't ask me this. She risked her life for me."

Micah's head lifted from the pillow, his gaze an echo of its former fierceness. "Adrian will bend for her. Promise me. Step up. Make it happen. You can free them all. Only you."

Lurching to his feet, Elijah stumbled out of the room.

"Blood oath, El," Micah whispered, holding up his

bloodied hand. Then he deflated into the bed, his chest rattling with every labored breath.

Elijah cleared the threshold. He looked at the lycans waiting outside the room. There were more of them now. A dozen familiar faces, all looking at him with somber, unwavering expectancy.

"You all put him up to this," he accused. "You told him where I've been these last couple of weeks."

Esther stepped forward. "Elijah—"

"You selfish fucking bastards."

He looked at his hand and the already healing punctures marring it. With a roar, he shifted. Bursting free of his clothes, he vaulted forward in a powerful lunge that took him almost to the end of the building.

He rammed through the door to the outside and ran.

Lindsay was still gasping, trying to regain the breath Adrian had knocked from her, when he landed on the other side of the house. She heard the slide of a glass door at her back; then she was being carried through it and into a room containing a massive desk and a wall of overflowing bookshelves.

Leaning back in his embrace, she looked at his face. His features were stark, the skin stretched taut with fierce determination. Another door closed behind her, this one an interior door, and she was pushed up against it, pinned by Adrian's hot, hard body. The drapes began their automated glide shut along with the sliding glass door, plunging the room into silence and darkness.

"Adrian . . ."

His mouth sealed over hers. He caught her wrists in his hands and pulled them above her head, one after the other. His tongue thrust into her mouth, a swift plunge that turned her on instantly.

The warm, vibrant scent of his skin filled her nostrils, wilder today than she'd remembered. Sexier.

She struggled against his grip and found her wrists tied to a coat hook on the back of the door. As his hands slid down her arms, she tugged to no avail, then grasped frantically with her fingers. Feeling lace, she realized he'd done that undressing thing with his thoughts and secured her to the hook with her own panties. A tentative squirm confirmed she was now commando in her jeans. "Let me go."

"You're not leaving me." His voice was low and deceptively even, but the rigidness behind it was as tangible as the thong around her wrists.

Lindsay tugged again. The lace tore and immediately something stronger bound her to the door. When Adrian's hands pushed up beneath her T-shirt and cupped her bare breasts, she realized it was her bra. A shiver moved through her. The only time she'd ever been held against her will was the day her mother had been killed. "Cut me loose, Adrian."

His mouth latched on to the side of her neck. His fingers tugged her nipples into hard tight points. "No."

Without volition, she arched into his hands, her breasts growing heavy and tender. "You're upset. We should t-talk. We *need* to talk."

"Not now." He gripped her hips, making her aware that she was now completely nude. When a hair-dusted thigh pushed between her own, she realized he was naked, too.

Her breathing was loud in the otherwise quiet room. Her heart raced with a potent mixture of fear and forbidden desire. If it had been anyone else restraining her, she would've lost it. But it was Adrian, and the feel of his hands against her skin kept the terror she might have felt at bay.

"You should think about this." She panted, attempting to wriggle away from his inflaming touch. "You don't want this. You don't want what's going to happen to you if you do this."

His cock glided between the slick lips of her sex. Lindsay froze. He was hot and hard, delectably long and thick.

"Does this feel," he purred, "as if I don't want this?"

She bucked when his lips wrapped around her nipple. The coat hook creaked in protest but held fast. Adrian didn't have the hollow particleboard doors that would have given her a chance to escape. The solid wood his architect had used was more than strong enough to take her weight and abuse.

He drew on her breast with long, deep pulls of his wicked mouth. Her good intentions started to melt away.

"I'm afraid—" She spoke the lie, hoping it would deter him.

"I know. You're on fire with it." He parted the lips of her sex and stroked a fingertip through the silken liquid of her desire. "You're always so fearless, but you trust me enough to be afraid."

Her moan echoed through the room. She was achingly aware that the hallway must be on the other side of the door behind her, along with a dozen or more angels who disliked and distrusted her for this very reason— she reduced their leader to a mere man, with all the weaknesses and lusts and desire for comfort that came with that mortal state. "Stop this."

"I can't." He kissed her again. A hot, wet, lush kiss that spoke of a man who'd crossed his limits at some point in the days they'd been apart. "I won't."

"God, Adrian." She writhed in his grip as he captured her neglected nipple in his mouth, his tongue licking and worrying the rigid peak. "Why won't you let me save you?"

He released her with a soft pop, then straightened to rub his temple against hers. "There's nothing to save. It's all falling apart."

The painful emotion in his words broke her heart. She longed to pull him close and embrace him, to soothe his torment. But she couldn't move, had only her voice with which to comfort him. "Tell me what happened."

"Later." He slid down her body. His lips brushed between her cleavage; then his tongue darted into her navel. When he nuzzled between her legs, Lindsay bit her lower lip to keep from crying out. Beneath her distress at being immobilized in the dark and her worry over Adrian's volatile mood, she was ferociously aroused. In an untenable situation. She couldn't forget how exposed they were and how many people—*angels*—were nearby.

"Don't do this. You'll regret it."

"I regret *not* doing it." He held her open with his thumbs. The tip of his tongue fluttered maddeningly over her clitoris. As her sex clenched in greedy hunger, a rough noise escaped him. "I should have finished what we started in Vegas. I should have ignored the damn door and fucked you until you'd never even *think* about leaving me."

His serrated voice revealed his anguish and cut her deeply. She wanted to push her fingers into his hair and hold him close. She wanted to gentle him with soft strokes of her hands down his back. She wanted to give him the freedom to put down his burdens in total safety, away from the eyes of those who needed him to be strong all the time. But doing so would make him confront what ate at him, when what he wanted now was the oblivion he could find in her body.

Oblivion she couldn't offer him. Not at the price he would pay for it.

Adrian caught her right leg behind the knee. He lifted it over his shoulder, opening her to the sudden thrust of his tongue. Her back arched and her head hit the door, the thud reverberating through the room and surely out into the hallway as well. He either didn't hear or didn't care. His mouth was buried in the slick folds of her sex, his tongue shoved as deep into her as he could go. He worked her tender flesh with rapacious hunger, as if he could drink her in. Consume her. Brand her body with his scorching, intimate kiss. She trembled and gasped, her toes curling so tightly they began to cramp. She hung on to that twinge of pain, fighting the orgasm he was determined to force on her.

His abrupt, drawn-out groan brought tears to her eyes, the sound so lost and desolate.

"It's not t-too late," she managed through heaving breaths. Hot tears fell onto her breasts, her heart torn because she knew it *was* too late. They were both too far gone to turn back now. They'd passed the point of no return the moment she killed the dragon in front of him. She could have walked away from the kill just that once, but she hadn't. She'd bared her most personal secret within hours of meeting him, as if she'd needed him to see her for who she really was.

Still, she fought the inevitable because she cared

about him. Deeply. So deeply that the thought of him suffering for her made her insane. "You can stop this, Adrian. Before it goes too far."

He growled then, a deep rumbling sound of aggression and determination. He latched on to her clitoris and sucked in rapid, forceful rhythm. A steady, drawing tempo that kicked her into an explosive climax. Her perspiration-slick body was wrenched by brutal spasms of release, devastated by a scorching pleasure she couldn't defend herself against.

Turning his head, Adrian wiped his wet mouth on her inner thigh. Then he shrugged out from under her leg and stood.

"What do you consider too late and too far?" he asked with dangerous softness. "I've already been inside you. With my fingers. My tongue. My cock."

Her eyes squeezed shut and her head hung limply. She struggled to regulate her breathing, to regain some control over her own body. Even shrouded in darkness, Lindsay felt raw and exposed, seared by his blistering emotional turmoil. "T-technically, yes," she managed between deep gulps of air. "But you stopped. You restrained yourself once. You can do it again."

"Technically, you say." His hands cupped the cheeks of her ass and squeezed roughly. His teeth nipped at the upper swell of her breast, over her heart, hard enough to hurt. The tightly leashed control she associated with him was gone. He was ruthless, predatory, single-minded in his need to dominate her from the outside in. "Neither of us came, so it doesn't count?"

He hefted her up and yanked her legs around his hips. A heartbeat later he was penetrating her with his **brutally hard erection. She shuddered and strained to** accommodate him, but he took a swift step forward and drove himself in to the root.

Pinned to the door, she whimpered in exquisite agony. Although primed by a half dozen nights of tender, erotic dreams, she still needed time to adjust to his size.

"Please," she whispered, although she didn't know what she was asking for. To stop? To start? To never give up, even though she begged him to? She couldn't say yes—not when she knew what he was risking. But she couldn't stem the selfish longing that wanted him to refuse to accept no for an answer. There was nowhere else she'd rather be than right where she was, but her refusal wasn't about her. It was about him and what was best for him.

She heard the rustle of Adrian's wings, felt the soft breeze they created as they unfurled and moved. That telltale kiss of air betrayed the emotions he fought to hide.

"No," she moaned, a final, futile effort to save him.

One of his hands went to her hair, lifting her head so he could take her mouth. His lips slanted across hers, his lungs inhaling her every gasping exhalation. He rolled his hips and screwed deep into her, grinding with just enough pressure to stimulate her swollen, sensitized clitoris. Lindsay's body tensed in heated expectation, her greedy sex rippling along the length of his throbbing penis.

His breath caught. His irises flared bright enough to delineate the sclera of his eyes and the thickness of his lashes in the darkness. He exhaled into her lungs. "No more technicalities."

Adrian came so hard she felt it like a deep, hard thrust inside her. The violent jerking of his spending cock . . . the wash of molten liquid that caused sweat to slide between her breasts . . .

Her orgasm took her by surprise.

She shook with the unexpected surge of pleasure, her blood roaring through her ears so that she barely heard him moan her name.

The need to sob and cry out welled inside her. Lindsay caught his neck in her teeth, biting down to stem the sounds she wanted no one else to hear.

"Yes," he hissed, thrusting mindlessly. "Fuck yes."

Her wrists were freed. Her arms fell to his shoulders, her muscles twitching and tingling from the strain of pulling for freedom.

He pivoted away from the door, carrying her unerringly in the dark—still joined, still coming. He sat, and Lindsay felt cushions beneath her knees. A love seat, maybe. Or an armless chair. Her jaw unclenched, releasing his throat, and her head lifted. Behind her, a soft glow built like a light on a dimmer switch—a barrister's desk lamp illuminating gradually until she could see everything in the room.

She looked upon his face, her heart thudding with joy at the sight of him. He was flushed, his eyes feverishly bright, his lips swollen from the ferocity of his kisses. But what ruined her was the moisture glistening on his lashes.

Tears. From her indomitable, implacable angel.

"It's already too late," he said hoarsely, wiping her own tears from her cheeks with soothing strokes of his thumbs. "Do you understand?"

She nodded.

He kissed the marks on her wrists left by the bonds he'd restrained her with. "I know you wanted to protect me from this. I tried to let you, but I can't."

"I'm sorry. I'm so damn sorry I—"

"Don't." His head fell back. Upholstered in black suede, the love seat they occupied framed Adrian's dark splendor and offset his rich olive-toned skin. "Don't apologize for caring enough to be strong when I'm weak. Don't be sorry for being the one thing that makes me happy."

"For how long?" she challenged.

"As long as we can beg, borrow, and steal. Don't deny me. I need you. I need *this*—your touch, your pleasure, your love. I can't think without you, can't feel anything. And I need to do both of those things to get through the shit I'm wading through right now. If you want to save me, you have to be with me."

"What about the other Sentinels?"

"What about them? There's not a one of them out there who doesn't know I just nailed you to my office door."

"Oh god . . ." Embarrassment flushed her skin.

"I *wanted* them to hear," he said vehemently. "I could have taken you miles away, but you and me . . . it needs to be out in the open. I'm not ashamed of how I feel about you. I'm not ashamed that I can't stop wanting you. It is what it is."

"They already hated me." She dreaded leaving the room and facing all those accusing cerulean eyes. "Now—"

"They heard you say no. They can't hold this against you."

Lindsay cupped his face in her hands. "I'm not worth all this. I'm not. I'm just a crazy mortal who has no self-preservation instincts."

"And I'm an angel who'd die for you. See? We're a perfect match."

Her heart fell into her stomach. *"Adrian."*

He caught her wrists, his face revealing so much emotion she wept at the beauty of it. "Stay with me, Lindsay. Be with me."

"How can I say yes, knowing what it'll do to you?"

"Just say it."

They were too stubborn, both of them. She'd gotten what she wished for. And again, she regretted it. She couldn't say yes, and he wouldn't hear no. "I don't belong anywhere else, you know. I've never fit in with 'normal' people. I don't fit in with your people. But I fit with *you*. I know it. I feel it. None of that matters, though, because it's forbidden. I'll be damned if I'm the reason you fall and lose your wings. I'd rather die than see you turned into a soulless, bloodsucking vampire."

He nuzzled his nose against hers. "*Ani ohev otach*, Lindsay."

Oh god . . . Now that she knew what that meant . . .

"Make love to me," he whispered, pulling her mouth down to his and teasing the seam of her lips with the tip of his tongue. "Show me you want this as much as I do."

Her hands gripped the back of the love seat.

"Take me, *neshama sheli*," he coaxed, flexing his still hard cock inside her. Sprawled beneath her in all his gorgeous magnificence and purring an erotic invitation, he looked every inch the sinful, decadent, unabashedly wicked fallen angel. "I'm yours."

Lindsay shook her head. "No."

Adrian's features lit with a glorious smile. He twisted swiftly and she found herself beneath him, filled with him.

"I know what it means when you say that," he murmured, hooking his arm beneath her leg and drawing it up, opening her so completely he hit the end of her.

Panting in exquisite torture, she managed, "It means run. Save yourself."

"All of which says, 'I'm falling for you, Adrian.'"

His tongue traced leisurely along his lower lip before he caught the firm curve in his teeth. He watched her with heavy-lidded eyes, gauging her reaction as he gave a practiced roll of his hips. The thick crown of his penis rubbed against all the deliciously tender erogenous zones inside her—a deliberate sensual assault.

She whimpered as he withdrew slowly, then thrust home deeply. Smooth and easy. He'd taken the edge off and was now settling in for what she knew would be a long, unhurried ride. Her fingernails dug into his tapered hips. "Adrian."

He bent his head and groaned into her mouth. "I'm falling for you, too, Lindsay."

Chapter 18

"It has to be her."

Syre pushed aside the slender female arms crossing his chest and slid from his bed. He exhaled harshly, fighting the growing hope that so often led to disappointment. "You're certain?"

"I wasn't at first," Torque said. "Even after meeting with her, I couldn't say absolutely. She's different this time."

"In what way?"

"In a lot of ways. For one, I'm pretty sure I got to her. There were a couple times when she looked at me funny, like she might know me but couldn't quite place me."

"That's not proof."

"No, but two hours after I met with her, she headed up to Angels' Point. Adrian returned shortly afterward."

Restless with excitement, Syre paced the length of his bedroom. "How will you get to her?"

"She has to come down into the city to go to work." There was a smile in his son's voice. "And she hired me, so I have an excuse to be in the hotel most nights of the week. It won't be long before the perfect opportunity presents itself."

"Sounds too good to be true."

"It's the best opportunity we've ever had."

Syre rubbed at the ache in his chest. "I should come to you."

"No." Torque's voice was sharp, his tone implacable. "Vash is here now, with Raze and Salem. I've got all the backup I need. Your coming here will only give Adrian the opportunity to take you out. You need to stay in Raceport and out of sight as much as possible for the time being."

"I won't hide."

"But you love Shadoe, and you want to see her again. I can't imagine it'll be more than a couple weeks before that happens."

Syre looked out the window at the moon, a sight he'd seen too many times to count. Too many times without Shadoe. Grieving parents didn't get opportunities to be reunited with the children that were lost to them, but his curse was also his blessing. He'd fallen from grace for siring Torque and Shadoe. Nephalim, they were called. Angel halflings. Yet it was that specialized hybridization that had spared her soul when he'd begun the Change to save her life. All of the nephalim vampires were unique in that way. Their souls survived the Change because they were as strong as an angel's, without the vulnerability of wings.

"Take as long as you need, son," he said quietly, stepping farther away from the bed as one of the two women occupying it rolled to the side with a disgruntled sigh. "It does me no good to lose one child while trying to recover the other. I need both of you."

"Dad." Torque laughed softly. "I didn't reach this age by making stupid mistakes. Don't worry. Just make arrangements for Shadoe's return. Before you know it, we'll all be together again."

"Micah says Vash had a rag or cloth . . . some bit of material with my blood on it."

From Adrian's elevated position on the stairs leading down into the sunken living room, he studied Elijah, who looked unusually agitated. "And she claims it came from the scene of an abduction in Shreveport?"

The lycan nodded. His arms were crossed and his stance was wide, as if anchoring himself for an expected blow. "The airport there. But I was with you in Phoenix then. The vamp was snatched a couple days before the chopper crash."

"How is that possible?" Jason asked from his position by the fireplace. "How would your blood end up states away from where you were?"

"Hell if I know," the lycan said. "In order to have been that readily identifiable, it couldn't have been more than a month old. Prior to hitting the nest in Utah, I haven't lost enough blood on any hunt in the last thirty days to leave some behind for someone to jack."

"Excuse me . . ." Lindsay began, drawing Adrian's attention. She sat on one of the sofas, looking petite and fragile in the massive room.

She'd been silent since she emerged from his bedroom, fresh from a shower and smelling like his soap and shampoo. Neither did anything to disguise the scent of sex with him, which was skin deep. Still, she'd been so embarrassed by the thought of everyone being able to smell his lust on her that he'd tried to comfort her the only way he could think of—he'd told her it would make perfect sense to smell like him if she used his toiletries.

"Yes, *neshama*?" he coaxed. Power was thrumming through him, his soul recharged by its growing attachment to hers. Added to the more primitive rush he felt from having made love to her for hours, he felt ready to take on anything. The Sentinels thought his love for a mortal made him weak, when the opposite was true. Lindsay gave him strength in ways he couldn't explain to anyone else.

"I'm sure figuring out *how* is important," she began. "But I'm curious as to *why*. Why would anyone want to set up Elijah? What do they get out of it?"

She looked at the lycan and offered him a brief, supportive smile. She seemed to have a fondness for him, which made Adrian determined to keep the beast close and safe for her sake. Whatever stability and grounding he could offer her in their present tenuous circumstances, he would.

"Maybe it's not him in particular," Jason suggested. "Maybe *any* lycan would have served the purpose. Anything they do reflects on Adrian."

Her lips twisted thoughtfully. "So someone sets it up to look like the vamp was snatched by Adrian . . . ? Why is that news? That's what he does. It's what you all do, lycans and angels alike."

Adrian relished an inner smile, pleased with her participation and clever mind. She enhanced him. Lindsay was a warrior, just like he was. Just as Shadoe had been. But Lindsay was cerebral about it, analytical, while Shadoe had used her sexuality as a weapon.

"Vash wouldn't retaliate for just anyone," he said. **"Did she say who was abducted?"**

A shadow passed over Elijah's face. "No name. Just that the vamp was a woman. A pilot and a friend of Vash's."

"A female pilot." Adrian looked at Jason, wondering if his second was reaching the same conclusion he was.

Jason whistled. "Can't say for sure, Captain. I didn't get a good look at her."

"She was diseased and unrecognizable. Sick like the vamp we caught in Hurricane."

Aaron entered the room. The recently returned Sentinel had already made his desire for retribution clear. In addition to Micah's deteriorating health, he'd lost his other lycan guard in Vash's attack. "Vash had Salem and Raze with her. They hit us in full daylight."

Three Fallen on the hunt together. Not unheard of, but rare. They didn't have many occasions to exert that much force at once.

Adrian remembered his conversation with Syre. *Nikki had one of the kindest hearts among us . . .*

Shit. He looked at Damien, who stood behind the sofa Lindsay was occupying. "Torque's wife. Nicole, right?"

The Sentinel nodded. "That sounds right. And she's a former Army pilot."

"Who's Torque?" Lindsay asked, her gaze darting from one face to another.

Your brother. Your twin.

Adrian looked at Jason, whose brows were raised in a look that asked, *How much are you going to tell her?*

Elijah replied. "Syre's son."

"And Syre is . . . ?" she prodded.

"The leader of the vampires," Adrian said, with an evenness that belied the twisting of his gut. She wasn't ready to hear everything yet. He would prefer that she never hear it. If the Creator was kind, Adrian would succeed in killing Syre. Then Lindsay would be freed from Shadoe's naphil gifts, Shadoe's soul would be freed from purgatory, and Adrian would be recalled for disobeying the standing order to keep the Fallen alive. It was the closest he could come to rectifying his mistake.

"The Watcher whose fall got you those crimson tips on your wings?" Lindsay asked.

He gave a brisk nod.

"All right. Before we move on . . . What's up with the superhero names? Syre, Torque, Vash, Raze . . ."

"Most of the Fallen gave up their angelic names when they fell. Syre was once known as Samyaza. Raze was once Ertael. As vampires, they have a proliferation of legal names they switch out every now and then as time passes, so they've established a culture in which there's almost a competition for the most outrageous handles."

"O-*kay* . . . To be clear, Vash—an important vampire— is involved because the gal who was abducted was important, because she's related by marriage to the leader of the vampires. Am I following so far?"

"Yes."

"Why don't they just call you and ask what the ransom terms are? It's not like they can't find you."

"They did."

"And they didn't believe you're innocent?"

"I killed her. I told Syre that." Adrian met her gaze unflinchingly, knowing she would understand such a brutal admission of murder.

Lindsay blinked in surprise. "When?"

He descended into the living room. "When did I tell him? In Phoenix. In the airport, right after I met you."

"So Vash knows this isn't a rescue mission. She's out for blood in retaliation for a death. She managed to corner Aaron and his two lycans. But instead of holding Aaron for ransom or targeting him because he's higher up the food chain than the lycans, she lets him go. I'm confused as to why a vamp who usually only hunts big fish would toss the biggest fish back." She looked at Elijah. "No offense to your friend."

The lycan met her gaze. "None taken."

Jason crossed his arms. "Killing a Sentinel would escalate the situation beyond what Syre would condone."

"His son's wife is dead, thanks to Adrian, but he balks at taking out one of the Sentinels?"

Damien looked at Adrian. "Go on, Lindsay. This is getting interesting."

Lindsay twisted on the sofa, bringing him more fully into the conversation. "I'm just trying to understand what's going on here. The vampire head honcho's daughter-in-law gets nabbed by Elijah. *Allegedly*," she qualified when Elijah opened his mouth. "Vamp dude calls Adrian to ask for her return and Adrian says he killed her. Yet Vash remains focused on the lycan involved and not the Sentinels. How come?"

Adrian's wings unfurled. "I accused Syre of sending Nikki to attack me. He didn't respond to the accusation as I would've expected, nor to my mention of Phineas, which led to me wondering whether he was losing control of his vamps."

"Is it possible that he thinks you're losing control of the lycans? I mean, the reverse is true. You probably didn't respond the way he expected. He called you because he was worried about his daughter-in-law, and you didn't even know who she was. You didn't recognize her. But the lycans who took her knew her identity— assuming she wasn't sick then. He's got to be thinking that the lycans made a pretty bold move taking some-one so valuable to him without you knowing about it."

"Told you," Jason said, looking at Adrian.

"Where are you all going with this?" Aaron asked.

Jason's brow arched. "It's possible the lycans are working on their own."

"But," Lindsay interjected, shooting a glance at Elijah, who gave nothing away on his face, "why implicate one of their own by leaving Elijah's blood at the scene?"

Aaron exhaled harshly. "Which resulted in the death of Luke—my other lycan—on sight. There was no attempt made to capture or speak to him. And Micah is as good as dead."

"They captured him, then let him go."

"They left him for dead," Aaron said. "There's a difference."

"Is there?" she challenged. "The whole leaving-someone-for-dead business is beyond me. Either something is dead or it's not, and if it isn't and you want it dead, you don't leave it to chance. Why would Vash—?"

A silence fell over the room as Lindsay abruptly stopped speaking. All eyes rested on her until she shrugged blithely and said, "Never mind. Too complicated for me. My brain hurts."

She stood and walked toward the windows, stepping through when one large pane of glass slid automatically to the side.

Resisting the urge to flex his wings, Adrian dismissed Jason and Aaron with an accompanying order to report to his office in the morning. He feigned nonchalance, but inside he was weighing the myriad possible reasons for why Elijah—the first Alpha to make an appearance in many years—had been set up to take the fall for Nikki's abduction. He knew Lindsay's mind had followed the same train of thought and she'd ceased her speculations the moment she realized how dangerous they were to Elijah.

Adrian studied the lycan as the living room cleared, noting how Elijah followed Lindsay as far as the window, guarding her still, yet making a pointed effort to stay within boundaries that wouldn't incite Adrian's fierce possessiveness. The lycan and Lindsay clearly had a friendship of sorts, which was why Adrian entrusted him with her protection, but that didn't mitigate the danger Elijah presented as an Alpha. Whether he had any culpability in the abduction or not, it appeared someone had gone to great lengths to bring the Alpha lycan to the attention of the vampires, and the vamps were taking the steps necessary to formalize that introduction.

The enemy of my enemy is my friend.

Collusion between the lycans and vampires would lead to the annihilation of the Sentinels. The numbers against them would be far too great to withstand.

Gauging Elijah's loyalty was more important than ever. Adrian expected that fidelity would be strongest with other lycans, but it just might be strong enough with Lindsay to make defection difficult.

Elijah met his gaze as he moved to follow Lindsay outside.

Adrian paused on the threshold. "What do you think, Elijah?"

"Vash was empty-handed after speaking to Micah. She was left with the choice of interrogating another lycan before my blood sample deteriorated or following Micah back to me. I think that's why she let him live."

"And what will you do should she come here?"

"Eviscerate the bitch." He growled, his eyes glowing with green fire. "Micah is my friend. He's like a brother to me, as Phineas was to you. And she killed him. I could've lived with that if she'd fought him for it. But to die like this, sick and broken in a bed—no lycan should have to die like that."

Adrian set his hand on Elijah's shoulder and swiftly searched the lycan's mind. A red haze of fury and grief washed over every sifting thought, none of which dealt with mutiny or treachery. Momentarily reassured, Adrian murmured, "May we all go down fighting."

He released the lycan and stepped outside, finding Lindsay standing a safe distance away from the railing while staring at the cityscape in the distance. He embraced her from behind, wrapping her within his arms and wings.

"Your participation helped immensely," he said with his lips to her ear. "Thank you."

"I hate that you're dealing with so much crap at once." She leaned into him, placing her arms over his. "You haven't had any time to grieve. And my being here is just making things worse."

Adrian's arms tightened around her. "Your being here makes things bearable."

"You're a glutton for punishment," she muttered. "He's loyal to you, you know. Elijah. And he's a good guy."

"That doesn't necessarily make him less dangerous."

"What does being an Alpha mean? What makes him different?"

"The beast within the lycans is powerful. They were created with demon blood—the blood of werewolves—

and it's very much like being possessed. They have two natures warring inside them."

"God," she breathed. "I can guess how that must be for them. I feel like I'm warring with myself sometimes. Especially with you. I know what I need to do, but it's hard to shut out the voice in my head that says, *To hell with the consequences*."

Shutting his eyes against her inadvertently accurate confession, he went on, "At times, the beast takes over. The lycan can't control the need to shift or the violence that comes with it. The Alphas are different. They have the power to decide which half of their nature is most dominant, regardless of triggers or provocation, and that power seems to extend outside of themselves. They can calm and subdue the beasts in the lycans around them. The others are drawn to that force of will, and their beasts subjugate willingly to the Alpha, but their allegiance must be with the Sentinels first and foremost."

Her head fell back into the crook of his shoulder, her silky golden curls brushing across his jaw. "What do you do with the Alphas?"

"We segregate them from the others and use them for assignments in which a lone hunter is required. The other lycans must work in teams."

"Who oversees that for you? Or do you do it?"

"The dispatching of the Alphas is delegated to Reese. I can introduce you, if you like. He can answer your questions more thoroughly."

Sighing, she tilted her head to the side. Her soft lips whispered against his chin. "I don't know how you carry the weight of everything you're responsible for, but I respect you for doing what has to be the most difficult job ever."

He'd noticed in Utah that Lindsay refrained from contradicting him in front of an audience, showing him respect and displaying a restraint that was unique to her. Although she was as strong willed and passionate as Shadoe, she was far less impetuous when it came to weighing the ramifications of her words and actions. She maneuvered well through group interactions, but in a way that minimized her presence and participation. While Shadoe had always been the most vibrant individual in any gathering, Lindsay could recede from notice when she chose to. It was a defensive tactic she must have cultivated to deal with her feelings of abnormality. Who would notice she was strange if they didn't notice her at all?

Adrian admired her ability to be circumspect, which made him ever more determined to protect her from further experiences that might erode her confidence. Lindsay Gibson was an extraordinary woman in so many ways. He never wanted her to question her worth for a moment.

Yet he'd put her in a position of being surrounded by those who distrusted and resented her. When he took himself out of the equation and thought only of her, he knew what had to be done. The sooner he killed Syre, the sooner she would be free of Shadoe's soul and this life of war that wasn't meant for her. But with every hour that passed, he fell a little farther and the thought of losing her gnawed a little deeper.

He knew he must have dreaded losing her with such ferocity before, but he was damned if he could remember when.

*   *   *

Lindsay sank into the chaise in Adrian's bedroom and stretched out. His personal space was surprisingly spartan compared to the bedroom that had been given to her. No art adorned the walls, and the furniture was Shaker in style.

This, she thought, was more like him. Although he appeared at home surrounded by the trappings of massive wealth, it was in this room that he fit best. As she surveyed the space, the affinity she felt for him deepened. She knew how it felt to wear a guise all the time. It was exhausting and wore away at a person after a while.

Adrian was busy unpacking his bags. It didn't escape her notice that he did it the old-fashioned way—with his two hands. Busywork hinted at agitation. Or avoidance.

Tucking her hands behind her head, she stared up at the ceiling. It was something she and her father had often done over the years—had lain on their backs and looked up at the sky, feeling the wind move over them as it whispered softly. Eddie Gibson never doubted that Lindsay heard voices in the air, even though he couldn't hear them himself. She was so grateful to him for that unconditional love. It enabled her to love others who were extraordinary, like Adrian.

"Thank you, by the way," she said, "for looking out for my dad. I know you need every hand right now, but I won't talk you out of watching his back. He's my rock. I couldn't get by without him."

"You're welcome."

She rubbed absently at the ache of homesickness in her chest. "You're being quiet. A penny for your thoughts."

"I'm thinking about the questions you brought up

earlier." He glanced at her. "You're quiet, too. What are you thinking about?"

"My dad, which led to me thinking about the lycans guarding him. I'm trying to wrap my mind around you enforcing this you-work-for-me-or-die rule. I can't see it in you. Commander of military forces, yes. An employer, yes. Even an angel—no problem. But someone who forces people to do things against their will under threat of death? No."

He exhaled audibly. Although his facial expression didn't change, she sensed disquiet in him.

"Are they slaves?" She looked at him again. "Adrian?"

He'd paused with his hands in his duffel bag, frowning. "I've always used the word 'indentured.'"

"That's a form of servitude."

"I don't abuse them. I make every attempt to see to their comfort. I try, in all ways, to be fair to them."

"But they can't quit? Or leave?"

His chest lifted and fell on a deep breath. "No."

"Yeah . . . I see a problem there."

"But neither can the Sentinels. Or the vampires. We're all trapped in our roles, which were established eons ago. This push and pull between us—it's bigger than all of us. The brutal fact of the matter is, if the lycans don't help me keep things together, there won't be a world to be free in."

Lindsay pushed her hair back from her forehead. "I understand what you're saying. But I still don't like it."

"You think I do?"

"No, I don't think you do. I don't think you have it in you to like it, which is why I wonder how you've done it for so long."

"I'm a soldier, Linds. I'm given orders and I follow them. It's all I can do."

There was something in the softness of his tone that made him seem so alone. As alone as she'd often felt over the years. She held her hand out to him. "I'd like for you to tell me what happened over the last week."

He crossed the room to her. *Not here,* he mouthed, catching her fingers with his own. He pulled her up, then tugged her out onto the wraparound deck.

Stepping into his arms, she said, "Wait a minute before you take off."

"Are you still scared?"

"Not right now, but I will be in a minute." She smiled, knowing there was nowhere else she'd rather be than with Adrian. All the restlessness that had been vibrating within her for the last week—and most of her life before that—was gone, replaced by a languidness that came from more than great sex. It came from him alone. He centered her. "I just love the way your body feels against mine when you're exerting yourself. And since this is pretty much the only guilt-free way to have you doing that, I want to make sure I enjoy every minute."

His hands slid to her hips and urged her against him. "Anytime you want me to exert myself against you, just ask."

Lindsay wrapped herself around him from shoulder to ankle. "You know I can't do that."

He looked down at her with eyes that were hot with desire and soft with affection. "Yes. I know, *neshama.* Ready?"

She nodded.

His wings snapped open and he leaped over the low

railing. They caught air and soared over the darkened hills with the wind singing softly. In the near distance, the lights of the city twinkled like a blanket of multicolored stars.

The flight was over too quickly. Adrian landed a few miles away, directly in front of a metal-sided building that sat unlit on a barren plateau.

"Where are we?" she asked breathlessly, her heartbeat still wild from exhilaration.

"One of the training camps. If you like, you'll be enduring it tomorrow."

He opened the door and the fluorescent lights flickered on automatically, revealing a large warehouse-type room with a half dozen bunk beds, two sofas, and walls covered in every weapon she knew of as well as several she'd never seen. It was like a giant man-cave great room, homicidal-style.

"Why," she queried, "do lycans and Sentinels, who have such awesome natural defense mechanisms, need any of these things?"

"Because the vamps use them. We need to know how to fend off attacks made with these weapons and to improvise, if any of them should fall into our hands."

Admiring a blade that looked somewhat like a scythe, Lindsay looked over her shoulder at him. "I'm worried about how the other Sentinels will deal with me training with them."

Adrian stood nearby, watching her with heated pride. "Let me worry about them."

"I don't want to cause problems for you, Adrian. And that's all I'm doing. I hate that."

"I woke this morning praying for the end to come

quickly. Now I have you, and the end is the last thing I want."

Lindsay couldn't stop the tear that ran down her cheek. She could be strong about a lot of things, but Adrian's tenderness had been devastating her from the beginning. He made her feel as if she was precious to him. It killed her that he would try to give her all of himself, but she would still have only a portion. There was nothing she could do about that except offer him what comfort she could, and refrain from asking for anything in return. "Talk to me. Tell me why you were ready to give up."

His wings flexed restlessly. The pearlescent backdrop showcased his dark beauty to breathtaking effect.

After her mother had died, she'd been so angry. She had railed at the entity other people believed in, the God others claimed was so generous and loving. She'd found little in life to redeem her lost faith in a benevolent higher power, but Adrian's existence softened that skepticism. If the same being who'd allowed her mother to be brutally murdered was also responsible for creating Adrian, then there was something magical and praiseworthy in the world, even if none of it was ever shared willingly with her.

"The Sentinel I lost was a friend," he said softly, inadvertently wounding her with his pain. "But more than that, she was a pristine example of what a seraph should be. She was pure of spirit and purpose, focused solely on our mission."

She moved toward him, reaching for his hand and clasping it in her own. So much death. He'd dealt with too much of it. "Another vamp attack?"

"That would have been kinder than the reality."

She stepped closer and he embraced her, settling his chin atop the crown of her head. Her connection to him in that moment rocked her. In a remote hillside warehouse, surrounded by implements of destruction and the arms of an angel, she felt at peace in a way she never had before. "You said you'd have to hurt someone you cared about."

"She fell in love," he murmured. "With a lycan."

"That's bad?"

"It's impossible."

"Why? Lycans aren't mortals."

He barked a humorless, bitter laugh. "Helena said the same thing, but seraphim aren't designed to experience mortal love. We're not supposed to have mates. She wanted my blessing. She hoped I would give it to her, because I have you. But it's not my place to make that decision. It's my responsibility to keep the Sentinels on the right path."

Lindsay felt the progress she'd recently made in regard to having some faith backslide again. How could love, in any form, be wrong? "What did she do?"

As he explained the actions Helena had taken, Lindsay's blood chilled and goose bumps spread across her skin. She relived the horror and agony of that night with him, her shoulders sagging under the growing weight of his despair. There was no greater proof of the impossibility of loving Adrian than the suicide of Helena and her beloved lycan.

"Jesus," she whispered when he was done. "I can't imagine."

"I can." His chest expanded with a deep inhalation. "I have."

Her heart stopped, then lurched into a double-time rhythm. She pulled back and glared up at him.

"I swear to you—" Her voice cracked, forcing her to clear her throat before continuing. "If you ever try something like that, I'll make you regret it."

His lips pressed to her forehead. "You worry too much about me."

"I'm serious." Her fingers dug into his waist. "Whatever consequences we face for being together is out of our hands. We don't need to borrow trouble on top of that."

"And we won't." For a moment, he looked so resolute and somber, giving her the impression there was something more he needed to say. Instead he said, "We should head back. You have an early day tomorrow, and I have to look into how Elijah's blood ended up in Louisiana."

"Do you have any guesses?"

"We take and store blood from each lycan for identification and genetic purposes. If any of Elijah's stored blood is missing, I have a traitor in my ranks. The alternative would be that someone collected his blood from a hunt at some point in the past and saved it, which would speak to lengthy premeditation. There's really no good way to look at this. Someone out there has an ulterior motive that can only cause me a lot of trouble." His thumb brushed over her cheekbone. "I know how you feel about the lycans, and I don't disagree, but there's no way one hundred and sixty-one Sentinels can contain the thousands of vampires in the world without their help."

"Let me help you, brainstorm with you. I want to support you ..."

"Yes, *neshama*. I look forward to it." He urged her toward the door. "But first, you need to get some sleep."

"That won't be a problem." She preceded him out of the building. "I haven't slept well since Vegas, and it's been a long day."

His mouth lifted in a half smile that charmed her. "Your definition of a long day may change after training tomorrow."

Lindsay looked at him through the lock of hair the evening wind blew across her cheek. "You can't scare me."

He turned off the lights and stepped outside with her. The wind kissed him, too, whispering across his wings. "You're fearless. That's one of the many reasons I want you."

A quiver of sexual awareness moved through her, heating her blood.

When they got back to the house, she didn't go inside, knowing it was best not to confront temptation directly. "I'm going to head back to the hotel. Is my stuff still out front?"

Adrian paused on the threshold of the sliding glass door leading back into his bedroom. "I want you to stay."

"That's not a good idea. Besides," she rushed on, when his eyes took on the glitter of determination, "I need to give two weeks' notice, and the sooner I do that, the better."

He weighed that a moment. "Once you quit, you'll stay here."

"Adrian—"

He took a step toward her.

She knew what would happen if he touched her. "Can we talk about it later? I'm beat."

After a brief hesitation, he nodded. "Tomorrow. Leave your suitcase here."

"I have—"

"—no idea what it did to me to see you putting that in your car." Catching her hand, he stroked his thumb over the back of it. "Leave it here."

"Fine." She squeezed his fingers, a faint echo of the constriction around her heart.

She couldn't say the words, but she could show him. That would have to be enough for both of them.

CHAPTER 19

"I knew they were going to have a hard time with this," Lindsay muttered to Elijah, watching as more and more Sentinels began to land in the field by the training warehouse.

The sun had just risen. Adrian had insisted Elijah drive Lindsay back to the hotel the night before, arguing that she was too tired to be behind the wheel. Since her Prius was a bit small for a large lycan, they'd taken one of the Point's Jeeps. She thought leaving her car behind might have been another way for Adrian to keep something of hers with him, something she'd have to come back for, so she'd refrained from arguing.

"Things have been the same for the Sentinels for a long time," Elijah said. "It's probably been a while since anything threw them a curveball."

She pivoted to face him. "Are you going to be all right, El? With the whole Alpha business and now the blood thing yesterday . . . Is there something I can do?"

He looked down at her. With his green eyes hidden

behind dark sunglasses, she couldn't get a read on what he might be thinking. "Just stick close to me. I'm supposed to keep you safe. If I fuck that up, I'm toast."

"I can't imagine you fucking anything up."

He snorted.

"Wanna talk about it?" she offered.

"Don't even want to think about it."

"Okay. I'm here if you need me."

Damien approached. While the morning was chilly and fog hugged the ground, he was dressed like the other Sentinels on the field: in loose pants and leather sandals. The women wore sports bras, but otherwise everyone sported bare torsos. Just looking at them made Lindsay shiver. She was wearing a lined jogging suit, but she was still just short of having chattering teeth.

"I've seen you with knives and a shotgun." The Sentinel raked her with a clinical glance. "You were fairly skilled with both. How are you in hand-to-hand combat?"

Her brow lifted. "Seriously? I'm human. That's what the knives and guns are for, to keep the inhumans from getting close enough to tear me to shreds. Plus knife throwing and marksmanship are solitary activities, so I taught myself— Whoa!"

Lindsay arched back and away from Damien's fist flying toward her face. The smack of flesh meeting flesh rent the air. She hit the dirt on her ass and stared up with wide eyes.

Elijah had blocked Damien's blow with the palm of his hand. The two men were in a standoff, their arms shaking with the force each exerted in a brutal sort of strong-arm competition.

"What the fuck?" she snapped.

The two men pushed away from each other, each taking a step back. They turned to her in unison, both extending a hand to help her up. She grabbed them both and let them haul her to her feet.

"Adrian said you were quick," Damien said calmly, as if he hadn't just struck out at her with a blow that would have shattered bone. "I didn't get a chance to see you move in Hurricane, so I had to gauge your speed."

Lindsay gaped at him, then shot a look at Elijah. A muscle was ticcing in the lycan's jaw. Maybe the test hadn't been just for her. Maybe they'd been testing him as well.

The rest of the Sentinels, about ten evenly divided between men and women, dotted the field around them, sizing her up. She felt like a raw slab of meat tossed to voracious raptors.

She rolled her shoulders back.

"If you get me squared away," she said to Damien, "Adrian will worry less about me and more about the shit you're dealing with. We all want that."

The Sentinel held still for a moment, staring her down. She didn't flinch.

Finally, he nodded. They might all want a pound of her flesh, but Damien would keep them focused on the big picture. Hopefully.

Elijah stepped closer to her. "I'm not going anywhere," he promised, in a way that sounded like a threat. A gauntlet thrown down for the others.

Damien gestured for her to join the Sentinels on the field. "Let's go."

She realized Adrian hadn't been kidding about revising her definition of a long day. This one was going to be endless, she knew. And it hadn't even started yet.

* * *

"Elijah's blood is missing from Navajo Lake."

Adrian looked away from the view speeding by the Maybach's rear passenger window and faced his lieutenant. "Fuck."

"Yeah." Jason returned his cell phone to his pocket. "Not the whole sample, just some of it. They had to weigh the bag to detect it."

The sun glinted off the Sentinel's golden hair through the panoramic glass roof, creating a halo effect. For a moment, homesickness was a deep ache in Adrian's chest.

The longest they could store blood before the cryopreservation affected the quality of the sample was ten years. Someone had accessed the blood, removed what they needed, and returned the sample.

"When we reach the airfield," Adrian said, "I want you to head to Navajo Lake and find the one responsible. Only Sentinels are authorized to access the cryogenic storage facility."

"You think it's one of us?"

"After Helena . . . who can be certain? I need to know for sure."

Jason sighed. "I never thought I'd have any sympathy for what Syre and the Watchers did. But it seems like the longer we're here, the more human we become. We want things . . . feel things . . . Well, you know."

Adrian studied his second for a long moment, looking at Jason with a thoroughness he hadn't employed for quite some time. He'd stopped paying attention to a lot of things, it seemed. Too lost to the apathy fostered by his grief and guilt.

"Do you desire, Jason?"

"Not to the extent you do and not for sex. My restlessness stems from frustration. I'm tired of carrying a yoke that can never be put down."

"I would ease your disquiet, if I could."

"Ah, well." Jason lifted one shoulder in a shrug. "I'll live. And I have hope that this vamp illness signals the end of our mission. God willing, it will take them all out and we'll be able to go home."

Adrian looked back out the window.

Home. For him, that was now wherever Lindsay was.

They reached Ontario and the hangar Mitchell Aeronautics kept there. They waited briefly as the massive metal doors parted; then they drove the Maybach inside. Jason set off to make flight arrangements for his trip to Utah. Adrian moved deeper into the building, heading down into the subterranean storage areas. The farther he descended, the easier it was to hear the growls and hissing. Unintelligible sounds mingled with shouted threats and profanities from those captives who hadn't yet been infected.

It felt very much like entering the bowels of hell.

"Captain."

A petite brunette approached him with a clipped, precise stride. Dressed in urban camouflage and sporting a pixielike cropped hairstyle, Siobhán looked too delicate to be formidable, which helped her immeasurably in battle. Her opponents always underestimated her. It was one of the reasons he'd put her in charge of rounding up infected vampires. The other reason was her fascination with science. This hunt had required someone who understood that capturing the vamps was only the beginning.

With gloved hands, she pulled down the surgical mask covering her face. "We've already lost two of the six I caught. Four is a very small pool of subjects, so I'll need to hunt again soon."

"Do any of the noninfected have useful information about when the illness was first sighted? Or how it might be spread?"

"One was willing to talk." She dug into the cargo pockets of her pants and withdrew a mask and gloves, which she handed to him.

"Are these necessary?" Sentinels were impervious to disease.

"I don't know." She gestured for him to walk with her, leading him to a room filled with a dozen silver-plated cages. "But you don't want their spittle on you, just for the ick factor."

He donned the protection without further questions. "What do we know?"

"The disease first appeared about a week ago. It infects at a varying rate. Some succumb swiftly and die within a matter of days. Others take longer to show symptoms and live up to two weeks. This group wasn't aware that there are other incidents of infection in other states, which makes me wonder how much Syre actually knows."

Adrian walked by the cages, examining the infected vamps with morbid fascination. Red-eyed and frothing at the mouth, they seemed mindless. They bashed themselves against the unforgiving metal bars and reached out with clawed fingers, grasping for Adrian and Siobhán with malevolent desperation. Their gazes were wild, yet lifeless. "Do they show any signs of intelligence?"

"No. They're like bad B-movie zombies. Aside from a fierce thirst for blood, there seem to be no lights on and no one home."

He exhaled harshly. "Are we testing their blood?"

"We took samples from both the infected and noninfected while they were still tranquilized on the plane. However ..."

Her pause caught his attention and he tore his gaze away from the macabre freak show to look at her. "Go on."

She crossed her arms. "Their metabolisms are extremely accelerated. While the noninfected vamps stayed under induced anesthesia for the duration of the flight, the sick ones woke up shortly after we took off. Malachai was bitten by one of them while drawing blood."

"Is he okay?"

"So far, he's fine. But I have him quarantined until I know for sure. The vamp that bit him was the first of the two causalities. I had to put him down to get him off Malachai."

Siobhán resumed walking, stopping before a cage in which a male vampire sat in the corner with his arms wrapped around his drawn-up knees. "This is the talkative one."

"So you're the great Adrian," the vamp said, his voice shaking. "You don't look so scary with that mask on. You look scared."

Crouching, Adrian asked, "What's your name?"

"Does it matter?"

"It does to me."

The vamp lifted a shaking hand to push back a grimy lock of dark hair that had fallen over his brow. "Singe."

"What is it you like to burn?" Adrian asked, recognizing the signs of withdrawal and knowing that the monikers vampires chose often had significance.

"Crystal dream."

Looking at Siobhán, Adrian asked, "Any possibility the drug is connected? Perhaps it affords a level of immunity?"

"Anything is a possibility at this point."

"Thank you for your help, Singe." Adrian stood and faced Siobhán. "Take me to Malachai."

They left the room and moved down the hall.

"I have a question for you," Adrian said quietly.

"Yes, Captain?"

"Lindsay Gibson mentioned that her blood has a negative effect against some of the beings she's hunted. Since she's taken down both vampires and demons alike, I assume it's the latter group that was susceptible." He thought of the vampress he'd interrogated in Hurricane. He'd had Lindsay's blood on his hands, but it didn't spark a reaction of any kind, adverse or otherwise. "Can you explain why her blood would allow a blade to slice into a dragon's impenetrable hide?"

She frowned. "Interesting. I'd have to think about it. I'd certainly love to test a sample."

"Is it possible that having two souls inside her would be the cause?"

Siobhán slowed before a metal door with a window. "Yes, it's possible. You know how powerful souls are. Two in one vessel likely creates a unique force we will probably never fully understand."

Looking through the glass, Adrian saw Malachai kicking back on a cot with his cell phone in hand. Adrian knocked. Malachai looked up, his face breaking out in a smile when he recognized his visitor.

"I feel fine, Captain," the Sentinel shouted.

"Good to hear." Adrian was about to say more when

a ferocious pounding came from down the hall. He looked over his shoulder. "What's that?"

Siobhán frowned. "I don't know. I don't like it."

A few more Sentinels appeared in the hallway as the violent thumping continued. They all looked to Adrian, who swiftly passed them en route to the source of the sound.

As the location of the noise became apparent, Siobhán said, "That's the makeshift morgue."

"Who's in there?"

"Aside from the corpses of the two infected vamps? No one."

The sound of glass shattering preceded a shout. *"Let me out of here!"*

They turned a corner into a short hallway that ended with a single door. A masculine face stared out through the broken window, amber eyes glowing with ire. "Fuck you, Sentinels," the man growled. "Either kill me or let me go. Don't fucking leave me in here with a rotting corpse!"

"He was a corpse," Siobhán whispered. "I shot him myself after he bit Malachai."

Adrian didn't take his eyes off the vamp in front of him. "He's made a miraculous recovery."

"But the other one is still dead . . . ?"

"So is the one I caught. Turned into an oil slick, I was told." He contemplated the seemingly cured vampire with narrowed eyes, the tempo of his heartbeat accelerating as he considered the possibilities.

"One of these things is not like the others," he murmured. "The only difference being . . . what? The ingestion of Sentinel blood?"

Siobhán made a choked noise. "Shit."

Yeah, deep shit.

"Are you feeling better?" Elijah asked as he watched Lindsay exit her adjoining bedroom.

He sat at the small desk in his suite, working on his laptop and trying not to feel like everything was closing in on him. That was pretty damn difficult, considering the wariness with which the Sentinels were watching him and the expectation that weighted the gaze of every lycan he crossed paths with. Everyone was waiting for him to make a move, one that would rip apart the well-oiled system that kept mortals blissfully ignorant. One side wanted to defuse his perceived power, while the other wanted him to blow up like a powder keg. He was fucked coming and going.

"Dude." Lindsay shook out her wet curls with her hands. "Did you get that vitamin water I asked for?"

"It's in your minifridge, Your Highness."

"Good grief." She stared at him with exaggerated shock. "Did you just make a joke?"

He refrained from smiling. "No."

"I think you did."

Elijah looked back at his laptop screen. He liked her. And after the multiple times she'd gone out of her way to save his sorry hide, he thought of her as a friend. He didn't have too many of those, which was why he'd been speechless when she'd said they were friends. Somewhere over the days he'd been guarding her, he had stopped thinking of her as just a principal and started thinking of her as just Lindsay. He was more relaxed around her than he'd been around anyone in a long time, because her friendship came without strings or expectations. She was crazy and fun, and blunt to a fault. She was just goofy enough to reveal that she hadn't socialized much as a kid. Like him, she probably had a very small group of people she trusted. He wondered if she'd ever shared her gifts with anyone else. Shit, why did she have them in the first place? She was a great big question mark, and everyone wanted a piece of her. And it was his job to make sure no one but Adrian got any.

She reappeared a moment later, swigging from a bottle of some neon-colored liquid that boasted its nutritional content. "Ya know . . . I feel like I got run over by a freight train while suffering a hangover."

The Sentinels had worked her hard all morning, so hard Elijah had had to step in a couple times. They hadn't liked that, but they knew Adrian would back him up. As for Lindsay, she'd put up with the brutal pace without protest, taking the occasional dirty hit and brushing it off.

The Sentinels clearly didn't understand the significance of Adrian's display of sexual dominance the day before, or they would have been more careful with her. Perhaps even Adrian didn't understand the entirety of the driving need he'd felt to claim, mark, and possess her, a need aggravated by her attempt to get away. Female lycans knew better than to flee. Rousing the beast by denying him his mate wasn't the smartest idea. Elijah had once assumed it was the demon in the lycan bloodline that made them so primal with their mates, but he'd been careful with Lindsay from the beginning, just in case. A smart move, if he said so himself. Now it'd been proven that the angels were capable of the same possessive and wild carnality. Perhaps the angelic contribution to the lycan genetic makeup was the largest source of that near violent covetousness.

Regardless, the lycans had gotten Adrian's message loud and clear. Unfortunately, Elijah feared the awareness of Lindsay's importance to the Sentinel leader only made her more vulnerable. Those who whispered about rebellion had been looking and waiting for a chink in Adrian's inviolate power, Elijah realized, and Lindsay was it.

Fuck. He scrubbed both hands over his face. How had he missed how fanatical the others had become? How long had Micah been filling the others' heads with the pipe dream of freedom?

"I can hear the wheels in your head turning," Lindsay said drily, setting her empty bottle on the dresser so housekeeping would recycle it. She was somewhat of a tree hugger, he'd noticed.

He needed to be hunting down whoever had set him up, but he couldn't leave Lindsay, and there was no one he could trust with her.

She went to the closet and pulled out her messenger bag, perfectly comfortable with walking around with an arsenal slung over her hip. "I need to go out."

He pushed back from the desk. "For what?"

"Seriously tacky touristy Disney and California stuff. Hats, sweatshirts, shot glasses, et cetera."

His lack of excitement must have shown on his face, because she laughed.

"I have to get my dad stuff he'll roll his eyes over," she explained. "But, lucky for you, we won't be gone too long. I've got an interviewee coming in at three."

Elijah looked at the clock and noted it was one. He had to hand it to her—she'd taken a beating all morning and kept on ticking. "Do you have plans tonight?"

"I need to get my car from the Point, but otherwise you're free to do whatever."

He nodded. "Good. Thanks."

Once she was settled in the hotel for the night, he could talk to Rachel by phone. He had to get some idea of how pervasive Micah's rebellion plans were. Elijah knew he had to rip that weed out by the root as soon as possible—a damn near impossible task when he was away from the rest of the pack most of the time.

"Why don't you have a girlfriend?" Lindsay asked him as they exited the elevator on the bottom floor. They usually took the stairs—all seventeen floors—but she was too wiped out to need the exercise today.

"Too complicated, too time-consuming, too much work."

"But you like girls, right? Or don't you?"

His gaze darted to hers, only to find her dark eyes laughing.

"Made you look," she teased.

He snorted in lieu of laughing, but it was a close race between the two.

Lindsay stopped abruptly just outside the revolving doors leading to the awning-covered bellhop and valet area. Bellmen were going through training in front of them, while gardeners put the finishing touches on the flower bed framing the crescent-shaped driveway. Life as mortals knew it was carrying on as usual, but the sudden stiffening of Lindsay's posture and her intense focus was like a dog on point, signaling the proximity of prey nearby.

Abruptly, his senses went on alert. Elijah scanned the immediate area again, just as he'd automatically done before they'd exited the lobby. The uncanny wind that always seemed to follow Lindsay blew past him, carrying the blood-rich scent of vampire. The beast inside him coiled in readiness, growling softly in anticipation of his order to attack.

The vamp responsible for their instinctive reactions appeared a moment later, strolling into the parking lot from the public sidewalk, blissfully unaware of the predators she'd roused.

Her looks hit him like a sledgehammer. She was tall and stacked, with curvy hips and full, firm tits. Her hair hung to her waist, straight as a board and blood red. She was clad like a goddamned dominatrix, with spiky-heeled boots, tight black pants, and a leather vest dipping in a low V that displayed the deep valley of her cleavage.

Elijah was blindsided by the insane urge to bend her over the hood of the Mercedes she was walking past, wrap her hair around his forearm, and drill her lush body until he came with a roar.

He fucking hated vampires, especially the females, who were more vicious than the males. Yet his cock was swelling with feral lust the longer he watched her.

She jerked violently, jolting him back to reality. She spun wildly, as if felled by a blow, then rounded back with fangs bared.

It wasn't until he saw the glint of sunlight on something metallic embedded in her shoulder that he realized what had happened.

"Shit," he muttered, barely catching Lindsay by the shoulder as she darted forward.

"Let me go, El," she snapped, yanking to be free of his unyielding grip.

"What the fuck are you doing?" he barked. "It's god-damned daylight. That's one of the Fallen."

Lindsay sliced across his forearm with her blade, eliciting a roar of pain and garnering her release.

She was halfway to the vampire when she answered him.

"That bitch killed my mother."

CHAPTER 20

Vash stared down at the burning pain in her shoulder and realized she'd been hit with a silver-plated throwing knife. Ripping the blade free, she looked up in time to catch sight of another volley a split second before it caught her in the bicep.

"Fuck!" she hissed, unprepared for a full-on attack in the middle of the damn day.

A blonde was racing toward her, another blade flying from her grip. Vash barely lurched out of the way in time, the smell of her own blood stirring the hunger in her.

A *human*. What the hell?

Vash charged, ready to take the crazy bitch down, when she smelled lycan. He raced out from beneath the shadow of the hotel's front awning, chasing the crazy blonde with the death wish.

It hit her then: *Shadoe.* Followed swiftly by the identifying scent of her guard dog . . .

The fucking bastard who'd kidnapped Nikki.

Stunned into senselessness, Vash skidded to a halt, earning her another blade in the thigh.

The two people she was in town to capture were coming straight toward her, and there wasn't a damn thing she could do about it. Not while she was alone. Not without her weapons. Not with witnesses.

Another blade nailed her in the shoulder, damn near dead center of the first hit she'd taken.

She had taught Shadoe how to throw like that. She had taught her how to hunt, how to kill. It was clear to Vash right away: Shadoe was deliberately avoiding hitting vital organs and arteries. The crazy blonde thought she was going to capture a vamp.

Vash grabbed a blade out of her shoulder and lobbed it at the lycan, then discarded the one in her leg and lunged forward, hitting Shadoe in the chest with her palms and throwing her backward several feet to crash into her lycan guard. The two went down, and Vash fled, leaping onto the hood of a nearby Jaguar and running up to its roof. She vaulted up and over the stone wall that divided the Belladonna parking lot from that of the dinner theater's next door, her rage so wild she could barely see straight.

She never ran away. She never took multiple hits. She never let anyone live who spilled her blood. But she couldn't take out Syre's daughter. She couldn't kill Shadoe.

"Goddamn! Shit! Fuck!" she shouted.

Her boots hit the roof of a Suburban on the other side of the wall, the alarm activating in an eruption of horn blaring. Her right heel broke off and stole her balance, sending her tumbling down the windshield, across the hood, and onto the asphalt.

She'd barely regained her footing when she heard another body hit the car behind her. Glancing over her shoulder, she saw the blonde hot on her heels. Vash took another hit in the shoulder, the sizzle of silver sending agony racing through her veins. Unable to pull a dagger out of her back, she could only run forward and hope like hell an escape route opened up. Ahead of her was a busy street, but that didn't seem to deter Shadoe. Whatever had crawled up Syre's daughter's ass was goading her like a cattle prod.

A white full-sized pickup truck bounced into the lot with too much speed, racing toward her. Vash was calculating the trajectory needed to leap over it when it spun out and swung around. Salem's head shot out the driver's-side window. "Get in!"

She jumped into the back and he hit the gas, kicking up loose asphalt and leaving behind a cloud that smelled of burning rubber. A throwing knife hit the rear of the cab with a sharp *ping*. Vash ducked with a curse.

The truck squealed into the swift-moving traffic to a chorus of angry horns and the crunch of metal and fiberglass. They were a good two miles away before Vash felt safe enough to pop her head up.

"You asked for reports of abductions."

Syre looked up from the spreadsheets on the monitor in front of him and met the gaze of the vampress in his office doorway. "Yes, Raven."

The dark-haired beauty entered with an unconsciously sensual stride. She wore mile-high black stilettos, a knee-length pencil skirt, and a button-down shirt that hugged full breasts. Apparently she was acting the role of naughty secretary, one of the many games she played to keep things interesting.

"There was a raid last night in Oregon," she said. "A group of Sentinels invaded a nest and took several minions with them."

Leaning back in his chair, Syre wondered at Adrian's growing boldness. To infect minions with a disease seemed unlike him. He was a warrior who engaged in and excelled in physical combat. Biological warfare wasn't a tactic Syre would ever have attributed to the Sentinel leader. Something had changed, or was in the process of changing.

For the first time in many, many years, Syre felt the clock ticking with brutal impatience. Torque had been pushing him to act, instead of react, for many years now. It looked like that time might indeed be nigh.

"Thank you," he murmured. "Send a team out to Oregon. I want to know every detail of the raid. And keep me apprised of any further reports immediately."

"Yes, Syre."

Raven left the room. He attempted to return his focus to the screen in front of him. The effort was futile. When the phone rang, he reached for it with relief, his thoughts still occupied by Adrian's offensive moves.

You have no idea of what I'm authorized to do, the Sentinel leader had said just a few short weeks earlier. Perhaps there was a wealth of threat in those words that Syre had been oblivious to.

The raised voice of the caller on the other end of the line was audible before he even placed the receiver by his ear.

"Calm yourself, Vash," he soothed. "Slow down. I can't—"

He stiffened as she continued spewing words in a

rush, all but one thought dissipating from his mind. *Act, instead of react.*

It was indeed the time.

"What the fuck were you thinking?" Adrian asked in that cool, modulated tone of voice that made Lindsay grit her teeth.

As wired as she felt, she'd prefer him to yell or raise his voice, pace or glower—*something*. Instead, he stood casually in front of his desk and spoke so calmly he might have been commenting on the weather. It was only the distant rumble of thunder that told her he wasn't taking the news of her reckless assault on one of the Fallen with anything less than total aplomb.

"I've been looking for that vampire my whole damn life," she bit out, "and there she was, strolling right by me. I had to do something."

"It was the middle of the day. You were surrounded by dozens of tourists."

Her arms crossed. "I don't have forever to hunt her down. If I have to wait another twenty years to find her, I might not be physically capable of doing anything about it. I might not even be *alive*. It's now or never."

Adrian's flame blue gaze bored into her, searing her with its heat. "You've now exposed yourself to the Fallen. They're going to come after you."

"I hope they send *her*," Lindsay shot back defiantly. "Next time, I won't play with her. I'll just take her down."

Damien made a noise that drew her attention. "If you could have killed her, why didn't you?"

"Because I need to know where the other two assholes are. She was alone when I first saw her. I didn't see anyone with her until she was rescued. And, by the way, the guy driving the getaway vehicle had the same crazy crayon-colored spiked hair I remember from the day they attacked my mother. If she's still hanging with that dude, I'm guessing the other one isn't far away."

"The ramifications of what you've done are going to haunt us. We don't hunt the Fallen. We can't. Their punishment is to live with what they are."

"She wasn't suffering when she terrorized my mom; she was having a damn good time. That bloodsucking cunt doesn't deserve to live." She shot a look at Adrian, whose impassive face gave nothing away. Her stomach knotted. God, she didn't want to cause him any more trouble. But what could she have done? Her entire life had been built around avenging her mother. "She left me alive, so it's her stupid mistake that I'm hunting her now. I guess she figured that, as a human, I wasn't going to grow up to be a threat. But that should absolve you of any blame. I'm not one of you. I don't operate under the same rules. What I do shouldn't affect you."

"You had a lycan with you," Adrian reminded. "That involves us."

"So cut me loose." She hated the soft note of pleading in her voice. "I can't bring you anything but trouble. That's killing me, Adrian. It's breaking my heart."

With a harsh exhale, Adrian leaned his hip against his desk and wrapped his hands around the edge. "When Vash shoved you into Elijah, she could have just as easily punctured your rib cage with her fist and ripped out your heart. You're only breathing now because she let you go."

"Why the fuck would she do that? *Again?* I got the drop on her; I can do it again."

"That was Vash?" Elijah's growl rumbled through the room. "I want that hunt."

Lindsay glanced at him and gave a curt nod. Vash had taken people they loved from them, and it was time to make her pay.

Looking back at Adrian, Lindsay said, "You told me you'd help me hunt her down. You dug around in my brain. You knew who she was. Were you lying?"

"No. But we need to provoke them into attacking us, not launch a war ourselves. We can take defense, not offense. There are rules and there are ways around those rules—" His cell phone rang, drawing his attention to where the phone rested on his desk. Frowning, he said, "Excuse me."

He answered with a clipped "Mitchell."

As she watched, Adrian's face took on the hardness of stone. She could hear someone speaking rapidly, but couldn't make out the words. Elijah exhaled in a rush and stepped closer to her, as if to stand with her. Support her. A chilly sense of foreboding swept over her.

A long, drawn-out moment passed. Finally, Adrian nodded. "Yes. Stand by. I'll make the arrangements."

Putting the BlackBerry down with far too much care, Adrian swept his gaze from Damien to Elijah. A silent communication passed between them, and the two men moved to leave the room. Elijah's brief squeeze to her shoulder and Damien's pitying look tightened the cold knot of dread in her stomach.

"What is it?" she asked when the door shut, leaving her and Adrian alone in his office.

He stepped toward her and gripped her upper arms in gentle hands. "It's your father, Lindsay. He—"

"No." The floor fell away from her and she swayed.

Her chest felt as if it had just cracked open, the pain so excruciating she would have sunk to the floor if not for Adrian's hold.

"He was driving and swerved off the road. He hit a tree."

"Bullshit." Tears streamed down her face. "I don't fucking believe it. My dad handles cars like a pro. This is Vash's fault. She's Syre's second. She could order this."

Which made this partly her own fault.

His wings unfurled and wrapped around her, sheltering her. He caught her close, gripping her nape and hip to press her fully against him. "I can't rule that out. I'll investigate until I know for sure."

A broken, serrated noise filled the room. Lindsay realized she was sobbing, her entire body racked by violent quaking.

Adrian held her, his warmth penetrating from the outside and sinking into her. No—*he* was inside her. Inside her mind like before, curling around everything like insidious tendrils of smoke. Her agonized grief began to fade, the sharpest edges softened by a strange sense of comfort.

Lindsay wrenched away from him, stumbling backward before crumpling to the floor. "What the f-fuck are you doing?"

Crouching beside her, he reached to brush her hair away from her face. His eyes flickered with preternatural flame and glistened with tears. "Taking away your pain. I can't bear it."

"W-what? How . . . ?"

"I can pull the painful memories from you, *neshama*. I can heighten your recollection of the happy ones."

"Don't you dare!" She pushed to her feet, shoving

away his hand when he reached to steady her. "If you ever steal a memory from me, painful or not, I'll never forgive you."

"You can't resent the loss of something you don't remember."

How she remained standing when it felt like a glowing-hot poker was piercing her chest was a miracle. "If you care about me at all, you won't take away the events that shaped me into who I am today ... God—" She gripped her pounding head in her hands, her thoughts tumbling through her mind in a chaotic deluge. Her chest was heaving in its struggle for air, her sobs half crazed to her own ears. "I have to go. I can't stay here."

"Stay tonight," he said quietly. "Can you do that for me? You're in no condition to be alone now."

"Adrian—" She couldn't even see him through the rush of tears that burned her eyes and throat. They'd made love in this room, held each other for hours. It was fitting that she would face the punishment for that transgression in the same space. "We're killing each other. Every moment we spend together comes back to us in torment inflicted on people we love. We have to stay away from each other."

"Yes," he agreed quietly. "I'll let you go. But not tonight. Not like this. One night in my home, where I know you'll be safe. I won't disturb you. Can you give me that?"

"You promise to let me go?"

"Yes, *neshama sheli*. I promise."

She no longer wanted to know what that meant. It was all too painful, the sweet and hot intimacy they shared. She nodded in acquiescence to his request, her mouth too dry to allow her to speak.

He bowed his head slightly. "Thank you."

There was something in the severe austerity of his features that unsettled her. A hint of grim determination. But she couldn't take any more right now. She was falling apart, shattered by a blow she'd never recover from.

Daddy . . . .

Without another word, Lindsay left the office and shut the door behind her. She was a mess. Her life was a mess. And she was fucking up the lives of everyone around her.

She retreated to her room and crawled into bed, crying herself into dark, restless sleep.

Adrian packed an overnight bag with quiet deliberation. He set aside a week's worth of clothes, but didn't anticipate needing all of them. God willing, Syre would be dead within the next forty-eight hours.

There was so little time. Vash had recognized Lindsay as Shadoe; there was no other reason for why she would've allowed Lindsay to live. At this very moment, Syre knew his daughter had returned. The Fallen leader would be weighing his options. He'd be consulting those he trusted, gathering data, and deciding what to do with it. Adrian had to get to him before that decision was made.

Then he had to get to Vashti. The attack on Lindsay's mother had been so unlike Syre's second that it could only have been done as a message to Adrian. Vash had to have known Lindsay was Shadoe and anticipated his learning of the murder when they inevitably met. The few decades in between were nothing to an immortal, the wait inconsequential.

The question was: why? If she'd known who Lindsay

was that long ago, why not tell Syre? Adrian intended to get the answer directly from the source.

Damn it. He hated hunting like this—too poorly thought out, too hasty. That was why, in all of Shadoe's past incarnations, he'd waited for Syre to come to him. Better to face his opponent on his home turf, where every advantage was at his fingertips. But sometimes a swift, foolhardy strike was just what was needed to slip beneath an enemy's defenses. He prayed that was the case this time, because he was going for it. Because this time was different. Lindsay was different. *He* was different with her. That was worth whatever price he would pay.

His gaze darted to the clock on the nightstand. It was shortly before midnight. Blessedly, Lindsay had stopped crying around ten, then fallen asleep. Every sob from her room had cut him deeper and deeper until now his heart bled steadily. It had never been like this between them. In the past, she'd always swiftly wiled her way into his bed and stayed there. In any other incarnation, he'd be in her arms now. Holding her, making love to her, choosing not to rush the inevitable confrontation with Syre, so that he could steal one more day with the woman he loved.

Now he had a flight booked that would take him to Raceport in a few short hours. He was traveling alone, flying commercial, and arriving just after sunrise. The time of day wouldn't affect Syre, but it would limit the number of minions Adrian had to contend with.

He was shoving another henley into his bag when he heard her whimper. He stilled, his senses zeroing in on the woman who was sleeping in the room next door. The mattress sighed as she moved; then a soft, sultry moan drifted over his senses.

Gooseflesh spread across Adrian's skin. He moved

away from his bed, stepping closer to the wall, although proximity wasn't required. He could be up at the lycan barracks and still hear her breathing as if his ear were pressed to her chest.

She began panting, then writhing. Another whimper shook him.

Incapable of resisting her when their time together was nearly at an end, Adrian left his room and moved the short distance down the hall to her door. He released the lock with an impatient thought and entered.

Her bedroom was shrouded in darkness. The drapes were drawn to block the views of the city in the distance. He closed the door behind him and moved silently toward the bed, his vision seeing her as clearly as if every light were on.

Lindsay had kicked off the covers. She twisted on the bed with sensual abandon, the lush scent of her desire going to his head and intoxicating him. Her hands cupped her breasts, squeezing through the satin of the tank top that matched the thong she wore.

Her back arched, offering up her beautiful breasts like a gift.

"Adrian ..."

He sucked in a sharp breath at the erotic invitation in her voice. Reaching down, he rubbed the aching length of his erection through his slacks, his blood flowing hot and thick through his veins. He was so turned on by the willingness she displayed while sleeping, a willingness she denied him while awake because she cared for him. He understood the affection that motivated her. If she didn't love him, she wouldn't deny the needs that haunted her even in dreams.

Knowing he shouldn't, he willed his clothes into a

haphazard pile on the floor. The cool night air felt good against his heated skin, almost like a caress from her hands. Lindsay gave another soft moan. His knee settled on the bed.

As the mattress dipped with his weight, her eyes flew open.

"Adrian," she whispered, rolling swiftly into his arms.

He groaned as her mouth pressed ardently to his, her tongue thrusting with a hunger that made his cockhead slick with wanting her. She pushed him back, tossing one silken leg across his hips and reaching between them to grip his cock in her slender hand. His neck arched with the pleasure of her touch, of her desire, of her lust given without reserve for the very first time.

She pressed down, the humid warmth of her sex soaking through the satin of her thong and searing the sensitive skin of his erection. Needing to feel her skin bare against his, he fisted her underwear, ripping it off her body. A hard shiver moved through him at how wet she was. The petal-soft feel of her denuded lips stroking along his length nearly brought him to climax.

"*Ani rotza otha,* Adrian." She purred, gliding her slick sex back and forth over him.

I want you.

He froze, his heart stilling in his chest. He knew that seductive tone all too well. "Shadoe?"

She reared up, her hands sliding into Lindsay's sexy blond curls, undulating Lindsay's body as she weaved her sensual spell over him.

But it was no longer lust he felt as Shadoe's soul stared back at him from Lindsay's beautiful face.

A shivering exhalation left him.

She'd lured him like this the very first time. It started

with a stolen kiss. Then the taste of her breasts, offered up to him with both of her hands, the dark brown nipples peaked tight in the open air. He'd begged her to leave him in peace, to respect the very law he had enforced on her father. He'd begged her to be strong for him because he had been so weak over her.

Instead, she'd grown bolder with every month that passed. She had played with her body in front of him, deliberately haunting the places he frequented, teasing him with the sight of her glistening fingers pushing in and out of her pouting sex until she climaxed with his name on her lips. He'd resisted her until she threatened to take a lover to her bed, then made sure he stumbled upon her fondling another man's cock through his clothes. Angry, possessive, tempted beyond reason, Adrian had given her what she'd been asking him for, taking her on the ground like an animal in heat. And once he'd fallen, there had been no turning back.

"Ani rotza otha," she said again, her hips rocking almost violently over him, riding him toward orgasm.

"No, *tzel.*"

He caught her by the hips and rolled her off him, then moved away. Gaining his feet, he ran his hands through his hair, painfully aroused by the feel of Lindsay, the scent of her, the sound of her voice.

But it wasn't Lindsay who called to him from the bed behind him.

"Ani ohevet otchah," Shadoe whispered, rustling the sheets with sinuous movements.

I love you.

Adrian squeezed his eyes shut. His wings burst free and flexed angrily. He should have known better. Lindsay would never seduce him. She would have denied him, as she'd been trying to do from the beginning. For his sake. Because she loved him.

He willed his clothes back on, then shoved his hands through his hair. When Shadoe's hand touched his bare shoulder, he grabbed it and spun, facing her.

"Take me," she whispered, standing naked before him, possessing the body that so perfectly fit his, that held him so sweetly, that gave him such pleasure he wept with the power of it.

It was only a shell without the woman he loved inside it.

Adrian cupped Lindsay's face in his hands, looking into her eyes, the windows to a soul that wasn't her own. Bending his head, he pressed his lips to hers, softly, chastely, his heart aching for the woman he'd once loved long ago. A woman so beautiful, fierce, and seductive she'd lured an angel to fall. He had loved her with hot, saturating abandon.

But Shadoe's time had passed, and he had since fallen in love with someone else. A mortal whose love was self-lessly given. A woman who accepted him just as he was, including the law and rules that had forged him yet also forbid them to be together.

His thumbs brushed over her cheekbones, and he pressed his forehead to hers. "I'm going to free you, Shadoe. I'm going to let you go."

"I want you," she said again, reaching between them for his flagging erection.

Adrian arched his hips away from her touch and sent a rush of languidness through Lindsay's body. He caught her as she sagged unconscious, lifting her and carrying her to the bed. He could do nothing about the thong he'd destroyed in the extremity of his need, so he covered her with the sheet. Brushing her hair back from her face, he kissed her forehead.

"Lindsay." He nuzzled his lips across her perspiration-damp skin. "Soon it will all be over."

He straightened and left the room with a purpose-driven stride. The beating of his heart was quick and heavy, but his mind was clear for the first time in ages.

The weight of the past dissipated along with his wings.

As he undressed again and stepped beneath a cold shower, it all washed away—the guilt and pain, the sorrow and remorse.

Why won't you let me save you? Lindsay had asked, unaware that she already had saved him in the most fundamental of ways. She'd given him the strength he'd lacked, and a sweet, precious love. There was so much she could teach him about how to love from the inside out. His biggest regret was that he'd never have the chance to follow her lead.

But at least he could free her from his past. All the fear and indecision that had plagued him for centuries was gone. He was no longer debating the wisdom of his decision to strike first, within enemy territory. Lindsay was unhappy and Adrian couldn't bear it. He couldn't stand being the cause of her pain. If it was in his power to end her suffering, he had to try.

All these years, he'd wanted to spare himself further self-recriminations. Instead of allowing Shadoe the peace of an honorable death in battle, he'd selfishly tried to bind her to him with immortality. It was not his place to intercede once the Creator decided it was time for someone to die, and his punishment for doing so had been long and agonizing. He'd intended to end the cycle as much for himself as for Shadoe.

Now he would act for Lindsay alone. He would give her back the life that should have been hers. A life of normalcy. A chance to be happy. The opportunity to find a man who would love her without all the chains that bound Adrian to his duty.

It was a gift he could give to her without strings. It wasn't equal to the gift she'd given him, but it would be given selflessly and out of a deep love, the likes of which he'd never known before.

CHAPTER 21

The moment Lindsay awoke, she knew Adrian was gone. The feeling of emptiness inside her was so pervasive, it was gnawing. She moved to leave the bed and realized she was nude. For a second, she wondered why. Then the memories hit her in a rush.

I'm going to let you go.

Soon it will all be over ...

With a gasp, she bent at the waist, her rib cage gripped in a vise of excruciating heartbreak. Her father was dead. *Daddy.*

And she knew, as only a woman in love could know, that Adrian didn't intend to ever see her again.

Her eyes closed, but tears leaked free. She'd lost the two most important individuals in her life at the same time. As she rocked with the pain, the echoes of her dreams came back to haunt her. She felt the burning desire coursing through her, so hot and powerful she couldn't resist it. Instead she had embraced it, amplified it, taken fierce pleasure in making Adrian bend like a reed beneath it. The power she'd felt in garnering his capitulation against his will had been heady and addictive. And sickening. She had felt almost as if she was watching herself from the outside, unable to control her own wild impulses. When Adrian had turned away from her, she'd been so relieved for both of them. So grateful that he possessed the strength she lacked.

But he hadn't turned away for a moment. He'd turned away from her forever. His voice in her dreams had been devoid of the aching tenderness she had become accustomed to feeling in it.

A half-crazed, half-sobbing laugh escaped her.

Pushing to her feet, Lindsay straightened and knew she had to get her head on straight. She had to return to Raleigh, and she expected to stay there for a while. She needed to get her bearings, figure out where she was going from here. She needed to regroup, then plan for how to hunt down Vash. The desire for vengeance was so pervasive she could barely think beyond it. That was a blessing in a way. Revenge gave her something to focus on beside her debilitating grief.

She showered and dressed. When she made the bed, she found her shredded panties. Whether she'd ripped them off herself in the throes of her erotic dream or Adrian had actually been with her and done it, the end result was the same—it was over between them.

"Be careful what you wish for," she muttered, wondering why she didn't just learn to stop wishing for things at all.

She stepped out onto the wraparound deck, noting from the position of the sun in the sky that it was late morning. There were no angels flying; no clouds, either.

It was a beautiful day, the kind Southern Californians enjoyed most of the year.

Lost in her misery, Lindsay took a set of stairs leading down the side of the hill to a smaller deck a few hundred yards below. From there, the city view was lost, leaving one with the impression that they were alone in the far reaches of the native SoCal landscape.

She set her elbows on the railing and began searching the contacts list on her cell phone. There were so many calls and arrangements to make. She made herself go through the motions, despite feeling so hollow and cold inside. Dead.

A massive winged shadow swept over her.

An angel's shadow, followed by the rustling of feathers as the Sentinel landed behind her. Feeling a desperate, futile hope that it might be Adrian and not wanting to let go of it, she hesitated a second before turning to face her companion.

A hand touched her shoulder.

"Good morn—" she began.

She fell into unconsciousness before she finished the greeting.

Adrian rolled into Raceport on a Harley he'd purchased just an hour before. It was early afternoon. Most of the minions were ensconced in the darkness somewhere, sleeping. Unfortunately, Raceport had one of the highest concentrations of Fallen in the country. After all this time, they still hovered around Syre like moths to a flame, even though they'd all already been burned and disfigured.

If he had a contingent of Sentinels with him or a pack of lycans, he'd be in a much better position. But even with the need for success being paramount, Adrian refused to involve anyone in his personal vendetta. This was his battle. The consequences for what he was about to do would fall on his shoulders alone.

He backed his bike into a spot directly in front of the general store. Syre's office was above it, as Adrian knew from vigilant and constant surveillance of the area—just as Angels' Point was watched. It was all part of the careful dance between them, the need to maintain a balance even as everything shifted and moved around them.

Dismounting, he withdrew a shotgun from its holster on the bike. He wore a pistol and a dagger strapped to each thigh, and his spine tingled with the need to employ his most powerful weapons. The rage of angels pumped hot and hard through his veins.

Before he reached the bottom step of the exterior staircase leading up to the Fallen leader's office, Adrian knew something was off. Raceport was crowded as always, due to its reputation for being a mecca for motorcycle enthusiasts from all over the country, but very few people glanced twice at him. Even when a group of chaps-wearing women across the street catcalled and whistled to him, it didn't divert much attention his way. If Syre had been nearby, security would be as tight as what Adrian employed at Angels' Point.

Grim faced and determined, he climbed the stairs without incident and stepped into the hallway at the top.

Two shadowy figures rushed toward him. He took them down with bullets, unable to utilize his wings in such a small space. Two more came up behind him just before he reached Syre's office. He threw open the door and darted in, hearing a scream from one of his pursuers as sunlight flooded the hallway behind him.

Kicking the door shut, Adrian shoved a chair beneath

the knob, all without taking his eyes or his pistol barrel off the vampress seated at Syre's desk.

"Hello, Adrian," she muttered, her lips curved in a smile that didn't reach her eyes. Sunlight fell over her pale bare arms and chocolate-colored hair. Her amber eyes glittered like tiger's-eye, but he remembered when they'd been blue like his own.

"Raven."

"He's not here."

"I can see that."

"He's not even in Virginia."

He moved to the closet door, opened it, and shot a cursory glance inside.

"It's just you and me," she assured. "And I have orders not to kill you."

"Ah. So we're playing by the same rules."

She stood in a singularly graceful movement, revealing an ultrashort denim skirt that she wouldn't be able to bend over in without exposing herself. Her top was gingham and tied in a knot between her full breasts, giving her a country-girl appearance he was sure went over well with the men visiting the area.

Rounding the desk, she trailed the fingertips of her right hand down her left arm and looked up at him beneath long, thick lashes. "You look good, Adrian. Real good. Having sex suits you."

He smiled, used to this game. The Fallen liked to taunt Sentinels with their sexuality. It was as if they wanted to flaunt the reason for their fall, as well as goad beings known for their abstinence. "Where is he?"

"What's the rush?" She sidled closer, licking her lower lip.

He whipped out his wing, forcing her to spin away to

avoid getting sliced. She ended up sprawled facedown atop the desk. He had her hands pinned behind her back before she could retaliate.

Bending over her, he hissed in her ear, "Where is he?"

"You don't have to manhandle me," she shot back, struggling. "He wants me to tell you."

Adrian knew why. His stomach knotted. "He's on his way to California."

"Actually," she purred malevolently, grinning, "he's already there."

Syre turned away from the bed upon which his daughter slept and exited out into the living room of the two-room hotel suite he'd reserved in Irvine. Torque sat on the couch with his elbows on his knees and his fingers steepled together beneath his chin. Vash paced restlessly.

"She's brainwashed," she hissed. "I don't know how long Adrian has had her, but he's trained her well. She tried to kill me!"

Torque met his gaze and shrugged. "I didn't see her in action, but I patched up Vash's wounds. Shadoe did a number on her."

Vash's long hair swayed around her hips with her agitated movements. "I don't think you have time to talk it out with her. It'll take years to deprogram her, and the lycan who was with her is the one who snatched Nikki."

Torque growled.

Syre ran a hand through his hair. His phone had beeped with a text message an hour before, telling him Adrian had made an appearance in Raceport. By now the Sentinel leader knew Lindsay Gibson was out of his safekeeping and a search would have been mounted. They didn't have long before it would be impossible to leave the state without Adrian knowing about it. If Syre hadn't Changed Shadoe by then, nothing would save them.

"You might have to turn her first," Torque said, "then explain later. Once she's back to being Shadoe, she won't have reason to hate us anymore. She'll remember what we are to her."

Syre moved to the adjoining door and waved them out. "Go. Both of you. Leave me alone with her."

"That's not wise," Vash said. "She might try to kill you."

"Without the lycan here to tell her what I am, how will she know?"

"You're assuming she can't tell. But I saw her run—watched her leap over a damn eight-foot-high wall. She's not entirely mortal, whatever the hell she smells like."

She smelled like Adrian, which turned Syre's stomach. He was ready for her to know why she'd suffered all these years. He was ready for her to remember just how much Adrian's desire had cost her.

"Then Shadoe is close to the surface in Lindsay Gibson," he said. "And I'm safer than you give her credit for. Now go. Help Torque track the lycan. Let's try to tie up all the loose ends we can while we're here."

They shuffled out the door into the connecting room, with Vash sending him a scowl over her shoulder. He turned the lock behind them, smiling. Vash hated to be bested in anything. That she'd been bested by a student of hers was chafing her mightily. If Lindsay Gibson hadn't been the vessel carrying his daughter, she'd be dead now.

He heard the soft creak of the mattress in the bedroom and turned to face the door leading into it, his heart thudding violently in his chest. He'd never been this close to having her back. Adrian had always kept her close, waiting for Syre to break down and come for her. The Sentinel had no idea how many attempts Syre had made over the years. Adrian was too precise, too methodical—a machine. It was next to impossible to break his code. But something was different this time. Something had prompted him to act rashly, to allow her out into the open, to leave her alone . . . It had to be Lindsay Gibson herself and how close Shadoe was to the surface in her. Maybe that's what Adrian had been waiting for all this time.

She appeared in the doorway, her gaze as sharp as a hawk's. A predator's gaze. The gaze of a huntress. It lit on him first, then swept around the relatively small space. "What are you?"

"How precise do you want me to be?"

He saw the shadow of confusion sweep across her features. She looked nothing like him, nothing like her mother or brother, whose Asian heritage was evident in their skin tone and sloe eyes. But something in her recognized him, and that perplexed her.

"Very," she said.

"I'm Syre. A vampire"—his mouth curved gently, with genuine affection—"and your father."

Lindsay stared at the seriously hot man standing a few feet away from her . . .

. . . and broke into crazed laughter that bubbled up from the stew of emotions inside her. She laughed until tears came to her eyes and coursed down her cheeks. She laughed until her chest was racked with harsh, hiccoughing sobs.

Syre, who actually managed to look alarmed, took a

tentative step toward her. She lifted up her hand to hold him off.

He stopped. The leader of the vampires, who'd somehow kidnapped her from Angels' Point, stopped at her uplifted hand.

He deferred to her. And she *knew* him.

It was a quiet surety inside her. She knew the fallen angel who stood across the room from her, looking far too young to be her father. He was gorgeous. Tall and elegant, like a Sentinel, but much darker. Definitely dangerous. Not just in his looks, although those were dark and dangerous, too. His black hair and caramel-hued skin were paired with eyes the color of toffee, making him stunning in a wholly exotic way.

God, the thought of him squaring off against Adrian was insane to her. They were too evenly matched.

"Where are we?" she asked, recognizing the brand of the hotel by its signature layout but unsure of where the property was located.

"Irvine."

"Why?"

He gestured for her to have a seat. As she did with Adrian, she felt an inexplicable pull to the suave vampire leader. She didn't trust it—didn't trust him. Vampires lured victims with seduction and a lulling sense of false security.

Lindsay moved to the wet bar instead and pulled the corkscrew out of the drawer. As far as weapons went, it was laughable. But beggars couldn't be choosy.

"There's no need to defend yourself against me, *tzel*," he murmured, taking a seat at the small dining table as if he had no concerns in the world.

"Don't call me that," she snapped, hating to hear

Adrian's term of endearment for her on another man's lips.

"Why not? It's your name."

Swallowing hard, she fought another wave of dizziness and intense déjà vu, so familiar now after the last few weeks but no less disconcerting. "My name is Lindsay Gibson. My father's name is—was—Eddie Gibson."

"Those things are true ... in regard to your mortal body." His amber eyes watched her with undeniable intensity. "But you carry the soul of my daughter Shadoe inside you."

Lindsay felt the blood drain from her face.

"Did you think it was just a pet name Adrian had for you?" Syre's slightly raspy voice was mesmerizing. "An endearment perhaps?"

His direct hit struck her hard.

"Ah, I see that you did." His smile was smugly knowing. "I bet he took one look at you and there was no getting away from him. He focused on you with an all-consuming intensity, didn't he? He pursued you swiftly and with a determination you couldn't deny. He treated you like the most precious thing in the world. And when a seraph like Adrian puts his mind to something, he never fails."

Leaning heavily into the countertop, she set one hand over her roiling stomach and tried to regulate her breathing.

"You're a beautiful woman, Lindsay. I'm sure he was sincerely attracted to the packaging. But the woman he covets is inside you—my daughter—and he's been keeping us apart since the dawn of time."

"That's not possible," she whispered through dry lips. "I'm not possessed by someone else's spirit."

His chin lifted. "So how do you explain your speed? How do you explain the first question you asked when you walked into this room—'*What* are you?' not '*Who* are you.' You felt the power in me with senses beyond the few afforded to your mortal body."

She stared at him, her right leg beginning to twitch and shake with her growing disquiet.

"You're wondering how it's possible," he said, still in that low, captivating tone. "You see, Shadoe was fatally wounded. You were a huntress even then. Adrian loved you so much, he couldn't bear to lose you. I'd already discovered that I could share immortality with others, and he brought you to me on the brink of death, begging me to save you."

Lindsay didn't realize she was crying until she felt the drops hitting her chest.

"I didn't hesitate," he went on. "I began the process of Changing you."

"Into a vampire?" She was sickened by the thought.

He gave a soft, humorless laugh. "Adrian's reaction was the same. He thought I could heal you without Changing you. You were too far gone for his blood to do the trick, but he'd heard that the Change took individuals to the very precipice of death, and he thought I could pull you back from it. Which I could, but as a vampire. When he realized what you would become, he finished you himself with a blade through the heart."

She flinched imagining what that would have cost Adrian—to kill the woman he loved in order to save her. But she understood it, too. Like her, every blow he'd been dealt in his life had come from a vampire. Of course he would rather lose his love than have her become a soulless, bloodsucking creature.

"But it was already too late. You were a naphil, one of the nephalim—a child born to a mortal and an angel. Your soul was stronger than a mere human's. It had the strength of an angel's, but without the weakness of wings. I'd given you just enough of my blood to immortalize that inhuman part of you before Adrian killed your body. So you've returned again and again, always in a different vessel but still my daughter."

Still the woman Adrian loved. A woman that wasn't her.

Her spine straightened. "A pretty s-story, but I don't believe you."

"Why would I lie?"

"To turn me against Adrian."

He made a soft *tsk*ing noise. "On the contrary, I can give him back to you. Fully, completely. I know you want that. I can see how much you love him."

"What are you saying?"

Pushing to his feet, he stepped closer. "I can finish the Change, Lindsay. I can give you immortality and re-awaken the soul in you that Adrian loves. I can take away the mortality that makes you forbidden to him. Everything can be what it should have been."

She laughed, but it came out a broken and painful cry. "Of course. Take Adrian's woman and make her a vampire. The ultimate revenge for the loss of your wings. It must kill you to see those crimson tips on his pretty feathers. It must be an agonizing reminder of how he mutilated you."

Syre was unfazed by her venomous outburst. "I didn't expect you to believe me. Will you believe him?"

Her heart stopped. "What are you saying?"

"Call him." His beautiful eyes glittered like gemstones. "Ask him yourself."

CHAPTER 22

Elijah watched the gates of the Navajo Lake pack entrance pass by the rear windows of the black Suburban he was in. He couldn't shake off the coiling apprehension rippling through him. Although Damien had assured him he wasn't being held responsible for Lindsay's abduction—which had technically happened under the Sentinels' watch—he'd been immediately returned to Navajo Lake instead of being allowed to assist in the hunt for her. All of Adrian's pack was being sent to the Lake and a new pack was being formed.

The extreme scope of that act spoke of deep suspicion. Lindsay had been taken from the Point, which meant someone there was undeniably involved. Quarantining the lycans appeared to be the first step in the attempt to find the culprits.

Despite understanding the precariousness of his own situation, Elijah's greatest fear was for Lindsay. Once he'd learned the identity of the vamp she'd attacked, his stomach had bottomed out. Vash had already been hunting him because of the blood in Shreveport; then Lindsay had been spotted with him—in the midst of launching an attack of her own. No matter how he looked at it, it looked bad for his friend. Real fucking bad. He doubted Lindsay would survive the day, if she wasn't already dead.

And he was states away, unable to help her. The beast inside him was pacing restlessly, growling its desire to be slipped free of its leash. If he weren't an Alpha, he would have lost control hours ago. As it was, he was debating mutiny for the first time in his life. He didn't have enough friends to callously disregard losing one, and Lindsay was special to him—she'd already proven she would die to save his ass. He had yet to return the favor.

The Suburban rolled to a stop in the center of the outpost. Elijah climbed out. A half dozen full-sized vans pulled up in a line behind the SUV, and the rest of Adrian's pack emptied into the courtyard.

Jason approached him. "You got here quickly. Good. I've narrowed the suspect pool to six individuals. One of them is responsible for stealing your blood. I thought you might like to question them."

Elijah stared at the Sentinel through his sunglasses, instantly put on guard by the show of camaraderie. Jason saw little value in lycans. They were occasionally useful, but always expendable—treated worse than dogs at times.

The Sentinel patted him on the back and smiled. "I thought you'd be pleased. Instead you're scowling at me."

Catching on, Elijah twisted away from the Sentinel's touch. He was being shown off as a lycan who was more connected to the angels than he was to his own kind. That was why they'd had him ride in the Suburban. That was why he was being singled out by Jason now. Elijah had thought they were keeping him close in preparation for punishment.

And he'd been right, just not in the way he'd expected.

Moving back toward the other members of Adrian's pack, he found them eyeing him with defiance and determination.

Rachel stepped forward and hissed. "Do you think you're one of them?"

"You're a smart girl, Rach. You know they're playing you and me both. They're playing all of us."

Jonas stepped closer. "You're Alpha, Elijah. What are you going to do about it?"

The impetuous young lycan gestured at the thirty-foot-high log fence around them. "If I were Alpha, I'd tear this place apart."

"And go where?" Elijah challenged.

Rachel's eyes glittered. "I don't know what you're afraid of, El. But you're going to have to make a decision about which side you're standing with. Don't let Micah's death be in vain."

"You can't put that on me."

"It's *all* on you," she said coldly. "More than you know."

He opened his mouth to retort, but she shifted and howled. The rest of the pack altered their forms en masse, circling him in a blatant show of subservience. The Sentinels nearby unfurled their wings, their eyes aflame.

Jason stepped closer, with his wings curled forward in the familiar battle-ready pose. "Elijah—"

The pack responded to the implied threat to their Alpha—a threat they'd instigated—by lunging forward in a writhing sea of multicolored fur.

Shouts shattered the mountain's tranquility. Angels took to the air. Lycans in lupine form poured from splintered doorways and shattered windows in an endless wave. Shots rang out and howls rent the air.

Elijah stood in the middle of utter chaos, watching everything he knew crumbling into pools of blood and fur and feathers. Screams reverberated through him, echoing in his horrified mind.

A bullet pierced his shoulder, the tiny bit of silver in it sizzling his flesh like acid. The lycans grew more frenzied and ferocious in reaction to the smell of his blood. With the choice taken from him, Elijah shifted and leaped into the fray, hoping to save as many lives as he could.

Adrian looked out of Syre's office windows at the town below. His blood had gone cold with trepidation. With every second that passed, he felt himself spiraling deeper into a primal state of rage.

His cell phone vibrated on the desktop. He felt Raven's wary eyes on him as he lifted it to his ear. "Mitchell."

"Adrian."

His breath exploded from his chest. "Lindsay! Where are you? Are you hurt?"

"Would you prefer to call me *tzel*?" she asked softly.

He sank into Syre's chair. "What did he tell you?"

"A long story, but the gist is that I carry the woman you love inside me. Is that true?"

He hesitated a moment, feeling the underlying pain in her voice. "You carry Shadoe's soul in you, yes."

Raven watched him avidly from the chair in the corner, her eyes sparkling with malicious glee.

"That's why you came up to me in the airport."

"At first it was for her," he admitted. "But that

changed. What's grown between us since then is because of you, Lindsay."

"In a few short weeks you got over the woman you've loved for ages and fell for me?" She made a choked noise, a sound so agonized his heart broke at the sound of it. "Forgive me if I don't believe you."

"I can prove it to you. Tell me where you are, how to find you. If I take Syre down, Shadoe's soul will be freed. It will just be you and me."

"But you said good-bye to me yesterday, Adrian. Not in so many words, but it was the end all the same. Is this why?"

"No, damn it." His hand fisted around a pen on the desktop. "It's because once I kill Syre, your body and soul will be your own. You won't feel evil around you anymore. You won't sense beings that aren't human. You won't have physical attributes that you'll have to hide. You can be normal. Lead a normal life. Enjoy all the precious mortal things you haven't had time for."

There was a long silence filled only with the sounds of their mutual labored breathing. He heard a door close on her end of the line. "Syre says he can fix this. He can make it right."

Adrian leaned forward. "Don't listen to him. He'll tell you whatever he has to in order to get what he wants."

"He says if he completes the Change, you can have Shadoe back. Forever this time. Immortally."

"Fuck no." The room spun around him. "That's not what I want."

"Isn't it? All those centuries ... all those incarnations ... You've found her and loved her. And lost her—over and over again. Now there's a chance to stop all that."

"He's wrong, Lindsay." Adrian heard the hoarseness

of his voice, the brutal desperation, and wondered why she couldn't. "He thinks Shadoe's naphil soul—a soul that's part angel—is stronger than yours. When she was alive, perhaps that was true. But she's not. She's a stowaway in *your* body. Your soul has a stronger hold on your physical form than hers does. You're not like the other incarnations of her. You feel her impulses, but you can ignore them. You have always been *you* since the moment we met. If you let Syre finish the Change, her soul will be freed, yours will die, and what will be left is a bloodsucking vampire. You don't want that. I don't want that for you."

He heard a soft sob.

"Lindsay." His eyes burned. His lungs were on fire. "Please. Please don't do this. Let me come to you, talk to you. You've been through a lot in the last twenty-four hours. You're reeling from your father's death—justifiably so. You need time to think. Time to heal. Let me be there for you, as you've been there for me."

"I don't need to think about this. No matter which way things go with the Change, you'll finally be free. Whether you're free with her or without her, this horrible cycle you've suffered through will finally be over."

The pen snapped in his hand. Black ink burst across the desk. "I can do the same thing by killing Syre. He started the Change; he's the only one who can finish it. Let me do it my way. Let me take care of this."

"Adrian—"

"I love you, Lindsay. *You.* Not her. I did love her once, but not anymore. Not like I used to. Not for a long time, I realized last night. And never like I love you. I'm begging you . . . with everything I am—with everything that belongs to you—don't do this."

"I believe you love me," she whispered, so quietly he barely heard her. "As much as you're able. But that's just another reason to finish this. As long as I'm out there somewhere, you're never going to be able to let me go—I can hear it in your voice. You're going to bash yourself against the rocks over and over until you're completely broken. I can't let you do it. At least once I've Changed, you'll let me go. You won't want me as a vampire."

Adrian shoved to his feet, his BlackBerry cracking under the strain of his grip. "Lindsay!"

"I love you, Adrian. Good-bye."

Lindsay stepped out of the bedroom, freshly showered and feeling cleansed inside and out. Syre waited patiently at the dining table. She had the feeling he was the type of man who could sit absolutely still for hours, waiting, his patience infinite and unyielding. So much control and power—it radiated from him as it did from Adrian. Adrian, whose beautiful voice had slashed and whipped with the force of his emotions. She was making him more human by the day, weakening him when he needed to be the strongest. Seeing Syre face-to-face proved that to her more than anything else. The vampire leader was a formidable force to be reckoned with, and his second was a homicidal manic. In the days ahead, Adrian would have to be at the top of his game in order to survive.

"Are you ready?" He stood in a display of sleek fluidity and grace.

She nodded. "Yes. I'm ready."

He gestured for her to return to the bedroom.

"Can you tell me what's going to happen?" she asked, lying on the bed as directed. Her heart was racing so violently she thought she might have a heart attack.

The vampire leader sat on the bed beside her and took her hand in his. He met her gaze directly, his perfect features soft with affection. Just looking at him told her what a stunner Shadoe must have been. An exotic beauty whose love had enslaved Adrian forever.

"I'm going to drink from you." His voice was as warm and intoxicating as heated brandy. "I'm going to drain you to the brink of death. Then I'm going to fill you back up with the blood from my veins and it's going to Change you."

"My soul will die."

He looked for a moment like he might lie to her. Then he nodded. "Mortal souls don't survive the Change. But if it's any consolation, I think Shadoe will have absorbed some of you over the time you two have been together. You might continue to exist in that way. I don't think you'll be completely lost."

"But you don't know."

"No," he agreed. "You are unique."

She exhaled a shaky breath. "Okay. I'm ready."

Syre brushed the hair back from her forehead. "You really love him. I wish I understood why. Every time you come back, you love him all over again."

Her eyes closed. "Please. Just get this over with."

She felt the humidity of his spice-scented breath against her wrist, then the sharp sting of his bite.

Lindsay floated in an oddly warm miasma. Like a swimmer on her back, she drifted languidly, all sense of time and urgency gone.

Around her, waves of memories rose and crested. Some were hers; most were not. She sifted through them with a lush fascination, watching reels of events like movies. So many versions of herself, as if she were the only actress in an endless play with multiple characters, settings, and time periods.

In the back of her mind, she registered a distant burning. Around her, smoke and fire licked along the shores of her memories, making the water boil until it was uncomfortable against her bare flesh. She tried to twist away, then to dip beneath the waters, but below the surface there was no bottom. There was only an endless void and the tickling sensation of that abyss suckling at her toes, luring her downward.

She broke the surface and returned to her horizontal position, keeping her legs away from the seductive pull below.

There was no escaping the growing heat.

"It'll go away soon."

Turning her head in search of the speaker, Lindsay discovered a woman floating nearby. An exotic and breathtaking woman. A woman whose rich beauty would make a stunning pairing with Adrian's dark magnificence.

"Shadoe."

Shadoe's mouth curved. "Hello, Lindsay."

She reached out and they linked fingers. A swift rush of cooling relief raced up Lindsay's arm from the contact. Her mind filled with images of Syre and a beautiful Asian woman. They were laughing. Playing. Chasing two young giggling children through a field of tall grasses. Syre had wings. Great, magnificent wings of azure blue that perfectly matched the color of his irises. They spread and stretched in a visible manifestation of his joy. He lifted the little girl high and kissed her forehead. Lindsay felt the press of those lips against her own skin, felt the rush of paternal love that accompanied it as if it were for her.

Syre set Shadoe down and chased his son, an adorable boy with chubby arms and legs. Shadoe moved to where her mother was laying out a picnic. She sat on the edge of the blanket and tossed small pieces of some kind of vegetable near the edge of the clearing, where the grasses began their domination of the landscape.

A small rabbitlike creature appeared, soft, fluffy, and white. It followed the vegetable trail to Shadoe, who stroked its trusting head with her fingertips. When the creature grew bolder and reared up to set its front paws on Shadoe's thigh, she laughed with delight and scooped it up like Syre had done to her only moments before. She nuzzled her freckled nose against the sweet animal's, then buried her face in its neck.

The creature's scream startled Lindsay so violently she jerked and sank beneath the waves. The memory slid away from her, getting caught in the churning surf near the burning shoreline, but not before Lindsay caught the ripe smell of blood and the beauty of crimson soaking into pristine white. Like Adrian's wings.

She kicked her way back up to the surface, gasping with a mixture of fear, fascination, and building hunger. The scent of the creature's blood drove her wild. Her mouth watered with the desire to drink it greedily the way Shadoe had.

Shadoe smiled at Lindsay's sputtering breaths. The naphil floated gracefully on her back with her hands tucked behind her head. Her dark hair fanned outward, as did the transparent gauzy skirts of her dress. She looked like a nymph, beautiful and seductive.

"You were already a vampire," Lindsay accused.

"No. The nephalim thirsted for blood before the Watchers fell. Our angel halves needed the energy found in the life force of others." There was no horror or remorse in the woman's voice. No shame or embarrassment.

Lindsay struggled to make sense of it all. The raging heat was slowly fading and languidness returned to her. She felt like taking a nap, like sinking into the silken embrace of the memories around her.

"He's loved me forever," Shadoe said casually. "Obsessively."

"I know."

New recollections lapped over her. She recognized some of them from her dreams. They made sense now. Every image and scene held Adrian in moments of lust and passion. Lindsay watched with a sharp, ferocious jealousy. She closed her eyes but still found no relief. The memories were in her head, her mind. Whispering. Crooning. Pleading. She was about to dive beneath the waves just to get away from them when she saw herself. She stilled her restless thrashing and took it all in, reliving the tender moments she'd shared with Adrian.

I need you, tzel.

Pain seared her at the understanding of what that meant: while making love to her, he'd been thinking of someone else.

The reminiscences continued unabated, giving her no peace.

Take me, neshama sheli.

She cried at the heated emotion radiating from Adrian as he asked her to take everything he offered her.

"What does that mean?" she asked Shadoe in a voice made husky by heartbreak and longing. "'*Neshama sheli*'?"

"It means 'my soul.' It's an endearment."

Lindsay absorbed that. As the memories swirled around her, spinning faster and faster until a vortex formed in a downward spiral, she noted how his endearments for her changed as their relationship progressed. Toward the end, he referred to her only as his soul. Not Shadoe's. His.

No, tzel. *I'm going to free you. I'm going to let you go . . .*

He'd been saying good-bye to Shadoe, not her.

Lindsay kicked upward, fighting the voracious sucking of the whirlpool. She was screaming, shouting for help, drowning with the sudden realization of how poorly she'd interpreted her dreams the night before.

Adrian loved her. And god knew she was crazy enough about him to die for his happiness. Which appeared to be what she was to him—the woman who made him happy.

She wouldn't give him up. She refused. He knew her inside and out. From the beginning, he'd allowed her to choose which direction she wanted to travel, and whichever road she chose—the hotel or the hunt, with or without him—he had made accommodations to allow her that freedom while still keeping her safe. She could be herself with him and he would love her that way. Cherish her.

With all her might, Lindsay fought the relentless pull of the now glowing abyss below her, but the cyclonic recollections around her rose higher and higher, and the reels of images in the sky above her seemed farther and farther away.

"Shadoe!" she yelled. "You'll never have all of him. Never again."

An arm shot out and grasped her wrist. Shadoe

leaned over the lip of the vortex, her long black hair hanging in a satiny curtain around her lovely face.

"Part of him belongs to me now." Lindsay whimpered, her shoulder separating from its socket as she was pulled in two directions. "You don't strike me as the type of woman who's willing to share."

"And you are?"

Lindsay's jaw tightened against the pain. "I'll take whatever I can have of him," she bit out. "If he thinks of you sometimes, I can live with that. Can you live with him making love to my body when he's with you?"

Shadoe's sloe eyes narrowed. Then her lush red lips curved in a smile. She released Lindsay's arm, and Lindsay fell toward the radiant light below.

"Shadoe."

Her rival dived into the vortex, racing past Lindsay with her arms outstretched and her hands clasped together in a narrow blade. She cut through the light and disappeared inside it. Instantly the whirlpool's direction changed, surging upward. As the moving pictures above Lindsay rushed down to meet her, she held her breath and closed her eyes.

She was spit out of the tempest with a gasping breath of cognizance.

Jackknifing up, Lindsay woke in a strange bed. She blinked at finding Kent Magus sitting in a chair beside her.

"Kent?" she queried, realizing she was drenched with sweat. So much sweat that the comforter and sheets beneath her were soaked with it, too. Something hard rattled around in her mouth. She spit it out, then another one. She winced at the sight of her two human canine teeth in her palm. "What are you doing in my dream?"

Kent stared at her, then frowned. "Lindsay . . . ? Where's Shadoe?"

"*You* have the hots for her, too?" Her gaze narrowed. Kent's handsome features echoed the woman's she had just said good-bye to in her mind . . . or soul—wherever. "She's gone. Not coming back. Off to a better place and all that."

"Shit," he whispered, running his hand through hair that had become spiky from his restless fingers.

"What are you doing here?"

He scrubbed at teary, reddened eyes. "I'm your— I'm Shadoe's brother, Torque."

"Oh. I thought you were my night auditor." She fell back into the wet bedclothes with a groan, certain she was both crazy and dying. No one could feel as bad as she did and live through it. Violent shudders wracked her body as if she were freezing, but she was burning up. Her mouth felt stuffed with cotton that tasted like an ashtray. Her stomach was churning as if ready to heave, and her head was throbbing so viciously she felt like something was trying to slam its way out of her skull from the inside.

But the reality she'd woken up to was worse.

She was still Lindsay, still crazy about Adrian, and she was one of the things they both hated and hunted—a vampire.

CHAPTER 23

Adrian saw the smoke rising from the remnants of the Navajo Lake pack miles before he reached it. When Damien pulled the Suburban through the gates, they entered a literal war zone. Very little remained intact. Fires burned untended. What had once been the cryogenic storage facility was a charred hole in the ground several meters deep. Not one window remained unbroken. Feathers dotted the ground along with dozens of naked corpses.

For the first time in two days, an emotion penetrated the thick haze of grief clouding Adrian's mind and heart.

Climbing out of the truck, he surveyed the devastation. He rubbed at the dull pain in his chest and asked, "How many Sentinel casualties?"

"Five, including Jason."

More losses in a matter of hours than they'd been dealt in centuries, plus two lieutenants lost in a single month. "How many lycans were killed?"

"Close to thirty." Damien looked pale and drawn.

"Although it's likely some fled and died from their wounds elsewhere. There are a few who stayed loyal to us, but I don't know how useful they'll be. The other lycans will kill them on sight."

Adrian wandered through the ruined outpost. This blow was the worst yet, one very likely to cause the destruction of every Sentinel.

And he wasn't at his best. Everything was murky, as if he were looking at the world through cracked, dirty glass.

Where was Lindsay? How was she? Had she gone through with the Change? Was Syre even now enjoying the return of his daughter after all these centuries apart?

The thought of crossing paths with Shadoe in Lindsay's body cut through Adrian like razors, yet he knew that day was coming if the Change had gone through as Syre predicted. He had no idea how he would survive such an encounter. He could only beg the Creator to spare him such agony.

He forced his scattered mind to focus on the immediate horror facing them. "Has news of this spread to the other packs?"

"Not all," Damien replied grimly. "But we haven't been able to reach the Andover or Forest River packs since early yesterday."

Adrian returned to the SUV for the tools stored in the back. "As per protocol, we'll burn the bodies, then level this place. We can't leave anything behind for the curious to find."

"Yes, Captain."

The use of his rank chilled him. "When we get back to the Point, you and Oliver should put your heads together and come up with some suggestions for how to proceed from here. By the day after tomorrow, you should have settled on a replacement for me."

"Adrian."

He felt the weight of Damien's gaze on his profile. The other Sentinels with them, Malachai and Geoffrey, stepped closer.

"I'm sorry," he said gruffly, his throat tight with remorse. It was his duty to support his men and give them encouragement and motivation when their morale was low. But he was lost himself. "I failed you all. I should have withdrawn from the mission the moment I fell. Perhaps this could've all been avoided."

Lindsay. Where are you?

"I've always believed your ability to feel human emotion is an asset to us," Damien said.

Beside him, Malachai nodded.

Geoffrey, a seraph of few words, shrugged. "I'd be lying if I said I've never found a mortal woman attractive."

Wings flexing restlessly, Adrian took several moments to decide what to say. "Perhaps we should recall all the Sentinels to the Point. Together, reflection may give us the answers and strength we seek."

"I take strength from you, Captain," Malachai said with quiet conviction.

How was that possible, Adrian wondered, when he didn't have any strength to give? He didn't know if there were hidden reserves left within him, he felt so tapped out.

Lindsay. Where are you?

The vein pulsed and throbbed with life, pumping nutrient-rich blood through the maid's industriously working body.

Lindsay heard every beat of the woman's heart as if she had a stethoscope to her ear. Her canines elongated and her mouth watered. Her hands fisted against the driving urge to feed.

Nearby, Syre sat on the love seat with his elbows resting on his parted knees and his forehead in his hands. His face was downturned, but Lindsay knew his gaze was bleak. He was grieving, his pain a palpable thing in the hotel room.

Torque stood in front of the small refrigerator at the wet bar, guarding the empty blood bags they'd used while watching her complete the Change. He studied her too closely, searching, as if he might find his sister in her, or some other miracle.

As for Lindsay, she sat at the small dining table and waited for the red-haired murderess to make an appearance. Impatient and anxious, the fingers of her right hand spun her cell phone on the tabletop. The red light blinking above the screen told her she had unheard messages from both Adrian and Elijah, but she felt no urge to listen. She was too far gone with hunger, like a junky jonesing for a fix. She was shaky and nauseous. Her body craved sustenance, but her stomach roiled at the thought of ingesting blood.

"It's all in your head," Torque had told her just that morning. "Have a taste and you'll see."

He was kind and considerate to her, as was Syre, but she felt like an imposter. As comfortable as she'd felt with Adrian, she felt equally awkward with the vampires. They didn't know she'd spent the majority of her life hunting their kind. They didn't know she wasn't going to stop until she took out Vashti.

That slaying would mark the end of her life, she was

pretty sure. They'd kill her then and that would be a blessing. There was nothing left for her anymore. Her parents were dead, she had to suck on veins to live, and Adrian would hate her if he saw her. He'd killed Shadoe—the woman he had loved to obsession and fallen from grace for—rather than see her become a vampire.

Outside the room, the wind moaned along the open hallway circling the inner atrium. The plaintive sound broke her heart—Adrian was in mourning, too.

The maid hurried out of the suite as if the hounds of hell were breathing down her neck. She couldn't fail to feel the tension in the room. Lindsay wondered what the woman would do if she knew she was being contemplated as a great afternoon snack.

As the door began to swing closed, it was suddenly thrust inward again. Vash strode in on four-inch-heeled boots as if she were queen of the world.

Lindsay felt bloodlust and aggression explode inside her. Her nostrils flared, her eyes zeroing in on the woman she'd been waiting forever to kill. Her senses were so powerful now they overwhelmed her, but she wouldn't get the opportunity to grow into them. She'd be permanently out of commission in about thirty minutes.

Vash tossed her long hair over her shoulder and shot a glance at Lindsay. She froze when their gazes met, her face taking on a look of disgruntled resignation.

"Aw, shit," she muttered, the instant before Lindsay launched herself across the room.

She tackled the vamp into the love seat, narrowly missing Syre, who darted up and out of the way with impossible speed. The sofa snapped down the middle, folding around them like a taco. Sandwiched in the middle, Vash could do little to protect her jugular. With canines extended, Lindsay bit deep. Her fist pierced the cushions of the love seat, her hand searching for a length of broken wood from the frame. Vash writhed beneath her, cursing in a gurgling voice.

The vampress's memories hit Lindsay with the force of Niagara Falls—Vash's history, carried in her Fallen blood. The life force both Sentinels and the Fallen needed to survive.

Lindsay released her in a rush, stumbling backward to sit heavily atop the coffee table. She wiped her bloodied mouth with the back of her hand and felt the room spin from the rush of feeding and the surprise of discovering Vash's innocence.

"It wasn't you!" She gripped her pounding skull, feeling dizzy and disoriented by the onslaught of eons of recollections that didn't include her mother's death.

Vash regained her footing, one hand pressed to her spurting throat. "That's your second free pass, you crazy bitch. Next time you come at me, it'll cost you."

"Whatever," Lindsay muttered, crushed by the realization that she was once again facing the task of finding a needle in a haystack. Subsiding on blood for years while she did so held no appeal. She'd become the monster she hunted, and while she searched for her mother's killer it would be the sickest hypocrisy to do to others what had been done to her. "Do me a favor and put me out of my misery."

"Fucking A," Vash said, just before nailing Lindsay in the head with a roundhouse kick.

Lindsay never saw the carpeted floor rushing up to meet her.

* * *

Adrian tossed his duffel bag on his bed and freed his wings, stretching them in an effort to ease the debilitating tension gripping his shoulders. He was heading toward his bathroom for a shower when a knock came to his open bedroom door.

Pausing, he faced Oliver, who looked as grim as every other face he'd seen over the last three days. "Yes?"

"You're going to want to deal with this, Captain."

The graveness of Oliver's tone renewed the painful tautness in Adrian's spine. "What is it?"

"There are vampires at the gate."

Seething, Adrian exited onto the deck and flew to the end of the driveway, setting down just in front of the wrought-iron barrier. The guardhouse was empty, his property devoid of lycan presence. His solitary approach was reckless and foolhardy, displaying how little value he placed on his own life at the moment.

A town car with dark window tinting waited out on the main road, its nose already pointed back down the hill. Torque stood on the other side of the gate, along with Raze.

"Where are your dogs, Adrian?" Raze growled. The massive vampire's lip curled as he surveyed the view from behind dark sunglasses.

"Don't need them to deal with you."

Torque rocked back on his heels. "I've got a present for you."

Foreboding spread with icy tendrils across Adrian's skin, but he affected boredom and said evenly, "Unless it's Lindsay Gibson, I don't give a fuck."

"It is. And she's dying."

Adrian's pulse skipped with life for the first time in

days. Torque would not have brought Shadoe here. Only Lindsay—a woman Syre had no real connection to. But still, Adrian had to be sure. "Shadoe?"

Torque shook his head. "She's gone. And Lindsay won't feed. Aside from a chunk she tore out of Vash, she hasn't drunk a drop. Her heartbeat has slowed to the point where I thought she was already dead by the time we got up here."

Adrian was over the gate and ripping the door off the car before Torque could say more. Lindsay lay across the backseat, her once golden skin now pale as alabaster. He shielded her from the sun with his wings, completely disregarding the easy target he presented with his back to two vampires. She was still as death, her chest barely moving.

"Syre returns her to you in honor of Shadoe," Torque said quietly. "She carried Shadoe's soul. We owe her something for that, and you get to collect."

Reaching in, Adrian shrouded her with the blanket tangled around her limp body and pulled her from the car. He held her close against him, then flew up and over the gate.

"You're welcome!" Raze yelled after him, but Adrian was already rushing into the house.

He took her to his bedroom and tucked her into the bed, willing the drapes shut to block out the sun. Lindsay was as cold as refrigerated marble, and just as lifeless. He shed their clothes with a thought and crawled in beside her, pulling her close to impart the heat from his body. A violent shiver moved through him as her chilled frame pressed against his.

"Lindsay," he whispered, burying his lips in her crown. She smelled wonderful, and he breathed her in with a shuddering inhale. Tears wet his face and her hair, the quiet of his room shattered by the serrated noises spilling unchecked from his aching throat.

He pulled back enough to examine her, his shaking hand pushing wayward curls away from her face. Her bloodless lips were slightly parted, revealing the tiniest tip of fang. His heart squeezed in his chest. "*Neshama*, don't leave me."

Adrian pushed his finger into her mouth, slicing the pad with the point of a razor-sharp canine. He slid the bleeding digit deep and stroked it across her tongue. "Feed," he coaxed. "Feed or you will die, and kill me with you."

He waited endless moments. When she didn't move, Adrian withdrew and slit the pad of a second fingertip, pushing both bleeding fingers into the cool recesses of her mouth.

Her lips quivered.

"Yes, *neshama sheli*. Drink. Come back to me."

A low, thready moan escaped her. Her throat worked on a tiny swallow.

"Drink of me," he urged. "Take what you need."

Another soft flex of her throat. Her eyelids fluttered, the skin so translucent he could see the fine network of blue veins coursing through them. They lifted, revealing the amber irises of a vampire. Her gaze was unfocused, her breathing still far too shallow.

He began to withdraw his fingers, but her tongue moved, pinning them to the roof of her mouth. She was too weak to hold him, and he pulled free, his lips curving with a grim smile when she mewled in protest.

Turning his head, Adrian traced his bleeding fingers over the thick artery in his neck. Her mouth followed blindly, open and rooting like a hungry babe. He caught the back of her head in his hand and directed her.

Her tongue licked back and forth over his pulsing vein, plumping it and arousing him in the process. When her fangs pierced his skin, his cock hardened instantly. Her mouth drew on him in rhythmic pulls, sending lust and desire radiating outward from the place where she fed. Her skin began to warm, her body gaining strength with every gulping swallow. Her groan vibrated against him and he jerked with the rush of sensation.

Lindsay began to rub against him, purring, succumbing to the sexual pleasure vamps found in feeding. Slinging her leg over his, she ground her sex against his thigh, leaving a slick trail of moisture behind.

He reached for her hips, further aroused by imagining the years ahead, endless days with the woman he loved forever by his side. "Put me inside you, Linds. Ride me till you come."

Her fangs slipped free of his skin. "Until *you* come," she breathed, mounting him.

Her tongue licked across the twin punctures, closing them. Reaching between them, she wrapped her warmed hands around his cock and positioned him at her entrance. She sheathed him in a deft, hard thrust of her hips that made him arch his back with a hiss of pleasure.

"My god . . . Adrian." She nuzzled her temple against his, her breath hot as it blew across his ear. "I've missed you so much."

Then she froze.

When she didn't move and barely breathed, Adrian lifted her torso away from his to search her face. "Lindsay? What is it?"

She covered her mouth with her hand, her amber

eyes darkening with shock and horror. "Oh! I'm sorry, Adrian. I—"

He took her face in his hands. "For what?"

As she shook her head, her eyes overflowed with pink-tinged tears. Her arms covered her breasts, a display of shame he couldn't bear to see. Her tight, wet sex slid upward along his cock when she moved to leave him. "I've changed. I'm not—"

Adrian rolled and pinned her beneath him. "I want you more now than I ever have."

"You can't . . ."

"Oh yes, I can. I do." He captured her arms above her head and kneed her thighs wider. He withdrew from her clinging depths with exquisite leisure, torturing them both. Then he hammered into her with a quick, hard thrust.

She gasped, her eyes wide and beautiful. A vampire's eyes, with Lindsay's pure, selfless soul shining behind them. Eyes that saw him as clearly in the darkness of his shrouded room as he saw her.

He pulled back and thrust again. "The feel of you feeding from my neck has me so damn hot for you. Feel how thick I am? How hard you've made me? You turn me inside out."

Her thighs tightened around his hips, clasping him sweetly.

His eyes closed in gratitude at her acceptance. Hunger curled like heated iron around his spine, and he groaned. The feel of her was so sublime it burned through him, restoring life to him just as his blood had done for her. "*What* you are doesn't matter to me. It never will. It's *who* you are that I love."

Her fingers dug into the backs of his hands, bringing a sharp bite of pain as newly formed claws pierced his flesh. That turned him on, too. His cock lengthened with his appreciation, filling her until she writhed. He was home, his soul completed by the proximity of hers—his Lindsay, so brave and selfless.

Enraptured by the feel of her beneath him, around him, he drove into her with powerful lunges. He watched the pleasure weight her eyelids and slacken her lush mouth. His wings spread out and away from the bed, quivering with the raging desire that built with every deep thrust.

"I can't live without you," he growled. "I won't let you make me do so."

She arched into his pounding hips, her sleek body even more powerful than before. Strong enough to take everything he had to give her and still demand more. "I love you."

Rearing back, Adrian yanked her up. He rested on his heels and urged her to rock against him. "Fuck me, Linds. Make me come."

She wrapped her silken arms around his neck and tucked her knees on either side of his. Thrusting her hips, she rode him, taking him swift and hard with fluidly graceful undulations.

She was formidable now and she devastated him with pleasure. The rhythmic slap of her pelvis against his was so erotic, he bit his lower lip to hold off the onslaught of orgasm. Not yet . . . Too soon . . . Make it last . . .

"Don't hold back," she moaned. "I'm waiting for you."

He caught her nape in his hand, pulling her mouth to his. Their lips sealed, their panting breaths mingling as they climaxed together. Quaking with the power of it. Shaken by the pure, unadulterated connection between them. No restraints.

At last.

"Elijah, too?" Lindsay asked, her fingers stroking across Adrian's chest. "He went with them?"

"His body wasn't among the dead, so I assume so, yes."

That hurt her. Elijah's actions could very well pit him against the man she loved. She thought of the message the lycan had left on her phone, the date of his call falling *after* the uprising. He wanted to see her, asked for her help. And because he was her friend, she wanted to give it to him. She was divided on all sides, beholden to damn near everyone for saving her ass at some point or other. "What will we do?"

Turning his head, Adrian pressed his lips to her forehead. "We recuperate and regroup. Then we assess the damage and start rebuilding."

"But there are so few of you now."

"We can do it." He sounded so sure.

"How well do you trust your Sentinels?"

"With my life."

She blew out her breath. "The person who snatched me from the Point and took me to Syre . . ."

"Yes?"

". . . sported wings."

Adrian jerked with surprise.

"I'm sorry." She attempted to soothe him with soft strokes of her hand over his chest. "I didn't get a look at who it was. I was knocked out from behind with some kind of Vulcan neck squeeze."

He was quiet for a long time, but the turmoil he felt

was reflected in the howling winds that surrounded the house.

"You hide your emotions so well," she said quietly. "But the weather gives you away."

He looked down at her with widened eyes. "How do you know that?"

"I feel the weather in you. I'm kinda attuned to that sort of thing. I feel emotions through the wind. It's like it talks to me. It used to warn me about inhumans, too, but I sense the differences on my own now. I guess my weather radar was truly mine and not an echo of Shadoe's abilities."

His mouth curved in one of his rare full smiles.

"What?" Lindsay was dazzled by that smile, and curious about its cause.

"I've prayed for a sign—any sign at all—that the Creator would absolve me of guilt for falling in love. When the weather began to respond to my moods, I thought it was to remind me of my shortcomings. But perhaps it was the sign I asked for, a gift to bring you to me."

"That's beautiful."

"And hopeful, which I need right now. We all do."

She hugged him. "When I was younger, I used to think my sixth sense made me a freak."

"No. It makes you mine."

They lay in silence for a while. Lindsay almost dozed, lulled by the steady cadence of Adrian's heartbeat and the feel of his warm, solid body pressed against hers.

"Do you miss her?" she asked after a while.

His chest expanded on a deep breath. He didn't pretend to misunderstand. "I should—I owe her that much—but it's been so long, and I need you so much. It's hard to see past you. Although, to be honest, I'm not trying very hard. I love the view."

"It's okay if you do think of her. I told her I wouldn't hold it against you if you did."

"You spoke to her?"

Lindsay set her hands atop the tight lacing of muscle that crisscrossed his abdomen, then set her chin upon them. "She was going to keep you. She was a pro at dealing with all those past lives and memories, while I was drowning in them. I had to fight for you."

His blue eyes flamed with the heat of his emotions. "You did?"

"I know, right? After all the times I tried to push you away, I finally realized I couldn't live—or die—without you. So I told her if she kept you, I'd still always have some part of you and she'd have to share. Apparently, she decided she'd rather have you be with me and think about her, than be with her while thinking about me."

Adrian's smile curled her toes. "That sounds like her."

"I'm grateful," she admitted. "She gave up her soul so I could keep mine."

"I will love her for that forever. But you have my heart and soul, Lindsay."

"I know."

After a drawn out moment, he exhaled audibly. "Maybe this ... experience was good for her, too. Shadoe wasn't a bad person, but she wasn't one to sacrifice her desires for the good of others."

"You're thinking she matured over countless lifetimes?"

"I'd like to think so. For her sake."

Lindsay looked down at her fingers as she traced the faint line of dark hair that bisected his abs and led to delicious places below. After everything he had been through and everything he'd lost, Adrian still had it in him to search for silver linings. She loved him for that, and countless other things. "I told her I'd take whatever I can get when it comes to you."

He twisted deftly, caging her beneath him. Framed by his unfurling wings, he was darkly handsome. Breathtaking. "Then you'd best be prepared to take all of me."

"Yes, *neshama*." She slid her arms around his neck. "All of you. Always."

CHAPTER 24

"As I feared," Damien said, "we've lost the Andover and Forest River packs. We're keeping a lid on the others for now, but if we're attacked from the outside while battling mutiny on the inside, more will fall."

Adrian stood at the railing of the wraparound deck and watched his Sentinels exercise their wings in the air above him. The early-morning sky of pink and gray was giving way to a soft powder blue. "We'll just have to find a way to be more resourceful. In the interim, the illness is spreading through the vampire ranks like wildfire. Perhaps all we really have to do is sit and wait. I won't count on it, but it's a possibility."

"You're better today," Damien noted.

"Stronger," he agreed. "Happier. Ready to take on the world."

"That's the sex talking."

Adrian turned at the sound of Lindsay's voice, finding her standing a few feet away. She reached over her head and pushed up to her tiptoes, stretching her lovely lithe body—much to his delight.

She straightened and wrinkled her nose at Damien. "I'm sorry. I really don't mean to flaunt the rules and be disrespectful. It's just that's such a guy thing to say the morning after he doesn't let his girlfriend get any sleep."

Morning after . . .

Adrian looked up at the sun in the sky, then shot a look at Damien, whose mouth hung slightly ajar. Lindsay seemed oblivious to the fact that she was standing in sunlight.

"I'd like to get back into training," she went on. "I'm going to need it so I can cover your ass *and* find the vamps who killed my mother. I'm not giving up on hunting those fuckers down and making them pay. And I need to know for sure what happened with my dad. If there's a score to settle there, I have to know. If it was truly just an accident, I need to know that, too."

"Whatever you require, *neshama*," Adrian assured her, concealing his astonishment.

Damien leaned closer and spoke under his breath. "She should be on fire in this level of sunlight. How is it possible that she's not?"

Adrian sat on the railing and watched Lindsay go through an elaborate and unwittingly sexy calisthenics routine. "I don't know, but I suspect my blood has something to do with it. Much like Fallen blood conveys a temporary immunity."

"Other vamps have bitten Sentinels before. They weren't then able to practice yoga on an uncovered deck."

"But only Lindsay has drunk Sentinel blood exclusively after being turned by one of the Fallen. Every cell in her body is nourished by blood that protects her. As long as she continues to drink from me, she might keep the benefits."

"A minion with the gifts of the Fallen." Damien lifted a hand to his brow, as if pained. "If Sentinel blood cures the vampire disease and imparts immunity to the healthy, and others were to learn of this—"

"—we'd be hunted to extinction. I know."

"Without the lycans, we're sitting ducks."

"Siobhán is testing whether lycan blood is an alternative. They were once seraphim, too."

Damien was silent for a moment. "I'll pray for a miracle."

"Pray for us all." Adrian set his hands on the railing and tipped his face up to the sun. The morning breeze blew across his feathers in a soft greeting from the new day. "We're going to need it."

Turn the page for a special preview of the
next sexy and thrilling Renegade Angels
novel by Sylvia Day

A HUNGER SO WILD

"We need to find out whether or not there are other Alphas." Elijah glanced at the lycan who walked beside him, wondering at how easily Stephan had stepped into the role of his Beta.

Instinct weighted heavily on everything they did as a fledgling pack, a truth that unsettled Elijah more than it soothed. He would have preferred that their destinies be shaped by their own hands and not by the demon blood that flowed through their veins.

But as he traversed the long stone hallway, the number of verdant gazes staring back at him was irrefutable proof of how dominant a lycan's baser nature was. Every one of them had the luminous green irises of a mixed bloodline creature. They lined the walls by the hundreds, staring as he passed them, forming a gauntlet through the red rock caves in southern Utah that he'd selected as his headquarters. They thought he was a damn messiah, the one lycan who could lead them into a new age of independence. They didn't realize that their expectations and hopes for freedom imprisoned him.

"I've made it a top priority," Stephan assured. "But half the lycans we send out don't return."

"Perhaps they're returning to the Sentinel fold. As far as quality of life goes, we had it better working for the angels."

"Is any price too high to pay for liberty?" Stephan asked. "We all know the Sentinels don't stand a chance if we take the offensive. There are less than two hundred of them in existence. Our numbers are in the tens of thousands."

The gentle prodding for Elijah to be proactive instead of reactive wasn't lost on him. He could feel it in the air around him, the crackling energy of lycans ready and willing to hunt. "Not yet," he said. "It's not time."

An arm shot out and grabbed him. "What the fuck are you waiting for?"

Elijah paused and turned, facing the brawny male whose eyes glowed in the shadows of the cave. The lycan was bristling and half shifted, his arms and neck covered in a grayish pelt.

The beast in Elijah growled a warning, but he held it in check, a control that made him Alpha.

"Are you challenging me, Nicodemus?" he asked with dangerous softness. He'd been waiting for this, had known it was coming. It would only be the first challenge of many, until he established his dominance through physical prowess in addition to a lycan's instinctive need to follow a leader.

The lycan's nostrils flared, his chest heaving as he fought against his beast. Lacking Elijah's control, Nic would lose.

Prying the man's grip from his arm, Elijah said, "You know where to find me."

Then he turned his back to the challenge and walked away, deliberately baiting Nic's beast. The sooner they got this over with the better.

Nic had asked him what he was waiting for. He was waiting for cohesion, trust, loyalty—the cementing framework that would hold all the packs together. Greater numbers or not, there was no way they'd win against a tightly commanded elite military unit like the Sentinels if they didn't work together.

A female approached him at a near run, agitation radiating from her tense frame. "Alpha," she greeted him. "You have a visitor. A vampire."

His brows rose. "*A* vampire? As in one?"

"Yes. She asked for the Alpha."

Elijah's curiosity was more than piqued. The lycans had been created by the Sentinels for the sole purpose of hunting and containing the vampires. The fact that the lycans had revolted from Sentinel control didn't mean they'd forgotten their ingrained hatred of bloodsuckers. For a vamp to walk into a den alone was suicidal.

"Show her to the great room," he said.

The lycan turned and ran back the way she'd come, with Elijah and Stephan following at a more sedate pace.

Stephan shook his head. "What the fuck?"

"She's desperate, for some reason."

"Why is that our problem?"

Shrugging, Elijah said, "Could be our gain."

"Do we really want to become a safe house for bloodsucking losers?"

"Let me get this straight: we rebel and we're better off, but a vampire bolts and they're a loser?"

Stephan scowled. "You know as well as I do that the pack won't take in vamps."

"Times have changed. In case you hadn't noticed, we're pretty damned desperate, too."

Elijah was stepping over the threshold into the great room when he heard the growl behind him. Lunging forward, he shifted into his lupine form before his paws hit the rock floor. He whirled around at the moment Nicodemus charged, taking a full-on ramming in the side that knocked the wind from him. Rolling over, he regained his feet, righting himself in time to catch his challenger by the throat midleap. With a toss of his head, Elijah threw the other lycan across the room. Then he howled his fury, the sound reverberating through the massive room.

Nic skid sideways on his paws, then found traction and attacked again. Elijah rushed forward to intercept him.

They collided with brutal force, their jaws snapping for purchase. Nic caught him by the foreleg and bit hard. Elijah went for the flank, his teeth digging in deep, his beast growling at the heady taste of hot, rich blood.

Kicking off his attacker, Elijah turned, ripping a chunk of flesh away. Nic yelped and came back around, limping. Elijah crouched, prepared to leap, when the lush scent of ripe cherries slid across his senses in teasing tendrils. The fragrance swept through him, burning through his blood and sending aggression pumping through his veins.

He was abruptly sick of playing with Nicodemus. Elijah vaulted ahead, twisting midair to avoid Nic's snarling maw and coming down on the lycan's back. Catching him by the throat, Elijah pinned him to the floor, his jaws clenched tight enough to wound and warn, but not enough to kill. Yet. Just the slightest increase in pressure would cut off Nic's air.

Nic writhed for a few moments, his limbs flailing in an effort to shake off his opponent. Then blood loss and exhaustion stole his strength. He whimpered for his release and Elijah let him go.

Elijah's low growl rumbled through the room. He turned, his gaze meeting those of every lycan in the room. They stood around the perimeter, their gazes lowering quickly as he dared any comers.

Satisfied that he'd made his point for the moment, he shifted and faced the arched doorway to the great room, his attention riveted to that ripe, sweet scent that was making his dick hard.

"Get me a change of clothes," he said to the room at large, uncaring of who did it, just that it got done. "And a damp towel."

He'd barely finished speaking when she appeared, looking just as he remembered her—black heeled boots, black Lycra bodysuit that clung to every curve, scarlet red hair that fell to her waist, and pearly white fangs. She looked like something out of a BDSM-laced wet dream and he wanted to fuck her nearly as badly as he wanted to kill her. The lust was instinctual and unwelcome; the fury was laced with grief and pain. She'd killed his best friend in a slow, agonizing death while trying to get to him.

Be careful what you wish for, bitch.

Baring his teeth in a semblance of a smile, he said her name, "Vashti."

Her gaze narrowed as she picked up his scent. "You."

* * *

Shit.

Vash stared at the naked, blood-spattered lycan standing across the room and her fists clenched. The lack of the familiar weight of her sword sheath on her back had already been driving her nuts, but now it pissed her off.

He'd killed her friend, and he was going to pay.

She stalked closer, her booted heels clicking across the uneven stone floor. They lived in a goddamn cave and fought among themselves like animals. Fucking dogs. She'd tried to talk Syre out of this fool's errand, but the vampire leader would not be swayed. He believed in the old "the enemy of my enemy is my friend" way of conducting a war and she might have agreed with that, if they were talking about anyone but lycans.

"The name is Elijah," he corrected, watching her with the focused gaze of a natural hunter zeroing in on its prey.

Another male approached him with a towel in one hand and clothes in the other. Elijah took the towel and began to wipe the blood from his mouth and jaw. His gaze never left hers as the cloth moved across his broad chest and arms.

Vash found her attention reluctantly drawn to the stroking of white terry cloth over golden skin. He was ripped with powerful muscles from head to toe, beautifully defined in a way she couldn't help but appreciate. There wasn't an ounce of extraneous flesh on him and his virility was unquestionable, even without his display of an impressive cock and weighty testicles. His scent was in the air, an earthy yet exhilarating fragrance of clove and bergamot that was rich with male pheromones.

He handed the towel to the lycan standing next him, then stroked his long, thick penis from root to tip.

"Like what you see?" he taunted in a deep rumbling voice that affected her physically. Blood oozed from a nasty gash in his calf, the scent so delicious her mouth watered for a taste of it.

She forced her gaze to lift from his groin with insolent leisure. "Just marveling that you don't smell like wet dog."

His nostrils flared. "You smell like sacrificial lamb."

Vash laughed softly. "I'm here to help you, lycan. You're safe while you're underground, but you'll have to surface at some point, and beneath the open sky is where the angels will slaughter you all. Since you're already fighting among yourselves, you won't have a chance in hell against Adrian's Sentinels without allies."

The lycans around the room rumbled their disgust at the very idea. She raised her voice and spoke to the assembly at large. "I absolutely agree with you. I don't want to work with you either."

"Yet you came when Syre sent you," Elijah said, stepping into a loose pair of jeans. "Walked straight into a wolf's den at his order."

She faced him again, her chin lifting. "We're more civilized than you, lycan. We know the value of a hierarchy of power."

He approached her, his barefooted stride sleek and predatory. The tight roping of muscles over his abdomen flexed as he walked, riveting her gaze. A surge of heat moved through her as his scent grew stronger.

Fuck. She'd been celibate too long if a lycan could make her hot.

Her hands fisted as he stopped in front of her. Too

close. Invading her personal space. Trying to intimidate her with his powerful body and sharply edged hunger. She saw the need in his eyes and smelled it in the air around him. He hated her, yet he desired her.

Despite her height and heels, Vash had to tilt her head back to look up at him. "Just tell me to fuck off and I'm out of here. I only agreed to present the offer. I really don't want you to accept."

"Ah, but I have no intention of turning you down until you go into the details." He caught a lock of her hair between his fingers and rubbed it. "And I want to see your face when you find out I didn't kill your friend."

Her breath caught. She told herself it was from surprise and not from the feel of his knuckle brushing over her breast. "My sense of smell is damn near as good as yours."

One side of his mouth lifted in a cruel smile. "Did you check my blood sample for anticoagulants?"

She stepped back in a rush. "What the fuck?"

"I was set up. The blood you found was from a stored supply. You, however, *are* guilty of killing my friend. Hopefully you remember him, since his murder signed your death warrant. The redhead you pinned to a tree and left for dead?"

He circled her. Dozens of pairs of emerald eyes watched her with open hostility. The chances of getting out of the cave alive diminished to zero.

"If you kill me now," she warned, "you'll have both the vamps and the Sentinels after you."

"That's problematic," he murmured, rounding her shoulder from the back.

"But there's something I want more than my life. If

you help me get it, I'll let you kill me in a way that looks like self-defense."

Elijah stopped in front of her again. "I'm listening."

"Clear the room."

With a wave of his arm, he gestured everyone out.

"Alpha . . . ?" Stephan questioned.

"Don't worry," Elijah said. "I can take her."

She snorted. "You can try, puppy. Don't forget I have a few eons on you."

In less than a minute, the room was emptied.

"I'm waiting," he said, his eyes glittering dangerously.

"One of your dogs killed my mate." Familiar rage and pain raced through her veins like acid. "If you think what I did to your friend was bad, it was nothing compared to what was done to Charron. You help me find the one responsible and let me kill him—I'm all yours."

His gaze narrowed. "How do you plan on finding this lycan? What are you looking for?"

"I have the date, time, and place. I just need to know who was in the area then. I can narrow it down from there."

"Such bloodthirsty loyalty."

She turned her head to look at him. "I could say the same about you."

"You'd have to stay with me," he pointed out. "I expect to be present anytime you question a pack member. It could take days, maybe weeks."

The scent of his lust grew stronger by the moment and she—damn it all—wasn't immune.

"I've been searching for years. A few weeks more won't kill me."

"No, but I will. Eventually. In the meantime, I don't have to like you," he said softly, "to want to fuck you."

She swallowed hard, damning the elevated rate of her pulse, which she knew he could hear. "Of course not. You're an animal."

He circled her again, leaning in and inhaling deeply. "What's your excuse?"